THE
PLOYS OF
Santiago

A LAND IN TURMOIL: BOOK THREE

E. PAUL BERGERON

Cover Art by Sandra Bergeron

Cover Design & Formatting by Gray Publishing Services

ISBN 978-0-9967013-7-2

SANTA YNEZ VALLEY

"It is beautiful this time of the year, is it not?" Francesca said.

William MacLeod watched as she stepped out of her saddle and walked to the edge of the stream. He couldn't help but thank the day she'd agreed to marry him ten years prior.

"I suppose I'd be a lot more appreciative if it would rain soon," he said as he watched her bend down and pluck a handful of yellow flowers.

"Yes, it has been another poor year. I know it worries you; I can see it in your face. It worries me also. But you must speak with me about it. I know you too well, William, you cannot keep all of your worries to yourself."

Mounting her horse, she guided it through the narrow path, among the cottonwood and willows, to a little patch of grass beside the stream.

"I don't. Well, maybe some," MacLeod stated, following closely. "You have enough to worry about. I hate burdening you with mine too. Especially when you can't do anything about them." Stepping out of the saddle, he let his reins fall atop the thick grass growing beside the stream. Unlike most other horses, MacLeod knew the little stallion he was riding wouldn't wander far.

Francesca dismounted and draped her reins over a bush. Few women in Alta California rode their own horses, often preferring to ride double. A woman riding solo was thought by many to be improper. Then again, so many things in her life were thought to be improper. She figured one more wouldn't matter. Besides, how many women in Alta California could say they had ridden almost the entire length of the land with a man she was not married to, as she had done years before.

Francesca sat by the stream on a small patch of grass, a place they came to often to get away from the children and the others. Folding her legs beneath her, she reached down and let her fingers trail in the water. "The hills are still green, though I can see the grass here in the valley is not as abundant as in past years. It is as if it does not have the strength to grow."

MacLeod grinned at her use of words. "Your English improves every day, Francesca. I thank you for wanting to learn it. And I'm happy you wanted the children to learn it also."

She smiled. "It is your language, William, and I have a feeling it may be ours here in Alta California someday."

"You might want to keep some of those thoughts to yourself. Others may not like your forward thinking."

"You say the same thing. What is it you write to that important man in America?"

Yes, MacLeod thought, *what have I been telling this man, this Senator Benton, about California? Is it a good thing I'm doing?* he wondered. "We've spoken of it before. He wants to know how the people feel about the government in Mexico. Seems things are unsettled in that Texas area of the country. What happens there could make trouble for the Americans living here."

"I am sure you are right, but I have heard the leaders here talk of this president we have, this Antonio López de Santa Anna, as if he were a king. Do you suppose he may also declare himself emperor like President Iturbide did?"

MacLeod laughed. "Well from what little I've heard about the man he'll probably try. He held out his hand to help her rise. "We best be going. Want to ride up to the far end and see how the cattle are faring before heading back?"

They rode through scattered groups of the thin, long-legged cattle that comprised most of Alta California's herds, keeping close to the banks of the stream. MacLeod was surprised how strong the flow of water was after what little rain they'd had the past three years.

"Did you hear the argument this morning?" Francesca asked, breaking the silence. "I do not know how you could have missed it."

"You mean Diego and Catalina?" MacLeod asked knowingly. "What's new, those two wake up every day complaining about on another? What was it about this time?"

"Oh, what else—she believes she should be treated as he is." Francesca giggled. "She comes running to me every time that son of yours laughs at her. He will not stop teasing her. If they were older, I would say they were attracted to each other."

"She's thirteen now, same as him. Hard to believe it's been that long?"

"Yes, and our two—Patricio and Laurita—five and a little over a year. My God, I cannot believe I have three children already."

MacLeod worked his horse around the cattle watering at the steam before pointing at a cow a dozen yards away. "That one's wandered a bit off course. It's the brand that new land owner is using."

"RS," Francesca said. "What is the name they call that place?"

"I hear it's called Rancho Santiago. I believe the name of the man who was given the land is Santiago."

"That was all mission land," Francesca muttered. "I understood it was all to go back to the Indians. I know my land was too far from the mission to be of importance to them. Besides, they had more than they needed."

"That's what this whole secularization process is about. Too many saw the land and all that the missions owned as a way to become rich, while doing nothing to earn it. It's not over yet, there may still be hope for some of the Indians. Sadly, the ones we've hired doubt it."

Francesca voiced her agreement and continued on about the problems she was having with a very strong willed thirteen-year-old daughter, who some days wanted to be treated like a princess, and other times like a boy. As they continued to talk, neither brought up the issue of Catalina's father, the Frenchman, Gaston Dupré, who MacLeod had shot and killed in a duel. They both knew the day would come that Francesca would have to address it with her daughter. Eventually, Catalina would discover it herself if they didn't have a conversation about it first, which was something they had both hoped to avoid. The one thing both MacLeod and Francesca had agreed upon in regards to Catalina was that she would not be married off to the first suitor who came along, as so many young girls were. Often times, they were coupled with an old widower needing a wife to take care of the hacienda and him.

As they rode along, Francesca continued talking about the children while MacLeod's attention remained focused on the land. It looked as if the land was overgrazed already, and there was still three months until *matanza*, when the killing season began. The cattle near the stream were few, meaning many were feeding further and further away from the water, returning only when they were in need of it. Reining in his horse, MacLeod waited for Francesca to come up alongside him, his eyes still glued to the pasture.

"What is it you are thinking?" Francesca asked, seeming to sense his concern.

"You know, the boundary marker for your land is just across that small ridge on the other side of the stream. I rode over there last week and took a look at the creek this RS uses to water their cattle. It looked pretty thin."

Francesca looked back at the nearby stream, a puzzled expression upon her face. "But ours does not look as if it has been reduced by the lack of rain. Why is that?"

"This stream comes from a series of springs further up in the mountains and runs down that narrow canyon. Add that water to the water from runoff, after the rains, and you have what you see here."

"I rode up there one day when you were away to see where this water comes from," Francesca admitted. "But I could not go further. It is very narrow and steep. You have seen these springs?"

"Yeah. Been a while. It's a pretty steep and rocky approach as you saw. Beautiful as I recall. The canyon opens up some for a spell with deep pools under a spread of cottonwood. But like I said, it's hard to get to. You wouldn't even know it was there unless someone took you."

"I would like to see this place. Will you take me? Maybe we can find a spot to bathe. Both of us this time," she said laughing, referring to the time he had watched her bathe in a stream years before"

"Sure, sometime," MacLeod agreed as he continued alongside the stream.

"I will remember you agreed to take me. Now, tell me what you know about this land next to Colinas de Oro."

MacLeod always referred to the land as hers, since by all rights it was. After Captain Fanning, from the trading ship out of Boston had married them, MacLeod approached acting governor Argüello for a grant of land in her name. Argüello, because of the favor he owed MacLeod for having rescued his nephew from a band of Indians, approved the land grant of close to 44,000 acres to Francesca. The fall of that year, in the late afternoon, as the sun crept down a cloudless sky toward the blue waters of the Pacific, Francesca saw it for the first time. The rays of the sun had turned the hills above her land a beautiful golden. She vowed that her land would hereafter be called Rancho Colinas de Oro, golden hills.

"Tell me more of what you know about this man who has been given this land next to ours. I have not heard you speak of him," Francesca said.

MacLeod rode a while, thinking back to what he had heard from a couple of their vaqueros who had ridden over to take a look. They said they had seen no buildings, but many Indians making adobe bricks and piles of the red tiles, like those on the roof of the nearby mission. MacLeod had seen the new brand on many of the cattle, so he assumed they had a crew of vaqueros doing their own round up, which MacLeod considered odd. The normal procedure was to inform nearby ranches, in case their cattle and unbranded heifers wandered over onto the other land grants.

"Very little," MacLeod admitted. "I've heard they're preparing to build, at least they're making bricks. I did hear this Santiago fellow was given the land grant by Governor Figueroa last year. I believe the man is from South America—Argentina, I think."

MacLeod turned away from the stream and led Francesca toward the center of their vast tract of land, not liking what he saw. The cattle were grazing far out toward the outer boundary line and into the foothills, searching for the dry grasses. He kneed his horse up a small rise, and stopped in the shade of a small grove of trees.

"I have been meaning to tell you—Esperanza is with child again," Francesca stated, following MacLeod to the spot he had stopped. "She is worried that Sean is drinking too much. She asks that you speak with him."

He had noticed it too. Sean had been doing very little, wandering off by himself, and not paying attention to his work in the little shop where he worked on furniture for the house, or taken to Monterey once a year and sold, or traded. MacLeod had often wondered where he got the wine, since they had little in the house, though he never asked.

"I'll have a try, but you know what he's like. He hasn't been himself since their little fellow died. You'd think her having another would bring him out of it."

Francesca walked her horse out from the shade and pointed at a large bull among the cows. "Even he is suffering," she said. "What can we do, before it is too late?"

Five years before MacLeod had purchased five heavy bulls from a rancho near the mission of La Purísima Concepción. The bulls had been selected from a handful the ranchero had that were producing a heavier calf. Over time, MacLeod hoped to improve the weight and tallow of his steers.

He knew he had to confront her with their options soon and now seemed as good a time as any. Especially since she had brought it up.

MacLeod and Francesca had become like partners in a business, as their good friend William Hartnell, had once said. He never made a decision about the ranch without speaking to her first. Well, most of the time. There was that matter of the loans, and the orders he had placed with the Boston ships for items to be brought out on their next trip.

"I wanted you to see for yourself, rather than just telling you— as I see it, we have three options. If we don't do something, there won't be enough grazing left for the cows. I say we send some people into the hills to start bringing in wood for the fires and we begin slaughtering sooner, rather than waiting until July. Every day these cattle feed is another day closer to starvation for some. If we don't get good rains this season many won't make it anyway. I think we should start slaughtering now and consider a good amount of the bigger two-year olds as well."

"It will cut down on what we have to offer next year. Will we suffer?" Francesca questioned.

"I can't see it mattering if we can't feed them."

"Very well, if you think that is what's best," she said.

"There's more," MacLeod began. "We should consider culling out the older cows and thinning out the horse herd."

"Oh, William, the horses too? What will you do with them?

"Well, I heard there's a group of Englishmen, from up in the north that work for the Hudson's Bay Company. From what I understand, they've been buying horses. You can usually find them trapping over on the San Joaquin River. We could drive a bunch over there and thin this herd out. Right now, they're eating up food that the cattle need."

Without a word, Francesca rode down the other side of the little knoll and worked her way through a few cattle, before returning to ride alongside the stream. MacLeod followed, knowing she was taking to heart everything he had said.

"I know you have thought about this for some time, and it's not an easy decision to make. When would you begin?"

"Sooner the better. We could get a few more vaqueros and round up the cattle, brand the youngsters. I'd say two, three weeks at the most. As soon as that's done, we can start slaughtering."

"I do not think we will have very much to celebrate after the round up this year. The other rancheros must also be suffering. Have you heard anything?"

MacLeod remained silent for some time as they rode the last two miles to the eastern edge of the land grant. Something was bothering him, but he said nothing. Finally, he spoke. "Everyone appears to be in the same condition; some are even worse, I suppose. In most cases, their water supply has dried up considerably. We're lucky in that regard."

Francesca reined her horse to a halt and pointed off to her right. "Look, there are a couple more of those cattle with that RS brand. Why do you think they have crossed over to our land?"

He had seen them. In fact, he had seen more and more of them as they neared the upper end of Rancho Colinas de Oro land. On the other side of the stream the land gently rose and formed a long, low ridge, the top being the boundary line of their land grant. If he rode to the top of the ridge, he could look down over a half mile to the trees lining the creek on Rancho Santiago land. In truth, he could see no reason for the cattle to be here.

"Must be our water tastes better," he shrugged. "As soon as we get back to the house, I'll have Sisquoc bring a few men up to push them back onto their land. I don't mind sharing water but we can't be sharing pastures. We don't have enough grazing space to feed our own cattle."

MacLeod's moccasins kicked up puffs of dust as he walked past one of the small adobe shops they had built some distance from the main house. It seemed they were always adding huts and small buildings as they continued to bring in more and more people to help with the ranch. In the past two years alone they had built shops for a combination tannery and saddle repair, as well as a blacksmith shop. Although the smithy was somewhat of a distance away from the other buildings.

As for the Indians he had hired, they lived in brush huts below Francesca and MacLeod's house. Many of them found themselves without a place to live after secularization and attempted to move back into their old villages in the tulle country. Sadly, many discovered their villages long deserted and all of their members no longer alive.

In one such case, an old man came by from the mission at the other end of the valley looking for work. It just so happened that he had worked there for years building and repairing saddles. Luckily, MacLeod was looking for a good saddle maker at the time and offered the man a job and a place to live. To which he gladly accepted.

"Señor Concannon?" MacLeod asked.

Without a word, the man pointed toward the end of the row of shops.

Nodding, MacLeod strode in the direction the man had pointed, stopping briefly to watch two women who were pounding corn. As he looked on, he made a mental note to plant more corn this year, even if he had to have people hand water it. Just then, a thought struck him. *We also need another vat for rendering the fat.* He vaguely remembered having seen one buried beneath a pile of broken adobe bricks and made a note to send Sisquoc and a couple of men with the *carreta* down to the old mission.

At times MacLeod wished he was back in the mountains with his friends, trapping. When he was there his only worries were keeping an eye out for wandering bands of Indians. Now he found himself waking in the night, the problems that needed solving and the hundreds of things to be taken care of weighing on his mind.

As he continued down the row of shops, MacLeod found Concannon sleeping behind the last dwelling in the ranch complex, an overturned wine jug at his head. Stepping closer, he nudged him gently with his foot.

"Oh, Jesus, Mary, and Joseph," Concannon said breathlessly as he held his head in both hands. "Is it not too early in the day to be rising?"

"Should have been up hours ago, Sean. I saw those Indians who are supposed to be making bricks sitting on their asses again, waiting for instructions. You know damn well they'll work well when they're told what to do. However, if you don't tell them, they're going to sit and wait. They're your responsibility."

Concannon pushed himself to his feet and wavered momentarily like a newborn colt. His hand went to the wall in an effort to support himself. "Right. I think I remember you saying something about that. If you'll be giving me a moment, I'll be getting to it." He reached down and picked up the overturned wine jug, swearing under his breath when he found it empty.

MacLeod's tolerance in the best of times had a very narrow limit. In the worst of times—there was no comparison. He and Concannon had shared many trials together since MacLeod had found the Irishman, at the time a deserter from a British Naval frigate, starving and in need of help. The little man barely came up past MacLeod's shoulder, and his carrot red hair and beard made him a minor celebrity in this land of black eyes and black hair.

However, it wasn't long before MacLeod discovered that the man had woodworking skills that proved a blessing and would stand up to anyone who might think to hurt Francesca. On a number of occasions, in the ten years or so since they all came together, Francesca had stood up for Concannon when the man's drinking had caused MacLeod to think about banishing him from the ranch. The man had done well—that is, until the fever had taken the life of he and his wife, Esperanza's, three-year-old boy this past winter.

MacLeod pitied the man, yet MacLeod had lost loved ones also so he didn't see that as an excuse for his behavior. In fact, he wondered if Concannon knew his wife was going to have another child. Somehow, he doubted it, especially with his recent behavior.

Just then, three Indian children raced past, screaming at a dog that had stolen the stick they were using in a game. Their high-pitched shrieks caused Concannon to wince, quickly covering his ears.

MacLeod paused a moment before softly whispering, "We'll be needing those bricks for the new smoke house we talked about, probably sooner than originally expected. We need to work on smoking as many tongues as we can this year. I would hate to see them go to waste."

"Aye, but we have the time yet, have we not?"

"Not as much as you may think. Get those Indians working and dunk your head in the water trough. We need to talk about a few things."

He watched Concannon shuffle over to where the workers waited, quickly getting them to their feet. Within minutes, he had them shouldering their tools and heading out to the area where the dirt and clay from down by the river had been piled high. Close by, a stack of hay waited to be mixed with the clay.

Yesterday's conversation with Francesca was forcing MacLeod to face problems he had hoped would work themselves out on their own. Sadly, it didn't appear that was the case. As it was, he didn't know how he was going to pay for the tools and goods he had ordered last year. By now, his order would have arrived in Boston, been filled, and on its way back. Already, there were loans due to merchants in Monterey. He knew they would wait to be paid, but for how long? This drought, and their decision to cull the herd and kill early, forced him to face a possibility he didn't want to face.

Francesca knew about some of the loans, but she wasn't aware of the gravity of the situation, nor did she know the total of the order he had placed last year. Nothing trivial—it was just more tools they needed that were currently unavailable here in Alta California; and, of course, books. His library in their little two-room adobe house already took up a good part of one wall. Even Francesca was struggling through a few of the easier books.

While MacLeod knew some of the goods were not essential, he also figured things would be better by the time they were delivered. Especially since from the time he ordered until a ship returned with his order was nigh on a year. Unfortunately, things were not better, they were worse.

With the workers having been given direction, Concannon dunked his head in the water trough before coming up, gasping for breath. After wringing the water out of his hair and beard he returned to where MacLeod waited.

"And now you'll be telling me why it is you're in such a hurry. Wouldn't have anything to do with these poor critters looking at starvation?" Concannon stated knowingly.

"Considering the condition you've kept yourself in lately, I didn't figure you'd have noticed," MacLeod countered.

Concannon looked away in shame. "I fear I'll not be capable of righting myself without help. Esperanza's told me to find a place in the shed to sleep if I can't come home without the wine in me. It'll be getting worse, I fear."

MacLeod didn't say anything for a moment before pointing at Concannon. "You had a reason to feel broken for a spell. I know what it feels like to have lost your child, though mine came back to me. You still have a good wife to look after, and we have our work here if we want to keep this place. It's up to you, Sean."

"What is it you want me to be doing then?"

MacLeod figured walking a spell might help clear Concannon's head. In truth, MacLeod always found he thought better when walking or in the saddle. As the two men walked, he filled Concannon in on what he and Francesca had decided they needed to do in an effort to make ends meet.

"These two-year olds you're to slaughter—will you be getting a good price for their hides?" Concannon asked, spitting into the dirt at his feet as he wiped his mouth.

"Shouldn't make a difference on hides. Tallow's another matter. We'll suffer there, but I don't think it can be helped."

"And Francesca's agreed to killing off breed stock?" he asked suspiciously. "Or did you even mention it? Somehow, I can't see her agreeing with you on this. You know how she loves her cows."

MacLeod nodded in agreement. "She not happy with it, but if we're to survive I can't see any other way."

"But if the rains come and there is another year in the future of the ranch, there will be less hides next year—possibly even the year after. Will there be enough to meet your obligations?"

Damn him for bringing that up, MacLeod thought. The only person MacLeod had to confide in, other than Francesca, was the Irishman. The problem was that Concannon had a way of getting right to the heart of any question without bouncing around the edges.

"Not sure. Whatever way it goes, I'll need some understanding from the merchants who hold the notes."

"Does she know?"

"Some, not everything."

Suddenly, a scream split the air as two horses raced out of the courtyard toward them. Diego sped by on his little black stallion, holding on to the horse's mane with one hand while looking over his shoulder and laughing. MacLeod and Concannon stepped back quickly as the bay gelding Catalina loved to ride raced past in pursuit of her step-brother, a look of pure determination etched on her face.

Concannon whistled. "That young lady will catch him one day and she'll never let him forget it."

MacLeod could only shake his head and laugh. "Francesca doesn't even begin to know how to handle her. I pity the man who falls for her."

"Back to your problem now. From what you told me a time ago, you have the money you'd need," Concannon said. "If you had a mind to go after it, I'd be glad to ride with you."

MacLeod slowly exhaled. Concannon was right. The money, or at least the silver, was there, buried in a cache among a high group of rocks, far out in the desert. Maybe five, six days ride with good horses and plenty of water, in case the springs were dry. But there were also other factors involved, ones MacLeod wasn't quite willing to face.

"Your little fellow you buried," MacLeod began, "you put him in the ground up there under those trees?"

Concannon looked up to the little grove of trees on a knoll where they had buried his son and nodded. MacLeod had watched him walk up there almost every day.

"Well, if you hadn't had a way of placing him in the ground; if you only had some rocks to lay over him and you couldn't be sure the animals wouldn't get to him, you might not be so anxious to go up there. I buried my Maria under a rock shelf of sorts. In hopes of keeping the animals out, I placed rocks around the opening and jammed them in as best I could." MacLeod paused a moment before continuing. "The silver is buried close by, but I fear going back and seeing that her grave has been opened. Don't think I could ever do it. It's best that she lie there the way I placed her."

"Then it will be a gamble of sorts," Concannon stated. "If you slaughter enough, and the market remains fair, will it be enough?"

MacLeod had added up the numbers far too many times to be wrong. "Not everything. I had figured on catching up next year, but now I'm worried prices may not hold if others see things the way I do. There could end up being more hides and tallow than the ships have room for."

Concannon reached down for a blade of grass and stuck it in his mouth. "Don't suppose you could have these things coming in on the ship sold elsewhere?"

"Fraid not. Few know how to use those tools you had a mind to tell me about. I was planning on surprising you. Thought you could build her some decent furniture. And some of the books I ordered would offend most, at least those without open minds. The Church frowns upon liberal thinking. Fellow called Voltaire is just one example."

"It may be a blessing in disguise. I could build two of everything and sell them in Monterey. Pay for the tools in a hurry."

MacLeod chuckled. "We may all end up building furniture or sawing wood if things don't improve. While you're thinking about other ways we can save this place, saddle a horse and find Sisquoc. We saw a bunch of cattle from this Rancho Santiago place up by the foothills. We need them all pushed back onto their own land."

Without a word, Concannon turned away and started for the saddlery.

"And, Sean," MacLeod called after him. "The women are worried about you. As much as you may wish you could, you can't bring the boy back. And speak with Esperanza—I think she may have something to tell you."

Francesca leaned against the door post, her arms crossed, watching the child play in the dirt. It would soon be time to call them in to wash before they ate, to avoid them bothering their father when he came home. William had so much to worry about lately and he didn't need to worry about the children running around screaming at one another, as Diego and Catalina usually did whenever they had nothing else to do.

The two children were so different. But what had she expected, they were with no common blood. In the cramped confines of the two-room adobe it was difficult enough not to step on each other, add in two rambunctious children and it was a recipe for disaster. Francesca shook her head. Just one more thing that MacLeod continued promising her, a bigger home. Sadly, the ranch always came first.

Francesca addressed Rosalie, the woman who had lived with her since Francesca had been cast out of her family home by her father who refused to believe she had been raped. "Have you ever seen it like this before; so long without the good rain?"

The old woman put down the dress she was embroidering for Catalina. "Yes, I have. I have also seen the years when there was too much rain. The rivers ran into the fields and the town. I do not know which is worse, but yes, I have seen the dry times too. When the rains did not come, the people in the pueblo would carry the Virgin Denvestra Senhora del Rosario through the town and pray for rain."

"I have heard them talk of this. Did it bring the rains?" Francesca questioned.

Rosalie shrugged her thin shoulders. "Sometimes. If it did not rain, they would keep doing it until it did."

Francesca watched MacLeod approach, stopping momentarily to speak with Concannon before continuing toward the house. "I worry for him," she whispered, her voice low. "He believes he is the only one that can save our ranch. He does not know how to accept the possibility of defeat."

"I saw that in his eyes when he came to our room with Father Fernández."

"Oh, Rosalie, that was ten years ago. He has changed. He no longer hates all the people he must deal with."

"He is a hard man and he will not change. He believes he is always right."

"That is true," Francesca agreed with a smile. Sometimes she didn't agree with him, but she knew how to make him change his mind without him knowing it. "There is something I must speak to him about and I think I must do it now."

Francesca walked toward him, watching as a smile wiped away the lines of concern etched upon his face when he saw her. When she was mere inches from him, she held out both hands to him, taking his rough hands in hers. "You must not look so worried. It frightens the children. They think you are angry with them."

"Can't be helped. It's mighty hard to smile during times like this. I spoke to Sean. Found him drunk again."

"Did you tell him that Esperanza will have another child, hopefully a healthier one?"

"No," MacLeod stated. "I figure that's her job. Though I told him she had something to tell him and that he can't go on the way he has been."

"He is a good man. We must have patience with him. But for now, I have something I wish to say. Come, let us sit a moment." She led him over to a wooden bench that sat beneath an olive tree she had planted when they first built their adobe house. Thanks to her insistence on planting cuttings from the mission orchards, they now had a number of fruit trees growing behind the house. Despite that fact, they didn't do well in their production and she didn't know why. MacLeod said he had sent word to a man in Los Angeles, a Frenchman named Don Luis de Aliso. He was said to have brought European grape clippings into Alta California. Where they would plant them or who would take care of them, Francesca didn't know.

"We spoke of some things yesterday, but there is something else I must speak to you about. I am worried about Diego. He has no interest in the ranch. In fact, he is only happy when he is on his horse or teasing Catalina. I wish he had a teacher so that he could learn more than just playing vaquero."

"Bothers me some too. I wish there was a school we could send him to. I haven't the time to try and teach him. I'd love to have sent him back to Boston for a proper education."

"Yes, but I would not like it if he was not here," Francesca added. She giggled. "Besides, what would Catalina do without him?"

"Probably start becoming a proper lady. Lord, that girl will have a hard time finding a man to marry. Although, she'll be a beauty."

Francesca folded her hands in her lap and turned to watch his face. "Do you think she looks like him?" she asked softly.

"Don't see him in her at all. I'm sorry, but she's going to be even more beautiful than you, if that's possible."

"You are laughing at me," she said, her face falling.

"He's gone, Francesca. He can't hurt you ever again."

"I only wish that she could have been ours," Francesca whispered sadly.

"We have two beautiful children of our own. There is no need to concern yourself with the other two not being our own. They're loved and that's all that matters."

"I know you are right. It is good that I hear it from you."

MacLeod smiled as he rose from the bench. "I told Concannon to find Sisquoc and ride up and drive those RS cattle back across the marker line. The more I think about it the more it bothers me. Don't know why yet, but it does. Was there something else you wanted to discuss?"

"Yes, I have been thinking since we spoke yesterday—about the cattle. I do not want to kill off any of the cows. I think we should try to find a way to feed them all until it rains and the grass is good again. Do you think the one who is next to us will kill his cows?"

MacLeod let out a slow breath. "Sometimes, Francesca, you ask the questions I should be asking myself. Would be interesting to know what he's planning to do, especially since he's in worse shape than we are."

She knew she had made her point, at least for the moment. She also knew this conversation would come up again if things didn't get better. And soon. Francesca couldn't help but wonder if Rosalie's remarks about the ceremony where everyone prayed for rain actually worked.

SANTIAGO HACIENDA

Cesario Santiago reined the big sorrel stallion to a halt and waved the others past. He had come down two days before on a trading ship, accompanied by two *gauchos* from Argentina. He needed a moment alone to contemplate what he saw before him. Much had been accomplished since the last time he was here, but there was still much to do and he knew he had to send a report back on the next ship. He knew those who had funded his ranch and cattle here in Alta California expected results, but this drought could very well ruin him, if not all of them. The money he had paid out in bribes, cattle, and supplies needed could not be recouped unless the ranch was a success.

"Doñ Santiago, it is good that you have come again."

"Pacheco, I see you have been busy," Santiago said. "What are those Indians doing over there?" he asked, pointing at the activity surrounding him.

"They are returning to the river for more water to make the bricks."

"Can they not take it from the stream?" Santiago asked in confusion.

Pacheco rubbed the side of his cheek. "Of course, but perhaps I can show you why I send them to the river."

Santiago felt he already knew the reason. He studied the thick-bodied man slouched in his saddle a few feet away. He was very dark skinned, meaning recent Indian blood, similar to many of the *gauchos* in Argentina. That fact made him wonder how this man would get along with those Santiago was bringing up from Argentina on the next ship. He had no doubt the vaqueros here in Alta California knew their way around cattle, but he preferred those he was more familiar with. He also wondered if the stories he had heard were true—about how the man had lost his eye. If they were, he owed the man who had passed the information along to him. Either way, Santiago vowed to find out soon.

He took some time examining the land around the spot chosen for his home and the ranch buildings. The land was much the same as he had seen on the ride down from Monterey. Although, it was possible the lack of rain had hurt this part of the land even more than in the north. *Such a beautiful valley, but far too dry now,* he thought to himself.

Pacheco pointed off to a grove of trees. "I have placed your tent on that small hill, away from the Indians and vaqueros."

"Very well. Ride with me, I wish to see what has been done."

Santiago surveyed the activity as Pacheco led him across the dusty courtyard area where the first layers of adobe bricks had been set for the house. Before they began building, he had been very specific about the thickness of the walls. In the heat of summer he wished the house to be as cool as possible. The old Indian, who Santiago had been told helped supervise the reconstruction of the little mission at the far end of the valley after the earthquake, had shrugged his shoulders and doubled the order for bricks.

"I have fifty Indians making the adobe bricks you will need," Pacheco explained as they rode. "As you can see, some are filling the forms and placing them in the sun. When they are dry enough, they will be removed so that we can make use of the forms again. I have others out in the fields cutting grass, and some digging the clay we found near the river below."

"And the water for these bricks. Is it from the stream?"

"I have *carretas* carry water in these jugs you see for the adobe."

Santiago pointed to a pile of nearby red tiles. "They were not here before. I had hoped to have some for the house."

"Yes. The administrator for the mission had given them to a friend," Pacheco explained. "He was too slow so we went down one night and carried them back here."

"And no one will complain to the authorities?" Santiago questioned.

Pacheco shrugged. "There is no way to tell where they come from."

The two men continued to ride across the area that would eventually be the courtyard while Pacheco pointed out the progress that had been made. Halting for a moment, Santiago pointed to the nearby trees lying on the ground, their roots wrapped in old burlap bags. "And those are my fruit trees?"

"Olive trees and fruit trees. We will stop making the bricks tomorrow and begin digging holes for the trees."

Santiago couldn't help but think about the water that would be necessary for the plantings to grow. "Have you seen anything like this before—the land, this lack of rain?"

"Many years ago, we experienced something similar," Pacheco said, leaning on the large fork of his saddle. "But maybe not like this. I will show you how bad it is when we are finished here. There is also a man you may want to speak with. He is here."

"I will speak with him later. For now, I would like to see the land."

Two hours later, Pacheco pointed to the creek where it flowed out of the mountains and onto Rancho Santiago land. "You see how low it is? They tell me in good years it covers those rocks." His voice was somber when he continued. "It is lower each time I come to see. There is something else I want you to see."

Nodding, Santiago followed him as they rode up and over a long-rounded ridge of land before descending down into a shallow valley. Another stream flowed out from a narrow canyon and ran down to where they sat on their horses.

Santiago rode to the edge of the stream and allowed his horse to drink. "This is good. We need to feed this water into the other stream. From the looks of it, there is plenty here."

"Yes, there is very much water here. It does not wet the land, but the cattle will not go thirsty. Although, it is most unfortunate that it is not on your land."

Santiago glared at Pacheco. "What do you mean it's not on Rancho Santiago land?"

Pacheco reined his horse around and pointed back up the small hill behind them. "Your land begins up there. We passed a pile of rocks—that is the line for Rancho Colinas de Oro land. This water is theirs."

Santiago kneed his horse through the three-foot depth of water and up the far embankment, continuing out onto Colinas de Oro land. Pacheco remained behind.

"I see some of my cattle are on this side," Santiago said when he returned. "Why is that?"

"I do not know," Pacheco said. "Perhaps they like the grass on this side. It is a shame more of them do not know about this grass."

Santiago had to admit the idea intrigued him. "It is time to return. I want to speak with this man you spoke of. After that, I want you to tell me when the house will be finished. There is someone I wish to bring out here, but she will not live in a house that is nothing more than a mud shelter.

After the two men returned, Pacheco left Santiago sitting under the trees where his tent had been set up. Santiago allowed the two Indian women to unpack his things and finish placing them in boxes. A few moments later Pacheco returned with a weathered-looking Mexican man who bowed deeply before squatting beside Santiago's bench.

"He came to me some days ago," Pacheco began. "I will let him tell you what he had to say."

With little prompting the old man explained how he had worked at La Purísima Concepión and helped to build the aqueduct that brought water down out of the hills to the mission. He explained that he had seen how the water in the creek had slowed in its flow and that perhaps there was a way to bring other water out of the mountains—assuming it could be found.

"Do you believe him?" Santiago asked Pacheco after dismissing the old man.

Pacheco scratched his groin and shrugged. "There is no reason for him to make up such a story. I did not ask him to come here."

"Very well. Find something he can do. I am sure there is a job for him somewhere. I will think about what he has said, but it may be of no importance."

Santiago watched Pacheco carefully, gauging his reaction to the next question. He knew that it would tell him much. Pulling a cigar from the pocket of his jacket, he lit it, watching the yearning in Pacheco's face. Tobacco was not readily available, so it was rare they could indulge.

"Do you know who owns this Rancho Colinas de Oro?" Santiago asked, offering a cigar to Pacheco.

Pacheco nodded, his eyes never leaving Santiago's, while he lit the cigar with the offered match. Pacheco had seldom seen a self-lighting match and was just as astonished as the first time. "I know them."

Santiago knew this, but he wanted to hear Pacheco say it. When he heard the story about how Pacheco lost his eye, he knew he wanted the man in his employment, especially with the reputation that accompanied him. Everyone had said he was a man who had no fear of breaking the law, since he was the law, or what there was of it.

"This—that you have shown me today—I know you are not a man familiar with cattle, but what do you think of my situation here?"

Santiago was pleased to see Pacheco did not hesitate with his opinion.

"I think you are in trouble. I think your cattle will not survive the year, at least not many of them. But I think you know this. Why are you asking me?"

"You are not a stupid man. You showed me what I needed to see." Santiago walked over to the opposite side of the grove of trees and pointed across to the low foothills in the distance. "That land, and that water over there, I will need it to survive. Tomorrow I intend to ride to this place and speak with the people who own it. I would like to meet them. You will come with me."

RANCHO COLINAS DE ORO

As if making up for its failure to saturate the land during the previous months, nature now bathed it with the glow from a brilliant sun. A sky of blue, that reminded MacLeod of the waters of a high mountain lake, stretched from the low mountains in the east to those that shielded the valley from the coastal storms. After reaching the last adobe hut in the little complex of shops they had built on the ranch, he waited for the man to finish repairing the old saddle on the bench in front of him.

"Can you fix it enough so I can still use it?" MacLeod asked. He hated using the one saddle worthy of riding to town to work the ranch.

"Señor, I think it will be good. But with this tool I can only do a little. The knife here is no good. You can find another, maybe?"

"I'll see what I can do. Do the best you can for now. When you're done with it have someone saddle a horse for me," MacLeod ordered.

Just then, Concannon came out of the little house he shared with Esperanza and shuffled toward MacLeod.

MacLeod stood waiting for him while mentally going over the list of chores he needed to accomplish before they began a round-up of their cattle and all the items he knew the ranch needed. He had no idea how he was going to pay for them yet, but they were necessary nonetheless. As Concannon approached he took in his appearance and wondered if he had taken their talk the day before seriously.

"You get those cows chased back yesterday?" MacLeod asked.

Concannon nodded. "Worked until it was too dark to see the brands. I have a feeling there's more than we found."

MacLeod felt a tinge of uneasiness. He had a feeling that might be the case. "Well, maybe you should run up there every couple of days and do what you can."

"I believe somebody's pushing them over. It's only happening up above where we can't always keep an eye on them."

"That's what I was afraid of," MacLeod said.

Concannon stepped to the side and looked past MacLeod. "Would you be expecting visitors by any chance?" he asked. "Looks like five riders."

MacLeod turned and peered in the direction Concannon was staring. From what he could tell, the riders were still a quarter mile off, coming from the direction of Rancho Santiago.

Neither man spoke as the riders closed the distance at a steady jog. "Couldn't be anyone other than the new one next to us," MacLeod finally said. "Seems an awfully big group just to say hello."

Concannon ran a hand through his hair. "You know, if you squint your eyes a wee bit, I think you might be recognizing the fat one on the right. I'm thinking he looks like the fellow I last saw walking down the road with no pants on."

"That was a long time ago, think you may be right. Doesn't look like he's wearing a uniform now though," MacLeod stated.

"Still a snake, just without the authority," Concannon countered.

MacLeod spit in the dirt at his feet. "Don't imagine he'll try anything unless I prod him. You suppose the other one is this Santiago fellow. That sorrel he's riding with all that silver on the saddle looks to be enough to pay off all my debts."

"Why would you be figuring they're here together?"

"Maybe this Santiago doesn't know about us. Least, I'll give him the benefit of not knowing. Why don't you slip into the house and tell Francesca we have visitors. And keep her there."

MacLeod walked out to meet the riders who brought their horses to a halt and spread out in front of him. Ignoring the one he knew as Pacheco, MacLeod focused on the big, clean-shaven man on the sorrel. Judging from his clothes, MacLeod surmised him to be Santiago. Without even speaking to him, he didn't like the man.

"I am Cesario Santiago. I have come to introduce myself," the man said, smiling as he touched the brim of his sombrero in a mock salute. "I am the owner of this land next to yours."

"Figured as much. The name's MacLeod, William MacLeod, though I figure you already know that."

"Ah, but of course you are. You are the Americano they talk so much about."

"That's right." MacLeod had no desire to give out any more information about himself than was necessary.

Santiago dismounted and handed the reins over to one of the vaqueros. Pacheco remained sitting on his horse, his hands resting on the pommel of his saddle.

MacLeod studied Santiago as he came forward. He was a large man, a good three inches taller than himself, and roughly thirty or forty pounds heavier with a trimmed mustache. The man walked forward with long, easy strides, unlike many Californians who spent most of their waking hours in a saddle.

The man offered his hand. "I have had the honor of entertaining many Americano sea captains when their ships port in our harbor in Buenos Aires. It was always a pleasure to discuss with them your American ideas."

Just then, MacLeod felt Francesca grip his arm.

"What is *he* doing here?" she asked, her voice dripping with disdain.

"Señor Santiago here has come to say hello. I doubt he knows about our relationship with Pacheco," MacLeod said, loud enough for Santiago to hear. Turning his attention back to Santiago, he nodded. "It would be a pleasure to hear about your plans for your land, Señor Santiago. However, if that man there works for you, I'd send him on his way. I will not tolerate having him on our land," MacLeod said, pointing directly at Pacheco.

Santiago smiled. "Of course. If he offends you. Perhaps, someday you can tell me why he offends you." Without another word he waved Pacheco away before turning to face Francesca. "I have heard from those in Monterey that the governor granted you this land. You are most fortunate. It is a beautiful valley."

"Yes, it is," Francesca agreed. "I hope you will be happy here."

"I am sure I will. Perhaps once my home is complete you will come and meet a woman I am taking care of. She will be staying with me when she is not in Monterey."

"Yes, it would be nice to have another woman nearby. We do not get a chance to visit often."

MacLeod watched Santiago take in their small adobe house and surrounding shops with a practiced eye, as if measuring their ability to make it through the year based on what he saw. He was about to ask the man how he came to employ Pacheco when Francesca turned to her husband. "We should invite Señor Santiago in for a cup of chocolate. Perhaps he can tell us about this country he comes from and why he has chosen to come here and live."

Francesca didn't wait for MacLeod to reply, instead opting to take Santiago's arm and leading him onto the house. MacLeod followed reluctantly, shaking his head at her ability to overlook the appearance of Pacheco in order to discover what they wished to learn about their new neighbor. MacLeod knew he would have balked at issuing such an open invitation.

When Francesca had seated Santiago in the one chair Concannon had fashioned for them, she sent Juana to make cups of chocolate for each of them before asking Rosalie to take the two young children outside to play. Rosalie gathered the children and strolled over to the door, glaring at Santiago as she passed. MacLeod covered his face to mask his grin. *It appears Rosalie has the same feelings about our new neighbor,* he thought to himself.

MacLeod pulled a bench over for Francesca to sit. He stood behind her and listened as Santiago began to talk.

"The first time I saw this country I fell in love with it," Santiago began, addressing Francesca. "I do hope the rains return this year and bring back its beauty."

Francesca smiled, squeezing MacLeod's arm. "Will you not tell me about this land you have been given? I had always believed it would be returned to the Indians for their use."

Santiago held out his hands and shrugged. "Coming from my country I was not aware of the promise made to the savages. I attended a meeting with your governor and asked for a grant. He was most gracious by giving me what is now Rancho Santiago."

"I understand that was Governor Figueroa?" MacLeod asked.

"Yes, Governor José Figueroa and I are related, in a minor way. When I came to this country, I did not know this. The good governor and I were discussing our families one evening and discovered a connection. It was most fortunate for me as you can see."

"Most fortunate," MacLeod muttered as Francesca's elbow connected with his ribs.

"You have come from Monterey?" Francesca asked. "You have seen our governor then? I have not had this honor."

Santiago paused for a moment before adding, "Then you have not heard? Governor Figueroa felt he needed time to recover from an illness. He appointed José Castro to take his place. Unfortunately, Governor Figueroa died soon after."

Francesca covered her mouth with her hand and bowed her head. "I had not heard this," she said.

"I believe I have met this Castro," MacLeod said. "He's a friend of Vallejo, I believe. It's just too bad about Figueroa. From what I've heard, he was one of the more competent leaders sent up here from Mexico."

"Yes, I have heard that also," Santiago agreed.

Francesca turned to MacLeod. "But Dón Castro—is he not one who believes Alta California should manage its own affairs and elect its own leaders?"

MacLeod nodded his head. "Oh, yes, he's one of the young firebrands. Hard to say what Mexico will do when they hear of his appointment."

Santiago turned to MacLeod and changed the subject. "You say you are still an American? You have not become a citizen of Mexico? How is this that you have been granted this land?"

"Rancho Colinas de Oro belongs to my wife. It was given to her by Governor Argüello," MacLeod explained.

"Most interesting," Santiago said, placing his hand over his cup when Juana appeared with more chocolate. "Is it not unusual to grant such a large amount of land to a woman?"

McLeod felt Francesca's hand tighten on his arm. "I don't know how unusual it is," MacLeod said. "At the time, there were far fewer people here in Alta California. The trade in cattle hides had just begun. In fact, the number of ships trading on the coast were few and far between."

Santiago placed his cup on the floor beside his chair. "It is certainly a splendid piece of land. I wish I had come sooner, before it was taken," Santiago said with a smile.

MacLeod couldn't remember seeing a less honest smile. He couldn't help but wonder how much of this information Santiago already knew. In truth, there were a few questions he would like answered.

"You seem to be running a lot of cattle on your land already. Were you able to buy them from the commissioner that was appointed when the missions broke up? As I understood it the priests were only allowed to retain their quarters and their gardens. The herds and crops were to be distributed to the pueblo."

Again, Santiago smiled and shrugged. "I was not made aware of the method of distribution. I met with this man who the Governor had appointed and came to an agreement on the purchase of the cattle."

And the man had taken the next ship south with the money—or so MacLeod had been told. He couldn't help but wonder what kind of agreement Santiago and the mission administrator had come to.

"You bring up the cattle," Santiago said. "How many are you managing on your land?"

"We're running about six thousand." For the time being, MacLeod intended to keep their plan to himself, at least until he discovered where Santiago stood.

Santiago's eyebrows rose a fraction. "Are you not worried about this weather we are having? I don't recall ever having weather like this in Argentina. Will you have adequate water and grass for so many?"

MacLeod folded his arms over his chest, a slight frown ceasing his forehead. The man had exposed himself without even realizing it. MacLeod knew that Santiago was aware of the water on Rancho Colinas de Oro land. *So why is he acting like he doesn't know?*

"I think we can manage. It looks like a tough year ahead, but our water is sufficient, I believe. Is it the same with you?"

MacLeod could tell Santiago knew they were both playing a game. He nodded, "But, of course. The grass is thin, but I have made preparations to obtain more water for the cattle. I am finding that much water is needed for the building of the hacienda, the crops, and trees I have brought here. I cannot afford to lose any of those."

Francesca spoke up, as if sensing the tension building between the two men. "Dón Santiago, when is it you expect to complete your home? I am most anxious to meet this woman you have spoken of."

Santiago rose and picked his sombrero up off the floor. Holding it at his side, he replied, "I believe she will be coming down on one of the trading ships soon. I have ordered my people to expedite the completion of the house. You can imagine she would not like living in a tent until it was complete."

"I am sure she would understand if it were not complete. We have all had the misfortune of living for a short time in places we did not like," Francesca offered.

Santiago gave the slightest bow and walked toward the door before turning back to face them. "Perhaps you can ride over to the hacienda when you have the opportunity. We may wish to speak again," Santiago said, addressing MacLeod.

MacLeod noted the lack of warmth in the invitation, an invitation unlike any he had received from Californios whose warmth and generosity had overcome some of his original contempt for them. "Perhaps," was all he felt the need to say.

"**I** do not like that man," Francesca said as they watched Santiago mount his horse and, accompanied by the vaqueros who had ridden over with him, ride away. Pacheco rode up and joined Santiago just before they disappeared over the ridge that separated the land grants. "Did you see who he brought with him? Why is this? Does he not know?"

"Been asking myself that same question since they rode up. Although, I expect he does know," MacLeod said. "The important question is why. Seems like he wanted to irritate us from the start, in spite of all the good neighboring he claims he came to do."

Concannon joined them from the spot he had chosen to watch the group, the shotgun cradled beneath his arm. "You should have killed that man when you had the chance. There be trouble ahead, I'd be betting."

"Expect you're right. Awful big coincidence this Santiago fellow hiring Pacheco without his knowing about our past. And assuming he did, why bring him along unless he wanted to stir up a hornet's nest."

Francesca took MacLeod's arm. "Is he not still a soldier?"

"I guess not. Military doesn't pay much; that is, when they do get paid. He's probably been making do by skimming off the duties collected from the ships. If I had to guess, Santiago heard about Pacheco and us and decided to hire him. Pacheco's no cattleman, so why hire him unless you have something else in mind?"

"I would still like to know why he came over here. I am angry and I do not like deceitful people," Francesca seethed.

"I assume he found out as much as he could about us by asking around and decided to come over and see if we measured up. Funny thing is, he asked questions he already knew the answers to. Seems like he wanted to add to what he already knew and give nothing up about himself or his ranch."

Francesca dropped MacLeod's arm and marched back into the house. It wasn't often he saw her as angry as this, but he couldn't blame her. Pacheco had done his best to rape her. The only thing that saved her was the Indian girl, Juana, shooting him. The patch he wore over an empty eye socket was the result of Francesca's ripping at his face while he wrestled her to the ground.

Just then, the sound of a horse, seemingly in a hurry, made MacLeod and Concannon turn. Young Diego was racing past the last of the little adobe buildings and reined his lathered horse back on its heels.

"Father, who was that man? Did you see his horse? I would give a hundred of ours for that sorrel with the golden mane."

"Well, son, first off you don't own any horses to give away. And second," MacLeod said, noting the Spanish style spurs on his young son's boots. "If I see you wearing those spurs again you won't be riding any horse. Hope you can walk real good with them on."

"But everyone wears them," the young boy argued.

"Diego, we've had this discussion before. I don't care what everyone else wears—I don't wear them and you won't either. When you learn to ride proper that horse will do as you ask. Probably better. You know my feelings about abusing horses. Now go and take them off. When you are done, round up your sister. Tell her that her mother would like to talk to her."

"I doubt she'll listen to me, she never does," Diego murmured.

"Well, try. And get rid of those spurs," MacLeod said firmly.

Once Diego was out of earshot, Concannon nodded toward the retreating group of riders. "He's got to be in as bad a shape as us, yet I know he has a hundred or more Indians over there working on that place of his. Wonder how he pays for their care?"

"Which makes his visit all the more troubling. Listen, the agent for Bryant, Sturgis, & Co. passed by day before yesterday. Said their ship from Boston should stop here in Santa Barbara by tomorrow. I think I'll ride over there and see if they brought those things I ordered."

Concannon scratched at his beard. "And what would you be wanting me to do while you're off traipsing around the country?"

"Well, I'd assign one of the trustier Indians to keep the brick makers working," MacLeod said with a grin. "But I'd feel a mighty bit better if you stuck around the house while I'm away. And keep that bird gun handy, which works just as well on skunks. I can still smell the odor of the last one that stopped by," MacLeod added with a chuckle.

Concannon looked away before adding, "Those RS cows you wanted pushed back—Sisquoc told me he sent three vaqueros up to take care of it."

"We'll need to keep an eye on it. Maybe check every couple of days to see they stay across the line. There's another thing...I'm thinking of giving the job of majordomo to Jesus Alvarado. We need one, and he knows cattle."

"What about Sisquoc?"

"He's happy looking after the Indians as their *alcalde*. The vaqueros and Indians respect Alvarado, and we're going to need good leadership in the months ahead if we expect to make it through."

MacLeod wasn't sure whether Concannon felt he should have had the job, but he knew Concannon's limits, and his drinking was a problem that had yet to be taken care of. "I need you close to the house, Irish. One of us should always be nearby from now on. Understand?"

"Don't you worry, Willie, I'll be doing what's needed."

MacLeod grinned at the nickname. It had been awhile since anyone had called him Willie. "And while you're about, round up all the hides we've been collecting. I haven't the time to run them to the coast right now, but I'll need to make good on a few promises as soon as possible."

"Going back to what I was saying about the three vaqueros we sent up to chase off the cows—only two came back," Concannon said. "Sisquoc figured maybe the other decided to go back across the tulles to his old village."

MacLeod could tell Concannon had more to say. "You don't?" he surmised.

"We've had problems with that one. Tends to look like he's working when he's not, always complaining about one thing or another. I even thought I caught him stealing once, but couldn't be sure. His village is not there anymore. It was wiped out with the last sickness. So, no, he's gone somewhere else."

"Well, keep an eye out for him. He knows where we keep everything so he could come back if he's a mind to. If you catch him doing something he shouldn't be, make a lesson of him."

Concannon nodded in understanding. "You have a good trip. I'll be looking forward to those tools you spoke of."

The day was still young when MacLeod entered their adobe to find Francesca still fretting about Santiago's appearance. After calming her fears about Pacheco's proximity, and informing her of his discussion with Concannon that one of them would remain close by, he told her of his plans to ride over to Santa Barbara and meet up with the ship. Francesca immediately ordered the Indian girl to wrap the leftover tortillas and cooked beef and prepare a travelling hamper for him. Within the hour MacLeod had his horse saddled, another on a lead line, and two pack mules. He knew he would need the mules if the ship had brought back the items he had ordered.

Dropping down into the valley, MacLeod crossed the Santa Ynez River, picking up the El Camino Real. The whole ride he couldn't help but think about their luck at having a full stream of water running out of the mountains. As he continued along, the road worked its way down through the narrow Gaviota Pass toward the ocean before turning south and travelling along the narrow strip of coast below the Santa Ynez Mountains. Having stayed in the area before, he already knew the spot he intended to camp.

Suddenly, his black stallion's ears flipped forward before letting out a snort, alerting him to their nearby guests. "Looks like we may have company tonight," he whispered, reaching behind his back to draw the pistol from his bedroll. With the old Bates of London .60 caliber flintlock hanging loosely at his side, he kneed the horse off the road and into the trees along the nearby creek. Just ahead of him, two horses stood dosing, their lead ropes snugged up to the bushes. A few feet away a spiral plume of smoke rose from a small fire burning beside the creek.

MacLeod reined the horse to a halt. "Howdy, mind if I sit and share your fire? MacLeod asked as he reined his horse to a halt.

MacLeod watched as an old man pushed himself to his feet and bowed his head. He recognized the dress of a Franciscan priest from one of the missions and immediately noted the shaved circle on his scalp.

"You are most welcome to our fire. We have brought little nourishment but we would be happy to share it with you. I am Father Avila."

MacLeod stepped down from the saddle, conscious of the big pistol held at his side. Discreetly pushing it back into his bedroll, he tied the horse to a nearby willow branch. "Much obliged. I believe the women packed enough for all of us," MacLeod said, untying the hamper bundle from off one of the mules.

The other man sitting on his haunches by the fire raised his head, the wide grin upon his face revealing a broken tooth smile. The stranger wore a threadbare poncho over his shoulders and his boots appeared worn thin by hard times. MacLeod took him for a vaquero, still hanging around the mission, hoping for occasional work. Without a word, the man rose and began gathering more wood for the fire. After placing the dry branches beside the priest he went and sat a comfortable distance off.

MacLeod untied the food package and spread it out on the ground beside the fire. "I'd be pleased if you'd share this fare with me."

The old Franciscan produced a small bundle of food of his own and added it to the pile before proceeding to bless it. "You are most kind," he said. Picking up a tortilla, the priest placed some beef and beans on it and handed it to the other man. "His name is Juan Gomez. He is travelling with me to San Miguel Arcángel. I wish to see my friend before he returns to Mexico."

"Juan, here, is one of the mission vaqueros?" MacLeod asked.

Father Avila nodded. "Yes, he has a wife and many children, but there is little for him to do now that the mission is no more. Juan was also in charge of the care of our orchards."

MacLeod nodded, watching in silence as the man ate. It was clear the man was still hungry. "Have you known him long?" MacLeod asked, thinking about the sad shape the fruit trees at the ranch were in.

"Yes, many years. He is a good man."

MacLeod knew that was as good a recommendation as he would get. "My wife and I own Rancho Colinas de Oro. There might be some work there for him when you're done with him—and he can bring his family. Perhaps he can look after my trees?" MacLeod suggested. "Lord knows they need looking after. Stop by and see me on your return. I'm sure the people there will be pleased to see a priest. I know my wife would like it very much." MacLeod knew Francesca often felt the need to speak with someone about her feelings. Sadly, he was not often the best listener.

"Ah, yes, I have heard of it. I believe we will pass nearby on our return. If your people wish, I would be pleased to see them and hear their confessions." Turning to Juan, Father Avila spoke in hushed whispers for a moment. The man's grin said it all. Still smiling, Juan rose and gathered more wood, nodding his head in happiness when he sat back down.

It was not often MacLeod had time to spend talking of things unrelated to the ranch or its problems. It was a breath of fresh air. For the next several minutes, he and Father Avila discussed the trials of secularization. Avila mentioned Father Fernandez's bitter condemnation of the process of breaking up the mission system, based on his years of observation of the Indians. MacLeod found Father Avila resigned to the loss of his life's work and said he now found contentment in his garden and studies.

"Did you know this very place we sit was the sight of a landing by our first governor?"

MacLeod grinned, knowing the good father wished to tell the story. "No, sir. I'm afraid I've not heard much about him."

"Yes, it was in the year of our Lord 1767. Gaspar de Portolá brought his ship into this bay with Father Juan Crespi. They camped here on this very stream. Father Crespi named this spot La Gaviota because of a seagull one of the soldiers had killed."

MacLeod sat by the fire and listened to the old priest tell of the struggle to establish the missions. It was obvious the priest seldom had the opportunity to tell his stories.

The next morning MacLeod woke to find his horse groomed and saddled. A still grinning Juan had stirred up the fire and warmed some tortillas and beans for breakfast. The night before, MacLeod figured he'd leave what food was left for Father Avila and Juan to help them along the rest of their trip. MacLeod knew he could wait until he reached Santa Barbara to eat.

Before riding out, he once again made Father Avila promise to stop at the ranch upon his return. After watching Juan ready everything for travel MacLeod knew he would make a great addition to the vaqueros. MacLeod wasn't sure exactly where they would house Juan's family. In truth, Rancho Colinas de Oro was quickly becoming a thriving little community of its own.

MONTEREY

The gentle sea breeze carrying the smells of Monterey Bay rustled the open curtains in the window of the three-room adobe house at the edge of town. Those new to Monterey often commented on the newly whitewashed home with the stables behind it, and the fence built to keep animals from feasting on its garden. Others spoke of the woman who lived there.

The woman, regal like in her long European style dress, stood at the window of her combination office and receiving room, watching boats fish the waters of the bay while other passerby made trips to and from the beach with people from one of the two ships lying at anchor. Busying themselves with their duties, one of her Indian servants stood nearby running a dust rag over the furniture, which she polished each day, while others walked from the cooking and cleaning room into the mistresses' bedchamber carrying fresh linens.

The woman, unaffected by the workers around her, watched as people gathered on the beach, waiting to be taken out to the ship to spend their trade profits. A boat, pulled through the surf by eight boatmen, rode the last wave onto the beach. Immediately, two men leapt out and pulled it further onto the sand. The woman watched intently as a man stepped over the side of the boat and began walking toward town. She knew within minutes he would be at her door. She let the curtain fall back and walked toward her chair, picking up a heavy leather journal that lay on a nearby desk as she passed. She placed the journal on her lap and crossed her hands on top of it.

Twenty minutes later a knock sounded at the door. A moment later, one of the servants rounded the corner into the office. "Señora, a man is here to see you," the young Indian servant girl announced.

"Yes, I was expecting him. Please show him in."

The man entered and removed his hat, exposing a head of thick gray hair to match his beard. "Doña Montero, I hope you are well," he greeted, offering a fleeting bow. "I would have come sooner but there was a lengthy meeting about the amount they are asking in duties."

Marisol Montero offered a smile and waved him to a chair opposite her. "Captain Jacobs, judging by the date, I believe your trip home and back was swift. And do not worry about not attending me sooner. It is to both our benefits that the duties are as low as possible. I hope you were able to strike a reasonable agreement."

"Most reasonable, I assure you," Captain Jacobs responded. He reached inside his jacket and extracted a thick envelope. "I have here the bills of sale for all the goods you ordered. I must say, ma'am, I would never have filled my hold with such goods, but the first women who came aboard left with their arms filled."

Marisol Montero smiled. All the ship owners, captains, and local merchants who were engaged in the trade were men. They failed to understand that the women often controlled the household purse and no one knew what the women wanted better than another woman, especially one who had been studying the trade in imported goods for the last ten years.

"I hope the women of Monterey have left something for those in other cities," she said.

The American sea captain laughed. "I believe I know where I can find an ample supply for them. It is unfortunate, that in order to make our trade profitable, we have to resort to subterfuge."

"Smuggling is common in this trade, Captain. None of us would make a profit without it," she said. "And the authorities know this. Governor Echeandía raised the duties so high it is the only way."

Jacobs twisted his pea cap in his hands. "You are right, ma'am. But many of us Christians don't like to go against the good book. We pay as much duty as we can, but we still need to make a profit."

Before taking a look at the list of goods she had purchased, Marisol Montero ordered one of the Indian girls to bring a cup of chocolate for the captain while she inspected the list of goods she had purchased. She had already reviewed her own notes before the Captain had arrived. Another ship, with goods of a lesser quality, would be arriving soon, allowing the women of Alta California, who had less purchasing power, to share in the enjoyment of improving their lifestyles.

"I must say, ma'am, your idea of having me round up patterns for the newest designs in New England was excellent. I would not have known were to start on such a venture, but my daughter lives in New York and when her mother wrote to her about your idea, she went to work immediately, talking to business people who knew what you wanted. I sold a handful of those patterns this morning, and the woolens and linens to go with them. When word gets out, the ladies will swamp my ship."

"Yes, we have always been able to purchase materials but not patterns. Now, I trust you have no problem with our original agreement?"

"No, ma'am," Jacobs said. "I've managed to make a fair profit on our agreement. I see no reason to change."

Marisol Montero rose and waved Jacobs back into his chair when he began to rise. She walked to her desk, placing the heavy journal on it and picking up a sealed envelope. With her back to him she said, "And our agreement—you have said nothing about this to anyone, I presume?"

"Doña Montero," he began, rising from his seat. "I am a man of my word. I will admit, I have been asked by others, about my cargo, but it remains between us."

"Very well, Captain. And you have not mentioned my name to anyone?"

Captain Jacobs took his pipe from his pocket and proceeded to fill it. He chuckled. "Ma'am, if the others knew how much profit I was making buying and selling for a woman they would be aghast. No, you will remain anonymous, as we agreed."

"And I trust," Marisol said, with her back still to Jacobs, "that no one besides you knows what I order?"

"As per our agreement."

"Very well, Captain," she said returning to her chair and holding out the envelope to Jacobs. "I have arranged to have a new contract written up, I trust you will approve of it and return it with your signature. I have also increased your share by two percent."

"Ma'am, that is most generous of you. I believe, between us, we will keep the ladies of your country well supplied with their needs."

Captain Jacobs rose with the thick envelope in his hand. "As we have agreed, I will tally my sales and give you a report when I am ready to return to Boston. You will also see that I have included a full financial report of your holdings in a number of Boston banks. I have found this the most prudent method of spreading the risk of bank failures. If I might say, ma'am, you are most certainly one of the wealthier people of Alta California."

"Thank you, Captain," Marisol said. She rose and held out her hand. "I will have a new order for you when we settle up. Good day, sir."

She waited for him to leave before walking over to her desk. Satisfied the servants were occupied elsewhere, she touched a panel at the back of the desk. Instantly, the panel sprung open revealing a compartment large enough to contain a series of small journals and envelopes. She selected one and sat at the desk to make a few entries before placing it back in the compartment, along with the report from Captain Jacobs. Marisol closed the panel and returned to her chair.

Even though she trusted Captain Jacobs, there was always fear of a ship being lost at sea. For this reason, much of her wealth was secreted away in a small iron safe located beneath the desk after being changed into gold or silver. The next ship to arrive would be bringing the coin she had requested. Alta California's financial transactions were regularly settled with notes based on hides and bags of tallow. These she used to pass along to the ship's captains when she gave them her new orders.

Marisol called for her meal while reflecting on her good fortunes in everything but love. When Vicente had taken ill, ten years before, he had called her in and shared with her his holdings, which he told her, if invested wisely, would enable her to live in relative comfort for the rest of her life. After his death she had ordered a few things not available in Alta California. Their arrival had caused a stir among the local women and Marisol, with her late husband's advice in mind, had invested in a small shipment of goods. Her trade had grown to such an extent that her paper accounts, along with her secreted coin, amounted to well over twenty thousand dollars.

A recent American arrival, and businessman, in Monterey, Thomas Larkin, had made it known that he intended on building a home in town of two stories with a sweeping balcony around the entire building. In truth, Marisol was anxious to see the home built and learn of the costs. What else was there to do with her secret fortune? Although by copying such a house she knew she would be revealing the extent of her wealth.

The thought of the American, Larkin, brought the other American to mind, the one who could have stolen her away if she had allowed it. A small smile creased her face. She had heard that the woman he had married had been granted a significant land grant by Governor Argüello somewhere in the south. She couldn't help but regret her last words to him on the sand in San Diego, with the Frenchman's body still unattended.

Marisol sighed, *How was I to know my husband would die so soon after? No, it was the thing to do at the time, but no one had ever made me feel as the American had.*

Marisol walked back to the window to once again look out over the harbor. She wrapped her arms around her body, knowing she would be asked to make a decision soon. Despite everything, these past ten years had changed little in her thinking. No one truly knew about her past. All they saw was a beautiful widow, who lived alone in a fine house.

Would I still have the line of suitors—from American ship's captains, to officials sent up from Mexico to govern Alta California, if they knew of my past? Would the good families of Alta California invite me into their homes if they knew? Who would accept me, knowing I had survived the streets of Vera Cruz by selling myself to eat? she thought to herself as her mind drifted back to the night she had met her husband.

One evening, in Vera Cruz, Vicente Montero had bought the rights to her body, but could not perform. When she took him in her arms he had wept as she offered him his money back. She remembered the moment, thinking it a cruel joke. The next night he found her on the streets and took her to his room and offered her a chance to climb out of the cesspool that was the backstreets of the city. Marry him and come to Alta California with him. He offered to have her taught the ways of the refined and have tutors teach her languages, as well as how to read and write. He even promised to cloth her in the finest clothes available. All she had to do was promise to keep his secret.

Montero spent six months in Vera Cruz while she went through her complete transformation. Regrettably, there was no one for her to celebrate with. She had no parents that she was aware of. In fact, she had no knowledge of who she was at all. Her only blessing was in her natural beauty and the very light skin of a true Spaniard.

After her husband's death she became tired of playing the game. She wanted to escape it all and a way had finally presented itself.

Cesario Santiago had presented himself before her in subtle finery, offering her his companionship. Not to marry, of course, as she had heard he had a wife in Buenos Aires. But, like all such men, there were the excuses of a loveless marriage, one of necessity. It was the type of marriage that could not be dissolved due to the church and the fact that his wife was from an important family.

But Marisol had made it known from the beginning of the courtship that her bed was hers and hers alone. Whether she chose to share it at some point was entirely up to her, and she had yet to make that decision.

Shaking her head, she walked through the house and out into her garden, taking a seat on a nearby bench in the shade of an olive tree. She was twenty-nine, she believed, and Santiago was much older, which was common in Alta California. Since she had never shared her background with anyone it was decided, for the sake of those who might be offended by her living in his house, that he was in fact her uncle, having recently discovered the lineage.

In spite of his argument that she would learn to love him, in a manner, she knew it would never be so. As the years passed since her husband's death, Marisol had put aside the romantic notion of love but wondered instead how a physical relationship would work. However, she would not decide that now. Perhaps in time.

SANTA BARBARA

The town of Santa Barbara had grown considerably since MacLeod first came here on the trail of his abducted son years before. He figured the town now had about a hundred little adobe houses built up around the old presidio. With the ocean at their front, the green clad mountains behind them, and the red tile roofs of the homes, it was a far cry from what he had seen in other towns. In the distance he could see a ship anchored about three miles out in the wide bay. He couldn't tell if it was the one he was told to expect, but he would soon find out.

A long adobe building, which featured three hand-hewn doors overlooking the plaza, housed the local *alcalde's* office; a man MacLeod knew from his first visit here ten years before. As expected, MacLeod found him at his desk upon entering the building.

"Doñ Peña, how is it I always find you working when I come to town?" MacLeod announced. It never failed—if MacLeod didn't mention how hard the man worked, Peña himself would.

"Doñ MacLeod. It has been too long since you have come to visit our beautiful little town."

"Seems so. I heard tell a Boston ship was due. Thought I'd ride down and meet it."

Peña rose from behind the large desk he had imported from the Sandwich Islands when he was appointed *alcalde*. He was a short man, thick-bodied, but well-groomed and now clean-shaven. Dressed in sharp contrast to the man MacLeod had met years ago, Peña walked around to embrace MacLeod. "Yes, that is the *North Star* in my harbor. Do you know Captain Butler?"

"Don't believe I do. But if it's a Bryant, Sturgis, & Co. ship out of Boston, I'm hoping it brought some things for me. Has the captain come ashore yet?"

"Yes, he and the other man with him, the one they call the supercargo, Señor Howard, I believe, they have gone to see the *comandante* at the Presidio."

"And how is your new *comandante*? Never had the pleasure of meeting him," MacLeod asked.

Gaspar Peña had been the *comandante* of the presidio when MacLeod first came, but rumor was he saw no future for himself in the position, and with a family that grew each year, he resigned his position in the military and soon became the *alcalde*. Peña now owned the finest whitewashed adobe home, which sat on the edge of town.

After heavy duties were placed on the ship's cargo by Governor Echeandia, it resulted in a marked increase in smuggling. Peña was thought to skim a percentage of the duties and drop a hint to favored ships' captains, or supercargos, when custom officials were about to pay a visit. As it so happened, the three islands that more or less enclosed the big bay provided a perfect repository for goods. Since the ships were required to go to Monterey first to pay the appropriate duties on their cargos, it was a common occurrence for ships to offload a large portion of their cargo before proceeding to Monterey.

Peña was not a greedy man and those officials in Monterey who were doing the same thing knew they were taking a chance that the person they appointed to replace Gaspar Peña would undoubtedly skim more, leaving less for Monterey officials to pocket.

Peña laughed. "He is learning that the position has its good moments as well as its bad. What can I say?" He gave a shrug. "Before I forget, I would ask—have you met this Doñ Santiago? He was said to be coming down from Monterey to construct his new home. This Rancho Santiago that Governor Figueroa granted him is next to yours, is it not?"

"Right next door," MacLeod stated, pausing for a beat. He needed to know where Peña's loyalties lay before being too open about his new neighbor. "He stopped by yesterday. Plans to complete his house and bring someone down to live with him."

"Yes, I have heard this also." Peña returned to his chair and sat down, leaning his elbows on the desk and steepling his hands. He stared at MacLeod for a moment before speaking. "Doñ MacLeod, I have known you since you stood in front of me and begged my permission to go in search of your son. I know you to be an honorable man. May I place my trust in you a moment?"

"I believe you can," MacLeod stated confidently, curious why the conversation had turned so formal.

Peña spread his hands apart. "This Señor Santiago that is coming to live on this ranch he is building—I have heard too many stories, rumors, whatever you want to call them. I have not made a decision about him yet. I will wait until he stands before me, much like you. That is all I will say about the matter for now."

MacLeod wasn't sure how much he wanted to divulge, so kept it vague. "Only met the man a couple of days ago, but I surely have questions about him after speaking with him. I guess we'll both have to wait and see. Did you know that Sergeant Pacheco is working with him now?"

A look of shock crossed Peña's face. "Pacheco? No, I had not heard. Though someone said he had left the military. Why would this man hire someone like Pacheco? Thank you, you have given me even more to consider. If he is there on that land next to yours, I would be most wary."

"Plan on it," MacLeod stated, eager to get back to the reason he was here. "I believe you said Captain Butler went up to the presidio.

If you don't mind, I'll step up there and catch him before he returns to his ship."

Alcalde Peña followed him to the door. "He will not be returning to his ship tonight. I have invited him to be my guest, he and the other man. You are also invited, of course."

"I thank you, sir, but I'd prefer to be returning to Colinas de Oro as soon as my business with the man is complete."

"Very well. I most certainly understand after what you have just told me. But please remember when you are in Santa Barbara, *mi casa e su casa.*"

After bidding Peña good day, MacLeod led his horse and the mules over to the water trough and let them drink before tying them to a nearby post. He found a place to sit with a good view of the gate to the Presidio.

He dozed in the warmth of the afternoon sun, coming awake with the sound of approaching voices. Two men lurched toward him on legs unaccustomed to walking on a motionless surface. If he had to guess, this was the captain of the Bryant ship that sat in the harbor. Clearly, they had been at sea for many months. Standing, MacLeod brushed the dirt from his pants and removed his wide sombrero, holding it at his side.

The two men approached. The first was tall, whip-thin, with a full beard, twinkling blue eyes and was wearing a peaked cap, which covered most of his long graying hair. The other man, much shorter, yet similar in appearance, seemed to be engaged in an animated conversation.

MacLeod stepped into their path. "Would you by any chance be Captain Butler of the Bryant, Sturgis ship, North Star?"

The tall man came to a halt and leaned back a beat before answering. "I am indeed Captain Jacob Butler. And who might you be? I believe I detect a touch of a New England accent."

"William MacLeod, sir, formerly from Boston, or thereabouts. Might I have a word with you?"

"That you may, that you may. This fellow here is Mr. Howard, my supercargo. He has some duties back at the ship that need to be taken care of, so he'll be off. I actually wondered how I might contact you. I have some things to pass on."

MacLeod nodded. "That's what I came to find out. I heard you had been to Monterey and were on your way here." Before he could continue, Captain Butler held out his hand to silence MacLeod.

Leaning forward, he peered out to sea. "I believe that is the *Makani* coming in now, out of the Sandwich Islands. See how she dropped her sails already. Their captain has never liked this anchorage. Though I can't say I blame him. Between November and April you have to be sure and have slip ropes on your cables. Be ready to put to sea first sign of a Southwester."

MacLeod couldn't help but grin. "I'll try to remember that the next time I anchor in the bay, Captain."

Captain Butler remained silent. After a few moments, he slapped his leg and roared in laughter. "By jove, you got me on that one, son. When you spend your life at sea with one eye on the weather every waking moment, you forget sometimes that you're talking to land lubbers."

71

Butler called out to halt his supercargo. "Give me a moment and I'll have Mr. Howard send your packages, crates, and mail back when he goes aboard. I always keep a boat and strong crew nearby when I'm ashore, just in case I'm needed aboard."

Mail. Could it possibly be a letter from my mother, or another from Senator Benton wanting more in depth information about political matters in Upper California? MacLeod wondered.

He hadn't received anything from home in over two years. The company had lost two ships at sea, and it was always possible that letters had gone down with them. Still, possible news from home made his heart beat faster. Then again, there was also a chance it brought bad news. For all he knew, his mother could have taken ill since she last wrote.

"Why, yes," Captain Butler continued. "Three letters, I believe, as well as half a dozen boxes and packages."

"Three letters?" MacLeod questioned, puzzled.

"You know, there were only two, but we sprung a leak in a couple of our water casks and I decided to port for water in San Blas. Well, now, just as I was about to return to the ship a young fellow came running up to me, said he had a letter for California and wanted to know if I would take it to Monterey with me."

"And it's for me?"

"Yes. It sat in my cabin until I anchored in Monterey and that's when I took a look at it. Since I had two others for you, I just kept it on board with me."

MacLeod scratched his head. *How would a letter for me reach San Blas, Mexico? There had to be a mistake.*

While they waited for the small boat to return with the boxes and packages, MacLeod realized this particular ship's captain might not take his note for the goods. He had left in such a hurry, his mind so consumed with seeing Pacheco and wondering what Santiago had in mind by coming to the ranch with his questions. Now, standing before Captain Butler, he wished he had said something before the man had ordered the goods be brought ashore.

"Captain, I left my place in such a hurry when I heard tell you would soon be in port, I hadn't the time to collect enough hides to pay for my goods. Should have mentioned before and not put you to this trouble. If you could hold those things until your next trip down, I'd be much obliged."

"Well now," the tall sea captain began. "I would hate to lose your things. You know sailing up and down the coast for a year or so, people all coming and going aboard the ship, it's almighty easy to misplace things. I believe they'll be safer in your hands. You can send your hides down and I'll pick them up on the next trip."

MacLeod never felt comfortable thanking people properly. He hated being in someone's personal debt, but he longed for the goods he had ordered. "Mighty obliged, Captain. I'll see the hides are rounded up and waiting for you."

Butler combed his beard with his fingers as he watched the little boat drop away from the ship and start the three-mile trip toward the beach. "Appears the *Makani's* in a hurry. They dropped one anchor and they aren't taking anything else down. You see that boat they're sending in? Don't think they plan on staying."

MacLeod wasn't paying much attention. All he could think about at that moment were the letters and goods he had ordered. A wide grin split his face remembering Concannon's struggle over the list of tools he would require in order to build the furniture and other items for the ranch. Augers of different sizes, rasps, mortise chisels, saws, compass, and wood plane, and of course the claw hammer and nails. In the very same order, MacLeod had requested books for himself, some items of clothing, and a special package of linens, silks, and ribbons for Francesca that she knew nothing about

The two men walked down to the beach in companionable silence as the boat from the *North Star* fought its way through the surf. As the boat was nearing the shore, two of the sailors leapt out and dragged the boat up onto the sand. Captain Butler stood and watched as the boxes and small crates were hauled out and placed on the shore. One of the men handed a small packet to Butler.

"Here are those letters I spoke of, son. Hope they bear nothing but good news. I'll pick up what you owe me on one of my future trips."

Tucking the letters into his pocket, MacLeod waved good-bye to Butler and carried one of the wooden crates up onto higher ground, returning a moment later for the others. He figured they would be safe until he returned with the mules and could get them loaded up. However, before doing so, he took a seat on one of the crates and tore open the packet Captain Butler had handed to him.

Immediately, he recognized his mother's writing on the top letter. A wave of relief flooded over him as he checked the date on the letter. Quickly scanning the four pages of small script, he felt a wave of relief to find she was still living near Boston and was doing well. She explained that she wanted to hear more about his new family and her grandchildren. Taking a moment, he tried to remember what he had told her about Francesca and Catalina. As he continued to read the letter, she went on to ask when he might return or if she could find a way to come out and see him.

A smile lit up his face at the thought of seeing his mother. *Why not?* he thought to himself. *Other women her age made long sea voyages.*

He heard a hail and turned to see the *Makani's* boat, manned by eight rowers, pull past the *North Star's* boat and run up onto the beach, its crew of dark-skinned Sandwich Islanders shouting and laughing as they leaped out barefooted and hauled it out of the surf. MacLeod watched as two people were helped out, standing by on the sandy beach as bags and small boxes were lifted from the boat and placed beside them.

Turning his attention back to the letters in his hand, he recognized the next to be from Senator Benton. He decided that letter would have to wait until he got back to the ranch and had made a decision about how much he wanted to tell the man. It was rare he got a thank you for what he did pass on anyway.

Needing to get back on the road as soon as possible, he stuffed the last two letters in his pocket and followed Butler toward town.

Half an hour later MacLeod rode back down to the beach with the mules. He let his horse stand and began hand-weighing the items to equal out the weight of the loads. When he finished, he threw a canvas over each load and secured it with a diamond hitch. He was just about to mount his horse when a meek voice hailed him.

"Señor, sir, I beg of you, would you be knowing of an Inn where my wife and I might find food and shelter?"

MacLeod turned to find a small man with wire-rimmed glasses, wearing a woolen vest and pants, holding a narrow brimmed hat in his hand. Behind him, a dark haired woman sat on a chest, using her hat in an attempt to cool herself.

MacLeod watched as the man turned to say something to the woman before turning back to face him. *"Por favor. Habla inglés?* I am sorry, that is all I know."

MacLeod grinned. "Reckon I do."

The woman laughed and tugged at the man's arm.

"Yes, Sarah, I will ask," he said. Turning back to face MacLeod, the man smiled. "Sir, my wife and I are in desperate need of a place to stay. We know nothing of where we are. Would you know where we might apply for shelter?"

MacLeod dropped the reins and walked over to where the two people stood among their belongings. "Well now, I might be asking why in tarnation that ship dropped you here. If you had a mind to come to Alta California, I would think Monterey would be a better place to start."

"Yes, I had heard that, but the captain of that ship said he was paid to bring us to California. The obstinate brute said this place was as good as any," the man explained.

"Well, this is a far cry from Monterey. Someone should have told you there are no Inns to speak of. Someone here might give you a spot on the floor to sleep and a meal, but you would need to be finding a way to Monterey if that's where you were bound."

The woman stood up and held out a gloved hand. "Sir, I beg your pardon. My name is Sarah Morgenthau, and this is my husband, Jacob. I'm afraid we had no choice in the matter. We were put on the ship in Lahaina and brought here. As you can see, we are in need of help and I'm afraid we do not speak their language."

MacLeod could only shake his head at the situation he'd found himself in. He had hoped to be well along the road by nightfall. The image of Pacheco so near his house had haunted him form the moment he left, but he couldn't leave these people here sitting in the sand. He shook the woman's hand. "William MacLeod, ma'am. Would you mind telling me why you're here?"

This time, Jacob Morgenthau spoke. "Well now, sir, we didn't have a say in the matter, I'm afraid, as Sarah has said. Her father saw fit to banish us from the island of Maui and this was where the ship was bound."

MacLeod held up his hand to stop the man. "Hold on a minute––you're telling me this young lady's father sent you away? Why would he do that?"

"It's a matter of differing opinions, sadly. He saw no other solution once we were married," the man explained.

"Differing opinions," MacLeod laughed. "I think that needs some explaining."

"You, sir, are of the Catholic faith?"

"No, never joined their church. Brought up Presbyterian, like my parents and Scottish forefathers. Wouldn't think of changing."

"Well, then you will understand. Sarah's father is a Baptist minister on the islands. He has a very narrow mind when it comes to religion."

"I've heard some do," MacLeod said, remembering the fiery sermons his stepfather had delivered, ones he seldom found time to honor himself.

"When Sarah and I decided that we wished to be wed I sat down with him and asked for her hand. When he spoke of having me whipped if this should happen, I took it to mean he did not approve."

"It sure sounds as if he didn't. But you said this lady is your wife? You married anyway?"

"Yes, we did. We eloped to another island and found a more lenient man to wed us."

"Well, maybe you can explain why her father was so against the two of you marrying?"

"It's a matter of interpretation. Religious interpretation, if I am being more specific."

MacLeod rocked back and forth on his feet, unsure of what he had gotten himself into. "Mind explaining?"

"Sir, I am Jewish," the man stated plainly. "Her father did not approve of a man marrying his daughter whose people murdered Jesus Christ."

"As my friend would say at this time—Jesus, Mary, and Joseph. So he shipped you both off to the land of Papist people—a place where they would practically burn you at the stake for carrying a bible. If I can give you one piece of advice...I'd keep that information to yourself. Maybe call yourself Morgan," MacLeod suggested.

"I will try to remember your counsel, sir, but as you can see, I cannot care for my wife as I should in this foreign situation. Do you have any advice I might consider?"

MacLeod watched the boat with the Sandwich Island rowers approach the *Makani*. While he could ask Captain Butler to take the couple to Monterey, he knew he wouldn't be sailing north for weeks. Behind him, his stallion pawed at the sand restlessly while both mules stood, supporting themselves on three legs, dozing. It always amazed him how mules seemed to be preserving their strength for the miles ahead and were never in a hurry.

"Frankly, I'm at a loss," MacLeod said. "I suppose I could walk you up and introduce you to the *alcalde.*"

"*Alcalde?*" Morgenthau asked in confusion. "Do you think he might have an answer for us?"

"Well, he's sort of the mayor of the town."

"Oh, that would be so kind of you," Sarah Morgenthau chimed in. "Jacob has learned to speak four languages in his teachings but has never needed to speak the Spanish tongue."

"So, you are a teacher of sorts?" MacLeod asked, wondering why the man would need so many languages.

Jacob ran his hand through his thick curly hair. "I am a teacher of languages and mathematics. That was my profession before leaving England. I too had a father with differing ideas so I chose to answer an advertisement. The English people in the islands of Hawaii were in need of a teacher for their children. That is where I met Sarah."

MacLeod rocked back and forth on his heels. *A teacher of language and mathematics,* he pondered, thinking back to William Hartnell who had started a school in Monterey when his business dealings failed. Regrettably, from what he'd heard its future appeared in doubt. "What will you be looking for here in Alta California? Could you not find passage to England from here?"

"I am afraid that in our current situation the necessary funds are not in our grasp. Somehow, I hope I can find employment of a sort to remedy this."

In that moment MacLeod made a decision. "Look here, my wife and I have a small ranch about sixty miles from here. We have two children in need of an education. I can't offer much beyond food and shelter for now, but you're welcome to it if you see fit. Frankly, I don't know how you will find much else hereabouts."

"Well, sir, that would be most kind of you. Are you sure your wife would not mind you bringing two strangers home?" Sarah asked in genuine concern.

MacLeod thought back to their recent conversation. "Ma'am, I think you will find her most agreeable. We recently had concerns about the children's education, so this will help to put her mind at ease."

Sarah Morgenthau smiled. "Oh, I do hope she will like me. Is she also from America as you appear to be?"

"No, she's from here."

"Oh, I will be sure to make every attempt to learn her language so we may communicate properly."

"Won't be necessary. She and the children speak both languages pretty fair. And I'm certain your company will be most appreciated."

Jacob Morgenthau placed his hat back on his head and straightened his woolen vest. "Well now, sir, if this ranch of yours is so far off, I believe we should be starting immediately. If you could direct us to a local market where I might purchase a few supplies, and point us in the right direction, you would be doing us a great service with your offer. Where might I hire a horse? I believe I can walk the distance, but I would prefer Sarah be comfortable."

"No need," MacLeod said. "Just wait here a spell while I find a cart to borrow. I'll leave the mules here to keep you company."

MacLeod returned an hour later, driving a squealing *carreta*, followed by a young boy who was walking beside a team of oxen. The mules had never been harnessed and MacLeod didn't want to begin what would likely be a riotous training session if he tried to put them in front of the cart. After searching in his pocket for a coin for the youngster, he loaded his packages and crates into the cart alongside the Morgenthau's luggage.

"If you're used to riding in a carriage, I can guarantee you this ride won't be the same. It's your choice, you can ride or walk alongside; these oxen don't hurry none."

Jacob was true to his word, he walked alongside the cart, helping Sarah on and off occasionally. As much as she desired to walk, she found it quite difficult to hold up her long dress and still keep up with the oxen. MacLeod, a switch in his hand, rode alongside the cart to keep the animals in motion. By that time, he had already resigned himself to the extra time it would take to get back to the ranch. However, he hoped bringing an honest to goodness teacher to help the children would make up for it. Still, knowing Pacheco was so close sent a chill down his spine.

Rancho Nuestro Señora del Refugio

The road they traveled ran down toward the water and along the coast. MacLeod had just pulled his horse to a halt to wait for Jacob and Sarah to catch up when he heard the first shouts. A thick cloud of dust floated up into the air from behind a low brush-covered rise on the inland side of the road.

"What is it?" Jacob asked in concern, taking Sarah's hand and helping her back onto the cart.

Then, another series of angry shouts sounded. "Not sure. There's an old pole corral the landowners built years ago. I've camped there a few times by the creek. Think I might go have a look."

"Whose land might we be on," Sarah asked.

"It's an old land grant given to a man way back by the name of José Ortega. It's called Rancho Nuestro Señora del Refugio. I heard our recent governor Figueroa granted it to Antonio Ortega. A relative I'm sure."

Jacob nodded before offering his wife a drink from the water barrel MacLeod had lashed to the side of the cart. "I see. And are you familiar with these people?"

"Nope, never met any of them. Might real soon though. I think I'll wander over and see what the commotion's all about."

"Would you mind if I accompanied you?"

"Don't see any reason for you not to," MacLeod said, flicking the switch over the oxen and driving them up the narrow trail.

At the top of the rise the pole corral came into view. Three men sat on the top railing shouting encouragement and laughing at the one inside the corral.

MacLeod reined his horse to a halt and watched as more swirls of dust rose into the air just as two men dropped off the top railing onto the ground inside the corral. Laughing, they circled a saddled sorrel stallion, its golden mane and tail knotted with burrs and streaked with blood. One of the men seized its lead rope and snubbed the horse's head up to a corral pole. Another raged in anger, as he circled behind the stallion with what appeared to be a braided rope.

Sarah, having joined the men at the top of the hill, uttered a cry when the man lashed the horse's withers with the rope. The stallion jerked its head back against the snubbed rope and danced away from its tormentor.

"Hate to see people abusing such a fine animal," MacLeod said.

"I believe Sarah's father would say, 'man is born with cruelty, but not all find it useful'."

MacLeod touched the rear of the oxen closest to him and urged the cart down toward the corral.

"Are you meaning to speak with them?" Jacob asked as he walked alongside the cart.

"Won't hurt to try. Would you mind reaching into the cart there and fetching my rifle," MacLeod asked, never taking his eyes off the activity in the corral.

The men in the corral failed to notice them approach. With another angry order from the third man in the corral the two men at the horse's head threw a sack over its head. The horse stood quivering, its withers running red with blood. Moving cautiously the vaquero with the braided rope moved to its side, then leaped into the saddle as the rope snubbed up to the post was dropped and the sack whipped off the horse's head.

"What are they doing to that poor animal?" Sarah asked, her hand pressed against the side of her face.

"Well, some folks here think that's the way to break a horse to the saddle. However, that's no reason to treat that beautiful animal in such a way." Macleod touched the flanks of his horse and trotted down toward the corral, the oxen lumbering along behind him.

More shouts arose as the man in the saddle waited for the horse's response. It stood, trembling, seemingly frozen, until the man on its back raked its sides with the heavy roweled spurs.

The stallion exploded, its head dropping toward the dirt, driving its rear hooves up above its shoulders in an attempt to rid itself of its tormentor. Clouds of dust rose and swirled about the spinning horse. Its rider pitched forward with the first buck. The horse then whirled around and rose up on its hind legs. The rider again rammed his spurs into the horse's flanks while clinging to the saddle. MacLeod swore as the horse dropped to the ground and sprinted toward the far side of the corral, spinning at the last moment and dropping its head again to lash out with its hooves. This time the rider rose high in the air, his arms flailing, before crashing down onto the top pole of the corral, and tumbling to the ground inside the corral. MacLeod watched the stallion's front hooves claw the air at the sight of its torturer. Suddenly the stallion charged the prone man who managed to roll under the bottom railing and out of the horse's reach.

The thrown rider climbed to his feet before stooping down to pick up a long braid whip lying nearby. With a determined expression upon his face, the man unfurled it and slipped through the gate, pulling it closed behind him.

"Please tell me he is not going to use that wicked thing on that poor animal?" Jacob muttered.

Shouts of encouragement and laughter at the rider's misfortune appeared to only increase his anger. Snapping the whip high over his head, he cast it out and back before bringing it down upon the stallion's rump.

MacLeod's eyes narrowed. *That isn't my horse nor is it my affair,* he told himself. Unfortunately, he also knew he would regret not doing something to save the poor animal. For the next several minutes, MacLeod watched as the horse was continually driven around the corral, the whip rising and cracking across the horse's back.

"Damn it to hell, that's just not right," MacLeod muttered pulling his pistol from his belt and firing a shot in the air. Tucking the spent pistol under his belt, he reached down for his battle scarred Kentucky rifle and laid it across the front of his saddle, not sure what exactly he was going to do yet.

Hearing the shot the man with the whip pushed through the swinging gate and stepped out, dragging the long whip behind him. He flicked it out in front of his feet and stood starring at MacLeod, his mouth agape.

MacLeod could see he was young, thin-faced, with the beginnings of a mustache. His black hair hung to his waist in a long, full braid. Despite the dirt from being tossed to the ground, his clothes appeared similar to those worn by the rich rancheros; much too fine to be worn while trying to break a horse.

MacLeod pondered the best approach, though nothing seemed to be a great solution. After allowing his temper to cool a moment, he said, "That horse hasn't done anything to deserve to be whipped. Looks like a mighty fine animal to me."

The young man flicked his wrist sending the tip of the whip to settle in the dirt behind him.

MacLeod blew out his breath and tightened the hold on his rifle. "Sure hope you're not thinking about using that whip on me. I wouldn't take too kindly to it."

Out of the corner of his eye MacLeod saw Sarah stepping off the back of the cart before pulling her husband close and whispering something in his ear.

The man glanced back at the others who were watching. Shaking his head, he turned back to face MacLeod. "Who are you to speak to me? You are on my land, this is my horse. I will do as I please with it."

"Just passing by on the road back-a-ways. Know it's none of my business, but I hate to see any animal treated in the manner you're treating that horse. I saw a lot of horses out there in the fields as I rode by, surely there's some you could ride that wouldn't give you any trouble."

Behind the man, MacLeod could hear the smattering of low laughter from the bystanders. Though none dared step forward to join the discussion.

The long-barreled Kentucky rifle in MacLeod's hands shifted a few inches coming to bear on the center of the man's chest. MacLeod watched intently as the man's hand holding the whip massaged the leather handle. "I'd sure appreciate it if you didn't try using that whip, otherwise I might be forced to shoot you."

The young man shook his head. "Do you know who I am?"

He knew the man expected to be recognized. "No, can't say that I do."

Feeling Jacob Morgenthau join him, MacLeod's eyes remained focus on the man with the whip when Morgenthau spoke. "I can recharge that pistol for you if you like. "I believe it's a Bates of London. My father possessed one similar to it."

MacLeod glanced down at the slender hand held out to him before turning back to the man holding the whip. Without taking his eyes off his target, he slipped the pistol from his belt and held it out. "Much obliged. And when you're done you might keep it handy. Don't expect trouble here, but young men seldom use caution. Know this from personal experience."

"I am Joaquin Francisco Ortega. This land is ours. I think you are that Americano who they say took some of our land."

How many times will I get myself in situations like this? MacLeod wondered. The more he thought about it, the more he wished he had ridden by. He still could, but he hated to see any animal punished.

Young Ortega shook out the whip again and started to bring his arm back.

"Hold it right there, son," MacLeod barked. "How fast do you think the ball in this rifle is? I'll bet it's a sight faster than that whip."

"You would not use it."

"You willing to bet your life on it?"

"If you shoot me, they will hang you."

"They might, but you won't be around to know about it one way or the other." MacLeod stepped out of the saddle, never taking his eyes of the whip. "Mr. Morgenthau—you will find another pistol buried beneath that stack of sacks on the cart. Be so good as to draw the ball? You'll find the tools where you found the powder. Expect you know how."

"Yes, sir, I have done so on a number of occasions. Shouldn't take but a minute," Jacob stated confidently before turning back to the cart.

"Soon as you're done you might take this Kentucky and keep an eye on our new friends," MacLeod suggested.

Just as he'd hoped, Ortega made no move as MacLeod walked past him and entered the corral.

The stallion backed itself into the far corner of the corral as MacLeod stepped through the gate and slowly eased it shut behind him. Remaining still for a moment, MacLeod allowed the horse to settle down and get used to his presence. When it appeared the horse had calmed, he began talking in a soft, hushed tone as he slowly walked forward a few steps.

In a voice not more than a whisper he continued to talk as he moved closer. When the stallion backed up along the fence, MacLeod halted and held his arms up, then slowly moved toward the head of the stallion. The horse shivered, backing up as MacLeod approached, its eyes wide with fear. MacLeod stopped and took a couple of steps back, still whispering softly while studying the horse's reaction. The horse responded, settling down. No longer feeling threatened, the animal began to move along the fence line. MacLeod cut it off, forcing it back the other direction. For the next half hour, MacLeod and the stallion shifted back and forth until the stallion stood quietly, its head hanging down in submission.

"All right, fella. Now, let's see if he's broken your spirit," MacLeod whispered, slowly moving back into the stallion's space.

The stallion backed up, feeling cornered. In an instant, he reared up, its front hooves pawing the air, uttering a fierce challenge to his would-be tormentor.

"Good boy," McLeod whispered. Slowly backing up, he slipped back through the gate and turned to Ortega. "I'd like to buy your horse."

Ortega remained silent for a moment before eventually bursting into laughter. Taking a moment to gather himself, he tried his best to regain control of the situation. "And what do you have that I do not already have?"

Ignoring his question, MacLeod walked over to Morgenthau and took the pistol from him. He slipped the flint out and palmed it in his hand. MacLeod knew how few of the soldiers had pistols, so he figured the regular citizens couldn't be much better off. At least he hoped that was the case, especially since he didn't have anything else of value.

"This horse is certainly not worth you killing me for," Ortega said, the look of bravado changing to one of fear as MacLeod stepped toward him, hand firmly gripping the pistol.

Unexpectedly, MacLeod twirled the pistol around and held it out to the man, butt first. "I could be wrong, but I don't figure you have one of these. I'll trade you this pistol for that horse. It's surely a better deal than killing it."

Cautiously, Ortega took the pistol in his hands, turning it over to inspect it. He pointed it directly at the horse and grinned.

"We got us a deal?" Macleod asked.

"You can have the horse. He will probably kill you anyway. But that is your problem. If he does not I will shoot you with this pistol if you ever come back." Ortega laughed again, pointing the pistol at one of the men behind him.

MacLeod went back and took the rifle out of Morgenthau's hands before untying a braided rope from behind his saddle. Seeing an astonished Morgenthau looking on, he smiled. "What would you have done if he had tried using that whip on me?" MacLeod asked.

"I believe I would have been forced to shoot him. Not to kill, you understand, but certainly to stop him."

MacLeod frowned. "You think you could separate the two?"

Morgenthau wiped his hands on his trousers. "Oh, most definitely. Your weapon appears to be finely balanced. I have no doubt that I could have shot him in the arm from this distance," he chuckled.

MacLeod turned to look at Ortega and his group. "And here I was figuring I might take a whipping if my bluff hadn't worked."

"You were bluffing?" Sarah asked in shocked disbelief.

MacLeod grinned. "Couldn't very well shoot the man, now could I? His horse, his land." He walked back through the corral gate and carefully approached the horse. Just as before, the stallion moved back a step or two before eventually calming enough to allow MacLeod to drop a loop over its head. Hoping to avoid terrifying the already distressed animal, MacLeod dropped the rope in the dirt and ran his hand along the stallion's shoulder, carefully removing the saddle. Freed of its binding, MacLeod backed away slowly and placed the saddle on the top rail of the corral.

MacLeod was pleased to find the once terrified horse calm and entirely unconcerned about his presence. After carefully retrieving the rope that was lying in the ground, MacLeod carefully led the now docile horse out of the corral and mounted his own horse. "Think it might be a sight better if we move on a ways before calling it a day."

MacLeod halted a couple of miles down the road and set up a dry camp. While Jacob gathered wood, Sarah, with gentle suggestion from MacLeod, did her best to prepare a meal. Doing his best with what he had, MacLeod took a ladle full of water and began washing the blood and dirt off the stallion's back, vowing to see the horse properly cared for as soon as they returned to the ranch.

Both Jacob and Sarah peppered MacLeod with questions about Alta California. It was clear they knew very little and what they did know had come from talking to men they met before sailing. MacLeod did his best to answer their questions and explain the political and religious situation in the country. In doing so, he confessed that the politics in Alta California were in constant flux. Something that would hopefully be changing soon…for the better.

RANCHO COLINAS DE ORO

As they made their way up the steep climb of Gaviota Pass, the cart unexpectedly lost a wheel, leaving them with no option but to stop. Fortunately, between the two men they managed to repair the damage, but it wasn't a sound fix and MacLeod was forced to remove much of the contents of the cart, which had to be transferred to the backs of the mule. Not wanting to risk any excess weight on the cart, MacLeod helped Sarah up onto the back of his horse and opted to walk alongside Jacob.

When MacLeod and his new companions made their way up from the river to the house, he was pleased to find Francesca standing in the doorway awaiting his arrival. Having long adopted the California lifestyle of riding everywhere, MacLeod's feet and legs ached from the long trek home. He could only imagine how the others felt.

Francesca stepped forward excitedly just as MacLeod helped Sarah off his horse.

"Brought a couple of guests. Hope you don't mind?"

As soon as Francesca set eyes on the young woman she rushed forward. "You have been hurt?" she asked.

Sarah Morgenthau stood by the horse and gripped the saddle to steady herself before answering. "Oh no, but I'm afraid my feet have been damaged somewhat. I doubt they make shoes for women to walk such long distances in," she said with a smile. "My name is Sarah Morgenthau, and that is my husband, Jacob. Your husband has rescued us from I know not what."

Francesca gave her a warm smile and took her by the arm. "Welcome to Rancho Colinas de Oro. I am Francesca. Come, you must sit and rest," she said. She was preparing to lead Sarah into the adobe when the new stallion caught her attention.

Calling out to Juana, Francesca instructed her to take Sarah and her husband inside and informed them that she would join them in a moment. With their guests being looked after, Francesca walked back to look at the horse. "William, whose horse is this?" she asked, taking in the battered appearance of the animal. "Who would do such a thing as this?"

"Well, he's ours now. I don't know how much good he is after the treatment he's had, but I intend to find out. With any luck, he might be a real fine horse with the proper care."

Francesca approached the stallion, talking softly and running a gentle hand over his body. The big stallion shivered, turning his head to follow her every move. "I can see where they put a saddle on him. Has he been ridden?"

Before answering, MacLeod summoned two of the ranch Indians to unload the cart, have the wheel repaired, and take care of the animals. He had promised to return the oxen and *carreta* on his next trip to Santa Barbara. MacLeod understood that his wife would have questions, but what he really wanted to find out was what had taken place in the time he was gone.

"I believe that's what they were trying to do with him. Didn't appear they had much patience" he finally answered.

"Did you trade something for him? I do not see how they would part with such a beautiful animal."

MacLeod wasn't sure how much he should tell her. *She will probably hear the whole story from Sarah anyway, might as well tell her everything,* he thought to himself. "Ahh, well, I traded that old pistol I keep in my bedroll. I'm almost certain the man thought I might shoot him if he didn't take it."

Francesca crossed her arms and narrowed her eyes upon him.

MacLeod waited. He had an idea of what was forthcoming.

"And would you have? Would you have shot this man even though he deserves to be shot?" Francesca asked, her tone serious.

MacLeod grinned and took her into his arms. "No, but I wasn't sure how to back away once I threatened him. That man you just met—he doesn't look like he would scare a crow, but he stood with me. I've taken kindly to him."

Francesca took the stallion's head in her hands and looked into his eyes. "I shall call him Bolivar. Yes, that is his name." She chuckled. "Wait until your son sees him."

"Afraid it will be some time before anyone can think about riding him," MacLeod stated knowingly as he gently ran a hand down the horse's head.

A few moments later, Juana returned to see if MacLeod and Francesca needed anything further. Needing the stallion tended to, MacLeod sent her in search of a vaquero. She returned a few minutes later with a young Indian boy named Malibu in tow. Without a word, the boy walked past MacLeod and approached the horse. The boy laid a hand on the horse's shoulder and trailed it along its side, talking to it in a language MacLeod had never understood.

The boy had shown up on an old black gelding one morning and spoke with Sisquoc, who later informed MacLeod that the boy knew horses and wished to stay.

MacLeod and Francesca looked on as the young boy inspected the cuts and abrasions on the horse's body. Without a word he took the lead rope from MacLeod's hand and walked off with the stallion.

"Is he ours?" a familiar voice asked in a hushed tone.

MacLeod hadn't heard his young son approach. "He's ours. Might take a spell to learn if he's been ruined or not."

"He is the most beautiful horse I have ever seen. Even better than the one that man rode who came with the others," Diego stated.

MacLeod put his hand on the youngster's shoulder. "He's not the only thing I brought back. I believe I have brought you and your sister a teacher."

"I want to be a vaquero, Father. What more do I need to know?"

"We'll talk about that later. For now, go and find your sister and bring her here. Both of you will begin to learn things you never dreamed existed."

"Why? She is only a girl, she does not need to learn anything else," the young boy asked in confusion.

"Son, you have much to learn. Your first lesson is to never let Francesca hear you say that," MacLeod whispered. "Now go and find Catalina for me."

Reluctantly, the young boy took off in search of his sister as Francesca approached and took MacLeod's arm in hers. "These people you have brought—what will we do with them?"

"Well now," MacLeod said with a grin. "I was telling Diego here. This man happens to be a teacher. He knows languages and mathematics. Thought he might prove useful."

Francesca's hand shot to her face as she covered her mouth in shock. "A teacher? Why is he here? There is nowhere for him to teach?" she asked in confusion.

"I'll tell you about it later. Better yet, have a talk with Sarah. I'm sure she'll fill you in as to why they're here. For now, I need to find Concannon and see about a place for them to stay."

Francesca nodded, making her way into the adobe to see to her guests.

It didn't take long for MacLeod to find Concannon. Just as he'd expected, he was in the last of the little lean-tos they used as shops. "Anything happen while I was gone?" MacLeod asked.

"If you be meaning our friend from the other side, no," Concannon said. MacLeod could smell the wine the man had consumed recently. He knew this wasn't the time to bring it up again, but vowed to have another discussion with him.

"You'll want to take a look at what I brought back. I haven't had a chance to open the crates or check the manifest, but I imagine they're pretty much what you and I talked about you needing. I also brought back a couple from the islands. We'll be needing a place for them."

Concannon stood up and stretched his back. "Then we'll be needing more building blocks than we planned. Where do you figure to put them?"

The two men walked out past the last little building and MacLeod pointed to a nearby spot shaded by a half dozen trees. "I don't know how long they'll be staying, but build it for a family. We can always use another house."

Concannon combed out his heard with a hand and sighed. "Meaning to tell you as soon as you got back—Sisquoc talked to a couple of Indians who came over from the other side."

"The San Joaquin valley?"

"Yep. Said they ran into a party of trappers looking for horses. Also says there's another bad fever in the Indian villages."

"Trappers?" MacLeod asked in confusion. "You mean another party like that Jed Smith fellow that came through here a number of years ago? Probably more likely that it's the Hudson's Bay Company. How long ago?"

"They just came over from the valley. From what Sisquoc said, these fellows need horses bad. Can't figure how to go back home without them," Concannon explained.

"They say how far north they are on the river?"

"From what I could make out, it was near where we found that old chief. You, remember?"

MacLeod took a few steps out past the last adobe. "That was some time back. You remember how we got there?"

Concannon shrugged. "Cross over and follow the river north. Can't miss it."

MacLeod blew out a breath. *So many things to be done in so little time.* "You know if Sisquoc or Alvarado have been able to find vaqueros for the *matanza*? We'll need to be starting the slaughter soon. Each passing day, the grass is less and less."

"Says there are some that might be available from the old mission. Both Indian and Mexican vaqueros."

MacLeod knew there was something else he needed to discuss with Concannon but he couldn't figure out what it was. "They'll do. Now, what say we gather up all the surplus horses and push them across to the river? See if we can sell them to those fellows. It would need to be done soon before they turn back," MacLeod said as he led the way back toward the adobe.

"Might even send someone ahead on a fast horse to tell them horses are available," Concannon suggested.

MacLeod turned back and studied the man for a moment. "You feeling up to it? Can't expect anyone else to get fair payment in return."

Concannon spit in the dirt. "We'll need Sisquoc to put trustworthy Indians to work on the adobe bricks since you're needing so many now. I'll get Alvarado to round up a handful of vaqueros, but I believe it would do me some good to get away for a spell."

MacLeod grinned. "Get it done and hurry back. I'll be needing you."

Before he could say anything in response MacLeod held up his hand to silence Concannon, pointing at the three riders approaching at a fast trot. "Sisquoc's clearly got something on his mind. Those horses are lathered up pretty good."

The big Indian reined his horse to a halt. The two vaqueros with him nodded to acknowledge MacLeod before riding off to their huts.

"Many RS cows on water and on Colinas land," Sisquoc commented, tilting his head back the way they had come.

"Didn't you push them back a few days ago?" MacLeod asked.

"Si. But this time many more. We moved them across again as they watched us."

"Who watched you?" MacLeod asked, his agitation growing.

"Vaqueros from over there," Sisquoc replied, pointing in the direction of Rancho Santiago. "And the one who was with us before but did not come back."

"You meaning the one we figured went back to his village?"

"Sisquoc nodded. "He did not go back to his village, he went over to them."

Another problem to be dealt with. "Guess it's time for another talk with our neighbor. Can't see how he doesn't know about it," MacLeod said, turning on his heel to leave.

On his way back to the house, MacLeod found Jesus Alvarado in one of the lean-tos discussing the treatment of the stallion with young Malibu. Stopping, he decided to fill his new majordomo and Sisquoc in on what he and Concannon had just discussed. All three men agreed to begin separating the cattle for the slaughter immediately and to round up the horses for Concannon.

For the time being, branding the young cattle could wait. Right now, he needed to focus on getting the horses rounded up and getting Santiago's cattle pushed back to their own land. In the meantime, MacLeod planned to go over and talk with Santiago about the RS cattle. Last thing he needed was a misunderstanding about whose cattle were being led to slaughter.

With all the men informed, MacLeod headed back toward the house to inform Francesca of what he had decided. However, before doing so, he reached into his pocket for the manifest from the shipment of goods he had ordered. Instead, his hand emerged with more than just the manifest; he also had the letter from Senator Benton and the final letter he had yet to read. He knew Senator Benton's question on the situation in California would take him days to analyze and answer. Tucking the letter back into his pocket he made a mental note to take the time to answer it as best he could.

The final letter, badly wrinkled from being handle, had only one thing written on the outside.

Doñ William MacLeod, Alta California.

He slit it open with his belt knife, the first thing MacLeod noticed was the date on the first page. It was dated two years ago. Quickly flipping to the last page, he spotted a familiar, largely looping signature.

He froze.

RANCHO SANTIAGO

Cesario Santiago looked up into a cloudless sky and cursed. Nothing had gone as planned since his arrival. Yesterday he had two Indian's whipped, and this morning Pacheco informed him four more had run off. Of course, he had sent Pacheco after them.

His instructions for the building of the house meant hundreds of new bricks needed to be made. As such, he didn't have time for workers to be running off. The adobe bricks being dried in the hot sun lay in rows in the fields, but there were still far too few for what he needed. It was nearing the point that he was contemplating setting a quota for each Indian.

Now he sat in the shade beneath a tree and watched Pacheco approach. He knew he would soon need to return to those at Colinas de Oro, but he hadn't yet made up his mind whether or not to bring Pacheco.

"Doñ Santiago—you have sent for me?"

"Yes, this man you brought to me, this old man you claim has worked with water—"

"They call him Ossio," Pacheco said.

"What have you done with him?"

Pacheco stretched his back. "I think maybe he is with the Indians down at the river bringing back water."

"Bring him to me. If he is so good with managing water, perhaps he can build me a dam so the water is not lost in the river. Perhaps you can take him as far as you can into the mountains to see where the water comes from."

Pacheco looked out toward the mountains in the distance. "You cannot ride to this place, I think. It is very hard to find where the water comes from."

Santiago hated to be questioned. "Remember who it is you are working for," he snapped. "You cannot return to what you were doing before I found you, I suggest you keep that in mind."

"I will take him there. It will probably kill him, but we will go. It is very hard to go up this canyon, you should know this."

Santiago nodded as he watched a group of Indians being led out into the fields where the bricks were being taken out of their wooden forms to dry in the sun. *At least these hot, dry day, are good for something,* Santiago thought to himself.

"Now tell me what you know about these people that have the land next to mine. This man, this Americano, how well do you know him? Can he be pushed?"

Pacheco eased his body out of the saddle and lit the stub of the cigar Santiago had given him. Santiago could see that the man was weighing his next words.

"This man you speak of—I will say this—if you push him, he will push you back."

"Are you afraid of him?"

Pacheco laughed. "He and I are known to each other. It is probable that one day one of us will kill the other."

"And the woman—you know her also?" Santiago questioned. He needed to know if the rumors were true.

Pacheco ignored the question, instead opting to change the subject. "I will go and find this man you seek. Perhaps he can help with the water and there will be no need to fight." Mounting his horse, he turned to Santiago. "So you know, we push many horses and cattle over onto the other side each night. In the day they return most of them."

"Is there anything else I should know?"

"A vaquero from over there came here. He wishes to stay, said he knows things we could use."

"Can he be trusted?" Santiago asked, a questioning look upon his face.

Pacheco shook his head. "Why is he willing to help us I ask? No, but he will be useful."

"Test him then. Have him show us what he can do. While you are at it, send the vaqueros to push the horses and cattle back across the line. Let us see what this man is made of."

Santiago walked over to where those in charge of planting the trees were digging holes in the dry soil before proceeding to the spot where the first layers of adobe bricks for the house were being laid.

She said she would come when the house was complete, but will it be worth the trouble of finishing the house and gardens I had planned without the water to quench the thirst of the cattle? And those waiting in Argentina for a report—what will I say to them?

He stood among the drying bricks, his thoughts running wild, while he waited for Pacheco to return with the water man.

"Tomorrow," Santiago said, as Pacheco reined his horse to a halt in front of him. "After you have shown this man what I want, we will go and see them again."

RANCHO COLINAS DE ORO

MacLeod found a secluded spot and sat down on a tree stump. His hands shook as he carefully unfolded the wrinkled pages. There was no mistaking the bold, scripted signature of Doñ Augustin de Cordero, Maria's father. The man began by saying he had received word of the death of his Maria, his last surviving child. He admitted to believing that MacLeod was responsible. He said it had taken many months for him to accept the fact that those who knew what had happened to Maria, would never allow her to live a normal life, after being sold to Romero, the renegade Mescalero

Apache. And who of them would believe the child was the Americanos, and not the Apache's.

Doñ Cordero went on to say that he was well, but his advancing years made him realize that he must make plans for his wife and property for when his time came. It was also in his aging that he had finally come to realize his animosity toward MacLeod must be put aside. His Maria had loved him and what had happened was in a great part a fault of his own. It was his pride and the refusal to believe that his daughter should have any say in whom she should marry that had set in motion the tragic events that followed.

Doñ Cordero went on to say that the rancho had prospered in the years since he and Maria's departure. With no other option, he put all his efforts into the growth and management of his growing empire.

MacLeod wiped the tears from his eyes and put the letter aside for a moment. In the distance, he heard the excited voices of Diego and Catalina. They had taken Jacob and Sarah out to show them the rest of the ranch. MacLeod could tell immediately that Jacob Morgenthau could educate his children in a way that he himself could never do. It thrilled him to watch Catalina leading Sarah by the hand out into the orchard. Diego, of course, wanted only to know how they came to bring the sorrel stallion back with them.

"I have watched you sit here for some time, William," Francesca said. "You appear troubled. Is it news you have brought back with you from Santa Barbara?"

He had not heard her approach. He smiled and rose to allow her to sit on the stump. "A letter from my mother. She says she is in good health and asks about you, and of course Diego and the other children."

"I am happy to hear this. Does she ever speak about coming to Alta California?"

"As a matter of fact, she did. I'm going to speak to one of the ship's captains the next time I see one."

Francesca pointed to the letter in his hand. "Is that her letter to you?"

Glancing down, MacLeod discovered he still held Cordero's letter in his hand. "No, this is from someone else. It was given to Captain Butler to bring up here. It was written two years ago."

Francesca tilted her head to the side in bewilderment. "And this person that writes this letter to you—you know of him?"

MacLeod looked back at the letter in his hand and nodded. "It is Maria's father, the woman who died in the desert—Diego's grandfather."

Francesca's hands went to her cheeks. "How is it he has found you? It has been so long."

"I wrote to him about what had happened. Maybe a year after. In truth, I didn't think he ever received my letter."

"But his words have troubled you it seems. What has he said?"

"Not troubled, no," MacLeod said. "He wants to see his grandson before he dies. He has no other grandchildren, only Diego."

Francesca folded her hands in her lap and waited.

MacLeod unfolded the last page and read the final paragraphs aloud. "*When my time has come, I wish to leave my property and ranch to Diego. If my dearest wife still lives, she is to be taken care of until the day she leaves this earth.'"*

"Oh, and this ranch, it is like Colinas de Oro?"

MacLeod laughed. "Doñ Cordero is a very rich rico in New Mexico. His lands are much bigger than ours."

"And did he say why he is doing this? Does he have no others to give his lands to?"

The last few lines in the letter reminded MacLeod of how well Doñ Cordero had kept up with the politics of Mexico and California. "As I said, he has no one else. He also believes that America will someday soon take over New Mexico. He believes an American would have a better chance of keeping the ranch."

The retention of land grants was a subject talked about often among those who followed the western expansion of the United States. Even in Senator Benton's letters he had requested information about Spanish land grants and their extent.

"But if it is their land how can the Americans take it?"

"Americans have different ways of marking their property. They have surveyors who measure it properly."

"We do not?" Francesca asked.

MacLeod shook his head. "We do it much better now, but old grants, like yours, were never surveyed. Back then you just drew up a little sketch to show where there was a creek on one side, a pile of rocks, or two big trees on the other. Hell, I'm not even sure where our boundary line is aside from that one pile of rocks on the far side of the stream."

"And this worries you?" Francesca surmised.

"Never mattered before because there was so much land available. But things change. You must also realize that Americans are different—they rarely honor the property of the people in the countries they take over. They believe it should all be theirs to take."

Francesca took the letter from his hand and stared at it a moment. "What will you do about this letter?"

MacLeod hadn't the time to think much about it. "I'll write to Doñ Cordero. Tell him a bit about Diego. He has given me the name of a man in San Blas who will forward him my letters. I don't see how he will ever meet his grandson though. I'll never make that journey again."

"And the other letter—is that one from the important man in America?"

He nodded. "Yes, another from that man. Should never have started answering his questions. The more I think about it, the more I question whether he is a friend of the people here."

"Did you answer the last one he sent?" Francesca questioned.

Macleod squeezed her shoulder gently. "No. I'll see what he's asking for this time, before I decide. Right now, I have other things worrying me."

They talked for a moment about where to house Jacob and Sarah until some kind of shelter could be built for them. MacLeod glanced up into the cloudless sky. "Least we won't need to worry about them getting rained on."

After MacLeod had told Francesca of his plan, she turned and headed back toward the house. Halting in her retreat, she turned back to MacLeod. "Will you tell Diego about this letter? He is old enough to know the story, William. He is no longer a child." Not waiting for an answer, Francesca turned on her heel and made her way inside. Despite how she may feel about the situation, the decision was his to make. When would he tell the boy the whole story?

Left with only his thoughts, MacLeod tried his best to gather himself before going out in search of Concannon. After all, he had other matters to attend to.

When he finally located Concannon he was pleased to see that he'd already saddled two horses and was ready to go.

"I'll step into the house a moment for the shotgun," Concannon said.

"We'll be leaving them behind this trip," MacLeod said, halting him in his tracks.

"If you'll be remembering, there's a fellow over there who would take great pleasure in killing you."

"I still have my pistol. Besides, I doubt he would do much with others around."

"Then you're more trusting a man than I."

They rode down to the river to see how the Indians were doing that had been sent there to gather buckets of a clay for the adobe bricks. Satisfied with their progress, the two men proceeded to follow the riverbank for a couple of miles before coming to a stop.

"Looks like we're not the only ones," MacLeod stated, pointing to where a dozen Indian workers labored.

"We have six and they have two dozen. How many people does this man have working this ranch he's to be building?" Concannon wondered aloud.

Kneeing the horse into a trot, MacLeod turned back from the river. "We'll know soon enough. Now remember, Sean, this is a friendly chat we're having with Doñ Santiago. I want to let him know we're going to be rounding up the loose, unbranded, youngsters."

"If you say so, but I wouldn't be trusting a word he will say."

"No, there's no way he'll admit they've been pushing animals onto Colinas de Oro land, so we're going to make them think those stupid critters wandered over here by themselves."

"Why?" Concannon asked.

"He's got something on his mind. He doesn't look like a stupid man. Clearly, he has less water than we do and we're the ones going to be slaughtering early. With any luck we might learn something about what he has up his sleeve."

RANCHO SANTIAGO

Cesario Santiago had chosen a spot in a wide valley with oak covered low-lying hills for his hacienda.

When MacLeod reached the top of the hill and could see the extent of the activity below, he reined his horse to a halt. He blew out his breath. "You have any idea about what's going on? Must be a hundred workers down there."

"Heard rumors from a vaquero or two, but never expected this," Concannon said in shock. "The man appears to have big plans in mind."

"Would appear so," MacLeod agreed. A glimmer of uncertainty churned in his belly. "Awfully big plans for the current size of the land grant."

They let the horses walk down through the oaks, wanting to take their time so that they could see all they could before speaking to Santiago. Neither man spoke as an uncomfortable silence filled the air around them.

"Looks like they've started the house he had mentioned," MacLeod stated, breaking the silence. "Said the woman wouldn't come out to live until it was finished. Sure looks like he intends on finishing it soon."

"Looks to be sawed lumber beside that pile of tiles. Where do you suppose he got that?" Concannon inquired.

"Must have had a ship bring it up from Mexico. Certainly wouldn't mind some of that."

Concannon scratched at his beard. "We'll be hopefully making boards like that with the new saw you bought. Might break a few backs doing it, but we'll have them regardless."

MacLeod pointed off to the right of the Indians that were laying the first layers of adobe. "He's planting trees already—three or four years old. Hope he has better luck than we have had with them." Suddenly, he remembered something that had been at the back of his mind and he had forgotten amidst all of the chaos. *The priest and his vaquero.* "Damn, between meeting those people on the beach and buying that sorrel, I forgot to tell Francesca something."

"What might that be—if I be asking?"

"Came upon a priest from the old mission—he had a man with him who took care of the mission orchards. Told them to stop by on their way back. Figured we might find a place for the man and his family."

Concannon simply nodded as the two continued to descend into the valley, the shadows lengthening before they found Santiago sitting under the shade of the oaks.

"Ah, you have taken my invitation to come and visit. As you can see there is still much to be done," Santiago stated.

"Doñ Santiago," MacLeod greeted. "Awful big operation you got going on here. Wish you luck." Compared to the growing accumulation of weathered adobe shelters and scattered lean-tos at Colinas de Oro, Rancho Santiago, when complete, looked as if it would rival even the finest ranchos in Alta California.

"Please, allow me to show you some of my plan," Santiago said as he stood.

MacLeod nodded and watched as the big man mounted his sorrel horse, leading them past the construction and planting to where the old man was inspecting the stream. MacLeod kept his eyes peeled for any sign of Pacheco.

"This man," Santiago said, pointing to the old man, "has worked at this La Purísima Mission. He is looking to see if we can build a dam and keep our water from flowing into the river. It will help the cattle but it can do nothing for the fields."

MacLeod felt it was time to talk about why he had come. "Doñ Santiago, the reason I came was to tell you that I'm going to be rounding up our cows and branding the young ones. If you want, you can send a vaquero or two over to separate any you think might be yours that may have strayed."

"Yes, I will talk with Señor Pacheco about this."

MacLeod watched Santiago's face, waiting for his reaction, but the man had turned away as if MacLeod's words meant little. MacLeod rocked uncomfortably in his saddle. He wanted nothing more than to rein his horse around and ride off since apparently his words meant nothing to the man, but there was also the other matter. "Might also mention to your man that more than a few of your RS cows are wandering over to graze Colinas de Oro land. I've had my vaqueros push them back more than once."

Santiago nodded and brushed the dust of his doeskin jacket. "Yes, I have been told this. I am also told many of yours come to drink my water."

MacLeod bristled at the obvious lie and underlying challenge.

Concannon, clearly irritated, whistled through his teeth.

MacLeod could tell Concannon was ready to explode so he decided to question the lie. "Don't know who's telling you this, but from what I've seen firsthand it's the other way round. I've got enough water, and don't mind sharing it with thirsty cows, but I don't take kindly when they stay around to eat my grass."

Santiago smiled. "Who are we, the owners of these beautiful lands, to question one another? I am sure these animals do whatever they wish. Although, it is most fortunate you have come. I wished to speak with you and was about to ride over myself and see you."

MacLeod waited impatiently for Santiago to continue.

Santiago remained quiet for a moment, appearing to gather his thoughts. When he spoke, his voice had hardened. "I do not believe you are a stupid man. I have seen Colinas de Oro and the condition of your fields and animals. I have also seen these little huts you build for those who do the work. You have also seen mine," Santiago stated, motioning to the buildings around them. "You have seen what I am prepared to do in order to retain my water. Regrettably, it is not enough."

MacLeod couldn't help but wonder where the man was going with his confession. If he were being honest, it made him quite uneasy. *The man clearly has a plan, but what is it?* MacLeod wondered.

"I have also heard that you will be needing to pay debts you have incurred," Santiago stated matter of fact, never turning his head to look at MacLeod. "I believe that if the rains do not come you will lose Colinas de Oro."

A chill crept over MacLeod. Where this man had gotten his information, he couldn't be sure. Californios kept financial matters to themselves, and their dealings seldom went beyond their word that they would pay the debts they owed. Often, years passed before a debt was repaid. The only possibility MacLeod could think of was that a ship's captain might have mentioned it to someone.

Santiago looked up into the cloudless sky and continued. "When I first came to this valley, I knew it surpassed every other place I had ever visited. They had told me about Colinas de Oro—said there was enough land for the both of us. At that time, the water was good and the grasses grew. But I see now that they were wrong."

MacLeod was only half-listening, his mind still racing with Santiago's last statement. *'I have also heard that you will be needing to pay debts you have incurred.'* The information the man had shook MacLeod to his core.

Does he know the extent of my debts? Where could this conversation possibly be headed? he thought to himself.

Santiago turned back to face MacLeod, his tone sharp. "I see now that there is not enough land or water for the both us."

Santiago's words rocked MacLeod. He waited for the man to continue.

"This woman you are married to—the land was given to her?" Not allowing him to answer, Santiago continued. "There are those who believe it may not have happened correctly. But that is another matter."

"What are you saying, Santiago?" MacLeod questioned, dropping all pretense of friendliness or titles.

"Oh, it is only a possibility that her land is not hers someone says to me. I say I would like to add this land given to Doña MacLeod to my own."

"Well, I wouldn't be counting on that ever happening. For now, I believe this talk is over." MacLeod reined his horse around before turning to face Santiago. "Just came by to let you know about the branding. I'll have my vaqueros push your cows back across the line. Seems a number of horses have wandered over too. Hate to think they all just got a mind to eat our grass."

"Before you go, I would like to tell you what I want. I would like to buy Colinas de Oro and all of its cattle."

"Not for sale. Not now, not ever. I'm afraid you've got the wrong impression, Santiago. We'll make it. Like you said, we have the water. From what I've seen, you'll be the one to fail."

Santiago's voice took on a brutal tone. "Consider my offer before it is too late. There is not much time, MacLeod. I never accept failure."

"Well then, I wish you luck," MacLeod stated harshly indicating to Concannon that they were done talking.

Santiago swung his horse around to block MacLeod's path. "I know about you, Americano. I have dealt with men like you all my life. You speak with your heart and not your head. Look around you," Santiago said, sweeping his arm around to indicate the valley. "What do you see? All this activity, all those people creating this rancho you see—I will not fail. Your Rancho Colinas de Oro is larger than what I have here and I will have it."

Not saying a word, MacLeod kicked the big gelding he rode, pushing aside Santiago's horse. "Hate to put a hole in your plans, Santiago, but that's not ever going to happen. You might think you know me, but there's much you're about to learn if you keep pushing me."

Santiago shook his head and smiled. "Fool. This offer I give you will not last. I cannot wait for my animals to perish from lack of water and pasture. You are in need of money and I am in need of your land."

MacLeod started to speak, but Santiago held up his hand, halting him. "Let me finish and then our business is complete. It is better to accept now than to lose it all. I will have Colinas de Oro, now or later. I may even keep some of your people. You do not know of the information I have about you. You and Doña Francesca have children, and others that we do not speak of."

Without thinking, MacLeod's hand went for the pistol in his belt.

"No," Concannon said, grabbing MacLeod's arm in a vise like grip. "There are other ways that are better than this."

"Listen to this little man," Santiago said. "You would be wise to accept my offer before it is too late. Your family needs a husband and father to look after them. Do not deprive them of that."

Santiago reined his horse over hard, jamming his spurs into its sides and riding off.

MacLeod wrenched his arm free of Concannon's grip and took a deep breath. When he spoke, his voice held a hint of promise. "I hate killing people; felt mighty sorry bout most of them. But I'll gladly kill that man if he pushes me much further."

RANCHO COLINAS DE ORO

The late afternoon sun bathed the hills with its golden rays. It was the same time of day when Francesca had first seen her land, albeit much later in the year. MacLeod had never seen the hills so brown quite this early.

What does that man know about my debts? Is he aware of how close Colinas de Oro is to ruin, if the rains stayed away another year? The thoughts continued to assault his ever-worried mind.

While MacLeod knew Francesca would never consider an offer to part with her land, he couldn't help but wonder if it was their best chance at survival. Although Santiago had not said how much he would offer, it had to be better than losing everything. If they didn't take his offer, what would they do in the meantime?

"Don't like having to thank people, Sean. You know how I am," MacLeod said, breaking the silence between Concannon and himself.

"Learned that about you long time back."

"Well, I would have shot the man if you hadn't stopped me."

"I know that. Wasn't thinking about you as much as the others," Concannon stated, his voice showing the restraint he'd held.

"Well, thank you anyway. The man sure stirred me up some." MacLeod shook his head. "We go over there thinking we know all about him and he's the one who knows about us."

"What do you figure his threat's worth?" Concannon asked in concern.

"Never believed in threatening a man unless I expected to do something about it. He didn't look to be a man to bluff," MacLeod said. "He has the man that would do it too."

"While you were talking, I noticed Pacheco had four men rounded up and waiting back a way. They weren't Indians or regular vaqueros," Concannon said.

"Think we had better take the man seriously," MacLeod stated as he mentally replayed Santiago's offer and the implied threat therein. He should have known Santiago would make a play for Colinas de Oro. But at least it made sense as to why the man wasn't as worried as he should be. "You heard him, what do you suppose he'll do? You know Francesca will never sell."

They rode up from the river a little further without speaking. Suddenly, Concannon broke the silence. "I were you, I'd plan on things happening. Keep your rifle ready. But remember, men like him don't fight fair."

"You ever wish you were back on your ship?" MacLeod asked in an attempt to change the subject.

"No, but there are times I would like to see the green hills of Ireland again. They're never brown like these."

"Unfortunately, we might not get any rain for another six months," MacLeod murmured. "I didn't need any more trouble than I already had, now this."

"How did he know about what you owe people?" Concannon asked, a puzzled expression upon his face. "And if he knows about that, what else does he know?"

Francesca was at the door of their adobe when the two men approached, Concannon continuing on to his own adobe. He dismounted and drew her over to the bench and seated her.

"You are troubled, I can see. Was this visit not good?" Francesca asked, her eyes filled with concern

MacLeod shook his head. "The man's worried about his cattle— as he ought to be. If the rains don't come, he'll be having water and feed problems long before the years out."

"Did you see the house he is building for this woman he spoke of? Do you know if she is from Monterey?"

"No idea, but it's awfully big looking. Trees are being planted all over for orchards and shade and he has maybe a hundred workers." MacLeod knew she needed to know about Santiago's offer. After all, she would find out soon enough.

"William, there is something you are not telling me," Francesca stated, seeing the worried expression upon his face. "How is it that he is not worried when he is building this home and has more cattle than we have? I do not believe he is a stupid man."

"I wouldn't say he's not worried, but he certainly has big plans. He believes this whole valley should be his. Figures to build himself an empire of sorts, I reckon."

Francesca rubbed her hands and brushed a fallen leaf off her skirt. "How is he to do this, William? Do not keep it all to yourself," she coaxed.

MacLeod took a deep breath. "He wants to buy Colinas de Oro. Somehow he knows of the money we owe and believes we can't last the year."

Francesca's eyes flared in anger. "Did you tell him it is not for sale?"

"Told him that."

"And what did he say?"

"It's not what he said so much as what he threatened to do," MacLeod stated.

"How would he do this?

"He indicated there might be a problem with your land grant or the money we owe, and some other things Seemed awful sure of himself. That place of his over there must be costing him a bunch of money. If you had taken note of his cows that we saw the other day you might have noticed. He has very few three-year olds. Most are another year away from slaughtering, so clearly he's not planning on using any hide money. How he is going to afford everything he is building I cannot understand. And now he's offering to buy Colinas de Oro and all of its cattle."

Francesca was shaking her head. "I don't understand this. How could there be a problem with our land?"

MacLeod kicked at the dust with the toe of his boot. "Well, when the governor granted you a good part of this valley it was never really surveyed, much like I said before. Not like they do so nowadays. At that time, we drew up what they call a *diseño*. Kind of a map stating where the boundary lines are and sent it up to the governor's office."

"Then there should not be a problem?"

"Did we make a copy?" MacLeod asked. He knew he should have taken the time and had the grant surveyed properly.

"I do not remember, but we know where the markers are, do we not?"

MacLeod scratched his head, feeling uneasy. "Well, most of them anyway. One was that big oak tree that came down in the wind a couple of years ago. The tree's still there on the ground. And there's that pile of stones we put up as a marker on the other side of the creek, below that long ridge."

Francesca sat looking at her hands in her lap for a while before eventually speaking. "I am nervous about this man. He is not one of us here in Alta California. What can we do to be safe?"

MacLeod had been thinking about it since talking with Santiago. "Suppose I can write to Monterey and have them check out the map we sent. Never entered my mind that someone would stoop low enough to challenge it."

"Do that, please. For me," Francesca whispered.

"I'll get to it soon as I can. Ought to ride up and check that other marker while I'm thinking about it," MacLeod said, hoping not to let on just how uneasy this whole affair was making him.

A week later MacLeod rode back to the house after checking with Sisquoc and the vaqueros about their plans to begin gathering the cattle. They needed to begin separating the cattle for branding and slaughtering.

As expected, his talk with Santiago had not stopped RS cattle from being pushed across the property line. The pasture at the upper end of the ranch was already overgrazed and the rest of the property would soon follow if they couldn't control the grazing cattle and horses. Sisquoc had spoken with a couple of Indians from a small village in the *tulles* who said the trappers were staying put until after the fall hunt. Based upon their new information, MacLeod and Concannon had decided to wait a couple of weeks before pushing the horses across to the San Joaquin.

As MacLeod rode up, a small group of people was gathered outside the house. He recognized the priest from the little mission.

Francesca came to meet him as he tied off his horse. "You should have told me you had invited Father Avila. I would have prepared and told the others. Many of them would like to be blessed by him."

"Sorry about that. Slipped my mind with all the things going on lately. Did he come alone?" MacLeod asked, looking around the small group of people surrounding the good Father.

"There is another man with him. He saw our trees and asked if he might take a look at them. I do not know why though?"

MacLeod wasn't sure how to tell her, so he just opted for the honest truth. "I met them when I went to Santa Barbara. Learned the man kept the mission orchards. I thought he might have an idea of how to care for ours."

Francesca clapped her hands together in excitement and took his arm. "Oh, then I am sure we can find room for one more, do you not think?"

"Well, I've been meaning to mention it, but he has a wife too."

"Very well, we shall manage. Perhaps she can help in the kitchen?" Francesca pondered aloud.

"And I believe they have a number of children," MacLeod added, his tone low.

"How many?" Francesca asked, a worried expression upon her face.

MacLeod thought the man had said three but he couldn't be positive. "Not sure exactly."

Francesca sighed. "It is so sad. So many good people can no longer work at the missions and yet, there is nowhere else for them to go."

"Well, we'll find them a place. If he can do anything for our trees it will be worth it."

"There is another thing," Francesca added. "Jacob would like to speak with you."

"About what?"

"I don't know. He was talking to Sean before coming to me."

"I'll go find him. In the meantime, make sure they eat well. Didn't appear they had much when I met them."

Francesca nodded before heading into the house while MacLeod went in search of Jacob.

As expected, MacLeod found Jacob sitting on a stump drawing letters in the sand for Diego and Catalina. "What was it you wanted to speak to me about?" MacLeod asked. Taking the opportunity for escape, the two children ran off allowing the men to speak.

"Well, I have been speaking to the red-headed fellow. He was telling me about this water problem they have next door and about the dam they intended to build."

Seeing Sisquoc riding toward them, MacLeod found himself not fully listening to what Jacob Morgenthau was saying.

"You should consider building yourself an aqueduct, of sorts, to help bring water from the stream to the house. I believe I could help" Morgenthau stated, pulling MacLeod's attention back to him.

"How would you do that?"

"Well, now, we have not had an opportunity to talk and I have not been entirely truthful. I told you I was a teacher, and I am."

"Looks like you could use some writing things to help you with the youngsters," MacLeod said, not realizing he was changing the subject.

"Yes, that would be a blessing. However, before I took up teaching in England, I worked for two years with an uncle who is an engineer of sorts. He builds things all over the country. Did I tell you my father is a doctor?" MacLeod shook his head, shocked by the revelation. "Anyway, after working for my uncle I went to a school of medicine for two years before realizing the profession was not for me. That was when I decided I would rather teach than heal."

Sisquoc rode up. MacLeod held his hand up for him to wait for a moment. "Are you saying water could be diverted from the stream up here to the houses?" MacLeod asked for clarification.

"Yes. And I don't mean to lecture, but the water from the steam is not as healthy as it should be. The cattle have contaminated it. I would highly recommend you boil it before drinking it."

"Why don't you draw me up something and we can discuss it later. It would be a good thing to have when the well runs dry as it is now" MacLeod suggested.

Jacob Morgenthau placed his hat back on his head. "Would it be too much to ask to have someone take me up to where this water comes from?"

"I can have someone take you part way. Might be hard to go all the way though. Right now I need to have something done before I forget."

McLeod took Sisquoc off to the side, MacLeod ordered, "Send someone down to bring back that pile of hides we've been collecting. Have them put in that *carreta* I brought back from Santa Barbara. I'll send it back with the priest. I need to pay that ship's captain."

Sisquoc nodded in understanding and set out to do as he had been instructed.

The young Indian boy, Malibu, came by with the golden maned sorrel as he had done every day since its arrival. Based upon the progress Malibu has been making with the animal, MacLeod figured the horse might be ready to ride in a couple more weeks.

When MacLeod returned to the house he found Francesca talking with the man from the mission. She left him and made her way over to speak to MacLeod. "William, the man says he can help our trees. He said it will take some time but that they can be saved and have much fruit."

"I hoped as much when I heard what he used to do. He can help with *matanza* too. I'm sure he's been around cattle before, and we're short-handed. That's the reason I haven't sent Concannon across to sell the horses. We need everybody we can get." Making his way over to where Father Avila and the man from the mission sat, he greeted both men and thanked them for coming.

Father Avila stood with the package of food Juana had prepared for them in his arms. "There are others from the mission who have attended many *matanzas*. If you are in need of some, I can send them up here for you," he stated, having overheard he and Francesca's conversation.

MacLeod grinned. "Sure could use at least half a dozen. All I can do is feed them and pay them in hides."

Father Avila bowed his head. "I will see to it then."

In the distance MacLeod could see Sisquoc and two others coming back from the hide curing area. From what he could see, it appeared as though the big Chumash had something draped across his saddle. Halting in front of MacLeod he dropped a hide on the ground and pointed at it. MacLeod spread it out. Someone had sliced the hide in a half dozen places.

"How many like this?" MacLeod asked, his voice tight.

"All."

"Everything we've got down there?"

Sisquoc nodded.

"Any idea when it was done?"

"Not long."

Each week they slaughtered a steer or two in order to feed the growing number of Indians and Mexican workers, along with their families. Because of that, MacLeod figured he had roughly seventy or eighty hides waiting to be taken to Santa Barbara.

"Any idea who could have done this?" MacLeod asked.

Sisquoc sent the two vaqueros off and stepped out of the saddle. MacLeod could tell the Indian had an idea who had trashed the hides. "The one who did not come back. The one who is now over there," he said, indicating with his head in the direction of Rancho Santiago.

MacLeod turned back to the house. *Was this something Santiago had ordered, or could it be Pacheco's work?* He knew there was no way to know for sure, but one way or the other, things were going to heat up.

RANCHO SANTIAGO

"Do you think he will sell?" Pacheco asked.

Cesario Santiago sipped a glass of rough red wine from the mission cellars. "Eventually they will see it is the only way. Perhaps he need only be encouraged."

Pacheco shuffled his feet in the dirt. "He does not push easily."

"You are afraid of this man?" Santiago asked.

"Afraid, no. I fear no man. But he is not to be misjudged. He is not like most you may push."

"He came to announce they are to begin their round-up and branding of their cattle. He wanted to know if we wished to participate."

"That is what the rancheros do. It is a little early," Pacheco said.

Santiago rose and stepped out from under the trees. "You have been up there to see how the land is. How long do we have?"

"They are already wandering far. Some we have found far beyond where they find the fields are not bare," Pacheco said. "You have too many cattle for this land."

"Yes, I did not believe this dryness would last. There is little time then. I cannot lose this land."

Pacheco stepped up into his saddle. "There are things that could be done, Doñ Santiago, but you must first tell me how far you will allow me to take this."

Santiago turned to look at the man. "I must have that land to survive. If I do not survive, neither will you," Santiago stated cryptically. "Someday you must tell me how you know this man and Doña MacLeod."

"Are you prepared for what will happen?" Pacheco asked, ignoring his final statement. "He will not run away without a fight and he has killed men before."

"He cannot survive if he has no one to work the cattle," Santiago stated, walking over and picking a cigar up off the table by his chair.

Pacheco leaned on the saddle horn and waited for him to continue.

"Perhaps if his people left him, he would begin to reconsider."

"Perhaps. But perhaps it will not be enough," Pacheco countered.

"You do what you feel you must, but we do not have much time. My cattle suffer already."

Pacheco reined his horse back. "Then be prepared for what will happen. I will not be the only one he will hold responsible." Pacheco spun his horse around and touched its sides with his spurs.

Santiago watched him ride off. He smiled. *Perhaps the man will have that woman yet,* he thought to himself. He had watched Pacheco when they rode over to Colinas de Oro; she had claimed his eye. It was clearly written upon Pacheco's face...he still lusted after her.

With the fuse lit, Santiago walked down to see what progress had been made on the house. Furnishings were set to arrive on a ship from Monterey soon and he wanted to see everything in its place before he returned to Monterey. He hoped this time *she* would return with him. While he was there he figured it would not hurt to visit this new governor. Perhaps he was a man who could be dealt with.

Rancho Colinas de Oro

Two weeks later MacLeod sat on the sorrel stallion and watched the vaqueros separate a cow from its bawling calf. This was the second day he had spent time on the horse, taking him out for a few hours to see what effects the abuse had done to its spirit. The day before, MacLeod let the horse set its own pace, quickly learning that the big stallion loved to run. With little urging, the horse broke into a long, ground eating lope, and kept it up until MacLeod returned to the corral and turned it over to young Malibu again.

Only once since taking the horse out had it shied and that was when the sound of a sudden loud crack from a whip a vaquero had used to drive a mother away from its calf. The horse had nearly thrown MacLeod. It took most of his strength to keep it from bolting. He knew it would take time, yet he felt the horse would eventually be worth the effort.

MacLeod grinned, watching as Diego whirled his *reata* above his head and hurled it at the back legs of a young steer. When the rope missed a laughing vaquero chased the young steer and turned it back for another attempt. Cheering rose when Diego's third attempt succeeded and the calf was thrown to the ground.

It had turned out that Juan, whose name was Juan Gómez, had more children than the three MacLeod expected. In fact, he brought a very large wife and seven children back to Rancho Colinas de Oro. Francesca could only shake her head before going in search of a place for the family to live. However, it wasn't all a disaster. It turned out, three of Juan's children were boys in their teenage years who had worked cattle with the mission vaqueros. After settling in, they quickly found themselves a string of horses and joined the other vaqueros under the supervision of MacLeod's new majordomo, Jesus Alvarado.

Since few Mexican vaqueros would consider a job in which they could not be on their horses, Sisquoc, as Indian *alcalde,* supervised the Indian workers in branding the young heifers. The brand was burnt into the skin on the left hip with a long heavy iron called *el fierro para herrar los ganados.* If the cattle were sold, another brand would eventually be placed on the left shoulder.

The Rancho Colinas de Oro brand was a CO with a wavy line through the O. Francesca said it represented the hills she had named the land after.

"Father, father, did you see?" Diego called out breathlessly as he loped over to MacLeod. "I caught that one over there," he said, pointing to a young steer looking for comfort from its mother.

"Saw it. You're getting pretty good with that *reata* since the last time I watched. Caught the heels and it only took you three tries."

"Cisco has been showing me how it's done," Diego said proudly. Cisco was Juan Gomez's sixteen-year-old son.

MacLeod watched as Cisco dropped to the ground and slipped the saddle off the little bay he had been riding. He reached for the trailing rope of the first loose horse he approached and threw his saddle up on its back.

MacLeod called out and motioned for the young man to join him.

The boy led his horse over to where MacLeod and Diego waited. He swept off his battered sombrero to reveal a head full of black hair framing a dust-streaked face. He held his hat with two hands against his chest.

"Cisco, right?" MacLeod asked.

"Si, señor," the boy said, his sweat streaked face split by a wide grin that revealed a row of pearly white teeth.

MacLeod had watched the boy work the cattle on a number of occasions since his arrival and knew he would make a first rate vaquero. With more work to be done, he quickly sent Cisco and

Diego off to chase more calves and bring them back to the branding area.

MacLeod watched as Diego raced back to help corner another calf. After the first few years he stopped worrying about the boy's development. The near death the boy suffered crossing the desert as a child had been a major concern for MacLeod. But now, Diego appeared to be as healthy as any other thirteen-year-old boy.

Far out across the pasture MacLeod watched the racing figure of Catalina, her long braid flying out from under her hat as she chased one of the shorthaired steers out of a shallow ravine and pushed it away from those gathered in a circle waiting for their turn to be branded. He grinned, remembering Francesca's concern that her daughter would rather be Alta California's first woman vaquero than a proper lady.

The smell of burnt flesh and the bawling of the cattle reminded him of happier times. Times when a *fiesta* would follow *matanza*. Even the Indians he employed on the ranch could feel the heavy doubt that had settled over the valley as the dry days continued.

Though just as he'd expected, Santiago had not sent any of his people over to help separate any RS cows from Colinas cows. MacLeod figured he had done his part. He rode over to where the Indian workers were preparing for the slaughtering to begin.

Sisquoc had managed to find one of the heavy iron vats at the mission and it now sat alongside the one they already had. An old Indian, who had wandered in one day looking for food, had remained and constructed a tiny brush shelter, finding something to do each day. For the past two weeks he had been driving a *carreta* down among the trees by the river and gathering dead wood for the vat fires. As such, a five-foot pile of dry wood waited beside the vats. It had turned out that Juan Gomez's wife had supervised the Indian woman at the mission in rendering the tallow so she had quickly taken over the same job at Colinas de Oro.

Nearby, two more of the Indian mission workers sat carving wooden pegs, using some of the ruined hides to strip leather thongs for pegging the green hides out in the sun to dry. Another woman began preparing the leather bags the solidified tallow would be placed in for transporting to the ships. Each bag, called an *arrobas,* held about twenty-five pounds of tallow, most of which was carried in the ships down to South America. MacLeod often found himself shaking his head at the lack of incentive among the Californios. They sold their hides to the traders, which were then shipped around Cape Horn and up to America to be made into shoes and other leather goods before eventually returning to Alta California for the people to purchase with more hides.

He rode further out to where Alvarado had separated the vaqueros into groups of *navajadores,* or stickers who would kill the steers, and turn them over to the *peladores* who would strip the hide and leave it for the butchers, or *tasajoras.* The actual butchering was usually done by Indian women.

Lost in his thoughts, he had not heard Concannon approach until he halted his horse right next to him.

"Looks as if we can have the branding finished in a couple more days. After that we can begin separating the three years olds and the biggest of the two year olds. I still need to get a count to see where we're at. Hopefully we can get a head start on the other ranchos while the price is still high," MacLeod stated.

Concannon grunted. "What's the latest prices you've heard?"

"Good, clean, well scraped hides are going for somewhere between one and a half and two dollars a hide. Tallow about two dollars a steer. As for those bigger two year olds—I'm thinking they're the result of those bulls we brought in a few years ago. They're finally starting to pay off."

Concannon simply nodded. Macleod waited for the man to respond. He had a feeling the Irishman had news but was in no hurry to share. He figured Concannon would tell him when he was ready.

"Been pushing horses up the far end of the ranch, closer to the pass, through the mountains, like you wanted. There's a little stream up there so they should stay put till we're ready to drive them over to the *tulles* and sell them."

MacLeod remembered the spot well. "Wish I could spare some vaqueros so you could do that right away. If there are Hudson's Bay trappers on the river looking for horses I wouldn't want to miss them."

"What do you figure I should do if they're gone?"

MacLeod watched as a young calf broke away from Diego's rope and raced back towards its mother. Almost instantly, a horse flashed past Diego who was busily attempting to recoil his *reata*. He let out a yell as Catalina threw her horse at the young steer and turned it back toward the fire and branding area. All around them, the vaqueros' shouts of encouragement could be heard.

MacLeod burst into laughter. "We'll be hearing about that this evening. She'll tell all."

"Something else you need to be hearing," Concannon muttered solemnly.

MacLeod waited.

"Came on something up there at the far end. Would never have found it if we didn't have to chase a bunch of steers out of a deep draw."

"Sean, you got something you want to tell me? Figure I'm not about to like it"

"One of them big bulls you brought to the ranch—found him in the ravine—his throat sliced open."

It took a moment for MacLeod to grasp what Concannon was telling him. "What do you figure happened? Went charging through the brush and tore it on a broken branch?"

"Not likely," Concannon said. "Looks as if someone used one of those long knives the *navajadores* use. Too clean to be anything else."

MacLeod remained silent as he processed the information. *First the dry hides had been mutilated and now a prized bull was found dead.*

"When you figure it happened?" MacLeod asked after a few moments.

"Last night. By the looks of things, it couldn't have been any earlier."

MacLeod nodded. "Full moon last night. No clouds. If someone knew whereabouts he was grazing it's an easy thing to drive him into that ravine. Little chance we would find him for a spell." He leaned over the front of the saddle and watched while he continued to digest this new information. "Any ideas?"

Concannon combed out his beard for a moment before speaking. "It's a war and you know it. Was me, I'd ride over there and shoot the man. Probably get shot myself."

"Just a thought, but when you were up at the far end did you see many RS horses?"

"There's a bunch of them. Why you asking?"

"I think we're about done branding. We'll need to start slaughtering here soon," MacLeod said. "Why don't you talk to Alvarado and have him give you two or three vaqueros. Take them horses over to the river and see if you can't meet up with those fellows. Might even run into another Irishman or two, you never know."

Concannon grinned. "You know, if I was a betting man I'd think you had some thoughts there. Mind sharing them?"

"Be sure of the men you take; don't want another situation like the one that went with Santiago. That being said—in all the hustle and bustle of rounding up these horses of ours it wouldn't surprise me a bit if a few RS horses got mixed in with ours. Be a crying shame, but what can you do," MacLeod shrugged.

"Hard to tell sometimes, what with all the dust they kick up. What do you figure might happen to them?" Concannon said with a wry grin.

"Well, we can't sell them, unless someone forgot to brand them. However, when it's discovered they're mixed in among ours we haven't got anyone to bring them back. So, as leader of this here party, what do you figure you would do with them?" MacLeod asked, a mischievous grin upon his face.

Concannon licked his lips and took off his hat to brush the sweat from his forehead. "Can't sell those branded ones, so we will probably take an iron with us for some of the others. I guess those we took by mistake we'll have to leave."

"Might have to," MacLeod shrugged. "Probably wouldn't discover them until you were a ways up the river, hundred miles or so."

"Be a shame, but what can you do?"

"While you're away I think I'll have Alvarado send vaqueros up to drive any steer back to RS. That'll keep everyone busy and on their own side."

"Then I guess I'll be telling Esperanza I'll be away a spell. She'll put some food together for us and be lecturing me for sure."

MacLeod wondered if she had told him they would be having another child. Though, based upon his behavior, he would assume not. *Maybe a week away will be good for him.* Sadly, he also knew they would be shorthanded until his return and everybody would be asked to work harder and longer. MacLeod made a mental note to make sure Francesca prepared the cooking crews for the long hours.

As he spun the horse around to leave, Concannon spoke. "If you don't mind me asking…what is it I'll be wanting for these horses?"

MacLeod mulled the question over for a moment. "Good ones, I figure are worth ten dollars a piece. They need horses bad enough they'll pay. Of course, whatever you can get is better than seeing the poor critters starve to death."

"How do suppose they'll be paying?" Concannon asked.

MacLeod hadn't thought of that. "I don't suppose they'll be carrying coin. It's always possible, but you'll probably be offered beaver pelts."

"Beaver pelts?"

MacLeod grinned. "It's the skin off one of those little critters with big tails you see in the streams sometimes. Two prime pelts for one good horse ought to be enough."

"Prime pelts? And how am I to know prime from whatever?"

"You got a point there," MacLeod said with a chuckle. "I were you, I'd inspect what they give you and throw back the first batch or two. They're bound to give you summer hides at first. Tell them you want fall hides—they'll be prime."

"And just what are you fixing to do with them?"

"We'll take them to Santa Barbara or Monterey. Any ship's captain will know their worth."

Concannon studied the sky for a time before speaking. "I don't like going off at a time like this. One of us should be nearby for the women."

MacLeod nodded in agreement. "This new fellow I brought up from Santa Barbara...you have a chance to talk with him?"

"Been meaning to," Concannon said. "We had us a few of them Jews back home. Pretty much kept to themselves."

"He'll surprise you, I believe. He's had experience with guns, and his wife is here too. I'll see to it that he has a weapon nearby at all times. We'll be okay."

"Then I best be starting," Concannon said reluctantly.

MacLeod knew Concannon was unsure about the situation, but he figured a word of encouragement would be appreciated. "Sean, anything you bring back will go a long way to helping out. I wouldn't ask you to go if it weren't needed."

"Esperanza said we should be expecting another in the fall. I believe it will help her after losing the boy. Will help me too," Concannon said.

MacLeod reached over and gripped Concannon's hand. "Hurry back. I'll be needing you here.

MONTEREY

Marisol Montero bent down and pulled a weed from her garden before walking out beyond the fence to gaze out across the sloping land toward the waters of the Monterey harbor. She watched as the gulls swooped down from their perches on the nearby driftwood logs, their cries filling the air. Three ships rode at anchor, one having brought the last of the goods she had ordered. Even with the fear of the drought, the women of Monterey managed to scrape together enough to purchase the silks and linens needed to follow the patterns of what women on the east coast of America were wearing. Her captains had also reported that sales in San Diego and Los Angeles were similar to here.

What was not sold from off the ships would be stocked in stores in all three towns. This year, her profits were less than those of her investments, which were made by a couple of her most trusted captains in Boston businesses. Marisol pondered this as she thought about this evening. Cesario Santiago had returned from the rancho he was building in the south. Tonight he would be coming for dinner to tell her of the progress he had made on this home he was building, which he hoped she would share with him.

Only one question remained—Would the story Santiago had spread, that she was a recently discovered niece, be believed by the people of Monterey? And would it truly concern her if they didn't? Had not the new American, Thomas Larkin, finally married the woman, Rachel Holmes, it was said he had bedded while on the boat coming here from America, despite the fact that she was married? The woman had found herself with Larkin's child. Though as it turned out, her husband died during a sea voyage to South America. Marisol laughed, remembering how the elite people of Santa Barbara had attended the wedding and welcomed the new couple into Alta California society.

She knew with absolute certainty that Cesario Santiago would pressure her to join him if this new house he had promised was complete.

Marisol sighed as she walked back through her garden and sat for a moment to reflect on his proposal. She knew of his marriage, he had never denied it. He had come out here to Alta California two years ago seeking a land grant from Governor Figueroa. The secularization of the missions had turned over most of the property and cattle to appointed administrators who were directed to portion out much of it to the Indians. However, Marisol knew the Indians had not fared well in the distribution, often selling their plot of land, or cattle, to the first person who made them an offer. In many cases, these same Indians ended up being employed by the buyer at a bare substance level. Rumors of Santiago's dealings with the governor's appointed administrator were ripe with speculation, especially when the recent administrator from that area had sailed for South America shortly after Santiago took possession of his new grant.

She looked around at her house and garden with the small orchard now bearing fruit. *What would I gain by going to live with him?* Marisol chuckled at the thought. She knew exactly why Santiago wanted her to come to his new home. He had made his desires perfectly clear—Santiago wanted her in his bed.

Cesario Santiago rarely failed to achieve what he went after. However, this time he would discover that he would not get his wish. She had no desire to share his bed, of that she was certain. In fact, her decision would be to remain in Monterey and tend to her business; possibly use her money to build a new home of her own.

This man, Larkin, had experimented with building a house with extended eaves to help keep rain from washing away the adobe of the walls. Despite it not being a problem the last three years, she knew that once the rains returned it would be a yearly battle with the destructive force of the rain. Whitewash only prolonged the need for repairs.

Calling out to one of her Indian servants, she asked them to begin preparing for his arrival. In the meantime, she steeled herself in preparation of the onslaught she knew she could expect from him at her refusal.

"I will need to see the governor tomorrow," Santiago stated matter of fact. Since his arrival two hours before, Marisol had noted his state of distraction. Whether it was the letter delivered to him by one of the ship's captains when he first arrived, or his concern for the welfare of the cattle on his ranch, she could not tell.

"Is this something to do with your land?" Marisol asked.

"Yes, I wish to verify the boundaries of Rancho Santiago."

"Is there a reason you believe they may be in dispute?" she asked, wondering if this was what occupied his thoughts all throughout dinner. Not once had he mentioned the progress made on the house he was building, or whether she would accompany him back when he left to return.

Perhaps, she thought, *he is taking it for granted that she would return with him.*

"That is what I wish to explore. This valley has limited water. As you can imagine, this has brought about a crisis for my cattle. The fields have not the grass, nor my stream the water, for my herds."

Marisol frowned. "And our governor has the answer to this problem?"

She watched his expression harden for a moment. Taking another sip of wine, his expression softened and he smiled.

"It is of no concern of yours. It is only business that we, as men, must conduct. I am sure he will simply direct me to the commissioner of lands for an explanation."

"Yes, as you say, it is for men to discuss business," she said signaling to one of the young Indian servants to remove the plates "If you fear there is not enough water or feed for your cattle what is it you hope to achieve here in Monterey?"

Santiago rose and walked over to her to assist her in rising. He escorted her to a nearby chair and seated her before speaking. "This valley where I am building my hacienda is large. It is one of the more beautiful valleys I have seen here in Alta California. Unfortunately, it is not large enough for two ranchos."

Marisol waited for him to continue. This was the first time he had made mention of a problem that might exist on the land granted to him. "Did you not realize this when you had the land surveyed?" she asked.

He clasped his hands together and rested his chin on them. "Of course. It was a concern for the future, but I anticipated a resolution after a few years."

"A resolution?" Marisol questioned.

"Yes. Once my herd had grown significantly I intended to approach those who own the rest of the land in the valley and make an offer to purchase theirs."

She ran her hands over her dress to smooth out a crease. His smugness infuriated her. He had come to Alta California and appeared to believe he could purchase, or take, whatever he wanted. If she hadn't made up her mind before, she knew without a doubt that she would never live with him in this new home he was building. "And if they did not want to sell their land?" she asked. She knew she would not rest until she knew where he stood.

"My dear," Santiago chuckled. "Everyone has a price. I would simply make it known to these people that they would be, what shall I say, more comfortable living elsewhere."

"I see. And obtaining this land next to yours would solve your problem?"

"Yes. Taking possession of this land is absolutely necessary for the survival of Rancho Santiago."

"When do you believe this will take place, taking this land away from those who own it?"

Santiago relit his cigar and offered up his cup to the young Indian girl to refill. "It must take place immediately. I have already made an offer to buy it."

"Then why do you appear so disturbed?" Marisol asked. "Have they accepted your offer?"

"Unfortunately, they have not. That is why I have come to Monterey to see the governor. And of course, to escort you back to Rancho Santiago. The house is complete and the furnishings will have arrived by the time we return. I know you will be comfortable there. You may bring a servant with you as well."

Marisol took a deep breath. She needed a moment to frame her rejection. If she had learned anything about him, it was that Cesario Santiago was not a man who accepted failure lightly. "This place which you have offered to purchase, does it have a name?"

"It was granted to a woman by Governor Argüello. It is called Rancho Colinas de Oro. But I believe you know these people already," Santiago said, dropping his cigar in the pot by his chair.

Marisol frowned. Clearly, he had assumed all evening that she would accompany him, not once asking if she wished to. "I know of these people? You are positive of this?" she asked in confusion.

Santiago sat back and used a table candle to light a fresh cigar. "Of course. I should have mentioned it before this, but I am told you were there when this Americano killed the Frenchman. It was said you had his son at the time."

RANCHO COLINAS DE ORO

MacLeod had filled Francesca in on his talk with Concannon. Well, part of it anyway.

"I do not like Sean going away at this time. There is no one to watch over him," Francesca stated, her tone soft.

"He's a grown man. Maybe a couple of weeks away from the wine will cure him." He paused for a moment before adding, "He did say Esperanza told him about them having another child."

Francesca smiled and nodded as the two of them watched clouds build up far out over the water in the west as they had most days.

Though just like those other days, they passed over and left brilliant blue skies in their wake.

MacLeod could tell that Francesca sensed something was wrong, though he wrestled with what he had to tell her. He couldn't keep it from her, she would find out soon enough.

"Sean was up at the far end of the pasture—you know, where that deep, dry arroyo comes out of the mountains. Found one of the new bulls with its throat cut."

Francesca's hand went to her mouth. "He is sure of this?"

"Asked him the exact same thing. He says there's no doubt someone had done it."

"What does this all mean, William? It is not the way things should be."

"Sean said it best. Says—this is war. I should have seen it coming. Although, I hoped it wouldn't come to this."

"I do not want to see people hurt," Francesca whispered. "It has never been like this before. Why are they doing this to us?"

"Clearly, the man is more desperate than I figured him to be. I can't say he didn't warn me, but I wasn't prepared for this. First the hides being all cut up, and now this." MacLeod shook his head.

MacLeod waved young Malibu over so he could see how the sorrel had responded to his run this morning. He didn't want to frighten Francesca about what was happening with their neighbor, but he had a bad feeling about where this would all lead. "He wants the land, Francesca. I don't want to admit it, but I agree with him when he says he can't survive without our land and its water."

"But what can he do if we refuse to give it to him?"

"We'll have to wait and see. In the meantime I'm going to have a talk with Jacob. Since he'll be spending his time nearby I want to make sure he'll keep an eye on you and the other women."

"And what can you do about the bulls? If they would do this to one, they could kill all of them."

"I plan on having the other four brought down here to keep closer to this part of the valley. You know, already I've noticed bigger calves."

MacLeod walked around the sorrel and inspected the scars on its back and sides. Francesca joined him, running a gentle hand down the sides of his body.

"It is such a shame they did this to him. He is so beautiful," Francesca said.

"He is that. Wish I could find a mare like him. Could produce some fine looking colts. Probably bring a good price too."

She ran her hand along the stallions shoulder and took his head between her hands. "Bolivar, you are so beautiful." She smiled up at MacLeod. "When might I ride him?"

MacLeod laughed. "He needs a firm hand. He's still somewhat spooked. Maybe when he's a little older he'll settle down some."

"What will you do about this other thing? I know you and I see it in your face," Francesca asked.

MacLeod took off the wide-brimmed sombrero he had recently taken to wearing, although he refused the other fancy clothing the men wore. "Need to ride over and warn him, I guess. Tell him that if it happens again there will be a reckoning."

Francesca took his arm in hers, her eyes wide with fear. "Do not go to see him alone. The man frightens me"

MacLeod spotted Alvarado talking with one of the vaqueros and waved him over to tell him about the bull. "I want the others brought in close to the ranch where they'll be safer."

Alvarado took off his sombrero and scratched his head. "We do not have enough people for all of this we are doing."

"I know, but get with Sisquoc and have his people that are working on the building bricks to halt for a spell. Just keep one up there to keep turning them over to dry. Use one of the younger vaqueros and take Gomez's son. They'll need to split up and locate those four bulls and drive them back. Shouldn't be a problem."

MacLeod was about to step into the house and retrieve his pistol and rifle when he spied Diego and Catalina sitting at the table with Jacob. Sending the children on their way, Jacob rose and approached MacLeod.

"Would you have but a moment?" the man asked.

MacLeod nodded as two young Indian girls walked by carrying large jugs of water from the creek. After pouring the water into a barrel beside the house the two girls trudged back to the creek for more.

"I have informed Francesca about the need to boil the water before you use it. Now, this man and his family you have brought from the mission, they speak of these reddish colored tiles they use to direct water."

"I suppose you're talking about the same ones they use for the roof," MacLeod surmised.

"Similar, I believe. He has said he knows how they are made," Jacob Morgenthau said.

"They're made out of the same thing as the bricks we build the houses with. They're called *tejas*. They form the adobe over a log that's been smoothed out so the clay won't stick to it and then put it into a kiln for days. That's what gives them the red color."

"Then it is possible to do this?"

MacLeod wasn't about to go over all the things needing done before he could think about a new project, but the man had brought up a good suggestion. "Well, we're molding adobe bricks for shelters right now. The tiles you're talking about take a lot of time and labor, but maybe it's something we can look at after we finish slaughtering."

"I have a few ideas when you get some time to speak," Morgenthau said.

"We can talk some later about your idea, but we've had a bull killed and I need to talk to some people about it."

"What can I do in the meantime to help?" the young man asked.

"There's another rifle in the house; I'd like you to keep it handy. Watch over the womenfolk until I get back."

Jacob took off his glasses and polished them with the end of his shirt. "I take it then that there is a certain degree of danger hereabouts?"

MacLeod doubted Santiago's threats would go beyond challenging the boundaries of the land grant or destroying property, but he knew better than to not be prepared. "Let's just say I'll feel safer if you're nearby."

He suddenly felt the exhaustion of the last few weeks overcome him. Francesca, seeming to sense his weariness, took his arm. "Come, Rosalie has prepared a meal. You will feel better after you have eaten and rested for a spell."

"I think you're right," he agreed. "I doubt waiting another day to talk to the man will make much difference."

As they approached the door Sarah came into view, her arms dripping from the blood of a newly butchered steer as she knelt by the door.

"We don't have enough Indians to do the butchering?" MacLeod asked, turning to face Jacob.

"Sarah does not mind. I have told her she did not need to do this, but she said she must find a way to help," Jacob explained.

Nodding, MacLeod ducked slightly and entered the house. On the long hand-hewn plank table the old lady had laid out a platter of tortillas and a bowl of meat and beans, spiced with hot peppers.

Francesca poured him a cup of water and rubbed his shoulders. "I think it is a good time to take a *siesta*—at least until the day is cooler." After everyone had eaten, Francesca shooed Diego and Catalina out of the house and led MacLeod over to the narrow bed in the lean-to attached to the house.

Lying down, MacLeod closed his eyes and attempted to rest.

Several hours later, MacLeod came to with a hand gently shaking his shoulder. Figures floated about the room. He had no idea how long he had slept.

"William, please you must wake," Francesca pleaded.

He noted the shadows climbing up the wall as the sun set out over the Pacific. He had slept away the entire afternoon. He sat up on the edge of the bed and buried his face in his hands. "Why did you let me sleep so long?" he groaned.

"It was for your benefit," Francesca said, kneading the muscles of his shoulders once again. "Señor Alvarado is here. He says he must talk to you."

MacLeod rose from the bed and brushed his hair back out of his face. After locating his boots that someone had removed while he slept he walked out into the late afternoon shadows. Outside, Alvarado stood with his hat in his hand a look of concern upon his face.

"There's a problem?" MacLeod asked?

"Si, they have brought the bulls back that you wished to hold near the house. But a boy has not returned."

"It's still pretty light," MacLeod said, taking a look around at the late afternoon sun. "Why are you worried?"

"His horse has returned," Alvarado stated matter of fact.

"Who is it?"

"The Gomez boy," Alvarado said

"Cisco?"

"Si."

"Find his dad and round up everyone you can find. The boy keeps riding some of those half broke stallions. I knew sooner or later this was bound to happen. Who saw him last?"

"One of the vaqueros said he saw him ride toward the top of the stream. He did not know why. We had found the bulls and were bringing them down."

MacLeod grabbed one of the young Indian boys that was standing nearby. "Fetch that little black stallion I ride and throw my saddle on him. He's sure footed as a mule and don't spook easy. Good thing we have a near full moon tonight."

Francesca, having heard the conversation, came out from the house with his Kentucky rifle in her arms and handed it to him. "Be careful."

MacLeod took the reins from the boy and stepped up into the saddle. He spoke to Alvarado "Spread them out. There's no telling where he might be. He's probably too damned embarrassed about being tossed from his horse and having to walk home. I'll follow the creek all the way up between here and RS land. Anyone finds the lad, be sure to let the others know," he said. "And don't get careless, there are bears feeding on fresh kill out there."

Alvarado nodded in understanding as MacLeod reined the little black stallion around and waved for the others to get moving.

He couldn't explain it, but he didn't like the way he felt.

MacLeod rubbed the sleep from his eyes as he worked his way through scattered oak trees that covered the land. The roots of the trees plumbed the depths of the land searching for any signs of moisture. Though it was clear that some the younger ones were showing signs of distress.

He kneed the black stallion up a low rise, stopping long enough to call out the lad's name. It wouldn't do to miss the boy if he had been tossed and hurt. Although MacLeod figured the boy's ego would take the biggest bruise. Especially after letting the horse return to the ranch without him. When he received no answer to his hail, MacLeod rode back down into the shallow troughs between the rolling hills, continuing along the edge of the stream toward the beginning of the low foothills that marked the upper boundary of the land grant.

As he rode in silence MacLeod found his thoughts returning to the problems at hand. Cesario Santiago's offer to buy Rancho Colinas de Oro would certainly resolve their financial problems. In truth, he envied Santiago's apparent well of unlimited resources.

He and Francesca had lived on the edge of poverty while they built up the herd in hopes that eventually the return from the yearly slaughter would give them breathing space. Still, this year and last year he'd had to borrow in order to replace broken equipment and household necessities. If this were Boston, the merchants he owed money to would be at his door, or they'd have sent the sheriff to collect. It was only because of the trust and patience of the Californios that verbal commitments for future payment were as good as the hides themselves. However, the captains of the Boston ships would not sail without payment for merchandise they had delivered.

And then there was his mother—what answer would he send to her about coming to California? He was pretty sure he would tell her to wait until the ranch was complete, assuming they still had it. By then, there would be room for her. Although that seemed to be a long way off.

Now that Jacob Morgenthau had agreed to take on the responsibility of teaching the youngsters, MacLeod felt some of the pressure removed from his shoulders. Alta California had far too many of their young men doing little more than gambling, drinking, or racing their horses about in a show of bravado. He wanted more than that for his son.

It was then that MacLeod remembered the other letter from the ship. Not the one from the American, Senator Benton, posing questions MacLeod felt needed more thought before he could answer them. No, it was the letter from Doñ Cordero, Diego's grandfather that posed the most thought. *How can I ignore the man's request to see his only grandson?* MacLeod thought to himself. *If what Doñ Cordero said was true, and I have no reason to doubt the man's word, he is making Diego the inheritor of his lands. He deserves to know his grandson.* While MacLeod had yet to answer the letter and had no real intention of crossing back over the desert to New Mexico again, he silently vowed to at least answer the letter and tell the man how the boy was doing.

Suddenly, the little stallion snorted, its ears twitching forward. Reining the horse to a halt, MacLeod listened intently. Only the night sounds of small critters scratching for food or the occasional call of an owl broke the silence.

The horse snorted again and shivered. Something had clearly caught its attention. Carefully slipping the rifle out of its leather sheath, he laid the barrel across the front of the saddle.

As he slowly continued forward, he spotted what had spooked the horse. About fifty yards ahead of him a black bear tore at the carcass of a newly killed steer. As of late, there had been far too damn many bears around, especially the short-tempered grizzlies. He touched the horse with his heels and pointed it up and around the low hill leaving the hungry bear to its dinner. The stallion didn't argue at the change of direction.

Still under the assumption the boy had been thrown from his horse, MacLeod figured he had probably wrapped himself in his serape and was huddled under a tree waiting for morning. That is, assuming he wasn't sitting at home eating his dinner already. Following the stream, they turned and wound their way through a heavy accumulation of deadwood. There in front of them, between two large tree stumps a log lay across the trail.

Again the horse crow hopped. Whatever it was, the horse didn't want anything to do with what was spooking it. Slowly urging the horse ahead, toward the largest accumulation of deadwood, MacLeod spotted the young boy's body lying on the ground on his back, a few feet from the stream with his arms at his sides as if he were sleeping.

MacLeod let out his breath and dismounted, letting the reins trail beside the horse. He walked over to where the boy lay and knelt down and checked for any sign of life. He reached down and touched the dark earth beneath the boy's head. He felt the wetness and raised his hand up to see the blood staining his skin. It appeared young Cisco's head had struck a rock when he was thrown from his horse. Taking off his hat, MacLeod let out a ragged breath.

How am I to tell the boy's father that his eldest son is dead? he thought in sadness.

MacLeod rose and walked over to the little stallion and removed his own serape. After covering the boy with it, he sat down to think about what could have possibly happened.

Gradually, the night passed as the sun climbed up from behind the mountains, bathing the little valley where MacLeod still sat. Something about the whole thing bothered him. *If the boy was thrown off his horse why is he lying on his back? It isn't a position I would expect to find someone who was tossed from a horse.*

He rose and walked around the body a few times before kneeling to inspect the earth at the boy's feet. Two shallow ruts led away from the boy's boots created by the worn Spanish spurs young Cisco wore. Glancing around, MacLeod searched to see if the boy's hat or *reata* lay nearby. He knew the boy didn't go anywhere without it and it wasn't on his saddle when the horse returned, he figured it had to be nearby.

Half an hour later MacLeod rose and walked back toward his horse from where young Cisco lay. There, in the dry earth, was a distinct set of furrows. He walked over to the black and slid the rifle out of its scabbard, checking the flint to be sure it had not been dislodged, then knelt down beside him and pulled back the serape. He was pretty sure he knew what he would find, but he had to be sure. Pulling the boy's sleeves up he saw the familiar raw burns caused by a *reata*. In fact, it looked as if two *reatas* had pinned the boy's arms to his side while he was being dragged. *Cisco Gomez had not been thrown from his horse; he had been dragged until his head had struck the rock, killing him.*

He felt the tears running down his cheek as he picked up the boy's body and laid it across his saddle, then walked the horse to the top of the ridge that separated the two land grants. From here he could looked back over Rancho Santiago land. He couldn't help but wonder why the boy had come this far out from the ranch. The only thing that made any sense is that he may have found some RS cattle on the land and took it upon himself to push them back across the creek.

The rock cairn before him stood four feet high, weeds pushing their way up through the rocks to entwine themselves around the pole MacLeod had placed among the rocks ten years before to mark their territory.

With one last look he turned and led the horse down the slope toward the far off ranch house. He was grateful that he had a couple of miles to think about what he would tell everyone. *This death needs to be paid for, but now is not the time,* he thought.

The Indians and the few Mexican vaqueros who made up their little community were not fighters, but MacLeod knew that if Juan Gomez found out what had happened to his son he would want immediate revenge. But at what price? He had a large family to look after.

No, MacLeod thought, *I will see to it that those responsible for young Cisco's death are paid back, one way or another. I could ride to Santa Barbara and see the authorities. Maybe file a complaint. But against whom? I have no proof that any of Santiago's people were responsible,* he thought to himself in defeat.

Several hours later, Juan Gomez and two of his sons saw MacLeod approaching and rode out to meet him. Unable to bring himself to tell the man the truth, MacLeod explained to them that young Cisco had probably been tossed when his horse spooked, and that he had fallen and hit his head on a rock. He explained that somehow the boy's *reata* must have gotten tangled around him and the horse dragged him some distance.

Gomez could only nod his head as he gently took the boy's body in his arms and climbed back up into his saddle. The youngest of his remaining boys began crying as the three rode back to the ranch to begin their mourning.

MacLeod mounted his horse and sat for a moment, wondering if he had done the right thing in making up the story. Before returning, he had taken special pains to wipe away any remaining traces of what had really happened. *He wished Concannon would finish what he had been sent to do and hurry back. Payment will be coming due––much sooner than originally expected.*

"You are sure of this?" Francesca asked in disbelief.

"No doubt. The signs were all there. They didn't even take time to cover them. Looked like maybe four of them if I had to guess," MacLeod explained as he handed the reins of the little black stallion to one of the Indian boys.

Francesca rubbed her hands down the front of her skirt. "And you told Señor Gomez?"

MacLeod shook his head. "No. Made up a story. Told him the young fellow got tossed. Nothing Gomez can do about it, except ride over there and get himself killed."

Francesca sighed before calling Rosalie to come and take the baby from her arms. When the old lady was finally out of earshot, Francesca asked, "What will you do?"

"Nothing for right now, except go over and talk with Gomez. Can't help but feel responsible. The entire ride back with that young fellow's body, I couldn't help but think, what if it had been Diego."

"You cannot blame yourself," Francesca whispered softly. "Señor Gomez was happy to bring his family here to live. He will understand that accidents happen."

MacLeod shifted on his feet. He felt the need for food and sleep. "Accidents, yes. But after this, what else can we expect from Senór Santiago? First the hides slashed, then the bull, and now this. Seems they're getting desperate"

"I also am afraid. Do you think they will come here next?"

"I don't know if Santiago knew about this, or simply authorized it. I have a feeling it's Pacheco's work, though I have no proof."

As the winds changed directions it brought with it the foul smell of putrefying flesh. High above the killing ground a flock of buzzards, their wings fluttering as they rode the breeze, waiting for their opportunity to land and tear at the sun baked flesh.

Francesca walked to the wooden bench and sat. "I will not sacrifice my family for this land, William. If you, or the children are in danger, I will part with Colinas de Oro."

"Won't come to that," MacLeod stated stubbornly. "I won't let this man drive us from our land, but I need time to finish the *matanza* and pay off some of our debts. After that he will have to answer to me."

"I will sell him the land," Francesca whispered, rising. Grasping MacLeod's arm, she added, "You do not need to fight him."

"I don't know what I ever did to deserve you, Francesca, but I can't turn my back on this now. I never have, never will. He must pay for what he has done."

Francesca took his face in her hands and kissed him on the lips. "Very well then. What is it you would want me to do?"

"I can't face Gomez knowing what I know, so I'd appreciate it if you would go over and speak with his wife."

"Yes, I will offer that they may place the boy up on the hill, beside Esperanza and Sean's boy. It is a beautiful spot."

"That would be good."

"And what will you do now?" she questioned.

"I'll ride down to the old mission. Father Avila has his little room and garden there—I'll bring him back for a proper burial."

"You will promise to stay away from the man?"

MacLeod nodded. "I promise. Before I go, I'll have a talk with Alvarado. Alvarado and Sisquoc need to keep everyone busy and get this killing finished. Soon as the hides are all staked out and dried, and the tallow is rendered and bagged, we can figure out a way to get it down to Santa Barbara."

"Do you think they would try and stop you?" she asked, her voice laced with concern.

"Why not. One of the things Santiago mentioned was how much we owe, and he's right. If I can't get these notes taken care of with the proceeds of these hides, we may be forced to sell."

Motioning for Rosalie to return the young child to her, Francesca scooped up the babe and said, "Then you will be careful and not provoke this man?"

"Not for a while anyway," MacLeod agreed. "Sean Concannon's due back soon and I'll feel better with him nearby."

"I wish to go and see the woman now," Francesca said. "I will take Juana to help her with the other children."

MacLeod nodded and rubbed the sleep from his eyes as his mind raced with thoughts. *Where will this finally end?* he wondered. *As far as I can tell, only Jacob and Concannon know how to handle a firearm. Santiago, on the other hand, had Pacheco and at least a dozen others who all appeared armed.* The odds didn't fare well for MacLeod.

RANCHO SANTIAGO

Marisol Montero rose from her chair, walked to the open door, and ran her hand over the rough texture of the still unfinished walls of the large hacienda Cesario Santiago had built to be the centerpiece of his rancho. She turned her head and covered her eyes as a fresh gust of wind blew more dust into the interior of the room. Dust covered everything. In the few days since her arrival she had spent much of her time attempting to keep her clothing from being covered in the fine silt blowing in off the dry landscape.

Santiago had said that eventually the trees and gardens he was having planted would take care of the problem.

But only if the rains come, Marisol thought to herself. *Why did I leave the comfort of my house and garden in Monterey to journey down here to this place?*

The two days it had taken them to travel along the coast and up through the steep canyon were enough to convince her that the promised comforts of nearby Santa Barbara were merely words to entice her to join him.

She knew the answer. She knew why, after having made up her mind to refuse Santiago's offer, she had said yes.

He was here—the Americano who had held her in his arms for that brief moment while they danced. The one whose child she had briefly thought would be hers to keep. The one who shot the Frenchman and saved her from herself. He was in this valley and she still loved him.

Marisol shook her head. She could not believe she had made the decision to travel here with Santiago. The Americano was married and she knew he probably would not remember the brief moments they had spent together. In truth, she had given up such childish foolishness many years ago. Yet, for some reason, she still longed to see him once more. His sun-bleached golden hair and blue eyes that had melted her heart ten or more years before had haunted her dreams in the years since their chance encounter.

Through the newly planted fruit trees she watched Santiago ride toward the house, gesturing to the man riding at his side; the one he called Pacheco.

She returned to her chair to await his arrival, her mind drifting back to the night before when she had refused his advances. She knew she would have to submit if she wanted to remain by his side.

"Ahh, Marisol—" Santiago began. "You should go out and walk among the trees I have planted. I believe they will bear fruit next year."

"But they will need the rain," she stated matter of fact. "I see you have people bringing them water."

"Yes," Santiago nodded. He dropped his sombrero on the chair and walked to the window, his back turned to her. "It is far worse than I expected."

"The water?" Marisol questioned.

"Yes. There is little water in the creek. Up there," he said, pointing toward the low hills in the distance, "there is more. The cattle are remaining close to the stream and drinking it nearly dry."

Marisol watched him brush the dust from his shirt and gaze out over the land. *Why is he not more concerned,* she wondered? "Is there nothing that can be done?" she pried, hoping to get some more information out of him.

Cesario Santiago turned to face her. "There is always something to be done. Señor Pacheco and I rode up into the foothills where the water comes out of the mountains. The one who came from La Purísima believes he could strengthen my source by diverting the stream up in the mountains somewhere else. He believes our water comes from the same place as Colinas de Oro's water."

Marisol studied him a moment, weighing her next words carefully. "And this is something you are exploring?"

"There is too little time," he said. "The cattle suffer already. But that is of no concern of yours. For now, you should learn to love this valley. Someday we can enjoy all of it together."

Marisol Montero bristled at his smugness. It was as if her thoughts were valueless. "They have accepted your offer to buy their land then?" she asked, knowing that wasn't the case.

"No, but there are other ways," He lit a cigar and waved one of the young Indian servants over to pull off his boots. "I am certain it is only a matter of time before it is all mine."

"This land you speak off—it is Colinas de Oro?"

He smiled and nodded. "Yes. They are friends of yours, are they not? Perhaps you should ride over and convince them it is better to accept my offer. After all, it is possible this offer will not last."

Marisol chewed nervously on her bottom lip. *What is behind these words of his? And why had he been so anxious to speak with the governor before we left Monterey?* "These people you speak of––I have not seen them in many years. It is possible they would not remember me. And why should they listen to what I may say about their land?"

Santiago laughed. "I am not a stupid man, Marisol. I would not have invited you here without learning as much as I could about you."

She shuddered at his words. "And what exactly have you learned?"

"Do you really want to know, my dear? Sometimes it is better to not know too much about what others know. What I will say is that I know the infatuation you had for this man. I also know that your husband could not satisfy you the way that I can. There are some who say the Americano may have satisfied you once." A devious smile played at Santiago's lips.

Marisol knew better than to respond in anger. If she did, he would win. She seated herself in a chair facing him and smiled. "These people you speak of, who have passed along this information, they know nothing of me. They can only imagine what it is like to be with me. And since you speak only to men, you should know this. Many have openly lusted after me and would gladly tell you stories to cover up their own indiscretions."

"There might be truth in what you say. However, we shall see what happens. They have turned down my offer and that is why I brought you here. Among other things, of course." Marisol noted the coldness that crept into his words as he continued to speak. "I will not make another offer. Perhaps you should speak with them before harm comes to them." He rose and threw aside the cup of wine he held.

She listened to the sounds floating in through the narrow window, not wanting to ask the questions forming in her mind. Instead, she waited for him to continue, as she knew he would.

"I cannot lose this land or these cattle. I have too much invested in this."

Rumors she had heard in Monterey suddenly came to mind, along with words passed on to her by the ship's captains that she dealt with. "This land and these cattle you speak of...are you alone in their ownership?"

He looked as if she had struck him. "Of course. Why do you ask such stupid questions?"

"It was nothing," she said. "Only a question I had." But she knew now some of the stories were more than just rumors. *There were others involved in the acquiring of these lands.* Then she remembered his reaction to some of the letters brought to him in Monterey. A wave of fear blanketed her. She knew there was more than sheer words in his threats.

"Do not worry yourself. Perhaps I have spoken too quickly." He smiled and bent down to retrieve his boots. "Besides, there is the possibility that another way exists and no harm would come to these friends of yours."

"As you have said, these people were at one time friends of mine and you speak of harm coming to them if they do not sell you their lands. Do you expect them to simply walk away from Colinas de Oro because you wish to buy it?"

Santiago laughed. "Return to whatever it is you do and let me worry about these matters. There are times when it is better you do not know how men solve their differences. I have changed my mind...I do not wish you to speak to them. Spend your time enjoying this house and the gardens I am creating for you. While you are doing this, prepare yourself for what I expect in return."

Marisol rose and walked past him, out through the open doorway. She would speak to him, the Americano, though she would have to do so without Santiago's knowledge

I must warn him. If I know him the way I believe I do, he will fight and he won't win. The odds are too great. As to preparing

myself—I will do just that as long as it gives me the time I need to warm them.

RANCHO COLINAS DE ORO

Francesca dipped the gourd into the barrel of water brought from the stream and handed it to her husband. "It is done now?"

MacLeod took the water from her and drank deeply. After wiping his mouth with the back of his hand, he said, "It's finished. Well, almost. The killing is over. Lord, the smell is terrible. Best not to ride out into the fields until the carcasses are stripped bare. Saw three grizzlies just yesterday."

She took the dipping gourd from his hand and carefully placed it beside the water barrel. "The people are exhausted. They walk as if they were all ill."

"There's still some fleshing to do on the last hides but other than that, we're done."

"Were you ever this tired when you were in the mountains, before you came to Alta California?"

MacLeod grinned and wrapped his arm around Francesca's waist. *How long was that, the time she is asking about? Ten years? No, more like fourteen.*

He had led the injured Charbonneau into Santa Fe, seeking medical help, and found himself arrested. And that was a month after burying his other friends somewhere near the place General Pike had built his fort to spend the winter. In fact, he had himself arrested by the same man. But then there was Maria, the beautiful daughter of Don Cordero, and the mother of young Diego.

"There were times, I imagine. Maybe not lasting as long as this. Right now I'm as bone weary as I can ever remember. Must be getting older."

Francesca jabbed him in the ribs lightly with her elbow. "You are not old! Look at you—even the Indian women look at you and grin. I must keep my eye on them so they do not try and steal you away from me," Francesca joked.

He watched as Jacob and Sarah took Diego and Catalina up to sit under the trees and read from a book. "Their studies have been neglected lately, but there'll be time to catch up, I hope," MacLeod said.

Two of the Indian workers shuffled past, their heads hanging low from exhaustion.

"They have done well, have they not?" Francesca asked.

"Better than I expected. We lost a few who went over the mountains. Didn't want to work so much. When they found their old villages were gone, they came back and got back to work without a word."

He needed to thank Father Avila for bringing over the half dozen vaqueros when he came for young Cisco's burial.

"And how is Senor Gomez?" Francesca asked, her voice solemn.

MacLeod paused a moment. "Better than I would have been. Never saw a man drive himself so hard. Though I expect it took his mind off his loss."

Francesca's tone turned serious. "Do you think he believed you––your story of how it happened?"

"Not sure. But when this is all done, I'll tell him. He'll need to know the truth. I know I would want to know if I were him."

Francesca pushed the sleeves of her dress up to her elbows and poured water over her hands, rubbing them together to wash away the dried blood from the butchering. "I am glad Sean has returned. I have not talked with him since he came back. Was he able to sell the horses?"

MacLeod, too, welcomed Concannon's return. The trip across to the San Joaquin was not the success MacLeod had hoped for. Regrettably, the few furs Concannon received for the horses were far from prime, but what he brought back would bring some value in trade. He couldn't blame Concannon; it seemed all the prime pelts went early in the spring to buy supplies for the trapping party. In truth, the English trappers from the Columbia River probably realized Concannon couldn't tell the difference, and opted to rid themselves of furs they might not keep.

"He sold what he could and left the rest, just as we had agreed. Hated to see some of that stock lost, but we can't feed them all."

Francesca hesitated a moment before asking her next question. "Was the time he was away good for him?"

Macleod didn't want to tell her the sad truth. Francesca tried to protect the little Irishman, always had, but it seemed the one thing the beaver men had in abundance was liquor. How the hell they got it, he couldn't figure out. Unless they had recently been resupplied. Nevertheless, Concannon couldn't pass up the temptation.

"I have him getting the last hides fleshed and staked out. They may be a little green but I can't wait any longer. The job is good for him."

She didn't question his response, though she knew he wasn't pleased. "Will it be enough, do you think? The hides, I mean?"

MacLeod had asked himself that very same question. "Hard to tell. Depends on the price. Bryant, Sturgis sent their agent up last week. Said he figured to ride back to San Diego and line up loads for the ship, but he wouldn't quote me any figures."

The winds shifted, bringing with them the overpowering odor of decaying flesh down from the killing fields. "Some say you get used to the smell after a while, but damned if I ever will. And in this heat, it will be months before we can count on any relief."

Francesca and MacLeod turned and walked toward the creek in hopes of finding fresher air. He knew something was on her mind. "Come on, Francesca, out with it."

Francesca sighed. "We have not heard from them in weeks," she muttered. "Do you suppose they have found another way?"

"If you mean our neighbor, I would say no. I have a feeling that something is coming soon."

"What more could he do?" she asked, her voice laden with fear.

"No idea. Frankly, I would have thought he would come back to press his offer. I rode up to the edge of their land where their water comes down that narrow canyon. I don't know how he's able to water all his stock; the stream seems to be running dry. Means he'll be pushing even more cattle over to our side at night."

MacLeod wasn't about to let her know how concerned he was that they hadn't seen or heard from Santiago or Pacheco. Sure, more and more Rancho Santiago cattle found their way over onto Colinas de Oro land. He would need to deal with it soon. How, he wasn't sure, but they had not slaughtered so many cattle only to have their land and grasses decimated by someone else's cattle.

"Rosalie said this morning that it will not rain again until later this year," Francesca muttered while ironing the front of her dress with her hands.

MacLeod shook his head. "I love the old lady, but you can tell her she'll be looking for a new place to live if it doesn't. All of us will. So for all of our sakes, she better be praying for rain extra hard."

A smile creased Francesca's cheeks. "You should not make fun of such things."

"Maybe she can start arranging one of those processions where everybody carries one of them dolls and asks for rain. Can't hurt and it should keep her busy."

"I will not. And I will never ask her to leave. You should not even make a joke of these things she does. She believes them."

"Very well, I won't. I'm sorry," MacLeod said with a grin. Francesca leaned over and kissed his cheek before returning to the house.

MacLeod was still thinking about what Santiago's next move might be. Was the killing of young Cisco on Santiago's orders? Or had Pacheco taken it *up*on himself? Did Santiago not approve? Could this be the reason they had not heard from him?

"No," MacLeod muttered to himself as he walked out toward where Concannon was working. "Something else was keeping Santiago from making a move, but what is it?"

Not knowing what Santiago's next move was left MacLeod uneasy and he needed everyone to be prepared for anything. Calling on one of Gomez's boys, he sent him off to find his father and bring him back, along with Jesus Alvarado, his majordomo, and Sisquoc.

"Is this a gathering of the chosen ones," Concannon asked as MacLeod led them over to where Concannon was staking down the last of the hides to dry.

"It's a parley of sorts," MacLeod said, inviting them all to sit. Hunkering down on his heels, he picked up a nearby stick of wood.

"Sean, you being at sea all those years, what kind of moonlight are we going to have the next few days?"

"We'll we having a full moon four nights from now. What you be having in mind, if you don't mind me asking?"

MacLeod proceeded to draw lines in the dirt while he explained his plan. "You all know the troubles we've been having, so I don't need to explain it again. These hides and bags of tallow we have are everything Colinas de Oro has in order to keep it going. But it isn't worth a fiddle string till it's safely in the hold of a Bryant, Sturgis ship."

"What is it you have a mind to do?" Concannon asked, slicing a damaged hide to make himself more ties.

"My thinking is that we have to get these hides and such to Santa Barbara quick as we can. I know everyone's tired, I sure as hell am, and you all have worked as hard as me. But I can't help feeling mighty exposed as long as everything sits here out in the open. Sean, those old *carretas* back behind the smithy's shop—can you repair them for one last trip?"

Concannon scratched his head before responding. "I'm thinking it might be something can be done, but it will take some doing."

"I want them ready to load in three days. Alvarado, gather all the mules we have and any mare that can be packed. Might have to rely on a few geldings too, but that can't be helped."

"Are you thinking of making a few trips?" Concannon asked.

"One trip. One trip and we're leaving at dusk in four days. We'll load everything down among that big grove of trees where we can't be seen."

Concannon combed his beard with his hand before asking, "You think they might try something?"

"If they knew what we were about, and they had the chance, they would. They've already shown what they're capable of doing," MacLeod said, hoping he hadn't said too much. "So now that we all know what needs to be done, let's get to it."

MacLeod had pushed everyone to the limit of their endurance and was now asking even more of their already exhausted body's.

Several days later, Francesca found MacLeod asleep on the hard packed ground right outside the door of their adobe. She shook him awake and led him to the bed where he slept for an hour.

The piles of folded flint hides grew by the hour. Heavy, swollen bags of tallow lay in rows, ready to be loaded onto the repaired *carretas*. MacLeod worked alongside the Indian and Mexican people who had never seen a *gente de razon* doing the work of a common Indian. Many took the liberty to comment on how well, or in some cases, how badly he performed the menial tasks. While everyone prepared the *carretas,* Jacob and Sarah spent hours in the kitchen area preparing food for the four-day journey.

As they continued to load the *carretas*, MacLeod looked toward the south, toward the land of Cesario Santiago. He had no doubt Santiago would try to prevent them from reaching Santa Barbara with enough hides and tallow to pay off the better part of their debts.

As the sun stood a hand's breath above the Pacific Ocean in the western sky, the last *carreta* received the remainder of the hides. With all of the hides and tallow loaded, MacLeod went in search of Concannon. When he finally found him, he was lashing a wrist thick branch to one of the poles on the side of a *carreta*. He turned as MacLeod approached. "It's the best I could do in such short time. There are some extra poles in each of these wagons, though if the wheels split or those wooden axels burn through them hubs you'll be needing to carry them loads on your back."

"Never believed you could fix them all," MacLeod said, awestruck.

Concannon pointed his chin at a pair of nearby horses that had no intention of having dead weight strapped to their backs. "You should be hoping they calm down some before we hit the pass or they'll cause the others to kick up their heels too."

MacLeod grinned watching the frustrated vaqueros attempting to control the animals. "I don't doubt we'll have a few loads thrown. My main concern is keeping the line as close together as possible."

"Where will we be stopping?"

"That's something I need to talk to you about. I need you to stay here and mind the place for the next few days. Jacob's staying too."

Concannon spit in the dirt before responding "And why is this you are leaving me behind?"

"I have a feeling they'll be paying a visit if they discover what we've done. You know yourself, Santiago knows about the money we owe. He'll do anything to see to it that we don't make it to Santa Barbara."

The little red-headed man walked off shaking his head. "Like you yourself are saying, he'll be after you if he finds out what you've done. I rather you not go without someone watching your back."

"The women need you here, Sean. I can't go off leaving them unprotected. Now, be off and let Francesca know. She'll feel a sight better knowing what is going on."

Concannon threw the rawhide straps he had been using to fix the *carreta* on the ground and stormed off without another word.

RANCHO SANTIAGO

The big sorrel stallion picked his way through the rocks in the narrow stream. Cesario Santiago followed Pacheco out of the canyon mouth and halted to wait for the old man on his mule.

Stepping out of his saddle, Santiago knelt by the stream, scooping a handful of water up and drinking it.

"So, what is it you think of his plan?" Pacheco asked.

The big Argentinian shook his head. "If there were more time, maybe it is possible. You say he went all the way to where the water splits into two streams?"

Pacheco shrugged. "That is what he said. I do not think he would lie. He has done this in other places."

The old man appeared on his mule, having just emerged from the canyon and took a moment to stop and take a drink of water. When he was finished, he grinned a toothless grin at the others and reached into his pocket, pulling out the stub of a cigar.

Santiago mounted his horse once again and touched its flanks with his spurs, urging it up the stream bank. Pacheco rode up alongside Santiago.

"This will take time and people. Of which I cannot afford to take away from what is currently being accomplished," Santiago stated. "The woman will drive me insane with her complaints unless the trees are planted and those windows that the ship will bring are installed. I have enough to worry about without this." Santiago sighed, taking a moment to compose himself. "Have you heard anything from them?"

Ever since Pacheco had told him about the boy and how a simple effort to scare him had turned ugly, leading to the boy's apparent death, he had been waiting to hear from MacLeod. Santiago had no feelings about the death; the only thing he was concerned about was the possibility of retaliation. While the gauchos he had brought with him were well prepared to defend themselves, he understood that the Americano could be dangerous.

Pacheco rode a distance seeming to contemplate his response. "I have heard nothing. They have told me he rode for the priest." He shrugged. "Perhaps they believe it was an accident."

"Perhaps. Though if he does not believe it was an accident do you think he will respond in some way?"

The two men rode along the edge of the stream with the old man trailing behind them until the house came into view. "He has been busy with other things," Pacheco said, breaking the silence between them. "Did you know he has taken his hides to the ships? When he is finished, who knows what he will do."

Santiago had completely forgotten the question he had posed to Pacheco, his mind occupied with the results of his meeting in Monterey. After a moment it sank in what Pacheco had said. "They have already left with the hides? When was this?"

"Two nights ago," Pacheco replied. "I sent someone to see how much progress they had made, but it was too late."

The news stunned Santiago. "And you are just telling me this news now?" he shouted. "Have you any idea what it will mean if he is able to sell his tallow and hides?"

Pacheco shook his head. "The one who told me this said they left at night. There was nothing we could do. By now they are already there."

Santiago had counted on them not being able to pay off their debts. In fact, he had spoken to a number of merchants in Monterey and made it known that he would see they were handsomely rewarded if they pressured Colinas de Oro for payment. After all, it wasn't completely out of the question to ask for money for two-year-old bills.

However, it wouldn't matter if this other effort paid off. Still, it would not hurt to add a little extra pressure. "Then he will not return for a number of days. Perhaps you should pay his woman another visit. I believe your last one with her was interrupted," Santiago suggested, his tone devious.

Pacheco kneed his horse causing Santiago's horse to pull up. "And if something were to happen you would not disapprove? You do not have a problem with this?" he asked in hopes of getting clarification.

Santiago reined the sorrel to a halt. He would have shot any other man for forcing his horse aside as Pacheco had done moments before, but the fact was he needed the man. He needed the man's brutal cunningness and his lust for the woman on the adjoining property. And now he had made it known that he would not stand in the man's way if he were to visit with this woman again.

Perhaps Pacheco would kill the Americano and his problems would be over, he thought, hopeful.

"We have not much time left. You may not get another opportunity like this. Take two of my people with you. Who knows, she may like more than one," Santiago laughed.

Santiago watched as Pacheco rode off. But after offering Pacheco a free hand with the woman he lusted after, his mind drifted back to the woman back at the hacienda. He wanted her in his bed, not some time from now, but now—today, tonight. What had she thought would happen when she agreed to come here with me? Was he not building her a home? So why has she refused to share her body with him? Santiago drove his spurs into the horse's flanks and raced toward the hacienda, wondering if he would have to be satisfied with one of the young Indian girls again this evening? They did not refuse him but neither did they show any passion. Instead, they lay on their backs until he finished taking his pleasure and then left without a word or show of emotion.

As Santiago approached the hacienda he found Marisol sitting outside the door of the adobe, fanning herself in the hot afternoon sun. He could not help but wonder if she had come with him because of this man, the one he suspected of having her heart, if not her body. Would she be more submissive if the Americano was gone? Santiago pondered the thought.

Santiago watched in irritation as four Indian workers rose lazily from the ground and made their way toward the gardens in an effort to busy themselves. Far too many workers were taking advantage of him, and Santiago was determined to see to it that it didn't happen again.

Scouring the grounds near the hacienda, Santiago searched for his majordomo. He had every intention of having the man round up the three men that had run away two nights prior and were found near the foothills, attempting to rope horses to make their escape. Unfortunately for them, Pacheco caught them and brought them back. The three would receive their punishment tonight.

Marisol rose as he made his way toward the front door. "Something has come while you were away." She walked ahead of him into the house and picked up a thin sealed package from where she had set it.

Santiago's heart leap. "From Monterey?"

She nodded and handed him the dispatch. Immediately, he recognized the Governor's seal. "I have been waiting for this. It may be the answer to my problems." He ripped open the sealed letter and walked to the back of the room as he read.

"Is it good news?" Marisol asked.

Santiago stood with his back to her. *The idiots*, he fumed. Surely the man who sat in power in Alta California could make a decision. Did he consider it out of his power? Was there no one in this country who would act? He crumbled the message up in a ball and threw it against the wall and stomped out of the room in anger.

RANCHO COLINAS DE ORO

“When will they return, Mother?”

"It will not be until tomorrow. They will travel slowly with the old people and the *carretas,*" Francesca said, parting Catalina's hair and beginning a new braid.

The girl turned on the stool to face her mother, a look of disappointment upon her face. "Why is it I was not permitted to go to Santa Barbara with them? It is always Diego who is allowed to do these things."

Francesca smiled. "You know the answer to this without asking me. Diego is becoming a man and must learn how these things are done."

"And me?" the young girl inquired.

"You are a young woman and will not find yourself a husband if you continue to act like a man. Men do not want their women to be riding all over the country alone in a man's saddle." This was the third time she'd had this conversation with her headstrong daughter.

How had she become so independent? Francesca silently wondered.

Catalina pouted a time before speaking. "I do not understand—I ride as well as any of the vaquero's. Well, almost as well."

Rosalie sat silently in her chair across the room sewing. While she said nothing Francesca knew what she was thinking. How could she convince the old lady that Catalina would never be the quiet, reserved young woman Alta Californios expected of their daughters?

She heard loud voices outside the hacienda. A young boy's voice appeared to be telling Francesca's servant girl, Juana, something. Francesca listened as Juana questioning the boy.

Suddenly, Juana burst through the door. "Señora, he said you must come. He said it is important."

Francesca wiped her hands on the sides of her dress and hurried out into the small courtyard. Outside, the boy had his hands on his knees, appearing out of breath from running. He looked up at her and pointed back over his shoulder. "Y–you must go there now, to the big tree near the water. H–he said someone is hurt and needs you," the boy huffed.

"Who is hurt?" She recognized Juan Gomez's young son.

The boy shook his head. "I do not know. He said you must hurry. He said there is no time and that I should find you and send you back."

Francesca searched for Concannon or Jacob. Unfortunately, neither man could be found. MacLeod had left both men behind in case of any trouble. Francesca shook her head. While she had not seen Concannon the last two days, she had heard Esperanza's constant barrage of screams at him. Her only assumption was that Concannon had found a way to hide his wine supply from his wife. Then she remembered Jacob had said he and the old man from the mission would be building a kiln to fire the adobe bricks for Jacob's water aqueduct.

With little time to waste, Francesca spotted the young Indian, Malibu, who cared for the personal horses kept near the hacienda. MacLeod had taken many of the horses with him to Santa Barbara so there were few other options.

"Malibu, hurry and saddle Bolivar for me," she called to the young boy. MacLeod had said she wasn't to ride him yet but the beautiful sorrel with the golden mane and tail was the first horse she spotted.

"Señora," the boy said, shaking his head, "I will go and find another for you."

"No, bring him here. And hurry," she instructed. She rushed back into the house and had Rosalie quickly tie her braids together before going in search of her wide-brimmed hat.

When she exited the adobe, Sarah was standing just outside the adobe. "Find Sean, please. Tell him I have been called to an emergency in that large grove of trees by the bend in the creek. He will know where it is," Francesca instructed.

"Francesca, are you sure? I can run and fetch Jacob if Sean cannot be found."

"The boy said to hurry. Watch the children for me and find Jacob. He may be able to help if someone is hurt." As instructed, the Indian boy stood holding Bolivar's head between his hands, speaking softly to him in an effort to settle him down. Francesca mounted the horse and swung him out, urging him into a lope.

The big horse shivered and tossed his head before eventually settling in under a strange hand on his reins. His long, powerful strides ate up the ground effortlessly. As she rode along, she chided herself for not seeking more information from the boy. Far ahead, the grove of cottonwood trees growing along the steam's banks came into view. A feeling of apprehension swept over her as she neared the trees.

Francesca eased the big horse into an easy canter and cautiously crossed the stream below the line of willows and then walked him forward. She saw no one.

She reined the horse to a halt and called out.

No one answered. She moved forward into the shade of the cottonwoods and halted the horse again. An uneasy feeling swept over her as the stallion's ears flipped forward before letting out a snort. A horse hidden behind the screen of willows answered.

Feeling the presence of others before she saw them, Francesca knew she had been drawn into a trap. Just as she prepared to rein Bolivar around, he shuddered.

Francesca watched in horror as two horses stepped out from behind the willows. Francesca recognized Pacheco. As she turned away from him another rider blocked her path.

"Señora, I see you have come to be with me again," Pacheco cooed.

"What is it you are doing on my land," Francesca said.

Pacheco laughed. "It will not be your land for long. I hope you have enjoyed your stay here."

"No one will take my land from me. Not you, nor the one who you work for. You have tried your tricks, but we have beaten you. Our hides and tallow are safe in the warehouses in Santa Barbara."

Pacheco leaned on the front of his saddle and nodded his head. "This is true, for the moment. But who knows what will happen. You should be more worried about what will happen to you, Señora. I think we have something that was never finished. Do you remember this?"

Francesca searched for an opening. If she could whirl Bolivar around the big stallion could drive past the one blocking her path. "I remember you lost something the last time. Perhaps you don't remember? My husband should have killed you when he had the chance," Francesca spat. "If you think you will live long after what you plan to do to me, you are mistaken."

"Ahh, but I think the years have made him more uncertain. He cannot fight us all. As you see, we are too many now. I think you should enjoy what will happen to you." Pacheco laughed. "My friends, they are very excited"

She knew this was not an idle threat. Only one question remained—could he allow her to live afterwards or did he plan on killing her? Whatever his intentions were Francesca knew she had time, but only if well spent. They were too close to the hacienda, which meant they would need to take her somewhere else, preferably back onto Rancho Santiago land. As it were, she felt she had the advantage of the better horse.

Pacheco nodded to the man behind her. Bolivar shivered with the strange horse approaching from the rear.

As Pacheco spoke to the two on either side of him, Francesca took in their dress. It was not that of the vaqueros she had ever seen. Both men carried long braided whips in their hands. Pacheco, on the other hand, carried a pistol in his belt.

Trying not to show her fear, Francesca held firm atop Bolivar. Though the lust she could smell on the men as they kneed their horses closer made it hard to contain her unease. She could see it in their eyes—they intended to have their way with her, whether she wanted it or not.

"Is this something you are all planning on doing to me?" Francesca asked, stalling for time.. "I did not think you are the type of man who would want to share me?" She knew there would only be only one opportunity to surprise them. "That boy will remember who sent him to find me. Or have you not thought of that?"

Pacheco ran his hand across his unshaven face. He grinned. "What does it matter? They will not know what happened to you. Besides, he is only a boy. He does not know who we are."

Francesca's hands ached from gripping the braided reins. She kept the stallion's head up, and waited for her opportunity. In truth, she knew they would never allow her a second chance. Suddenly, her mind drifted to her husband and the children.

It did not matter what this man did, MacLeod would know who was responsible. Sadly, what Pacheco said was true. They had so many more men than those on Colinas de Oro. Deep down, she knew MacLeod would fight them. But was Pacheco right when he said that time had made MacLeod less likely to fight them all.

She could only hope he would think about Diego and Catalina, and their two? Would he worry about who would take care of all the children? Would this make him less likely to fight? The more she thought about it, the more she wanted him to kill this man for what he was planning to do to her. On the other hand, she wished MacLeod would think about the children first.

Francesca watched as Pacheco spoke to the others. As soon as he had finished, the two men spun their horses around and started up the stream toward Rancho Santiago land. Not letting her guard down, she watched intently as Pacheco reined his horse in alongside Francesca while the one behind her fell back and followed.

Francesca listened closely as the man behind Pacheco joked about what he would like to do with her. Pacheco laughed and turned his head to respond.

This is my chance, she thought to herself.

Lashing the face of Pacheco's horse with the end of her reins, Francesca drove her horse into him, forcing the smaller horse to turn aside.

Bolivar leapt at her frantic urging and in three strides he opened up a narrow lead, his hooves tearing up the dry earth beneath him. Francesca hung on to the front of her saddle, never daring to look over her shoulder. She knew Bolivar would prove to be the stronger horse, but in a close race the others would not lose much distance.

As she frantically rode back toward the hacienda, she heard Pacheco shouting out commands behind her. A moment later she heard the crack of a whip as it broke the air above her head. Then a second whip cracked. With each snap of the whip Francesca felt Bolivar shudder. She increased her grip on the saddle, and drove her heels into the horse's flanks. As expected, the horse needed no further encouragement.

Despite Pacheco's screams of abuse the two horses closest to Francesca began to fall behind. She knew they would have to turn back soon. The hacienda buildings were only a little over a mile away and everyone would see her being chased. She reached down and gently ran her hand over the horse's neck in encouragement.

Francesca heard the retort of a pistol. Before she could even grasp what was happening, the stallion dropped his head and leapt into the air. She lost her grip on the saddle and felt her body rising into the air. As the horse came back down to earth, her hands still remained wrapped in the reins. For an instant she felt completely weightless before eventually slamming into the ground, her body rolling over several times before coming to a stop.

Sarah Morgenthau shielded her eyes from the brilliant glare of the afternoon sun. At first, she didn't seem certain about what it was she was seeing. It wasn't until the horse whinnied that reality set in. She didn't seem certain at first, then she cried out and ran to the horse and quickly gathered its reins out of the dirt. At first, the lathered stallion shied away from the strange hands on its reins before allowing her to lead it to the house.

Hearing Sarah's cries the old woman hurried to the door, "Is that not the one the Señora rode today?"

"It is," Sarah called out for young Catalina, who still sulked about not being allowed to go to Santa Barbara with the others. "Catalina, hurry and find Jacob, and bring him here right away, your mother must have been thrown." A look of panic graced the young girl's face before she rushed out the door in search of Jacob.

A few moments later Jacob Morgenthau hurried over, his hands thick with the adobe mixture he had been working with. "What is Bolivar doing saddled?" he asked.

"A boy came with a message that someone was in need of help. Francesca had him saddled and rode away. She must have fallen and could not catch up with the horse."

Jacob placed a gentle hand upon the shivering horse's flank and slowly walked around him. "Look at this," he said, pointing to a thin trail of blood along the stallion's flank. "If I'm not mistaken, that looks like a musket ball crease," he stated, his voice tight.

Sarah's hand went to her mouth. "Francesca is still out there. She may be hurt."

Jacob nodded. "I'll find Concannon—he'll need to go and look for her. Damned if it wasn't his responsibility to keep her away from that horse." He grabbed the arm of a nearby youngster, he and sent him after the Irishman.

A moment later the boy returned. "The Señor say no," the boy said, shaking his head.

"Damn that man, he's probably drunk again. I'll go and fetch him," Jacob's voice was laced with irritation as he strode off to retrieve the drunken Irishman.

A short time later, the two men returned. Concannon walked unsteadily alongside Jacob. He nodded to Sarah and grasped Bolivar's trailing reins and ran his hand down the horse's neck in an attempt to calm the frightened animal.

Jacob pointed out the bloody crease behind the saddle. "That looks like a musket ball crease, does it not?"

Concannon appeared to sober as he grabbed one of the young boys standing nearby. "Fetch me a horse, boy." He spoke to Sarah. "Where did she go, do you know?"

"The lad that brought the message said something about the big trees up at the bend in the creek."

"Probably just got thrown and is walking back now. I best ride out there and bring her back myself. Lord knows what Willie will say when he discovers I didn't stop her from riding this beast." Concannon climbed into the saddle of the leggy bay the boy had brought for him. "Knowing the lass I'm sure she'll be begging me not to tell her husband."

Concannon trotted past the small bands of cattle, which hurried out of his path, their hooves kicking up little plums of dust. He stopped for a moment, shielding his eyes from the sun's glare and searched the landscape. About a mile from the hacienda he spotted something, a dark image, but it wasn't a figure walking as he'd expected to see. He kicked the little bay into a gallop and closed in on the object.

"Jesus, Mary and Joseph. What have I done," Concannon muttered, leaping from the saddle to kneel by the inert figure lying on its side in the dirt. As gently as he could, he rolled her over and carefully brushed the dirt from her face. He tried to sit her up but her body refused to remain upright.

Concannon laid Francesca back on the ground and untied a small leather water bag from his saddle. He poured a few drops on his hands and wiped her face as clean as he could before attempting to give her water. Instead of drinking it, the water simply ran down her chin onto the ground.

"Oh Lord, what have I done?" he muttered again in a panic. "Oh, Francesca, pray be well." Tears welled up in the eyes of the little red-bearded Irishman as he knelt beside her.

A gust of wind stirred up a dust-devil sending it whirling over them. He slid his arms beneath her and held her close, shielding her from the flying dirt as best he could until the wind subsided, then picked her up and approached the bay.

Unfortunately, nature had bestowed Concannon with a small, wiry body but failed to give him height. He stood beside the horse with Francesca in his arms, unable to mount his horse while he held her in his arms. Neither could he bring himself to drape her over the saddle, not knowing her condition.

Without another thought he began walking, gently singing an unknown Gaelic tune that no one would have recognized.

As soon as Concannon appeared from behind the blacksmith's shop, Sarah spotted him. She shouted for Jacob. "Oh my God, he is carrying her! She's hurt, Jacob. Hurry."

Together they ran to meet them. Seeing his exhaustion, Jacob carefully took Francesca in his arms. "Run to the house and have her bed readied," he instructed the old woman, who had remained with them since the horse had been found. "And heat water," he called after her.

"Oh, Jacob, can you help her?" Sarah pleaded.

"I don't know. It looks like she struck her head when she fell. We can do little for her until she wakes. The best thing right now is to make her comfortable and pray for her."

"We will need to send someone for William,"

Concannon stood, swaying, sweat and tears running down his cheeks, dripping from his beard. "She will be all right, will she not?"

Sarah reached over to support him. "You carried her all the way? You could not ride with her?" she asked.

He shook his head. "My legs are too short and I could not regain the saddle. It is all my fault. She rode that horse, beautiful as it is, and I knew it wasn't safe. He will never forgive me if she is badly hurt," the man sobbed.

Sarah laid her hand on his arm. "I'm sure William will understand, Sean."

Concannon grimaced. "Not this time, I fear. It'll be the last of me here on Colinas de Oro. Though I cannot bear to leave until she wakes."

Jacob emerged from inside the house. "We have put her in her bed. For now, that is all we can do."

Catalina stood by herself listening while they all spoke about sending someone to find her father and hurry him home. Glancing near the stables, she spotted her little gelding, fully saddled and ready to ride.

Exhausted, Concannon found a spot in the shade beneath the olive tree and sank to the ground, his face buried in his hands.

"Find Señor Gomez and have him saddle a horse," Jacob instructed Catalina. "We'll have him ride for your father. Be sure he knows that he'll need to ride hard."

"He is with the vaqueros," the girl stated. "There is no need to send for him...I know the way." Without another word, the young girl vaulted into her saddle and dug her heels into the gelding's side.

EL CAMINO REAL

MacLeod dozed in the saddle, the fresh salt air carried by the cooling breeze a sharp contrast to the days of insufferable dry heat that had gone on for weeks. Behind him, the squealing *carretas* carried those who were returning to Colinas de Oro. Some walked beside the carts, others rode, but none were in a hurry. MacLeod had told Alvarado to let the people come along at their own pace, they had all worked hard to get the hides and bags of tallow prepared for the delivery to the Bryant & Sturgis warehouse in Santa Barbara.

When MacLeod awoke, he reined his horse to the side of El Camino Real to let the others catch up. Two of the Gomez boys rode together, still suffering from the loss of their brother. He knew he needed to tell their father that his son's death was no accident; he just wasn't sure when to do so.

Distracted by his thoughts, MacLeod hadn't noticed Sisquoc had rode up beside him. "I think someone is coming fast," Sisquoc stated, pointing up the road.

Turning in the direction Sisquoc indicated, MacLeod could see the rider was bent over, urging the horse on, the horse's flanks heavily lathered.

"Can't be one of ours," MacLeod said. "There was no one left who could ride a horse like this one coming."

"Señor, I think maybe it is the girl," Sisquoc said. Both the Gomez boys broke into wide grins and waved their sombreros in the air in greeting. "Si, it is Señorita Catalina."

"What in tarnation would be making her ride her horse into the ground like that," MacLeod murmured. He touched his horse's sides and rode out to meet her.

The girl reined her horse in hard, sending up a pillar of dust. Though before MacLeod could speak, she blurted, "Father, you must come quickly, mother has been hurt."

"How badly, Catalina?" MacLeod asked in concern.

"I do not know, but she will not wake up. Señor Jacob said she must have hit her head when she fell from her horse. You must go to her now."

MacLeod leaned over and wrapped his arm around his adopted daughter. Turning to face one of the boys who sat on his horse nearby, he said, "Son, go back and bring up that spotted gelding, I'll need to change horses on the way. How did it happen?" he asked the girl.

Fresh tears ran down through the dust caked on the young girl's face. "Someone told her to come quick, and she had the boy bring her Bolivar. Then later Bolivar came back without her."

"Damn it all," he shouted, dismounting his horse and stripping his saddle off and putting it on the back of the gelding. "I told Concannon not to allow her to ride that damn horse. In fact, I told her the same thing."

Alvarado, having noticed they had stopped, rode up to find out what was going on. "Gather them all up and take your time bringing these carts through the pass." He turned to the Gomez boy who had brought up his horse, "You look after the Señorita here. Don't be letting her go wandering off by herself."

The boy grinned and took off his sombrero. "Si, Doñ MacLeod. I will try what you ask, but it will be hard with her. She will not always listen to me."

MacLeod nodded. "Catalina, you mind now and follow home with the rest."

MacLeod stepped up into his saddle. Though it didn't go unnoticed that his stepdaughter's face was a mask of indignation at having someone appointed to look after her. Not wasting another moment, he kicked the gelding into a ground eating lope hoping beyond hope that Francesca's injury wasn't as bad as it sounded.

By the time the sun neared its furthest arc and dropped into the Pacific, MacLeod was entering the narrow defile known as Gaviota Pass. The pass took El Camino Real through the coastal mountain range and into the valley beyond. Early explorers had thought the pass too treacherous and often found themselves clawing their way through the chaparral and steep slopes of the coastal mountain range. In times of rain, the rocky stream that flowed through the canyon made travel impossible.

When MacLeod arrived at the hacienda he could see the candlelight flickering in the windows. Quickly stepping out of the saddle he dropped the gelding's reins and hurried toward the door. Sarah met him at the door wiping her hands on her apron

"How is she?" he asked, not wasting any time with pleasantries.

"She is the same. I fear we do not know how badly she is hurt."

MacLeod brushed past her, his hat held in two hands, fearing what he might see. Jacob sat beside the narrow bed.

"William, I am glad Catalina found you."

"My God, she looks so pale. Do you have any idea why she has not come around?"

Sarah came around the opposite side of bed with a cloth and pan of water. She dipped the cloth in the water and carefully bathed Francesca's face.

Jacob shook his head. "With my limited medical experience, the best I can conclude is that she has suffered a concussion. You can see the bruising on the side of her head," Jacob added, indicating the dark patches on the side of her face.

MacLeod knelt beside the bed and took her hand in his. "There must be something we can do."

"Perhaps a real doctor would have better knowledge,"

"There are none in Alta California. Not enough people to support one, I suppose."

Jacob stretched and rubbed the back of his neck. "We had one on the ship Sarah and I came in on. Do you suppose all ships carry one?"

Juana, the Indian girl MacLeod had rescued from two of the guards from the San Diego Presidio, slipped into the room and placed a bowl of meat and beans in front of MacLeod.

"By God, thank you, Juana. I have not thought of food since Catalina brought the news," he said. Famished, MacLeod peeled a tortilla off the stack and folded it into a scoop. Halfway to his mouth with the tortilla and beans he stopped. "What did you just say about a doctor?" MacLeod asked as if just registering what Jacob had said.

"I was only wondering if all the ships carry one?" Jacob explained. There was a man on the ship that brought us here who they called Doctor?"

MacLeod placed the bowl on the floor beside his chair and stood up. "I don't know about all ships, but I do know Bryant & Sturgis ships have one. The ship that was still in the harbor when we left was British. There's a good chance they would have one aboard."

Juana picked up the bowl and thrust it into his stomach. "Doñ MacLeod—you eat first."

MacLeod grabbed a tortilla and heaped the bean and meat mixture atop it. "Jacob, run out there and have one of those boys saddle my black stallion. Tell him to pick another also. I'll need to be riding hard."

"Will you not wait until morning?" Sarah asked in concern. She knew he had to be exhausted after such a long haul and then having to hurry back so quickly.

"No. Where is Concannon? I need to see him before I leave."

Twenty minutes later the horses were saddled and ready to go. Before leaving, MacLeod went back for one last look at Francesca. At the sight of her pale skin his heart skipped a beat. He leaned over and kissed her forehead. "I will be back as soon as I can. Just hold on," he whispered.

Concannon stood outside the hacienda adobe, twisting his hat in his hands. Tears streaked his cheeks and saturated his beard.

"William, it is all my fault. I should...."

MacLeod held up hand. "No. It was a simple thing I asked you to do. I suppose you were drunk again? I warned you, Sean. I kept allowing myself to believe you would find a way to give it up, but you haven't. I don't know where you're getting the drink and honestly, I don't give a damn anymore. You've about ruined your own family now look at what you've done by your drunken negligence. Francesca, who has loved you like a brother, lies in there and may very well never come back to us."

MacLeod climbed up on the horses back. "Be gone before I get back," He spun the horse around and raced out of the courtyard back the direction he had come only hours before.

Thankful for a partial moon and a clear sky filled with stars, MacLeod made his way back through the rock strewn pass and down onto the main track. Hours before dawn he rode through the sleeping camp, stopping for only a moment to pass instructions along to Alvarado and Sisquoc.

The gentle sea breeze lulled him into a fitful sleep. Luckily for him, the black, seeming to sense his need, continued down the well-travelled road without his guidance.

Later, he would determine there were signs he would have read had he been awake.

In spite of the drought, the berry bushes benefitted from the coastal moisture. Although the crop wasn't what it would be in wet years, it still drew the attention of hungry bears and their young cubs.

The black's sudden sidestepping woke him just as he felt the lead rope for the other horse torn from his grasp. He tried to steady the black, whose ears were laid back as far as they would go, but it was no use. The horse had the scent of the bear and wanted no part of hanging around.

As his eyes scanned the area surrounding them, MacLeod spotted the two cubs pushing their snouts into the berry filled bush.

The cubs weren't the problem; it was their mother who was sure to be lurking around. MacLeod needed to locate the mother bear. And fast. He eased the rifle out from under his leg and cocked it.

Just as he was beginning to wonder if he could slip past the two cubs before his presence was known, the roar of the female grizzly split the air. MacLeod turned in the saddle as she charged through the bushes and slammed into the black stallion, sending MacLeod flying through the air and into the thick growth of bushes. As he fought to regain his breath, he listened as the horse screamed in agony. Finally able to take a deep breath, he crawled out of the bushes and began to search for his rifle, assuming it hadn't been tossed far. He knew the mother grizzly would come looking for him as soon as she was satisfied the horse was no longer a danger to her cubs.

From where he lay MacLeod could hear the bear thrashing about. He could smell her foul odor as she continued her attack on the horse. On his hands and knees, MacLeod frantically searched for his rifle while trying his best to remain silent. He took a deep breath and tried to imagine it flying out of his hands as the horse went down and he rose into the air to crash into the bushes.

The rifle could be almost anywhere, he thought to himself as the panic began to set in. Left with no other option, MacLeod felt for the knife at his belt, knowing it would be useless against the grizzly's rage.

From the corner of his eye he watched the bear rise to her full height and paw at the air. He knew it didn't matter if she saw him or not, the bear's sense of smell had already told her exactly where he was. Hidden or not, MacLeod knew he only had a matter of seconds before she dropped back to the ground and came after him.

Then he saw the rifle lying in the road. He started to scramble towards it but his movements attracted her attention. She threw her head back and roared again before dropping down onto all four legs and charging after him. Left with little time to react MacLeod drew his knife and rolled over on the ground to face her, while trying to scoot backward toward the rifle. Rising above him, mouth open wide, the flesh from the black stallion dangling from her jaws, the bear threw back her head in challenge as she pawed the air and took a swipe at him, missing him by mere inches. MacLeod knew one swipe of that huge paw could rip an arm off. He had previously witnessed the devastation an angry female grizzly could do, and now he found himself faced with one.

MacLeod scooted back another foot, his left hand reaching behind him for the rifle and knowing that only a well place shot would stop her, even if it didn't kill her.

The bear's paw lashed out at him again. In a fight for survival, MacLeod struck out with the knife but the tremendous strength in her front leg ripped the knife from his grasp as a terrible burn, followed by agonizing pain tore through his arm. Glancing down, he could see where her claws raked his arm, ripping his shirt into shreds. Angry at the wound his knife had caused on her leg, the bear rose to her full height. Without taking his eyes off of her, MacLeod swept his hand along the ground until he touched the barrel of his rifle. The last thing he could be concerned with was whether the fragile flint had been damaged or knocked out of its pocket. If he couldn't bring the rifle to bear, and fire into her, she would rip him to shreds in her fury.

MacLeod slid the rifle from behind his back and brought it up to his waist as she charged. He thrust the rifle into her chest and pulled the trigger.

The bear howled in pain before swiping the rifle out of his grasp, shattering the stock. MacLeod quickly pushed himself to his feet, his arm hanging at his side as the blood ran down his arm and off his fingertips. Frantically, he searched for his pistol, hoping to find it and finish her off before she came at him again. He backed away and turned slowly. The black horse lay on its side, weakly attempting to rise. There, among the low brush, MacLeod saw the pistol. With a quick look at the bear, he convinced himself he could turn his back on her long enough to quickly retrieve the pistol. He scooted over and picked it up, finding the flint still seated in its place. Cautiously he approached the bear as she thrashed about, attempting to rise. MacLeod watched as her eyes filled with the rage he knew she felt. He raised the pistol and shot her in the eye. She thrashed a time or two then fell onto her side and lay still.

Macleod sank to his knees in relief, cradling his arm with his good hand. Somehow he needed to keep going.

Once he located the bag with his powder and ball, he placed the pistol between his knees. His hand shook as he tamped the powder down inside the barrel and placed the ball on the muzzle. He slid out the wooden ram and seated the ball before pushing himself to his feet. Mere feet from him the black stallion that he loved to ride still lay on its side, its haunch ripped open by the four-inch claws of the grizzly. MacLeod placed the muzzle close to the horse's head and fired.

The pain in his arm continued to increase. He stripped his bedroll off the saddle and found a shirt. Holding the shirt in his teeth, he ripped off several long bands, then using the water from his water bag he cleaned off his arm and bound it tightly with the shirt.

He wondered how far his spare horse had run, doubting the animal would stop for some miles. All around him the smell of the deceased grizzly hung in the air. MacLeod cast his eyes around trying to locate the two cubs he had seen earlier. They were too young to be a problem. That would come later, assuming they survived.

Beside him, the broken rifle lay in the dirt, its stock splintered. He picked it up and hid it behind a large rock on the side of the road before going in search of his sombrero. It lay among the weeds beside the road. Picking it up, he placed it on his head and began walking the thirty-five or so miles to Santa Barbara.

With the sun beginning its downward arc MacLeod spotted his runaway horse grazing alongside the road. He approached as carefully as he could, talking to the chestnut gelding as he edged forward, stopping every few feet until the horse returned to nibbling at the dry grass. It backed away from him a few feet and stopped. Searching the surrounding area, MacLeod spotted the trailing lead rope, which had snagged on a roadside bush, but with the smell of the grizzly still on him, he couldn't risk the horse suddenly bolting and pulling the rope out of the bushes. He edged closer, talking to it as he did. Without admitting it to himself he knew he would never make it to Santa Barbara on foot. He needed to get ahold of his horse before it was too late. He inched forward another step, the horse, still wary, moved sideways, its nostrils flaring at the familiar smell of the grizzly. MacLeod knew he would only have one chance to wrap his hand in the horse's mane and leap onto its back.

He shuffled over to the horse, who stood trembling, its eyes searching and nostrils seeking the presence of the bear.

MacLeod whispered softly to the horse, gently running his good hand along its flank. He would have to grab the horse's mane in order to try and vault onto its back. He couldn't remember whether the gelding had been ridden or just used for packing, but he would find out soon enough, assuming he could get on its back.

Panicked, the horse side-stepped away as MacLeod slid his left hand along its back. The lead rope hung loose. If the horse spooked now MacLeod knew he would never get another chance. MacLeod moved cautiously toward the horse's head. Slowly, he reached for the dangling lead rope. Instinctively, the gelding threw its head back causing the rope to swing further away from MacLeod's outstretched hand. He tried again, his right shoulder and arm throbbing from the cuts caused by the bear's claws.

MacLeod took a deep breath. He ran his hand over the horse's neck before firmly grasping its rope halter, then pulled gently, causing the gelding to turn its head and bring the dangling lead rope within reach.

This is it, he thought to himself. He tied a loop in the lead rope and thrust his arm through it.

MacLeod continued to talk to the frightened animal. Each time he stroked the animal it shivered under his touch and kept sidestepping away from him.

The pain in his arm persisted. He ignore it and concentrated on mounting the gelding.

Three times he had readied himself to vault onto the horse's back but each time the gelding seemed to sense his intentions and hip-hopped away.

His arm had stiffened as the blood from the deep gouges coagulated. MacLeod knew the wounds would need to be treated...and soon. As he looked around, he spotted a large boulder beside the road, giving him an idea. Using the horse's halter, he slowly led the animal over to it and carefully stepped up onto the rock. Once the horse had calmed slightly, MacLeod eased himself forward until he could throw his right leg over the horse's back.

The gelding shuddered and hopped about as it felt MacLeod's weight settle upon its back. With his arm still in the loop he had made in the lead rope, MacLeod wrapped his hand in its mane and gently tapped its side with his heels.

After several half-hearted attempts to rid itself of the weight on its back the horse settled down and began walking down the rutted road in the direction of Santa Barbara.

M acLeod dozed in the saddle on the way to Santa Barbara, only to awaken some time later with a pulsating pain from the claw marks of the grizzly. In his more lucid moments, he knew the wounds needed cleansing. After all, there was no telling what the bear may have carried on her claws. Unfortunately for him, not much could be done until he reached his destination.

Having drifted back off, MacLeod wasn't sure how long he had been out when he suddenly awoke to the sound of voices. Trying his best to focus on anything other than the pain in his arm, MacLeod watched as a squealing *carreta* came to a stop, blocking the road and a man walked toward him, talking softly to the chestnut gelding.

"Senor, I think you are hurt, maybe," the man said after beckoning an old woman over who had been sitting in the back of the rickety old *carreta*.

The woman looked at MacLeod's arm and shook her head in disbelief.

Behind them, three young children hung back watching as the woman demanded MacLeod dismount so that she could treat his wounds.

Doing as he'd been asked, MacLeod dismounted, allowing the couple to tend to his wounds before helping him back on his horse and three hours later, MacLeod caught sight of the first red-tiled roofs of Santa Barbara through the fading evening light.

Once more his troubled thoughts returned to the bedside of Francesca; her face as pale as snow, her breathing barely noticeable. All thoughts of the struggle with Santiago were long forgotten. Only the question of Francesca's survival mattered. To help keep his mind from dwelling on what might happen he focused on what he loved about her...like the slight tilt of the head when he tried to explain a new plan he had. Or the frown that furrowed her brow, which meant she was about to question his idea. Although she never voiced her disapproval at the time, he knew it would come later in a series of questions that were meant to persuade him to rethink his plans. Though despite what she may think and the fact that it was her land, Francesca never said no outright.

MacLeod had always assumed that if he joined her church and became a citizen of Mexico he would be entitled to do with the land as he pleased. However, he knew he would never give up his right to be an American citizen.

But what will you do if she dies? the voice in the back of his mind whispered.

MacLeod couldn't be sure of the answer to that question. Francesca was his guide, his future, his strength.

Shaking his head in an effort to clear the morbid thoughts, MacLeod's eyes focused on the ship anchored in the harbor, silhouetted against the setting sun. The fading light was too weak for him to make out the ship's flag; he could only hope it kept a doctor as part of its crew.

MacLeod turned down the path toward the landing. A boat sat a few feet above the lapping water, its four-man crew resting nearby in the sand.

"What ship?" MacLeod asked.

"She's the Belfast, out of Liverpool. What is it you'd be wanting?"

"Your captain—is he ashore?"

One of the crewmen stood up and brushed sand from his trousers. "Aye, he's arranging for our trading to begin. Captain Lancaster's his name. You'll find him up at this *alcalde's* place. He and the doctor."

MacLeod felt a wave of hope.

"I'm in need of a doctor. You say they're up at the *alcalde's* house?"

A chorus of muted laughter came with the response. "You'll be needing to sober him up first. Highly doubt he's been fully sober since we left Glouster."

MacLeod tipped his hat in thanks and kneed the gelding back onto the track that led to town.

MacLeod was met with open arms, quickly escorted into the house. An ample woman who had been standing nearby curtsied when MacLeod was introduced, then showed concern at his crudely bandaged arm. She shooed away a half dozen children.

MacLeod removed his hat. "Señor Peña," he said to the man whose house he had entered. "I understand the captain of that ship out there is here."

"Si, he and the doctor have come to visit. I will bring them to you."

MacLeod leaned his back against the white-washed adobe wall in exhaustion, questioning how much longer he could function without sleep.

A few moments later a short man, some would say had failed to push himself away from the kitchen table sooner, came forward. "Captain Lancaster, sir. How may I be of service?"

MacLeod quickly rethought his first impression of the man. The eyes buried beneath a full head of black hair never wavered as MacLeod offered his hand. "I understand you're carrying a doctor. My wife has been injured and requires a doctor; I've come to see if I might have him ride out to our ranch."

The man ran his hand over his chin and squinted at MacLeod before chuckling. "I believe I'm familiar with you and your wife."

MacLeod couldn't remember having ever encountered the man before. Especially since the hide trade had been dominated by Boston ships for quite some time.

"I'm sorry, Captain, I doubt we've met. I rarely go to Monterey, even less to Santa Barbara."

The twinkle in the ship captain's eye made MacLeod somewhat uneasy. "I'm sorry to not have introduced the situation of our meeting, but it was about ten years ago as I remember. I had the honor of attending your wedding. I was first mate under Captain Fanning."

MacLeod grinned. "My apologies, sir, I didn't remember."

The Englishman brushed aside MacLeod's embarrassment. "Nothing to apologize for. If I were to wed such a beautiful young woman, I wouldn't be remembering those standing around on the quarterdeck and wishing they were in your shoes. Now, did I hear something about you being in need of a doctor?"

"It's not for me, Captain, it's for my wife. She's taken a terrible fall and has not regained her senses."

Captain Lancaster pursed his lips and ran his hand over his chin again. "Well now, a doctor it is. If you be needing one, you shall have one. But not before first watch in the morning, I'm afraid."

The aroma of cooking emanating from the fires caused MacLeod's stomach to revolt, reminding him that he had not eaten since the morning before. Concerned that every minute might be crucial to Francesca's survival, he decided that food would have to wait. As if having a sudden moment of clarity, Captain Lancaster's words penetrated the fog that fatigue had caused to his mental faculties. "I'm sorry, Captain, I was under the impression that the doctor was here with you."

"Oh, that he is. Unfortunately for you, the good doctor is somewhat enamored with our host's ample supply of wine. We carry only rum on the ship. I'm afraid he has over indulged. I'm sure the effects will have worn off somewhat by morning."

MacLeod felt his temper rise. Francesca lay in her bed because the one person asked to watch over her had failed, due to his excessive love of wine. And now, the man who might be able to save her lay in a room unconscious, due to his over indulgence of the very same wine.

MacLeod thought about his next words for a moment before speaking. "Could you spare the man for a few days? I'm afraid the situation has scrambled my thinking."

"No need to apologize, young man. I also carry a very efficient loblolly boy to back up our surgeon." Captain Lancaster laughed. "Fortunately for us, his religion will not allow him to partake in our daily ration of rum, or any spirits for that matter. I'll send for him immediately to look after that arm of yours. What may I ask caused such wounds?"

MacLeod raised his right arm as far as he could and inspected the newly formed scabs. "I'm afraid I crossed paths with a mother Grizzly."

The ship's captain shook his head. "Afraid I can't relate to that. Heard about them, but they're somewhat rare in England."

"I appreciate your offer of assistance but if it's all right with you, I'll have Doñ Peña rouse the good doctor while I find him a horse."

Lancaster chuckled. "I'll warn you, the man is an obstinate brute when sober."

Doñ Peña, having overheard the conversation, motioned to MacLeod. "I will provide you with horses," he said. "I wish I could do more for the lovely Señora."

"That is most kind of you," MacLeod said. "I'd like to be on my way as soon as possible." *How am I supposed to force an unwilling doctor to ride the miles to the ranch while attempting to remain awake myself?* MacLeod though.

Seating himself on a nearby wooden bench while waiting for Doñ Peña to round up the doctor, MacLeod quickly fell asleep.

He couldn't be sure how long he had been asleep. It wasn't until he felt a hand shaking his shoulder.

"Señor MacLeod, the doctor is ready."

MacLeod jerked his head back, wiping the sleep from his eyes, and attempted to focus on the bent figure being supported by Captain Lancaster. The man pushed his long gray hair out of his eyes and stared at MacLeod a moment before speaking. "I'll not be treated like this," he shouted, his words thick and slurred. "If you would be so kind as to unhand me, I'll have the boat take me back to the ship."

In as pleasant a tone as he could muster, MacLeod explained the situation and his need for the doctor's assistance.

The man swayed while attempting to tuck his shirt into his trousers, the heavy stubble on his cavernous cheeks gray in the candlelit room. He bent down to put his feet in his shoes, muttering to himself as he did so. "I'll not be dragged away in the middle of the night to attend to some Mexican female who fell off her horse. If anything becomes of her there are dozens of other women heaving their skirts up for a looksee to replace her. To bloody hell with her, whoever she is."

Without a word MacLeod crossed the room in two strides, drawing and cocking his pistol in his pursuit. "Your tongue, sir, is about to put your life at my mercy," MacLeod seethed. "Once you have sobered up I expect an apology for those remarks."

Doñ Peña and Captain Lancaster both stepped in to intervene before the situation could escalate any further. Lancaster pushed the doctor up against the adobe wall while Peña placed a hand on MacLeod's arm and gently persuaded him to lower the pistol.

A shaken doctor sputtered out an apology before flopping down onto the floor.

MacLeod took a deep breath and allowed his temper to subside, fully aware that Francesca's life might very well be in this man's hands. Once he was calm he un-cocked the pistol and thrust it back under his belt. "Captain Lancaster—I'll have him back as soon as possible. Down by the beach I have a warehouse full of hides, most are committed to Bryant & Sturgis, out of Boston, but a good amount of our hides and tallow are in that smaller building by the hide house. I'd be pleased if you would consider making me an offer on them."

"Well now, son, that's considerate of you. I'd be pleased to take them off your hands since that's what I'm here for. First thing in the morning I'll have my men come ashore and tally what you have."

A still shaken doctor steadied himself before making his way out of the house to the already waiting horse.

MacLeod, following behind the doctor, took a moment to thank everyone before stepping outside in preparation of the long ride back to Rancho Colinas de Oro.

As he stepped outside a young boy sprinted out of the gathering darkness. The boy rushed over to the *alcalde* and pointed back toward the beach. "Doñ Peña, there is a fire."

Santa Barbara

Hearing the boy's words, Doñ Peña rushed past MacLeod to see where the fire was coming from. There had been a few occasions where lightening had set the surrounding hillside ablaze, threatening to engulf the town itself. However, this night, there had been no lightening. Even though, a fire of any kind could do a great amount of damage before water, hand carried from the shore, could contain it.

Doñ Peña's youngest son grasped MacLeod's hand, drawing him toward the door. Instantly, MacLeod's eyes caught the glow of the flames. Captain Lancaster stood to one side as others came out of their nearby dwellings to watch.

Peña shouted out orders, sending the men who had gathered, rushing to carry buckets down to the water's edge.

"Not right sure what might be burning," Captain Lancaster said. "I believe those hide houses are empty this time of the year."

"Not all of them," MacLeod said. He swung up onto the borrowed saddle and turned the horse toward the row of warehouses Bryant & Sturgis used to finish preparing the hides before filling their ships hold. Fatigue had been put aside for the moment.

"Oh God, please don't let it be our warehouse," he muttered to himself as he closed in on the flames. Although deep in his heart he was pretty certain it was his warehouse.

As he drew near, the heat from the flames enveloped him. Within seconds, the putrid smell of the burning hides caused him to pull his shirt up over his nose. Although it wasn't long before the smell and the wave of heat from the roaring flames forced MacLeod to retreat.

It was almost too much to bear when he thought of their losses. Sure, there was still the other warehouse, not much more than one quarter the size of this one. They had used it as a back-up when they couldn't get any more hides in the large one.

He dismounted and sat on the ground as the voices of the men attempting to save the warehouse filtered through the crackle of the flames. He thought back to the tremendous effort his people had put in to get the hides this far. *What will I tell them now? What will I tell those who held my debts? And Francesca—what will I tell her when she wakes up?*

With no answers to any of the looming questions, MacLeod decided to worry about that later. Right now, before fatigue overwhelmed him, he needed to get the doctor on the road to Colinas de Oro.

The miles slipped past as a new day dawned. MacLeod had taken the precaution of leading the doctor's horse in case he developed the idea of turning back. The man had made faint protests until he realized the futility of it.

MacLeod was quickly jarred awake when his horse pulled up and laid its ears back. No matter how hard he tried, no amount of coaxing could get the horse to move. Behind him, the doctor's small mare pulled on the lead rope.

On the road ahead lay the bodies of his black horse and the grizzly.

Carefully slipping off his horse MacLeod began searching for the spot he had cached his rifle. He figured he would have Concannon try to rebuild the stock, or wrap it in a wet hide like he had seen others do. It was then that he remembered he had told Concannon to be gone before he returned.

After mounting his horse once again, he coaxed the horses around the two carcasses and continued down the road, past the dead bear's cubs who were waiting patiently for their dinner.

Up through the pass in the moonlight he began thinking again of what he might find when he finally returned to the hacienda. *Will Francesca still live?* he wondered.

A short while later, MacLeod and the doctor approached the small adobe house just as Jacob was exiting, a lantern in his hand.

MacLeod waited patiently for Jacob to speak, praying the words that follow were not that his wife had perished.

Jacob shook his head. "There has been no change, William. She has not recovered her senses as of yet."

MacLeod sighed, slipping down from the saddle to lean against the horse until he felt he could walk without falling.

"Is this the doctor?" Jacob asked.

MacLeod nodded. "Was somewhat reluctant to come."

Jacob Morgenthau grinned. "Imagine you were quite persuasive since he's here."

"Would you be so good as to show him where he can clean himself up while I go and see her?" Jacob nodded before leading the doctor away.

When MacLeod entered the bedroom he found Francesca lying on their bed, framed by candlelight. He knelt beside the bed and took her hand in his. "I've brought a doctor back. He'll be here shortly to attend to you."

Sarah stepped into the room, a bowl of water in her hands. Nodding his approval, she approached the opposite side of the bed and dipped a cloth in a bowl of water before proceeding to sponge Francesca's face and arms. "I don't know if it is of any comfort for her, but it helps me."

MacLeod nodded as he laid his head on the bed and quickly gave in to exhaustion.

Rosalie woke him as dawn broke over the mountains to the east. She led him to a bed fashioned out of robes in the far corner of the room and stripped off what remained of his shirt, then proceeded to bath his wounds in warm water. She explained that she was worried about what dirt lay beneath the scabs on his arm and shoulder. After applying poultices to his wounds and rewrapping them in clean cloths she allowed him to return to Francesca's side.

All the while the doctor continued his examination of Francesca before eventually beckoning for MacLeod to follow him outside. MacLeod, who had not spoken to him since they arrived, waited, fearing for the worst.

"I won't address your actions in bringing me here," the doctor said. "You haven't asked, but my name is Wellington. Doctor Wellington. I was a student of medicine at Cambridge."

MacLeod wondered why this man, educated as he was, had been brought down to serve on a British trading ship.

"Will my wife recover?" MacLeod asked.

The doctor shrugged. "For all we know about medicine we know very little about what goes on inside the human head. She has obviously suffered a severe blow. From what I can tell, there appears to be some swelling, but to what extent it might have affected her brain, we'll have to wait and see. By the way, I watched the old woman tend to your arm. It amazes me sometimes to see what the uneducated can achieve. It appears her poultices were made from local weeds. Who's to say which are better? Hers or mine." The doctor shrugged.

"My wife, Doctor, will she recover?"

"I don't know. Only time will tell. However, there is something else that could be serious that I would like to address. Of course, it won't matter if she fails to regain consciousness."

MacLeod waited, wondering what could be so serious. "Are you saying there's something else wrong with her?"

Dr. Wellington ran a hand through his hair. "I have noticed a certain degree of swelling in her lower spine area. I don't like it."

"Your concern is apparent, Doctor. What does it mean?"

"She may have broken her back in the fall. Unfortunately, we won't know for sure until she comes to."

"If she did, would it heal?"

Doctor Wellington shrugged. "It very well could mean that your wife would be paralyzed. If that is the case, she would never walk again."

MacLeod wondered where it would all end. The implications, along with all the other issues he was facing, made decisions about the future of Colinas de Oro that much more difficult.

Or did it?

"So, Doctor, are you saying she would have to be kept in her bed?"

"Well no," the doctor said, taking a seat on the bench Francesca loved. "I would say that is a possibility. Though it greatly depends upon the person and how much they are willing to devote themselves to learning how to live without the use of their legs."

MacLeod watched Juana, the young Indian woman who was devoted to Francesca, round up the children. He had yet to discuss Francesca's injuries with them.

"My ship will be in the harbor for a number of days, if you can find a place for me to sleep I would like to stay and keep an eye on her," the doctor stated, pulling MacLeod's attention back to him.

His thoughts running wild, there was something MacLeod had to ask. "What if she doesn't wake soon?"

"The swelling in her brain would have to be addressed. In order to do that I would need to open her scalp and attempt to reduce the pressure."

MacLeod was simply too exhausted to understand exactly what the doctor was saying. Sensing his continued exhaustion, Rosalie took him by the arm and led him toward the house. Jacob, who had come to check on Francesca, stood near the doorway.

"Concannon?" MacLeod asked before entering the house.

"He has left as you told him."

"Where to?"

"I understand he's living with Father Avila at the old mission."

MacLeod stood there for a moment before speaking. "Esperanza can stay. Be sure to tell her that. But I don't want to see him again."

RANCHO SANTIAGO

Marisol Montero shaded her eyes from the early afternoon sun as she walked around the recently completed adobe house. She found a rough wooden bench and pulled it into the shade of the house. The heat, and the lack of even a faint breeze, brought back her thoughts of what she had left behind. She had brought it up with him last night but as expected, he had refused to allow her to return to Monterey. In effect, she was his prisoner. She now needed to consider her options. Assuming she had any. She watched him now as he talked with this man she had heard of often, this Pacheco, who had once worked for the military command in Los Angeles.

Nearby, her maid watered the flowers Marisol had recently planted. If cared for properly, they would soon appear. Turning to the young woman, Marisol beckoned her over.

"Si, Señora."

"You will say nothing to him about what was delivered. It is between us."

"Of course, Señora," the girl replied in understanding. "May I ask if we will be returning to Monterey?"

Marisol would rather keep Santiago's refusal to herself. "We will see. Now remember, this letter is our secret." Without another word she dismissed the woman and removed the letter from the journal on her lap. It had been delivered this morning, hand carried from Santa Barbara. She recognized the important looking seal of the Governor's office.

Upon opening it, she recognized that it was a map of this very valley. She couldn't help but wonder how much this had cost Santiago. The markings on the map were undoubtedly the boundaries of a land grant. In script across the top of the map was written *Colinas de Oro. What is Santiago going to do with a map of the Colinas de Oro land grant?* Marisol wondered.

She watched him wave Pacheco away, and quickly tucked the letter back in her journal as Santiago walked toward her, his boots scuffing up clouds of dust that rose and fell back to the ground in the listless air.

"I am waiting for a message from the Governor. Has it arrived yet?" he asked.

So he was expecting it, she thought. She knew she would not be able to cover her theft for long. "No, there has been nothing since the last one. Are you expecting something of importance?"

Santiago stood by her side and swept his hand across the breadth of the valley. "Soon, all of this will be mine. I want you to remain here with me and enjoy it."

"So they have agreed to sell their land? Is that what you are saying?" Marisol asked, knowing that wasn't the case.

"It does not matter. There are other ways."

"Could it have anything to do with the woman being injured?"

Santiago's head snapped around to look at her. "What have you heard about this?"

"Only that she was injured. They do not know if she will live." She knew by his reaction that he was somehow involved. She needed to see his reaction when she asked the next question. "Did you have anything to do with it?"

Santiago raised a hand in her direction. She was sure he was about to strike her.

"I am told the woman fell from her horse. How could I have been involved? It is most unfortunate, but maybe it will convince these people to leave."

"Do you think they will sell their land now?" Marisol asked.

This time Santiago smiled. "It must be soon, otherwise they will discover it is far too late."

RANCHO COLINAS DE ORO

"Señor, señor, please. She is awake," the boy's voice broke through his dreams.

MacLeod pushed aside the hand that shook his shoulder. Sleep had been so rare lately and he hated to be disturbed. He rolled over onto the makeshift bed Juana had prepared, he thought only of returning to the blissful slumber that shielded him from the mounting mountain of problems.

"Señor, please, you must come!"

Damn, there it is again. Doesn't anyone understand how much I need the rest? he thought to himself. Reluctantly, MacLeod pushed himself up into a sitting position. "What?"

"She is awake. The Señora is awake," the boy spat out.

Awake? Could it possibly be true? MacLeod leapt to his feet and sprinted across the small courtyard toward the house. Sarah Morgenthau waited by the door.

"Is it true?" he asked.

"Yes, the doctor said you could see her now. He will speak with you after."

MacLeod ducked under the low doorway and entered the room. Francesca lay propped up with cushions, a thin blanket across her legs. Rosalie sat beside the bed holding Francesca's hand in her own.

MacLeod rushed to the other side of the bed and took Francesca's other hand. "I worried so. The doctor thought you might not wake. How are you feeling?"

MacLeod felt Francesca weakly squeeze his hand. "I don't know. I am so tired. Though I imagine I should be after what they say has happened to me."

Francesca removed her hand from his grasp and brushed a strand of hair away from her eyes. "Have you spoken with the doctor yet? He has asked to speak with you. Then you must tell me how I have the attention of a real doctor."

"I'll talk to him later. Right now, I only want to hear about you."

"Please, William, go speak to him now and come back," she urged.

MacLeod rose and headed for the door. "I'll be right back."

Just outside the small adobe, MacLeod found the doctor sitting in the shade. "You wanted to see me?" Macleod asked.

Doctor Wellington nodded. "It is what I feared. Your wife has no feeling whatsoever below her waist."

MacLeod tried to remember what the doctor had said earlier. "Will she recover over time?"

"No, I'm afraid she will never walk again. Her back has been broken. She will live in her bed, or in a chair, for the remainder of her life."

The impact of the doctor's words devastated him. What would life be like without her constant presence? Everything that surrounded him was in jeopardy. And all their troubles had been brought about by Santiago. How many of them mattered now?

"Would she be better off living away from here, maybe in Santa Barbara or Monterey?" MacLeod asked, hoping the doctor would help to make his decisions about the fate of Colinas de Oro easier.

"It would make no difference as long as she has those who would see she was properly taken care of."

A few moments later they were joined by Sarah, who had already heard the doctor's prognosis. "She is very tired, but she would like to speak to you before she sleeps."

MacLeod nodded before turning to the doctor once again. "Does she know?"

"Yes, I have told her."

When MacLeod returned to Francesca's bedside, she held her hand out to him. "Please, sit."

"Are you sure you don't want to rest? Diego and Catalina would like to sit with you," he said.

"They have been here already. Did the doctor tell you about me?"

MacLeod could only nod. He couldn't bring himself to speak the words aloud. "I've thought about it—I thought perhaps you would prefer to live in Monterey. It might be easier for you."

Francesca smiled. "No, this is our land. I have changed my mind…I do not want to leave our land. We must find a way to save Colinas de Oro."

The memory of the blazing hide warehouse flooded his mind. Sooner or later she would learn of it and he knew it would be best if she heard it from him. Though for today, he wanted her to concentrate on gaining her strength.

"Where is Sean?" she asked. "I thought he would have heard I was awake and come to visit by now."

"He's no longer here. I told him I didn't want him on Colinas de Oro land again. I left orders that you were not to ride Bolivar. He knew that. He disobeyed me."

Francesca shook her head and reached for his hand again. "You are a hard man, William. Forgiveness comes hard for you."

"He was drunk again, Francesca. Sober, he might have stopped you."

"It was I who chose to ride Bolivar. I am sure he would have stopped me if he knew."

"He was told not to let you ride the horse. He is as responsible as you."

Francesca waited a moment before speaking. "Do you know that place on the way to the stream where those two trees grow?"

"What about it?" MacLeod asked in confusion.

"Has Jacob or Sarah not told you?"

"Told me what?"

"That Sean carried me back in his arms from that place."

"Not possible. That's close to two miles."

Francesca shut her eyes for a moment and sighed. MacLeod thought she had fallen asleep when she didn't say anything else. "Sarah told me what happened," she finally said. "He couldn't get back on his horse with me in his arms, so he carried me. When he reached the house he collapsed. She said he lay there weeping and repeating something in that language he sometimes uses."

MacLeod couldn't help but wonder if he were in the same situation if he could have carried someone in his arms for two miles. Still, he had been explicit when he told Concannon not to let her ride the stallion. "What are you asking, Francesca?"

"I want you to go and ask him to return."

"I don't even know where he is," MacLeod said.

"I am sure someone knows. Ask Jacob. Perhaps he knows."

MacLeod pushed away the weariness that held his body captive. The dark secret he withheld from them all hung heavy on his mind. Dr. Wellington had been sworn to secrecy to keep the fire at the warehouse to himself. At the time, MacLeod had no idea of the implications the fire brought to light. No one did. In truth, they were ruined. No money from hides or tallow could be counted on until the following year. And then it would be limited, due to his culling of the two-year-old steers.

"William?" she said. "Will you do this for me? After that you need to speak to the children. They will need to know what they have to do now."

It wasn't a discussion MacLeod looked forward to, but he knew she was right. There was also the matter of the letter. It was time Diego was told about his grandfather.

Francesca touched his hand. "Do this for me, William. It was as much my fault as it was Sean's."

God, how he hated to apologize. "If it's what you wish," he finally agreed.

"Do you know where he went?"

Jacob ran his hand over his face. "At least in Hawaii we had a breeze to combat the heat. But yes, I believe I heard Father Avila has taken him in at the old mission."

"Well, maybe a few confessions will help his soul. God knows he could use it," MacLeod said. He reached out and caught the arm of one of the Gomez boys. "Saddle up two horses and bring them here."

"Would you want me to accompany you?" Jacob asked.

"No, I think it's best I do this alone, but thanks for the offer."

McLeod rode down off the small rise leading a short-legged bay mare. He couldn't help being amazed at how neglect had caused so much damage to the mission buildings. It was only ten years ago that most of the missions were well cared for by the two Franciscan or Dominican priests that had been in charge. Of course, the bigger missions, like Santa Barbara or San Gabriel, had as many as a thousand Indians to do the work.

As he looked around at the mission buildings he remembered that one of the smaller missions, much like this one, had been sold to an individual who turned it into a barn for his milking cows. He thought about the overworked priests, like Father Fernandez at San Gabriel mission. Had God given up on his past houses of worship? MacLeod wondered.

As he approached a sudden gust of wind sent a spiral of dust into the air. Even in the heat Father Avila greeted him in his traditional woolen garment.

"Have you come to ask me to perform the rites of burial for that poor woman?" Father Avila asked, sullen.

"Not exactly, Father."

"Then she lives?"

MacLeod felt himself choking up. He waited a moment before speaking. "She is alive, yes."

"Thank God. We have been praying for her diligently."

"Well, you got a partial answer to your prayers, Father."

A movement on the far side of the mission chapel caught his attention. "If that's you back there, Sean, I need a word with you."

Father Avila shuffled over and placed a hand on MacLeod's leg. "Please be kind to him if you have it in you, son. He has little left in the way of hope. We have spent many hours on our knees in prayer for your wife."

A moment later Sean Concannon walked out from the shadow of the chapel.

"What is it you be wanting of me? You have already given me all that I could ask for. She is alive you say?"

MacLeod knew there was no reason to keep the truth from him. "I brought a doctor out from a ship that was in Santa Barbara. He has determined her back was broken in the fall."

Concannon seemed to shrink before MacLeod's eyes. He sat down on the ground and buried his head in his hands. When he looked up, MacLeod could see the tears staining his eyes. "But she will live?"

"The doctor said there's a reasonable chance she will. Unfortunately, she'll never walk again."

"Oh Mother of God, what have I done?" Concannon moaned as the tears began to fall.

MacLeod remained on his horse thinking about Francesca's request. How could she be so forgiving? he wondered. Though despite his feelings, she wanted Concannon to return. They'd always had a special bond he could never understand. It was part of what made him love her so.

Deep down, he knew he could not go back without taking Concannon with him. He could either forgive him for what had transpired, or live and work side-by-side and let the blame fester in his mind. Though stubborn as he was, he also recognized that the days ahead would try his soul and he needed a friend to watch his back. As it were, there was none better than the little Irishman.

"You saved her life, Sean. Francesca has asked me to come and get you. I don't know what it is between you two, but right now I'll do anything she asks."

"Is this true? I'm forgiven?"

"Get your belongings together. I brought a horse. We've things to talk about on the way back."

While Concannon gathered the few belongings he had brought with him to the mission MacLeod stepped out of the saddle and spoke to Father Avila.

"I don't know how she's going to accept where she's at, but I suspect she'd like to see you, Father."

"Then I will ride with you. Allow me a few moments to prepare." MacLeod nodded.

On the ride back to Colinas de Oro a few dark clouds had begun to gather in the west. Though just as all the times before, they soon dissipated. Once again, false hope unspoken.

Father Avila's grey-backed mule soon fell behind, which suited MacLeod. He needed to fill Concannon in on their latest setback and now seemed as good a time as any. "I brought the doctor here from a hide ship, English, that was anchored in the harbor in Santa Barbara."

Concannon seemed to know this wasn't all MacLeod had to report and remained silent.

"They burnt down our hide house," MacLeod said, realizing there was no easy way to break the news. "Everything we worked so hard for went up in flames."

"Now what could possibly start a fire there—unless someone wanted it destroyed? Do they know who did it?" Concannon asked.

"No, no one saw a thing."

"Of course they didn't," Concannon stated. He lowered his voice, making sure the faint breeze wouldn't carry his words back to Father Avila, he asked, "What will you be doing about it?"

"Not much I can do except accuse the man I believe had something to do with it. No proof though, so we can't be sure he's involved."

"Did they burn everything?"

"There was a small building we used for the overflow that was left unscathed. Not enough to keep us going though."

"Does she know?"

MacLeod shook his head. "No. I haven't told her yet. There's still plenty of time. Last thing she needs is another worry. I just want her to focus on regaining her strength."

Concannon glanced over his shoulder again. "What are you planning? Never struck me as someone to sit by when things go against you."

"So many things lately. I haven't had time to think clear," MacLeod admitted.

"Have you noticed if they've started branding their heifers yet? Seems there may be some of their young mixed in with ours."

MacLeod's face broke into a wry grin. "You know, sometimes your mind contemplates deceitful things. I was wondering the same thing myself."

"I believe if you ride up the canyon the stream follows, where we held the horse, not a far piece, it narrows quickly. There's a side canyon runs into the main one."

They rode awhile before MacLeod finally said, "Don't recall this place you're talking about. Seems I would have seen it. How'd you come by it?"

"Jacob and me rode up as far as we could one day. There's a bunch of trees and things covers the way in."

"So what are you proposing? Would it be what I'm thinking it is?"

"I were you, I'd send some of us out a couple of nights to round up those unbranded youngsters and drive them up there. Happens there's a couple of large meadows back a ways that could hold them for a spell."

MacLeod grunted. "Mighty dangerous. It's rustling anyway you want to look at it. There would be a war over it for sure."

"Just a thought."

"Well, can't say I won't consider it. Right now I need to figure out a way to tell her about the fire."

"It'll break the poor lass's heart. She loves this land so."

"Well, she'll need to bow to reason," MacLeod said. "We can't live on credit forever."

"I'd like to see her before you break the news." MacLeod nodded in agreement.

Francesca was sleeping when he and Concannon rode into the courtyard. Not wanting to wake her, MacLeod sent Concannon on to see Esperanza. He would see her in the morning after she'd had a proper nights rest.

When he brought her breakfast the next morning he told her she was looking better. This pleased her greatly. As was expected, Rosalie managed her meals while she and Juana took turns washing and dressing her. Still, MacLeod wondered if the consequences of her damaged back had sunk completely sunk in yet. It was one thing to be thankful you had survived, but another to accept the fact you would never walk again.

Despite his desire to do so, MacLeod knew he couldn't keep the terrible news from her any longer. He knew she would eventually hear it from someone if he didn't tell her. He took her hand in his, he held it tightly "Francesca, there's something you need to know," he began. Taking a deep breath, he continued. "While I was in Santa Barbara our hide house was set on fire. Everything in it was destroyed."

He watched the implications of what he had said begin forming in her expression. She shook her head in disbelief. "Tell me it cannot be true, William."

"It's true."

"How could this happen?" she cried.

MacLeod felt his rage return to the surface. "It didn't just happen, Francesca. Somebody did it on purpose."

"Do you think Señor Santiago is responsible?"

"I know he is."

"Can we not tell the authorities?"

"No, Francesca," he said, standing and walking to the open doorway. "I have no proof to show them. The Governor is the main authority. He would want proof."

"Then what can we do if he is to blame?"

"Not much without a fight."

Francesca sipped her water from a cup that sat on the small table next to her bed. "There must be another way. People will be hurt if there is a fight. I know you, but you cannot fight them alone."

"I'll go and see him. I can't let him get away with this without him knowing I blame him. He'll bluster and deny it, of course."

"Do you think that well help?" she asked.

"No, but it's all I can do until something else comes along."

MacLeod walked out into the courtyard and sat on the small bench. How could he convince her it would be better to turn the land grant back over to the government and sell off the cattle? Though that wasn't what he really wanted to do. What he really wanted to do was ride over to Rancho Santiago and shoot the son of a bitch.

From his seat on the bench, MacLeod watched as Jacob Morgenthau gestured to two of the Chumash Indians that were making adobe bricks. Already three courses of the three-foot-thick bricks had been laid for the new house he and Sarah were to live in. A flood of guilt flooded MacLeod at the knowledge he still hadn't told them about the fire.

Concannon, who was just rounding one of the lean-tos spotted MacLeod and walked over to where he sat. However, before he could say anything, MacLeod spoke.

"I need you to do something for me."

"And what might that be?" Concannon asked.

"I want you to take the doctor back to his ship. If it's not in the harbor yet, wait for it. I'll give you a note for the Captain. His name's Lancaster. Clean out the little warehouse and give everything to the Captain for a credit. He may have already done it, but if not, make sure it gets done. There are a few things in the note I want from him. I know he's got some new muskets on board so I want you to buy three—powder and ball included."

Concannon combed his beard with his fingers. "And all the fixings that go with them, I suppose?"

"Take a couple of pack animals with you."

"Are you planning on a fight?" Concannon asked.

"Pays to be ready. Just the other side of our overnight spot you'll find a dead grizzly and my little black stallion. Pull them into the brush off the trail. My saddle's cached behind those big boulders off the road, as is my rifle. Stocks been smashed all to hell. I'm hoping you can do something with it."

"I'll be telling Esperanza and have her prepare some food to take."

"And Sean—" MacLeod called after him.

Concannon shook his head. "Haven't touched a bottle since it happened," he stated, knowing exactly what MacLeod was going to ask.

MacLeod walked up into the now flourishing orchard, thanks to Juan Gomez.

Juan Gomez. The man's name reminded MacLeod of what had happened to his son. He knew soon he would have to tell Gomez how his son had died.

Taking in the orchard trees, MacLeod found it hard to believe how much of a change they had made. Each day one of the boys carted water up from the stream to nourish the trees. Before the accident, Francesca had often walked here, telling MacLeod how fortunate they were to have someone so knowledgeable to care for their trees.

Since Francesca's diagnosis Diego and Catalina appeared to take heed of Rosalie's demand that they keep their arguments out of Francesca's hearing. The two younger ones, as expected, were often found in their mother's bed seeking her attention.

Five days later, Sisquoc, MacLeod's big Chumash Indian *alcalde*, rode up from the river to inform MacLeod that half a dozen uniformed riders were turning off El Camino Real and would soon be at the house.

MacLeod waited in the courtyard, wondering if this was an official visit? And if so, why? He grabbed Diego by the arm as his son ran past. "Hustle up to Sean's place and have him come down." The boy nodded as he ran off in the direction of Concannon's adobe.

The riders came out of the woods below and rode toward the house. Even from such a distance, MacLeod could see there was something familiar about the lead rider.

Concannon sidled up to MacLeod carrying his shotgun. He had returned the night before with three new muskets, along with powder and lead.

"What might these fellows be wanting?" Concannon asked.

"Don't know, but that one in the lead there we might have met before."

A moment later Concannon grunted. "That's the little fellow from down in San Diego I be thinking. Figured himself all high and mighty."

"I believe you're right," MacLeod said. "Our own little Corporal Rodriguez. Wonder what he's doing up here."

Concannon grinned. "Esperanza spoke of him."

"Yep. He brought me to San Diego from the San Gabriel Mission. Proud as a peacock, that one. Told her he had captured me. I was still carrying my old Kentucky riffle. She laughed at him and asked why I had a gun and he didn't. He rather fancied her. She would just laugh at him."

"I wonder whether he'll remember us. It's been a while."

MacLeod chuckled. "Oh, I'm sure he knows all about us, but I doubt this is a come calling type of visit. Bringing along those other five fellows means it's an official visit of some kind." MacLeod turned to Sisquoc. "They come from the south or the north?"

The Indian pointed toward the north.

"Then it's Monterey they've come from then," MacLeod surmised. I wonder what it is he's wanting?"

The group of horsemen halted in front of MacLeod.

"You're a long way from the Presidio, Corporal. How can I help you?"

"Yes, and it is Captain you are looking at now."

"That may be so, Rodriguez, but you're still a runt," Concannon countered.

Rodriquez's hand flew to his sword.

"I wouldn't do that, Captain. My friend here is a little out of line."

Rodriguez straightened up and said, "He will apologize to me then. I am the military authority sent by our Governor. I want this insult removed."

"Well now, Señor Rodriguez," Concannon began. "We can discuss that between us at a later time."

MacLeod's impatience began to show. "What is it you want? You come here with five armed soldiers—must be something important."

Rodriguez unbuttoned his coat and reached inside, pulling out an envelope. Without a word, he handed it over to MacLeod.

MacLeod took the paper from the man and scoffed. "What's this? Must be important to send you and half the garrison to deliver it."

Rodriguez puffed out his chest. "They did not tell me. Only that I was to wait for what they request."

MacLeod tore open the dispatch and quickly read it. The secretary for the Governor was requesting them to give Rodriguez their copy of the *diseño* for Rancho Colinas de Oro. The letter mentioned a dispute had arisen over the boundary lines.

Santiago, MacLeod thought to himself in anger.

While he and Francesca had looked, they never found the copy they were supposed to have.

Jacob Morgenthau stepped out of the shadows of the nearby tree in the courtyard. "The letter worries you, William? I can see it in your face."

"It appears our neighbor's reach is long. He is grasping at anything now. He believes he's found our weak point."

Rodriguez leaned over the pommel of his saddle. "If you will provide me with what it is our Excellency the Governor wants, I will return immediately. He requested I travel as quickly as possible."

MacLeod folded the dispatch and tucked it in his pocket. With each passing day their problems mounted. "Tell his Excellency that I will consider his request and get back to him."

"I have been instructed not to return without what is requested. I know you, Americano, and I know how little you regard our laws. That is why I have brought these men to assist me if you refuse," the man explained, motioning to the men on either side of him.

"Afraid you're going to be forced into a decision to use them. You're not getting what you want." *Because I don't have it,* MacLeod thought to himself. He felt someone at his shoulder, he turned his head slightly not wanting to risk taking his eyes off of Rodriguez.

"I thought you might be needing this," Jacob said, passing MacLeod one of the British muskets Concannon had brought back with him from Santa Barbara. "I believe Sean has also armed himself."

MacLeod watched as Rodriguez mentally reviewed his options before speaking to those behind him. In an instant, the other five riders turned their horses around and started back toward the river. "I will tell his Excellency you will be following me to Monterey. If not," Rodriguez said with a shrug. "I am certain he will have me return with more troops." With that, Rodriguez spun his horse around and galloped after the others.

MacLeod exhaled loudly. "Thanks for covering my back," he said to Jacob as he handed the musket over to him. Turning to face Concannon, he asked, "Sean, you thinking you can repair my rifle stock?"

"I'll be needing to make you a new one. In the meantime, I've wrapped it with wet hide. This sun will dry it out soon enough. If I might ask, what did the little fart want?"

"Oh, nothing much, except the map of Colinas de Oro boundaries."

"Why did you not give it to him?"

"Don't have it," MacLeod said with a shrug.

"Will that possibly pose a problem?" Jacob asked in concern.

"If the Governor sent that little fellow down here for it you can bet we're looking at another problem."

MacLeod turned back toward the house knowing the encounter would have been reported to Francesca and she would want to know everything. Due to Mexican laws, which gave all possessions the woman might have at the time of a marriage to the husband, he could then do with them as he pleased. However, MacLeod had always sought her input before deciding any action concerning Colinas de Oro. In his mind, this was still her land, laws or not. While he still wanted her to consider moving to Monterey, he very well may still be able to save the ranch if he could find a way to pay off their debts.

MacLeod had a decision to make. *Should I ride to Monterey to answer the Governor's summons or have it out with Santiago first? Not Monterey,* he eventually decided.

One of Gomez's sons trotted by. Embarrassed he had forgotten the boy's name, MacLeod grabbed the boy by the arm, embarrassed he had forgotten his name.

"What's your name?"

The boy grinned. "Jesus, Señor."

"Ok, Jesus. Round up the big stallion and saddle him for me."

The boy took off like he had been shot out of a gun. It was then that MacLeod realized he had not told young Jesus not to ride Bolivar.

Sure enough, fifteen minutes later, the boy rode up, his feet too short to reach the stirrups, and a grin that would warm a cold room.

MacLeod couldn't help chuckling. Everyone on the ranch wanted to be seen riding Bolivar and he knew the kid would be the envy of them all.

An hour later MacLeod reined the horse to a stop and searched the area where the pillar of rocks marked one corner of the land grant. All that remained were a few weeds surrounding a bare patch of earth.

MacLeod rode back to the stream and let the horse drink. The many hoof prints on this side of the stream told him all he needed to know. They were still pushing the cattle over at night to water and graze. Not all, just enough to make a difference in Rancho Santiago's sparse grazing lands.

He crossed the stream and rode toward the Northern marker, not expecting to find the downed oak tree in its usual place either. Though he also hadn't expected to see ruts in the ground where the tree had been dragged off a mile into the foothills where someone had used an axe to break it up.

MacLeod didn't even bother checking on the other markers down by the river, he was pretty sure they would have been tampered with also.

MacLeod took off his sombrero and fanned himself with it. *How did they know what markers designated the Colinas de Oro grant?*

Unless— Suddenly, realization struck. *They have seen the original diseño, which was filed somewhere in Monterey.*

Concannon looked up from his workbench as MacLeod rode up. "You wanting to take a ride with me?"

Concannon put aside the piece of oak he was carving. "If you can find another, I'd prefer to continue with this little thing I'm working on."

"Doesn't look like something we might be needing. What is it?"

"Oh, just a piece Esperanza has twisted my ear about."

"Well, I'll see if I can't stir up Jacob. By the way, keep those people busy on those adobe bricks. We need a root cellar. I've had a mind to build one, but haven't found the time."

"Sounds like you're planning on staying," Concannon said.

MacLeod stepped out of the saddle. "She won't leave. She says as long as we have enough to feed everyone, she's staying."

Concannon grinned. "And those you owe money to—how long does she figure they'll wait?"

"Yep, that's the problem. She keeps saying she knows I'll find a way."

He walked over to the house leading Bolivar. Jacob sat on the bench with Catalina and Diego. They looked up from their lesson when he approached. "Could you spare a moment?" MacLeod asked, addressing Jacob.

"Certainly," Jacob said. That was all the children needed to hear before galloping off.

"You ever get the feeling asking them to learn something is painful to their minds?" MacLeod questioned.

"Wouldn't be young ones if they didn't."

"How are they doing?"

Jacob took a moment before answering. "I am very pleased with their progress. It's a pity Diego cannot attend a real school. He's a bright young man."

"Wishing that were possible. Not likely out here though. Sadly, they don't go in for much book learning."

"Well, I'll do my best for them. Least I can do with what you have done for Sarah and me."

MacLeod dropped the horse's reins and let it wander in search of any grass it could find. "Jacob, think about what I'm about to ask. I don't want you to feel obligated," MacLeod finally stated. "I'm riding over to see the man who has this land next to us and I'd like to have someone watching my back when I'm talking to him."

Jacob Morgenthau nodded once in understanding. "I'll be telling Sarah then."

MacLeod gave a nod and smile before entering the house to tell Francesca.

"She is asleep," Rosalie said.

"When she wakes tell her I'll be back before sundown." Rosalie nodded. After picking up one of the new rifles along with a bag of balls and powder, he exited. Just outside, Jacob stood outside with a saddled horse. MacLeod handed the bag to Jacob, MacLeod said, "Make yourself familiar with it."

Jacob turned the rifle over and felt the balance. "It's a Baker rifle."

"You've seen one before?" MacLeod asked in astonishment.

"Indeed I have. Had one of my own back in England. It's their latest military rifle. Used it during the war with that French devil, Bonaparte."

"Is it any good?" MacLeod asked. He wondered how it compared to his own Kentucky, but had yet to test it out.

"Oh, very. I've hit targets at a hundred and fifty yards with mine"

"Good, then it's yours." MacLeod walked out into the field to catch the stallion, going over in his head how he would confront Santiago.

After mounting their horses, both men rode in silence while MacLeod continued going over his options.

Finally, Jacob said, "I've been wondering—with the loss of all the hides, I'm feeling Sarah and I might be an added burden. Perhaps you can help us get to Monterey; ease your burden a bit. I'm sure I can get some sort of work there."

MacLeod swept his sombrero off and wiped the sweat from his forehead. "No, no. You needn't be thinking that. We've got vegetables in the garden, fruit this fall, thanks to Gomez, and plenty of beef. I've a few hides left so I'll be buying all the beans and flour we'll be needing."

"If you're sure. You will not hurt our feelings by sending us on our way," Jacob said.

"Maybe I have another motive," MacLeod admitted. "I kind of fancy the idea of having another who can handle the guns I bought."

As they rode along, MacLeod filled Jacob in on young Gomez's death, making him promise to keep it a secret.

"Yes, I can see what that news would do to the lad's father."

"Don't get me wrong, I'll be settling the debt someday soon. Just not now."

They rode the last few miles in silence once more. It wasn't until they started down the slope into the shallow valley that MacLeod could see all the work that had been done to the house Santiago was building. His first impression of the rancho after coming into view was the tree's Santiago had planted.

"Must take a great deal of hand watering," Jacob said.

"Yep, and I'm wondering if the woman he spoke of has come out yet," MacLeod said.

As they approached the courtyard MacLeod slid his rifle out from under his leg. The last time he was here strong words were spoken. This time, he felt it would be better to be prepared, unwilling to underestimate the lengths his enemy would go to.

Santiago stepped out of the doorway as MacLeod pulled his horse to a halt. Santiago spoke to a young Indian girl. She ran off toward an area where other buildings were being constructed.

"Ah, I see you have come to visit once again. It is a shame you could not bring your lovely wife. I understand she has recovered from her fall."

Leaning across the pommel of the saddle, MacLeod scanned the grounds before answering.

"As well as can be expected. She'll never fully recover, but that is neither here nor there. This isn't a social call, Santiago. I'm here to deliver my last warning."

Santiago grinned as three riders appeared from behind one of the roofless adobes and rode toward them. Now MacLeod knew why the young Indian girl had left in such a hurry.

Santiago laughed. "A warning. *You* are issuing *me* a warning?"

Never taking his eyes off of Santiago, MacLeod muttered to Jacob at his side, "Keep your eyes on that fat fellow in the lead."

"The one with the eye patch?" Jacob asked.

"That's the one. Sneakier than a sidewinder. Name's Pacheco. The eye patch is compliments of Francesca."

"Surely not our gentle Francesca?" Jacob said in shock.

"One and the same."

"I believe that's a story I would like to hear."

MacLeod felt Jacob drift away, the Baker rifle now butt down on his thigh.

It was obvious to MacLeod that Santiago was rarely the receiver of warnings.

"Take it as the only one you'll ever get from me."

Santiago held his hands out, palms up, and turned to the three riders fanned out behind him. Roaring in laughter, he sputtered, "He is giving me a warning. How do you suppose I should act?"

The door to Santiago's house opened and a figure walked out, though MacLeod could not chance taking his eyes off Santiago.

"Guillermo, you have come to visit?"

The voice shook him to his core. *It couldn't be. It's not possible. Still, there could be no mistaking it.* He turned and saw her. *Marisol.* Somehow, the years had failed to dampen her beauty. If anything, she was more beautiful than when he first met her.

"Señora Montero," he said, sweeping off his sombrero. "Your presence is a most welcome surprise. I would not have believed it if I was told you were here."

MacLeod watched the anger build in Santiago's face. He turned back to look at Marisol, the question he so desperately longed to ask burned through his thoughts. *What had brought her here? And why is she with him?*

RANCHO SANTIAGO

Her presence only increased the tension between the two men. MacLeod felt it, but he wasn't leaving. Not until he had said what he needed to say. Santiago needed to know he had gone too far and there was a price to be paid for the crimes he had committed.

"I have heard Señora MacLeod was injured. How is she?" Marisol asked kindly.

"She is as well as can be expected, thank you. I will tell her you asked."

Santiago walked over and roughly grasped Marisol's arm. Spinning her around, he gave her a light shove. "You will return to the house now. This is not a conversation for you."

Marisol wrenched her arm out of his grasp, her eyes flaring with rage. "I will not do as you ordered. I have known these people for years." She turned back and addressed MacLeod directly. "Now what is this reasoning that brings about a warning?"

MacLeod still couldn't get over her being here and living with Santiago. "We've had a number of things happen on Rancho Colinas de Oro land, including having to herd Santiago cattle off our pasture."

Santiago sneered. "That is a false story. It is Señor Pacheco here who has chased *your* steers off my property."

"Stop the bullshit, Santiago, it may not be you personally, but I'd bet a ton of tallow it was under your orders."

"There were other things as well?" she asked.

MacLeod searched Santiago's face as he listed those things he knew were Santiago's efforts to drive them off their land. "Yes, ma'am, there are many more."

"Tell me about them," Marisol urged.

"Well, one of his Indians rode over, with others I presume, and slashed about a hundred hides. A breed bull had its throat cut. And a young lad who went out in search of our other bulls was dragged to death."

Marisol's hand went to her mouth in horror. She turned to Santiago. "Tell me you had no part in this."

Santiago shook his head. "I know nothing of these accusations. You have accused me of these vile incidents with no proof. My reputation is at stake. As you can see, I am not armed so you have me at a disadvantage. In my country I would be allowed to shoot you for such accusations."

MacLeod waited a moment before accepting the challenge. "Then arm yourself. I'll wait. Be better than having one of your people shoot me in the back."

"You will pay for this insult," Santiago spat.

"Why wait? But don't count on Pacheco there to back you up. I assure you, the man behind me is quite capable of shooting him first."

"I am sorry to hear these stories," Marisol said, hoping to diffuse the situation. "I would hope they are only coincidence."

"I wish they were too," MacLeod said, his hand resting on the Bates of London Flintlock pistol in his belt. "But then somebody put a torch to our hide warehouse in Santa Barbara. We lost everything."

"Madre de Dios, how will you survive?" Marisol muttered.

MacLeod's eyes never left Santiago. He wondered how the man would react when he informed them that they weren't leaving. "We'll manage. We've got our orchards and plenty of beef. We've enough corn and beans."

"Bah," Santiago muttered. "You should have accepted my offer to purchase Colinas de Oro and its animals."

MacLeod was the one to laugh this time. "As I understand it, the land would revert to the Government of Alta California."

"Enough of your nonsense. Turn your horse around and leave. Do not return to Rancho Santiago, ever." Without another word, Santiago turned and waved Pacheco away.

Marisol walked over and placed a gentle hand on MacLeod's leg. "It is strange that we meet again, although I now believe this was in his plan all along. Tell Francesca I will come and see her soon."

Her hand resting on his leg sent tremors racing throughout his body. He desperately wanted to reach down and kiss her beautiful lips. Though for their sake, he hoped she would now return to Monterey.

"I will tell her," MacLeod said. "She will welcome your visit; but come alone."

"Keep your eyes on that skunk, Jacob. He'd as soon shoot you in the back," MacLeod said, loud enough for everyone could hear.

"I don't believe he feels the time is now, but you're safe to turn and ride away," Jacob said.

MacLeod nodded before spinning the stallion around and digging his heels into its side. Jacob had positioned himself a dozen yards beyond. He followed MacLeod up the gentle rise back toward Colinas de Oro.

MONTEREY

MacLeod knew he couldn't put off the trip to Monterey much longer. It had been five days since Rodriquez's visit and his demand to present their copy of the *diseño* and the written boundaries of Colinas de Oro.

The problem was that they couldn't find their copy and hadn't seen it for years. Fact is, there were few places in a two-room adobe to hide it.

"What will you tell our Governor?" Francesca asked, the concern etched across her features.

"I'm just wondering why he wants to see ours. The original is with whomever keeps these things." MacLeod was happy to see Francesca propped up in a chair he had fashioned. She said there was little pain in her back now, though he doubted greatly that she told the truth.

Francesca pushed a lock of hair aside and sighed. "Did Doña Montero say when she might visit?" she asked, changing the subject. "It would be wonderful to see her again, though I am sorry she has had to do this thing and move in with this man."

MacLeod had relayed little of the encounter with Santiago, swearing Jacob to secrecy. "I am unsure," he replied. "But I will need to go and answer the Governor, though I dislike leaving you while you are so weak."

"No." Francesca said, laying her hand on his arm. "It is something you must do before they come again."

Before he left he had instructed Concannon and Jacob to have the Indian gardeners plant a second crop of vegetables while other workers continued digging the large hole for the root cellar.

Riding north on El Camino Real, a packhorse on a lead rope, MacLeod had packed enough supplies for a five-day trip in case of delay. As it turned out, the trip gave MacLeod plenty of time to worry over the problems concerning the ranch, as well as the sudden reappearance of Marisol Montero. MacLeod had heard that she was living in Monterey after her husband died, but he never expected to see her at Rancho Santiago, so close to his own home.

He had hoped that Vicente Montero had left her enough to live off of, but apparently that had not been the case and she had sadly been forced into living with Santiago.

"Damn it all," MacLeod muttered to himself. *Why did she show up now?* He couldn't keep his mind from straying back to the time he had held her in his arms so long ago.

Nothing had happened between them, but they both came to the same conclusion—the less they saw of each other, the better.

On the second night of his travels, MacLeod opted to camp near the quickly decaying adobe mission of San Luis Obispo de Tolsa. The following night he found himself near San Miguel Arcangel and decided to camp there for the night. In truth, he had wanted to take some time to again view the magnificent painting behind the altar.

San Miguel had been the last mission to be secularized, only a couple of years prior. The painting, which hung behind the altar, still retained its true colors, despite the outside walls already showing decay. Once the Indians had heard what secularization meant they no longer bothered fearing the priests and stopped helping maintain the mission buildings.

Once past Nuestra Senora de la Soledad, where ten years before he had learned the prodigal priest had passed with the baby Diego, he took the turn off to San Carlos Borromeo de Carmelo and Monterey.

The one they called the Carmel Mission had suffered severe neglect, as had all the others. His memories of this place included rescuing Francesca from imprisonment for shooting Pacheco. Though, in truth, it was the young Indian girl, Juana, who had actually pulled the trigger.

MacLeod swore softly at the memory and silently wishing the girl had been more accurate.

When MacLeod finally arrived in Monterey, the cool ocean breeze helping to dissipate the heat of the day, he immediately took notice of the new buildings going up in a number of locations.

He found the Governor at his desk when he entered the office.

Removing his hat upon entering, MacLeod greeted, "Your Excellency, I believe you sent for me. My name is William MacLeod."

The Governor looked up before pushing the paper he was working on aside. "I know nothing of this," he stated in confusion.

"You sent Corporal Rodriquez down to Colinas de Oro. He wanted our copy of the *diseño* ," MacLeod clarified.

"Yes, yes, now I remember. Captain Rodriguez," the Governor said laughing. "He practically begged me to send him when he heard of the assignment."

"I'll bet he did," MacLeod said.

This new man, sent up from Mexico to govern California, had not been at the job long enough for the merchants of Monterey to get a feel for his politics. Recently, a new movement had begun to have native Californios placed in charge. What that meant for this man's position he could not be sure.

MacLeod watched the short, stocky figure behind the desk shuffle through a stack of papers before he found what he wanted.

"Yes, here it is. It is desired you present the papers of your land grant so that it can be prepared with this original. You will need to present this to Señor—whatever his name is. He is in that building over there," the Governor said, pointing across the plaza.

Thanking the governor for his time, MacLeod stooped down and walked out through the low doorway he'd just come in. *Why must these people built houses with such low door openings,* he wondered as he made his way across the plaza and entered the office the governor had indictated. Though unlike the governor's office, MacLeod hit his head on the doorway, cursing his own stupidity.

Inside, a man sat behind the narrow counter, his ill-fitting vest stained with bits of food and wine. Clasping his hands together at chest level, the man raised his eyebrows. In a way, the man reminded MacLeod of a scarecrow,

MacLeod quickly informed the man that he wished to see the original copy of the map of Colinas de Oro, which brought about a questioning look from the man's face.

"No, Señor, it is not here. It was sent for many days ago and has yet to be returned."

"Who sent for it?" MacLeod asked in confusion.

The man could only shrug. "I think maybe it was our Excellency, the Governor, who sent his man to ask for it."

MacLeod knew it would get him nowhere to brow beat this old man so he headed back across the plaza again, anger welling up inside of him at this wild goose chase the governor had sent him on.

A guard, who now stood in front of the door, tried to prevent MacLeod from entering. Having lost control of what little patience remained, MacLeod shoved him aside and threw the door open. To his surprise, the governor showed his own anger as MacLeod leaned over the man's desk.

With both hands on the desk MacLeod thrust his head forward. "Damn you, you already knew it was not there. You sent someone down for our copy and you have nothing to compare it with. That is, unless you're sitting on the original."

The governor, angered, pushed his chair back and stood, shouting for the guard.

The man MacLeod had pushed aside rushed in and came to a halt beside MacLeod. He rammed the butt of an old musket on the floor and saluted.

The governor once again took a seat and pulled his chair back up to the desk. "Now, perhaps we can discuss this without you threatening me any further."

MacLeod let the rage that was building up inside of him gradually down before speaking. "I'm sorry to barge in on you, Your Excellency, but I have a feeling this sudden request for our *diseño* has been requested by someone and has nothing to do with you."

The governor nodded. "Very well. Now if you would show me the copy of yours we can settle this matter," the governor said, holding out his hand.

"Afraid ours is missing also."

At this, the Governor dismissed the guard.

"May I ask again why everyone's so interested in our land all of a sudden?"

"Yes. Doñ Santiago, owner of this grant next to yours, was questioning the finding of those who were sent to survey his land. These men could not complete their duty because they needed the information on the land grated to your wife by the acting governor at that time."

"So what did they decide?" MacLeod asked. He was having a problem with the fact that was something that could have been solved very easily by checking the original Colinas de Oro map, which was kept here in Monterey.

"Yes, I sent for this map that was supposedly in our files. However, it was not so. Now you are telling me yours has also disappeared."

MacLeod studied the man's face for any sign of dishonesty. "Ours would have only been a copy. It is the responsibility of the government to keep the original."

"Ah, yes, so it is. But you must understand, back in the time you say the Colinas de Oro land was granted it was one of the few issued in many years. And this acting Governor could be said to be lacking in knowledge of the need for safekeeping such documents."

A sudden gust of wind brought with it the smell of the sea and sound of gulls hunting for a meal as MacLeod pondered what to say next. "So what happens if you can't locate this map?" MacLeod asked.

The governor beat a tattoo on the desktop with his fingers. Turning his attention to a stack of papers on his desk, he began shuffling them about. Without looking up, he replied, "Then what am I to believe? Perhaps you are mistaken and it never actually existed. Perhaps this acting governor, whatever his name was, said he was going to grant this land, but never filed the appropriate paperwork."

MacLeod stood silent. *What would this mean if it were true? What if the map he had helped draw was never officially filed?* Land surveys didn't come until much later as more grants were issued to some of the wealthier Californios.

"Then how do we go about reclaiming Colinas de Oro?" MacLeod questioned. "We have upwards of twenty or so people and three to four thousand head of cattle. What's the process?"

"Well, if there is nothing to show you were given this land it still belongs to California. You could apply to me for this, but I am afraid someone else has already done so in the event the land was free of legal binding."

MacLeod didn't even need to ask who was lining up to claim it. Now he was positive this governor was lining his own pockets. "And who might that be? Surely it would have come up long before this?"

"I am new here in Alta California. They appointed me the governor because I am Mexican and not Spanish. Shortly after I arrived, Doñ Santiago came to me to ask about this land you claim is yours. He believes the water you are using belongs to him."

MacLeod knew they had once had a copy of the *diseño*, but what did it matter now that the original was lost? He fought to keep his temper in check. "Your man across the plaza said you sent for it and that he produced it. Appears to me it's somewhere. Not like you saying it never existed. But you say it's lost?"

"Yes, what he sent me was an old map of the lands around Santa Inés Mission. Someone had placed it in the file and named it Colinas de Oro."

MacLeod remained in front of the Governor's desk pondering what to do next. Someone had bought the man off, that much was clear. "How much did Santiago pay you, Governor? How much was stealing our land worth?" MacLeod muttered.

The man's face burned red as he leapt to his feet and called for the guard once again while shaking his fist at MacLeod.

"Never mind, Governor, I'll see my own way out." Without another word, MacLeod stormed out of the office and made his way to the water's edge to think.

Santiago had once again attacked them, but this time it might very well prove to be the last. He wondered how long they had before the order to leave the land was granted? Or had the order already been given? Could Santiago have known their copy of the map was missing? He didn't know the answer to that question, but he fully intended to find out.

RANCHO SANTIAGO

"Yes, go over there if you wish," Santiago said through gritted teeth. "But you will take Pacheco along for protection." He laughed. "Yes, you will certainly be received with much favor with him at your side."

Marisol Montero bristled. "I will go as I wish and not with that man at my side. You are not an uninformed man and you know the history between this man, Pacheco, and Francesca MacLeod. It is too bad she did not kill him."

"You ask to go and visit this woman? Is it not he you wish to see again? I am sure he had you because it is known your husband could not."

Marisol picked a new glass vase off the serving table and threw it at him.

Santiago dodged as the vase shattered and fell to the floor.

"No man has had me since I married the good man that was Doñ Vicente Montero. And you will not be the one to change that. Send for your wife, show her the place you built for me." Brushing past him, Marisol retrieved the wide brimmed hat from her Indian servant. The hat would serve to shield her face from the burning rays of the sun. In her other hand, the small bag she carried held her gloves. She had also slipped something else beneath her dress, where it lay within her breasts.

As she stepped into the carriage that could take her to Colinas de Oro, Santiago stepped outside and shouted after her. "Give my regards to the woman and their little half-breed bastards."

Marisol was not delusional. She knew she would need to find a way to Santa Barbara, and soon. But she would need help in order to do so.

When Marisol arrived a short while later there were three people standing outside the adobe hacienda while others walked between the buildings carrying baskets. She brushed the perspiration from her forehead, silently wishing she had bathed before she came. Then again, there was so little water brought to the house unless it was for cooking.

A short, redheaded man walked up to the carriage and held out his hand. "Doña Montero, I am Sean Concannon. I believe we met once in more dire circumstances."

Marisol smiled. "Of course. You sat on the beach that day when we came off the ship. You also stood beside Guillermo in front of the Frenchman." She allowed him to help her from the carriage where a young woman stood waiting to greet her.

"Doña Montero, this is Sarah Morgenthau," Concannon introduced. "She will take you inside to see Francesca."

Marisol looked around the overcrowded adobe. Compared to her own home in Monterey, or Santiago's new hacienda, this home was less than adequate for the family living here. But to her surprise, there were nothing but smiles to greet her.

She found Francesca propped up with pillows on her bed. Her hair looked freshly brushed, but lacking the sheen she remembered. Her face was pale, and there appeared to be pain hidden behind the smile that greeted Marisol.

"You have come!" Francesca said excitedly. "William said you wished to visit."

Marisol noted the weakness in her voice. "As soon as I heard of your accident I could not stay away." Marisol watched as something she could not explain reflected in Francesca's eyes. *Was it an accident?* Marisol wondered.

Using all the strength she could muster, Francesca attempted to push herself up from the pillows, nearly toppling from the bed in the process. "I am sorry William is not here to greet you. He has been summoned to Monterey by our governor."

"It was you I wished to see." Marisol smiled. "It is a most inconvenient time to go off and leave you, is it not?"

The Indian girl at the side of the bed dipped a cloth in a basin of water and began wiping Francesca's forehead.

"Thank you, Juana. Now would you please go and find Diego and Catalina for me?"

"You say he was summoned by our Governor?" Marisol asked.

"Yes. They sent down this arrogant little man to request we deliver our *diseño* into his hands. According to him, he was not told why."

From the corner of her eyes Marisol noticed Francesca reach under the thin blanket and move her legs, the effort bringing a look of pain to her eyes.

"Is it your legs that were injured when you fell?" Marisol asked, changing the subject.

A thin laughed escaped from Francesca bringing forth another spasm of pain. "He did not tell you?" Francesca asked. "William did not tell you about my injury?"

The only thing Marisol could remember during their brief conversation was the fear that the two men were about to kill each other. "No, only that your horse was to blame."

"Yes, well, he still has hope, despite the doctor from the ship saying otherwise. This doctor said my back was broken. I am to be carried everywhere. He said I would need to learn how to live without my legs." Francesca wiped a tear from her eye.

"Madre de Dios, I was not told this." Marisol's thoughts went to the item she carried in her bosom. *Would it not be better for this poor woman to go and live in Santa Barbara and let Santiago have his way?*

A few short moments later young voices could be heard entering the adobe, engaged in an apparently ongoing argument. A young girl, almost a woman, burst through the bedroom door and walked to the bedside where her mother lay. In truth, Marisol had never seen a more beautiful girl. Marisol watched as the young girl turned, arms folded, and glared at the door. One could only assume she awaited her brother's arrival.

Marisol heard the young boy before she saw him. With laughter still in his voice Diego entered and swept his sombrero off of his head. Marisol gasped. He was the exact image of MacLeod, but with jet-black hair.

"Diego, do you remember Doña Montero?" Francesca asked, motioning to her. "She once looked after you for a short time."

Diego turned, his blue eyes flashing as he shook his head.

Marisol smiled and held out her hands to him. "Come, let me look at you. You are the image of your father."

Diego's dark features turned even darker as he shifted from one foot to the other while she held his hands. Behind him, Catalina smirked. When Francesca finally introduced young Catalina, she gave a poor imitation of a curtsy.

Dismissing the children with a wave of her hand, Francesca sank back into the pillows.

"I should go and let you rest," Marisol said.

Francesca held up her hand. "No, please stay. I have something to say."

Marisol nodded as she moved the bench closer to the bed and took a seat.

It was then that a thin man wearing a pair of glasses entered the room. Taking in his appearance, Marisol recognized him as the man holding the gun on Pacheco

"This is Jacob," Francesca introduced. "He is Sarah's husband. He is teaching the children. We are so happy they are here," she explained, smiling kindly at the man.

Marisol tilted her head and studied the meek looking man. It was odd. He had not appeared at all nervous when he protected Guillermo. "You are an American?"

"No, ma'am. Sarah and I come from England. I'm afraid we were banished from the Sandwich Island and were rescued by this fine family."

"You received an education in your country?" Marisol asked, a thought coming to mind for the future.

"I did, ma'am. At one time I thought to study medicine, however, the idea of helping the young minds learn about the world sent me off in another direction. Instead, I became a teacher."

Turning to Sarah, who was still situated beside Francesca, Jacob leaned down to whisper something in her ear before they both exited.

Francesca beckoned Marisol to come closer. "There is something you should know, but you cannot say this to anyone. If William found out terrible things might happen. Do you promise?"

Marisol nodded wondering what secret this woman could have to pass on, and why?

Francesca took Marisol's hand in hers and took a deep breath, as if to stay her nerves. "You have a man that works for Señor Santiago—his name is Pacheco. Do you know of this man?"

Marisol nodded slowly. "Yes, he was there when your husband came to warn Santiago. Why do you ask?"

"He is an evil man. It was I who took out his eye and caused him to wear that patch."

"I remember a time when it was said a woman was brought to Monterey for attempting to kill a soldier. Was that you they speak of?" Marisol asked in shock.

"Yes," Francesca stated firmly, the effort appearing to tire her. The Indian girl, still at her side, wiped her forehand once again. "You must stay away from him," Francesca choked out.

Marisol managed a weak smile. "He has not spoken to me. thought they are always together."

"It is true I was thrown from my horse. I have told no one of what I am about to speak." Francesca took a deep breath, remaining silent for a beat. "It was this man, Pacheco, along with three others who caused it."

"I cannot believe this," Marisol gasped. "You are sure?"

Francesca nodded. Marisol had wondered why Santiago kept Pacheco. He did little work around the Rancho. She knew there had to be another explanation.

"You have asked me to mention this to no one—I assume you have not told Guillermo?"

"No. He would try to kill him. But Santiago is never alone. The others with Pacheco that day all carried these long whips. But it was this man, Pacheco, who fired his pistol and struck my horse. That was what caused my horse to throw me off."

Marisol suddenly remembered something else MacLeod had said in their brief conversation. "Your husband mentioned something about a boy being killed?"

Francesca shook her head and asked the Indian girl to go and prepare chocolate. Francesca waited until the girl had left the room before speaking. "Yes, but that is something that is not spoken of. William knows the boy was dragged along the ground until he hit his head on a rock. There were many horse tracks which led back to Rancho Santiago land."

Now Marisol began to understand the need for secrecy. She knew MacLeod and she knew his refusal to back down. She had seen him challenge the Frenchman, Dupré, a known duelist who had challenged many to face his pistol.

Francesca continued. "You see now why he cannot know about Pacheco's involvement. He would not ask Jacob or Sean to risk their lives; he would do it himself. And there are too many of them."

"But if he knew of this," Francesca continued. "He would go alone. Our land is in danger of being taken from us," Francesca admitted. "I can no longer walk or look after the duties of a mother and wife. I cannot take the chance of losing him too."

"Would it not be better for you to live in another place?" Marisol asked, squeezing Francesca's hand.

"I cannot bear the thought."

"I have heard of the things that have happened. I have lived in the house that he built and have heard of the threats he has given to others. I believe now he is capable of all you blame him for. Why do you want to remain here?"

Francesca looked down at her hands. For a time she said nothing. Marisol thought she might be too exhausted to continue this emotional discussion, but before she could say anything, Francesca spoke.

"Because it is all we have. This land was given to me, yet my husband can do with it whatever he wants, except sell it. It cannot be sold. Santiago knows this. If we were to leave it would return to the state."

"If he made an offer to buy your land, he could not, he could purchase your cattle only." Marisol explained. The more she thought about it, the more she could see why Santiago wanted to drive them off the land. He had made arrangements with the new governor and the land would be taken and added to Rancho Santiago.

"But how can you survive? As I understand it, all of your hides and tallow were destroyed in a fire."

A bitter smile creased Francesca's face. "We have enough to make it until next year. After that God will decide if he thinks we deserve to remain. William has gone to see the Governor to find out what it is he wants and why he would want to see or *diseño*."

MONTEREY

MacLeod walked back to where he had left the horses, his thoughts tumbling around inside his head, finding no place to come to rest. Without realizing what he was doing, he checked the sky, looking for the dark clouds that might bring rain. As it had been for almost two years now, the sky promised only more sunshine and hot days ahead. A humorless chuckle that only he heard brought him back to reality.

What does it matter now if it does not rain? It would be someone else's problem, he thought to himself.

Atop the hill, above the town of Monterey, the Presidio's guns protected the bay, probably manned with few who had ever loaded them or fired off their charges.

MacLeod untied his horse and prepared to mount. To this point, he saw no reason to postpone the long ride back to Colinas de Oro.

Suddenly, a heavy boom sounded from out in the harbor, giving him pause. Another cannon from a ship approaching the harbor followed. There would be a series of cannon shots to follow, as well as the Presidio's answer—providing they had enough powder.

From where he stood, MacLeod couldn't make out the flag of the country it represented. Though it certainly wasn't a ship in the hide and tallow trade, not with the cannon it apparently carried.

All around the street that housed government offices, and trading stores bustled with activity. The current drought had not appeared to interfere with business, but he assumed next year would probably be different if the number of hides available for trade decreased.

MacLeod climbed into the saddle and retrieved the packhorse's lead rope. He hadn't reached the middle of town when he spotted a familiar figure approaching.

William Hartnell, dressed in a frock coat and heavy shoes, had come out to California a few years before. He and his partner, Hugh McCulloch, worked for John Begg & Co. Later, they formed their own company to begin trading in this brand new business of hides and tallow. The business had failed, leaving Hartnell eighteen thousand dollars in debt.

MacLeod had met Hartnell shortly after he had arrived in California, with a six-month-old child, whose mother had perished in an Indian attack along the Colorado River. When MacLeod's baby son, Diego, was kidnapped by a mission priest, Hartnell had vouched for MacLeod, allowing him to remain in the newly independent Mexican state of Alto California. Given a job by Hartnell, MacLeod was required to travel up and down the state gathering promises of trade from the priests in charge of the chain of missions from San Diego to Yorba Buena. At the same time, it allowed MacLeod to search for his son. For that, MacLeod felt he would forever be in Hartnell's debt.

"Well, well, now, if it isn't William MacLeod," Hartnell said. MacLeod stepped down from the saddle, holding out his hand to the Englishman. "And how is that lovely wife of yours?" Hartnell asked.

MacLeod felt no need to hold back the information. "I'm afraid she is not well," he said before relaying the information about her fall.

"I am sorry to hear that. She has had more misfortune in her young life than most have in a lifetime."

"I'll be certain to tell her of your concern."

"And what brings you so far from home?" Hartnell questioned.

MacLeod hesitated a moment before answering. "What do you know about our current governor?"

"Well now, he appears competent. Not like so many appointed before him. In what way are you asking exactly?"

After MacLeod finished telling Hartnell about the lost *diseño* and the governor's implication that there may never have been one filed properly, Hartnell drew him aside to speak. "It is possible that he has been given false information and acted upon it. It is said he loves this new position he has and is often surrounded by those who cater to his love of authority."

"So you believe money night have had a hand in it?"

The two men walked for a while, both remaining silent. Seeing two men approaching, Hartnell waited until they had passed before answering. "That I don't know. It is too early since his appointment to tell. However, he does appear easily susceptible to flattery," Hartnell laughed. "And knowing your normal approach, I would guarantee your words to him were lacking in flattery."

MacLeod stopped, unsure if he should ask his next question. "Is it possible that this man Santiago, who has the land next to our, could persuade him to turn over a land map to him?"

"I don't believe so. But there are others working in the government offices here who might."

"Damn, I hadn't thought of that. These people aren't paid much. And I'm sure Santiago has the money. Gives me something to think about," MacLeod said.

Hartnell paused a moment, then said, "Listen, there's no reason you should return today. There is a man I'd like you to meet, an American fellow from your part of the country. His name is Larkin. Thomas Larkin. Came out here to meet up with his half-brother. You probably know the man—John Cooper?"

MacLeod nodded. While he knew of Cooper, he had never met the man. Word had it that Cooper sold his ship to a former governor, and between the two of them they damn near put the other boats trading in hides and tallow out of business. Now Larkin, he was another matter altogether. Seems he got a woman named Rachel Holmes with child while on the boat coming out to California. Holmes's husband was at sea and never made it back to California. He died, leaving Larkin and Rachel to wed. MacLeod remembered this because they had been married in Santa Barbara and the wedding was attended by many.

MacLeod accepted Hartnell's offer to come for dinner. It would be good to talk with someone from back home.

Hartnell filled MacLeod in on what he had been doing since they had last seen one another. He had joined the church and become a Mexican citizen. He also married the sixteen-year-old daughter of Doñ Jose de la Guerra y Noriega. After the failure of his business, Hartnell opened the Colegio de San Jose school.

At the mention of the school MacLeod thought about the need for Diego to further his education and decided to mention this to Hartnell.

"Unfortunately, I have had to close the school. My two preachers were Jesuit priests."

"Why is it you must close?" MacLeod asked.

"Well now, the government in Mexico has forced all Spaniards out of California. My teachers were both Spaniards."

"I had heard something about that," MacLeod said.

"Well, here we are," Hartnell said. "I do hope you two get along."

"Is there a reason we shouldn't?" MacLeod asked.

Hartnell paused at the door. "No, no, but Thomas is somewhat taken with making money. An American quality I suppose. Although the Lord knows I've tried to do the same with little success."

When they entered they found Larkin sitting in the front room of Hartnell's house reading a newspaper.

"Thomas, I have a countryman of yours here. Meet William MacLeod. William, this is Thomas Larkin."

Larkin rose and offered his hand. "And whereabouts would you be from?"

"Walpole, Massachusetts," MacLeod replied.

"Walpole? By God, that's a bit south of Boston. Charleston myself."

MacLeod nodded. "Sure is. Right across the Charles River."

"So what brings you out to California? What ship did you come out of Boston on? A whaler or one these hide traders?" Larkin inquired.

MacLeod shook his head. Hartnell had mentioned the man wasn't in the best of health. Though seeing him helped to put things into perspective. Larkin was at least a head shorter than MacLeod, quite thin, and when he spoke he held his hand up behind his ear. Obviously he was hard of hearing.

"Came by way of New Mexico and across the desert," MacLeod explained.

"Yes, I've heard of others that have taken that frightful journey. Let me see now," Larkin said. "I believe that fellow Jedidiah Smith was the first. And then there was Pattie and a fellow named Walker, I believe. So you followed them?"

MacLeod wasn't in the mood to get into a revising of history so he simply said, "Came out just like them."

"Indeed now. Were the Indians pacified by then?"

"Not quite," MacLeod said. To go any further in his explanation would bring Maria Cordero, Diego's mother, into the conversation and the story of her death. That was a story he didn't wish to relive.

Larkin didn't press the issue any further and retreated to his chair, easing his slender body down into the cushions.

Hartnell spoke up. "I've been meaning to have that chair repaired for some time. You know, a resourceful fellow could do a good business here building solid furniture. Lord knows the Californians won't"

"Why is that?" Larkin asked.

"Oh, their culture primarily. A hundred years or so of small rancheros, cattle being new as far as a source of income. The young men are completely satisfied with their horses, flashy outfits, and gambling. There's little enterprise here."

Larkin turned to MacLeod. "Is this your opinion also?"

"I've seen what Thomas here speaks about. Pretty much the same thing I saw in New Mexico. But the people are happy with this way of life. And in truth, it grows on you. My own son would rather spend all his time on his horse than do anything else."

"That's interesting," Larkin said. "And these domesticated Indians. Can they be civilized?"

"Civilized? I believe you would need to explain your version of civilized. I've got about two dozen mission Indians working for me."

"I see, and how are they to control?" Larkin asked in curiosity.

MacLeod sat on low stool in front of the fireplace and thought about his response for a moment. "I'll admit, they come and go at times. It's their nature. But in the end, they come back. Where else can they go? The *Tulernos* from the villages along the San Joaquin River, they're all gone, but some still go back. I suppose they are hoping."

"Why is that?"

"White man's disease. The Indians catch them and can't fight them."

Larkin looked puzzled. "Where did these Indians go to mingle with white men, I don't quite understand?"

"Probably fur trappers from the Hudson's Bay Company up north of us brought it to them. I've seen whole villages wiped out."

"You say these Indians you have working for you are useful then?"

MacLeod laughed. "Very. Many have been well trained at the missions. You should visit a few of these old mission buildings while you still can."

Hartnell interjected. "Yes. When Governor Figueroa finally signed the secularization bill I don't believe he realized the uproar that would follow."

"How so," Larkin asked.

"You have to understand, the missions were built to help populate California and civilize the Indians. Supposedly, it was to take sixty years or so. After that, the land and cattle were to be distributed equally to the Indians. Now this secularization process is in its infancy, but already there are signs that it won't work. That is, it won't work as far as the Indians are concerned. With the explosion of the hide and tallow trade, the California people want the land and cattle for themselves. It's easy to convince an Indian to sell his portion of the land."

MacLeod knew a little bit about this. "The governor appoints an administrator to oversee this. Unfortunately, no one is overseeing the administrators. Or so it seems."

Larkin turned to MacLeod. "What brought you out to California?"

"Had no real intention of coming here at all. Has your family lived in Charlestown always?" MacLeod asked in hopes of changing the subject.

"They have. In fact, my grandfather supplied the horse for Paul Revere."

"Mr. Larkin here is building a house in town," Hartnell explained. "It will have two stories and has everyone talking about it."

MacLeod thought about the small adobe they all lived in and wondered if he would ever be able to build a proper house for Francesca.

"I understand you have a substantial land grant in the south? I assume you joined their church and became a citizen."

Just then, Hartnell's wife came in to announce that their meal would be ready soon and asked if Doñ MacLeod be staying.

"For myself, I doubt I'll seek citizenship," Larkin continued as if he hadn't heard. "Can't bring myself to join their church."

MacLeod could see this statement didn't sit well with Hartnell, so MacLeod sought to change the subject. "Our land grant was given to my wife. She is the legal owner of Colinas de Oro. There is something I would like to ask. What do you know of this fellow, Benton? He's a U.S. Senator I believe."

"You would be talking about Thomas Hart Benton, Senator from Missouri?"

"That's the fellow," MacLeod nodded in agreement.

"Well, let's see, he's a Jacksonian Democrat. They call him Old Bullion. Hates paper money and would like to see all commerce done with gold coin."

"What's his interest in California, if any?" MacLeod questioned.

"Oh, he's all for western expansion. In the early days he thought the U.S. should expand all the way to the Rocky Mountains. But now he's saying the Pacific."

Now MacLeod could understand why the Senator was asking all the questions about California. "Is President Jackson of the same mind?"

Larkin responded. "Now, that I don't know. He has said he might run again, but there's a growing group that oppose him. It's the anti-masonic party. Jackson is apparently a Freemason."

"My father was one, a Freemason. Never asked me to join though," Hartnell said.

MacLeod had a little understanding of such things. His father had once said Freemasons never asked someone to join the fraternity. The person had to ask.

"What business will you be taking up here in California?" MacLeod asked, changing the subject.

"Timber for one thing. I see a need for it. And with commerce growing so rapidly with the trade ships scouring the coast and bringing goods, these people never dreamed of having debt collected."

Hartnell's wife called them to dinner. Larkin rose and handed MacLeod the newspaper. "News from Boston. You might be interested in it."

U pon hearing the news that debt collection was one of Larkin's new employment interests, MacLeod went to bed in Hartnell's spare room. Wondering how long before some of his debtors would prevail of Larkin's services?

Not focusing on it too long, MacLeod put the thought aside. He knew that if they lost the ranch they had more than enough cattle to wipe the slate clean.

Before going to sleep MacLeod asked Hartnell for paper, a quill pen, and ink. He sat for a while mentally composing the words he would use in a letter to his mother. Hartnell had promised to hand it over to the first ship returning to Boston.

MacLeod figured his mother didn't need to know the situation they'd recently found themselves in. Instead, he told her she had three grandchildren and another by his marriage to Francesca. He included stories of the kids and how big they all had grown. At the end of the letter he informed her that he would write again soon and mentioned the possibility of her coming to California, dependent upon her health.

With the writing of the letter his thoughts turned to Doñ Cordero. He knew he had to write him. He also knew Diego deserved to be told about his grandparents in New Mexico. He hoped it wasn't too late.

With sleep hard to come by, MacLeod decided to ride out of Monterey before dawn, grateful for the wealth of stars to help guide him. His best guess was that he had three days to find a way to tell Francesca of his findings. He knew her feelings about Colinas de Oro. After all, she was one of the first women to be granted land. At the time it had been a way for the acting governor to repay MacLeod for rescuing a member of his family. MacLeod, not being a citizen of Mexico, could not buy or be given land, so Francesca was the next logical solution in MacLeod's mind.

The mission, San Antonio de Padua, had not been secularized yet. When MacLeod arrived he shared a modest meal with the two priests and picked up two fresh horses. People traveling El Camino Real seldom paid for fresh horses. They were too numerous to bother.

He rode for a time alongside the Rio Salinas, normally finding spots where the river rose to the surface for a time before sinking back down into the sand and flowing underground. Only this time, he rode for miles without finding a spot to drink or water the horses.

A punishing sun beat down upon him relentlessly, the temperature rising quickly with each passing hour.

MacLeod rode as hard as he dared without riding the horses into the ground. By the beginning of the third day MacLeod knew it was high time to exchange the horses once again.

He was almost at the rancho when someone recognized him and ran to the house to announce his return.

"Doñ MacLeod, it is good to have you return," Gomez shouted. MacLeod dismounted and handed the reins to the man's eldest son

"How is she?" were his first words to Sarah.

"She is good, William. Very anxious for your return."

MacLeod removed his sombrero and ducked under the low doorway.

Francesca sat up in bed with the aid of pillows and held her arms out to him. "You are back. I could not believe it when they told me you were here so soon."

MacLeod bent down and kissed her, holding her in his arms gently.

How could he tell her what he had learned? he thought in sadness. The truth he held onto was eating away at him. Where will all these people go who depended upon him?

"Tell me, was our governor happy with our story? Will he not send those men back again?"

Was now the time to tell her or should he wait? he asked himself. *Surely the governor wouldn't send people down to demand they leave for some time. Possibly even weeks. And by then Francesca would have regained her strength. She was still so pale.*

MacLeod came to a decision. Fact was, the people who worked and lived at Colinas de Oro would need time to make arrangements. They would need to find a place to live.

He took her hand in his. "I saw this new governor we have. He said that when he was asked to review the boundaries of Colinas de Oro, he called for the original copy to be sent to his office. The man who handles such things sent him one that was recorded as ours."

Francesca's eyes brightened. "Then everything will be as it should be. I am so happy now," she said.

"No, Francesca, it's not okay. It was not for your land. They cannot find the one for Colinas de Oro."

MacLeod could see the confusion in her face.

"What does this mean?" she asked, her voice not much more than a whisper.

He couldn't think of a way to make the answer any easier, so he just told her the hard truth. "When I spoke to the governor he questioned if you were ever really given the land at all. He said that without the *diseño* there was no proof."

"And you believed him when he said this?"

"Santiago is the one who started all of this. He wants this land and is willing to do anything to get it."

Francesca closed her eyes and leaned back into the pillows that helped to support her broken body. "Are you thinking Señor Santiago has somehow convinced our governor of this? He is so new there in Monterey."

"There's no other explanation. Santiago and he must be in this together."

"I wonder if there is another explanation," she muttered. "You said whoever was asked by the governor sent the wrong *diseño* to him. Is it possible that this is in fact the person who Señor Santiago went to see when he went to Monterey?"

MacLeod was prepared to say that was not possible, but then he remembered the clerk who he'd spoken to about the Colinas de Oro's original boundary map. He hadn't spent much time looking for it. In fact, he didn't look for it all. "I was so sure the governor was to blame, but then, William Hartnell said much the same as you have."

"What will we do, William?"

"Not certain there's anything we can do. We've no way of proving you have the land grant legally," MacLeod stated. Shaking his head, MacLeod let out a calming breath. "Let's change the subject. How are you feeling?"

Francesca's grim look told him more than words could ever say. "They take such good care of me, but I am such a burden to everyone. I lie here at night and cry myself to sleep. Our two little ones cannot understand why I am here in bed all the time."

MacLeod felt helpless. What could he say to make her see that her life meant everything in the world to him?

Francesca took his hand again before speaking. "I had a visit while you were away. Doña Montero came to see me. She was sorry you were not here."

The last thing MacLeod needed right now was the immediate presence of Marisol Montero. Seeing her only a short time before had brought back memories better left buried. "She said she wanted to visit you. I'm glad she did."

"She had me call in Diego," she said with a chuckle. "Catalina came also." Francesca shook her head. "That child does not like to be left out of anything."

"Did Diego remember her?" MacLeod inquired.

"I don't know. I believe I saw a tear in her eye when she saw him. Why does she not remarry and have children of her own?"

MacLeod shrugged. "Not sure. Though she doesn't appear happy with the decision to come and live with Santiago. Did she say anything about that?"

Francesca took the cup of water Juana offered her. "There were other things she said, but I was so tired. I believe I fell asleep before she left."

MacLeod stood. She looked tired and she had enough to think about now. As he turned to leave Francesca held up her hand to stop him.

"You should rest," he said with a smile. "We will talk later."

"No, there was something else I had forgotten."

"Rest now. You can tell me later."

"No, no. She said it was important—that you would know how to use it."

"What was it?" MacLeod asked in confusion. He couldn't think anything Marisol might have given Francesca that would be useful. Unless it was something about Santiago.

Francesca called for Sarah. While she waited, she closed her eyes. MacLeod was about to leave when Sarah appeared in the small bedroom. He was surprised when Francesca spoke. "Doña Montero had something for me. Do you know where it is?"

"Yes, you asked me to put it away before you fell asleep again," Sarah said.

"Fetch it for me, Sarah, and give it to William."

Sarah returned a moment later and handed the piece of paper to MacLeod.

"Read it to me, William. Is it important?" Francesca pleaded, her eyes still closed.

Carefully unfolding the paper MacLeod's eyes scanned its contents before he whispered, "My God, it can't be."

RANCHO COLINAS DE ORO

"What is it?" Francesca demanded, her eyes now wide open.

MacLeod didn't answer as he continued to study the document.

"William, tell me. What is it?"

Once he was sure of its validity, he replied, "It's the *diseño* for Colinas de Oro. The original *diseño*."

"Are you sure?" Francesca asked, trying her best to sit up. Finally Sarah helped her.

MacLeod nodded. "It's the one that's supposed to be in Monterey. It's even got acting Governor Arguellos's signature on it."

"I don't understand. How did she get it?" Francesca appeared to be just as puzzled as MacLeod.

"Not sure. Unless it was sent to Santiago and somehow she found it."

Francesca clasped her hands together and in a hopeful tone asked, "This will save us, will it not?"

MacLeod continued to study the hand drawn map for a moment, recognizing each of the places indicating the boundaries of the land grant. Unfortunately, two of them had been removed.

"William, this is what you need to take to the Governor?"

Finally, MacLeod spoke. "This is it. But what if Santiago was expecting it and I go to Monterey with it?"

That's when realization struck. "He will know she took it," Francesca whispered. "What will he do to her if he discovers this?"

"She has to leave before he does," MacLeod stated matter of fact.

"But she cannot. Doña Montero has said he will not let her go."

"Figures. If he went to all this trouble to get her here, just so he can use her, he's getting desperate|"

A moment later Sarah returned with Jacob in tow. He could tell she had something to share, but he opted to let her wait.

Her voice strained, Francesca held up her hand and urged, "William you must save her somehow. She did this for you."

"She did it for both of us," MacLeod countered. Francesca's last statement made him nervous.

"William," she said, squeezing his hand. "I have always thought she was in love with you, and you with her also. But you married me and you have been the best husband I could have ever asked for."

MacLeod could only shake his head. "I married you, Francesca. My meeting Doña Montero had to do with the Frenchman and Diego. If she had not agreed to return to France with him he said he would kill me and my son. For that, I'll always try to help her. I love *you.*"

Francesca smiled. "Thank you, William. When you shot that man you also saved me. My parents never believed he had raped me and that I was with child."

Uncomfortable, MacLeod wished to end the conversation. No one had ever brought such immediate feelings to the surface in the way Marisol Montero had. At the time, they had both agreed that being apart was the best way to handle their mutual feelings. Now, years later, she had visited his home and put them in debt to her. Possibly at the risk of her life. He knew he had to help her escape from Santiago's grasp.

But how?

The other major problem was the governor. How long would he be willing to wait before he came to collect?

Jacob Morgenthau, who was patiently standing nearby, placed a hand on MacLeod's shoulder. "William, Sean is outside. There is something that you and Francesca need to see."

MacLeod had not thought to ask about Concannon or what he had been up to. "Can't it wait?"

"It will only take a moment. Can you carry Francesca out into the courtyard?"

MacLeod looked at her. "Have you ever left the bed?"

"No, only when Juana sits me in a chair for a moment to change my bedding."

MacLeod turned to Jacob and asked, "Is this important somehow?"

"I believe it is. You will believe it is also once you have seen it."

Francesca pulled aside the thin covering and held her arms out to MacLeod. "It is such a great day today and I have not been out of this room since the accident. Carry me out, please."

MacLeod lifted her into his arms and carried her out of the room thinking it strange that no one was in the other room. As they approached the entryway, he began to hear voices filtering in from out in the courtyard.

The bright sunlight momentarily blinded him as Francesca covered her own eyes with her hand.

At first, MacLeod could only see the large number of people and children gathered round. When they finally came into focus, he spied Sarah and Jacob standing off to one side, both with huge grins upon their faces. Rosalie came away from the small cooking fire, wiping her hands on her apron. He turned his head. Gomez and his wife, and the smaller children stood on the other side of the courtyard. Esperanza waited in the back, the new child beginning to show, her hands resting on her belly.

At first, MacLeod hadn't noticed the absence of Concannon. It wasn't until he heard the Irish brogue and everyone turned to watch.

Concannon came out from the shadows cast by the ranch house wall. In front of him, he pushed something that was covered by a woolen blanket.

"Francesca," Concannon began. "I know I am responsible for what happened to you. I should never have allowed you to ride that horse, but I was too drunk to stop you."

Francesca reached over and tugged on his beard. "I have forgiven you, Sean. Did I not tell you this already?"

MacLeod wondered why Concannon's voice appeared so shaky.

"You saved me from myself and I can never repay you for that," Sean muttered, his voice filled with emotion.

"How did I do that, Sean?" Francesca asked in confusion.

"I have not had the wine since the accident."

Francesca closed her eyes a moment before asking, "How did you manage this? You have tried to do this before but never had any success."

Concannon's face lit up. "I had something to take my mind off the wine."

Francesca leaned her head back against MacLeod's shoulder as she pointed to the blanket wrapped object beside Concannon. "Is this the thing you have been working on? The reason you have not come to visit me?"

Concannon's face broke into a wide grin that lit up his eyes as he nodded.

MacLeod mentally reviewed the list of things Concannon was supposed to be working on while he was away. As expected, he figured they had probably been left undone. Just another issue to be brought up when they were alone.

MacLeod could tell Francesca was getting tired and needed her rest. "Well, show us what this thing is you've been working on. I can't stand here like this all day."

Concannon reached over and slipped the blanket off the object he had toiled over for days.

MacLeod frowned. The odd looking chair had been padded with a number of folded blankets. For the life of him, he couldn't understand how the wheels attached to the chair were of any significance.

Concannon walked up to them and held out his arms. "May I take her a moment?" he asked.

MacLeod nodded.

Scooping her up into his arms, Concannon walked back to the chair and gently lowered her onto the seat. He then walked to the back of the chair and began pushing it around the courtyard.

MacLeod folded his arms and grinned as Francesca's face told the story. Jacob excitedly relieved Concannon and continued to circle the courtyard before being pushed aside by Juana. Her comments made it obvious this was to be her job.

Francesca could hardly control her excitement. "Oh, Sean, I thought I would forever live in my bed. I wish to sit out here every day in this new chair you have made me."

MacLeod felt the need to thank Concannon but as usual, found it difficult to admit, even to himself, that he was wrong. "Where in tarnation did you find those wheels?' MacLeod asked.

"When I went to Santa Barbara I saw them on the ship. Captain said he brought them for someone who wanted to build himself a small carriage." Concannon shrugged. "Didn't want them when he saw them."

The wheeled chair had brought Francesca back to them. "It's wonderful, Sean. I thank you for it."

MacLeod walked around the chair, inspecting the way Concannon had built it. The joints were snug, the wooden slats of the arms and back smooth. It was perfection.

Concannon watched intently as MacLeod inspected every square inch of the chair.

"Mighty fine work for such a short time," MacLeod said. Then he remembered something Hartnell had said when he was visiting. "You have a fine hand with wood, would you consider doing more of it?"

"What's your meaning?" the redheaded man asked in confusion.

"Take you out of all the other things you're doing and allow you to build good things to sell. There's few in this country can do the work you do, and there's people with money wanting it."

"What things would you be meaning?" Concannon asked.

MacLeod walked around the chair running his hand over the smooth wood. "Furniture, Sean, good furniture. Tables, chairs, sideboards, cabinets, you know. According to William Hartnell, there's a need. And as you well know, we could use the money."

Concannon combed his beard with his hand. "Well now, what you say might be true, but there's more to what you be asking than just building this chair."

MacLeod watched as Juana and Sarah carried Francesca back into the house, leaving the men to talk while she rested.

"What would you need?" MacLeod asked, turning his attention back to Concannon.

"Let me think a moment. It's not a thing that's been on me mind, you understand."

"Tools, saws, things like that?" MacLeod prodded.

"Aye, and wood, dry lumber. It would have to be dry. But, William, that's not something that happens overnight."

"I realize that. But if the ranch is safe for the time being, we have the time."

"And how will you be paying for these things? Or have you forgotten the people you already owe?"

Concannon always had a way of bringing up the obvious.

"I'll think of something. Maybe make an agreement with the ship's captain to give him the first pieces you make?" he suggested. "He can trade them in San Diego, Los Angeles, Santa Barbara, and Monterey. Come to think of it, we can give Bryant & Sturgis the contract to trade them after we clear our debts."

"So how should we do this?" Concannon asked excitedly. Esperanza, seeing the excitement upon her husband's face, came over to listen after giving MacLeod a hug.

MacLeod called Jacob over. He and quickly told him of his idea. "Help Sean here prepare a list of everything he would need. I believe we could also ask whichever ship's captain we send the order to Boston with to inquire about what other tools and items we might have missed."

"I'll be needing to go into the mountains and fell some trees down," Concannon said. "The sooner they're down, the sooner they'll be drying."

"Soon as you have that list put together I'll ride to Santa Barbara with it. After that we can go and look for the trees you'll be needing."

RANCHO SANTIAGO

Marisol Montero knew she had failed as soon as Santiago walked through the door and threw his travelling bag on the floor and poured himself a glass of wine.

She felt her body constrict in anticipation. *Does he know? Is his anger due to the knowledge that I had intercepted the diseño?*

She watched in nervous anticipation as Santiago seated himself and called for all of the servants to make their presence known.

Panicked, Marisol tried to remember which of the Indian servants had seen her accept the dispatch.

One by one the servants stood in front of him and denied having accepted anything.

It was then that Marisol remembered it was the young Indian girl, the same one who happened to be Santiago's choice when he wanted a woman and she wouldn't give him his way. Marisol could tell the girl was petrified. Marisol had to admit she was also.

The girl stood, trembling in front of Santiago. Marisol waited for the inevitable outburst that she was sure was to follow.

To her surprise, it never came. When Santiago dismissed her, the girl passed by Marisol on the way out of the room, her eyes rising to meet Marisol's as she passed. Marisol took a deep breath and internally thanked the girl for her silence. For the moment she was safe.

"You have not said what you went to Monterey for. Were you successful?" Marisol asked, hoping to put an end to the interrogation of the servants.

"The man was not there. I cannot believe the laziness and complete lack of initiative in these people."

"So you were unsuccessful?"

Santiago poured himself another cup of wine. "I spoke with this new governor and he is going to authorize another survey of the land next to us." Santiago laughed. "How they will know where to begin eludes me."

She waited for him to continue. Now she knew for certain that someone in Monterey was helping him. How else could he have been sent Colinas de Oro's *diseño*? They should have destroyed it. That was their mistake, Marisol thought to herself.

A moment later, one of the servants came for Santiago to inform him that Pacheco wished to speak to him.

Marisol's body tensed when Pacheco entered the house. After everything she had heard from Francesca, she could almost feel his one eye strip her naked. In truth, she knew only his fear of Santiago kept her out of his filthy grasp. But there was still one question that burned through her mind. *How can I save myself from Santiago?*

Marisol watched in nervousness as the two men walked to the door discussing the situation of the cattle. It was apparent to her that things were quickly unraveling. And from what little she knew about Santiago, he was a man who did not recognize failure.

Santiago lit a cigar as he stood in the doorway and watched as Pacheco mounted his horse and rode off. When he turned back to look at Marisol she could feel his eyes almost scrutinizing her.

"This survey you speak of, how will this affect Rancho Santiago?" she asked.

Santiago tapped the ash off his cigar and waited a moment before answering. "It is my belief that I can convince them my land includes the water that runs through the land of your friends. If this is true, they cannot survive."

"And if it does not?"

"There are other ways," he said cryptically. "I am not finished with them. Not in the slightest."

She felt the chill envelope her at his words. In that instant it became abundantly clear that this man was willing to anything in order to get his way.

Rancho Colinas de Oro

MacLeod stepped out of the house and looked toward the west. It was his normal routine each and every morning, and just like every other day he was greeted with a sky of blue, filled with a smattering of puffy white clouds. MacLeod shook his head. *When will I see the dark clouds that carried the life giving rain?* he wondered.

He knew Francesca often liked to come out and sit in her new wheelchair before the sun chased away any cooling breeze, but he was so focused on his own thoughts that he had not heard Juana carry her outside.

"Rosalie has told me not to bother looking for the rain. She says it will not come for some time," Francesca stated sadly.

"It's a good thing these cattle can't hear the old woman," MacLeod joked. "They would probably just lie down and die now, instead of a few months from now."

"You should not be like that, William. We must have hope," Francesca chastised.

MacLeod pushed her chair over to a shaded spot beneath the olive tree. "If hope would bring rain the fields would be green with new grass and the creek would overflow its banks. All I've been doing for months now is hoping."

"Do not give up, please. I could not live if you gave up."

MacLeod grinned. "As long as I have you, I'll never give up hoping. How is your strength today?"

"Each day is a little better. I do not know what I would do without Juana and Sarah—and of course Rosalie. She is like a mother to me."

Juana had been at Francesca's side since MacLeod rescued her from two San Diego Presidio soldiers hell-bent on raping her. As a run away from the San Diego de Alcala Mission he could not send her back for the punishment she was sure to receive. As luck would have it, Francesca had wanted to keep her. And it was fortunate she had.

When Pacheco had tried to rape Francesca, Juana found the pistol MacLeod had left and shot Pacheco in an effort to protect her. Juana had been with Francesca ever since.

"We have been lucky with the people who are with us. Many others have had troubles with their Indians," MacLeod said.

"They are treated well here. You do not punish them if they do wrong. And they have no other place to go."

The couple watched as two of their Indians from the Chumash village led horses carrying jugs of water toward the hacienda. They had been hand watering Francesca's fruit trees and the vegetable garden. Without the vegetables, MacLeod could see no way they would all be survive.

Francesca must have been having some of the same thoughts because she said, "Rosalie tells me we will need mores supplies from Santa Barbara. With all the new people living with us we have not enough flour or beans. Is it possible to get more?"

"We'll need to plant more corn next year also, make enough to last us. We still have some hides we can trade for what we need this year, but I don't want to be running up more debts with the people in Santa Barbara. They won't wait forever to be paid."

"Will you not need to go to Monterey soon?" Francesca asked.

"I was thinking the same thing myself. Though I'd like to put it off as long as possible—for Marisol's sake."

"I fear for her, William."

"I do too," MacLeod admitted. "If Santiago discovers what she did there's no telling what he might do to her."

Francesca pushed on one of the large wheels on her chair and turned it to face MacLeod. "You must help her, William."

A time passed before he finally responded. "There's also Pacheco to consider. It'll mean a fight. I doubt greatly they'll let her go without one."

In the distance MacLeod could see Concannon and Jacob talking. *Another thing to think about,* he thought to himself. *Do I go ahead with placing an order for whatever would be needed to begin preparing to build furniture or do I wait until matters are resolved?"*

Francesca broke into his thoughts. "What are you thinking about?"

"Everything. Trying to figure out where to begin on this furniture thing we discussed."

"Well, you said Sean would need to have dry trees to work with—why not begin there?"

MacLeod smiled and leaned over to kiss her. "You always were the one to put things in order. I'll speak to him and figure out what's needed. We can go tomorrow."

After Juana returned to take Francesca inside to rest, MacLeod called for Concannon, Jacob and Sisquoc to join him. Together, they decided on what to take with them into the mountains.

With a list compiled the men went back to work. Before Jacob could get too far, MacLeod pulled him aside. "I'd like you to stay behind. And keep your gun close by. We shouldn't be gone but a day or so."

Jacob nodded. "That will be fine. This house Sarah and I are building will need much work done before the winter comes."

"Take Gomez aside and show him how to use one of those Baker rifles. Sooner or later he'll find out how young Cisco died and I have a feeling he'll be needing it."

An hour before dawn the group rode out toward the low-lying hills. Before leaving MacLeod had made certain all of the gear and supplies they would need were secured on three pack animals. In case they were needed, the group also led a number of extra horses. Sisquoc had chosen four of the Indians to remain to fell and trim the trees.

Along the way Concannon marked a number of large oak trees for cutting.

"You think we can cut those into usable planks?" MacLeod asked.

"Woods tough as nails, but with the proper saw anything's possible. They'll make mighty fine furniture."

"Well, you'll be needing those four tough young men to do the sawing."

Concannon climbed back on his horse and continued along the pathway stopping occasionally to mark more trees.

Half an hour later, Concannon rode up alongside MacLeod. "Appears they've been pushing more and more cows across the line."

They rode into the middle of a bunch of grazing cattle. There were at least half a dozen heifers feeding alongside their RS mothers while others grazed off by themselves.

"You notice anything peculiar about these youngsters?" MacLeod asked.

A knowing look appeared upon on Concannon's face. Separating a couple of the mothers and babes, he rode around them. "Don't appear they carry an RS brand."

"What's that tell you?"

"Either those fellows he has got over there are too lazy to do the work, or they don't see any need to get it done."

"That's what I'm thinking." MacLeod pushed a couple of young steers away from their moms and watched them graze for a moment. "These are fine by themselves. She doesn't even seem to mind."

Sisquoc sat watching the two men before riding his big stallion over and joining them.

"What be you thinking here?" Concannon asked. "Appears it's not the first time you've had these thoughts."

"You remember that box canyon where you parked those horses, as well as that other place you spoke of?" MacLeod questioned.

"It's up a spell from the foothills...other end of the ranch land. Why?"

"It's not on Colinas de Oro land, correct?"

Concannon removed his sweat-stained sombrero and wiped his forehead. "I believe you are right."

A dozen more RS cows moved aside as MacLeod pushed his way through the small herd. "They're all losing weight—nothing but skin and bones. Is there any water up in that canyon?"

"Come to think of it, there is. At the upper end. There are a bunch of cottonwoods and a small pond. Comes out of some rocks nearby and seeps into the ground mostly."

"Maybe you can go up there and see if you can shore up that pond some, keep more of the water." MacLeod suggested. Before Concannon could respond, he turned to Sisquoc. "Let's not be pushing any more RS cows back across the line. I figure grass will be getting hard to find on Santiago land, so let's just see what happens." Turning back to Concannon he said, "The entrance to this canyon can be defended?"

MacLeod could tell Concannon was trying to remember what the entrance to the canyon looked like before responding.

"You put a couple of those young bucks of Sisquoc's that I saw practicing with them bows of theirs, yes. I believe they could hold off quite a spell."

"Is there another way out if someone blocked the entrance?"

"They could climb out easy enough, assuming they had to."

MacLeod smiled. "Here's what I'm thinking—we post these two Chumash boys you been talking about and give them a week's supplies. After that, have a couple of our vaqueros pick a dozen or so at a time of the unbranded RS heifers and drive them into this canyon. Let Santiago's boys drive as many of their cows as they want over onto Colinas land. We'll have someone go up there once a week and put our brand on them before bringing them back as Colinas de Oro cows and integrating them into our herds."

Concannon rubbed his chin and looked over at MacLeod. "Could start a war if they ever found out."

"It's coming anyway. Just a matter of time the way I figure. Might have to take it to them first though since there aren't as many fighters on our side."

They rode up out of the foothills and began climbing into the pine and fir carpeted mountains. Along the way Sisquoc pointed out the route they would need to follow in order to drag the logs back down the mountain.

By dusk, Concannon had marked roughly fifty trees. Pine and cedar alike. The job of felling the trees and trimming them down would take most of the summer, but at least they had a start on the process.

By nightfall all were exhausted and for the first time in years MacLeod threw a blanket on the ground and slept beneath the stars. He had nearly forgotten the smells of the forest, the whisper of the wind through the trees, the smell of meat cooking over a small fire.

Lying in the silence of the forest gave him time to think with no distractions. Everything was coming at him like a raging river overflowing its banks. How long he had, he could not be sure. How long before Santiago discovered the *diseño* was intercepted by Marisol? And how could he get her away safely before something bad happened to her?

Before his mind could ponder the issues at hand any further, Concannon squatted down beside him. "What we did today is surely a beginning, but how do you figure on getting past tomorrow and next week, if you don't mind me asking?"

"Well, we got by today. See what happens tomorrow. Hope I can get to Monterey in time. Hope we can save Doña Montero."

Concannon snickered. "You best be praying for rain too, else it won't matter none."

"The old lady's doing it for me," MacLeod stated dismissively. "Said it's not likely to happen soon though."

"How's she figuring her prayers aren't being answered?"

MacLeod had wondered the same thing, but didn't dare ask the question. "I think she feels something as big as asking for rain takes a lot of praying. I surely hope it works."

He made a mental note to have Francesca send a note to Marisol and ask her to visit again. Maybe together they could come up with a plan to save her. With that, MacLeod rolled over and pulled the thin blanket over his head. The animals had finally settled down and accepted the picket line strung between two trees, he prayed that sleep would claim him soon. He could only hope that tomorrow would bring forth a solution.

After the men had returned from their trip, MacLeod went in search of Concannon to find out how he was doing in fashioning a new stock for his Kentucky rifle. As he approached the tiny adobe home Concannon had built, he noticed a small fire sending up spirals of smoke into the still air from the open hearth outside the tiny adobe home Concannon had built. MacLeod tipped his hat to Esperanza.

"He has gone to get me wood for my fire," Esperanza said with the smile that had given hope to many of the men in the San Diego

Presidio before Concannon had swept her off her feet. MacLeod's first meeting with her came when she brought his meals to his cell in the jail. He was grateful for her kindness.

The aroma of the meat simmering in the large copper pot hung over the fire made MacLeod's stomach rumble. With all the attention being paid to Francesca lately he often found himself missing meals.

"I need to speak with him a moment, if you can spare him," he said, returning her grin. "I'll see you get your wood if you promise me a bowl of that *puchero* you have cooking in that pot."

Esperanza placed her stone roller aside and stood, leaning back and stretching. "You can have a bowl, but come before him," she said, and laughed. "He will eat it all if you are late." MacLeod laughed knowing she was telling the truth.

When Concannon returned a short while later the two men walked off by themselves. Unconsciously, MacLeod reached down and broke off a handful of dry grass. "Seems all a waste if the Lord don't send us some rain soon. Mighty soon at that."

"There were times we wished it would stop raining. Across the seas that is," Concannon clarified.

"Hard to believe." Changing the subject MacLeod said, "You happen to see Sisquoc lately?"

"No. Haven't seen the big fellow come to think of it."

"I would have thought he'd be back by now. I know he wanted to be sure those fellows we left behind knew what they were doing."

Concannon tossed a pebble at a small lizard sitting in the shade of a dying shrub. "Seems a long time to stay with them. Noticed some of his Indians not doing much of anything."

"Tell you what," MacLeod said. "Get us a couple of horses saddled and I'll go tell Francesca. In fact bring an extra horse. Something doesn't seem right."

An hour later, the two men rode out. The old lady, Rosalie, insisted on packing a lunch of tortillas and beans neatly wrapped in cornhusks.

"The water's down a mite, I'm thinking," Concannon said.

"Appears you're right. Still, it's enough, for a while anyway. Could also be because so many more cows are watering on it."

They rode in silence for a spell, deep in their own thoughts. Finally, Concannon broke the silence. "You given any of your thinking to our friend, Pacheco? Seems too long for him to be silent."

"Think about him all the time," MacLeod admitted.

"You should have killed the arsehole when you had the chance. Told you that before."

"I know, you've told me that a dozen times already. However, these women have made me think twice before shooting people."

Concannon shook his head. "It'll be the death of you if you don't be changing your ways."

MacLeod laughed. "You know, Sean, there are times I wonder why I saved your sorry ass. Should have let the British capture you. Wouldn't have had to spend ten years listening to your opinions."

"How many you suppose he has with him?"

MacLeod was taken aback. "Who? Pacheco?"

"Who we been talking about?"

"Well, as of late we've been discussing my shortcomings," MacLeod said.

The sun had just reached the top of its arc, the shadows dwindling before starting down the opposite side. MacLeod had been wondering about the same thing. "Don't rightly know, but it's sure to be more people than we have. Why, what are you thinking?"

"I'm thinking there needs to be a way to give us a chance. If it comes to that, of course."

MacLeod thought about what Concannon had said. "I doubt they'll start anything yet. Unless they think they have the advantage. But Pacheco on the other hand, may think differently."

Concannon pulled his horse to a halt and shielded his eyes with his hat for a spell. "Appears to be something going on out there by that small grove of trees." Concannon continued watching for a moment.

"Your eyes are a sight better than mine. What is it you're seeing?"

"Not sure, but I think we might wander over and take a look."

"Way ahead of you," MacLeod said. He reached under his leg and pulled one of the new Baker rifles from its scabbard. "I somehow doubt it's any of our people."

They rode down into a shallow valley with scattered oaks along its side and flats before following it a quarter mile out of sight of the gathering Concannon had spotted.

It was that distinct crack of whips that assaulted their ears first.

MacLeod kicked his horse into a canter and guided it up the side of the shallow slope. Concannon followed close behind, his scattergun in hand.

A whip cracked again, accompanied by loud yells and laughter.

"That's Sisquoc they're whipping," Concannon shouted.

"Give them a warning. We'll see how much they want to continue living." MacLeod kicked his horse into a full gallop as Concannon's gun went off.

Two men stood on either side of Sisquoc, whom they had tied to a tree. Blood ran down his back and puddled in the dirt at his feet. He had not uttered a sound.

At the sound of the scattergun both men broke away and quickly raced for their horses. Though before they could reach them MacLeod pulled his horse up and leapt to the ground, bringing the rifle to his shoulder as he knelt. Concannon, eyes trained on the men, raced past. The ball from MacLeod's Baker rifle struck one man in the leg. The man screamed and fell to the ground, clutching at his shattered leg. The other turned and raised the hand with the whip. He didn't seem to know whether to run, help his partner, or stay and fight.

Unfortunately for him, Concannon reduced the man's options.

Sliding off his horse, Concannon drew his knife as he hit the ground. In a flash Concannon's knife buried itself in the man's shoulder. The man dropped to the ground clutching at the hilt of the knife while the other RS man continued to scream in agonizing pain.

"Forgotten how well you use that. Reminds me of that day I found you."

"You were lucky I felt no need to kill you that time," Concannon said with a grin. He grabbed the hilt of his knife and pushed the man back to the ground with his foot, then wiped the blade on his trousers.

"Grab that water off my saddle and see to Sisquoc. I've a mind to hand him this here gun and let him put these fellows out of their misery himself," MacLeod called over his shoulder.

A big grin split Concannon's face. "Now you're seeing the light, as my Pa would say," Concannon called as he began untying Sisquoc from the oak they had lashed him to.

MacLeod caught the big Chumash as Concannon cut away the last of the leather thongs that had bound him. As soon as he was free they could see Sisquoc's chest was scraped raw from the rough bark of the tree.

Behind them the two injured RS men continued to send up a plaintiff wail. Sisquoc had not uttered more than a grunt as MacLeod slowly lowered him to the ground and held the water bag for him to drink.

"What you be thinking you want to do with these fellows?" Concannon asked, motioning to the two injured men. "Was me, I'd leave them where they lie. You being so soft of late, you'd probably want to bind their wounds and give them a pat on the head before asking them not to be doing this anymore or you might get mad."

"You are a cold-hearted man. All your people like you?"

"Oh, no. Most would have cut their bleeding throats already and buried them deep to nourish the land." Concannon shrugged. "Who knows, couple of years from now might have a couple of flower patches out here. Of course, we would need it to rain once in a while."

"Not a bad idea I want them to take a message back to our friends over yonder. We'll hoist them up and lash them to their saddles. I imagine sooner or later someone will find them. First though, I want to find out who sent them."

MacLeod pulled his knife from his belt and stalked over to where the two lay on the ground. He grabbed the long braid one of the men wore, he sliced it off. Switching to Spanish and placing the razor sharp blade at the man's throat, he said. "Who sent you, or was this your own idea of having a good time?"

Fear shone in the man's eyes as he tried to shake his head, stopping only when he felt the knife cut the skin of his neck.

"One more time, Amigo, who sent you?"

The man desperately tried to back away from the pressure of the blade by gently pushing himself away with his good hand. MacLeod's knife followed him.

"I'll make it easy for you—was it Doñ Santiago?"

The man shook his head.

"Was it Señor Pacheco?"

MacLeod could see the fear reflected in the man's expression. He had his answer. "So it was Pacheco who sent you."

"He will kill me, Señor," the man cried.

"I don't doubt he will, but you could have chosen to leave Rancho Santiago at any time. You have a horse. Got nobody to blame but yourself. Both of you. You tell him I saved your life so you could tell him who did this to you. Tell him it was El

Americano. He'll understand. Course he might kill you before you get the chance to tell him." MacLeod shrugged.

Concannon and MacLeod hoisted the two men onto their saddles and bound them to their horses. Both men pleaded to be let loose so they could escape their fate. Sadly, their pleas fell upon deaf ears.

In spite of wanting to do it himself, MacLeod and Concannon helped Sisquoc up onto the saddle of the extra horse they had brought along. The whip had flayed the Indian's back and blood still seeped from the cuts.

"Have Jacob look at him when you get back. Rosalie will want to participate, I imagine. She has a ready supply of dry herbs and plants for everything imaginable. I will be back as soon as I can."

Concannon climbed up onto his horse. "You be careful now, going over there. They'd just as soon shoot you and you don't have me protecting you."

MacLeod grinned. "You're like an old woman, Sean, always minding out for me."

"Oh, blarney It's not you I'm caring about, it's that wife of yours. How would I be explaining to her if you up and hurt yourself—or worse?"

MacLeod knew every time Concannon talked about Francesca he was reliving the accident and the part he played in it. What he needed to be thinking about was the one growing in Esperanza's belly. The one that was meant to replace the son they had lost. If they lost another MacLeod wouldn't give a peso for Concannon's chances.

MacLeod watched as Concannon and Sisquoc rode off toward the hacienda before mounting his long-legged bay gelding. Retrieving the lead rope attached to the horses of the RS vaqueros he made his way toward Rancho Santiago, the men wailing in pain with each step forward.

The sun lay a hand's-breadth above the horizon when MacLeod finally turned the horses loose nearly half a mile from the Rancho Santiago hacienda.

The sound of distant thunder reverberated over the valley. A carpet of dark clouds momentarily blocked the intense rays of an unforgiving sun. All heads turned and faced the west in hope. They knew that if the rains were to come it would probably come from the west or southwest.

The tension grew as everyone awaited the next peal of thunder. Sadly, no one was surprised when it appeared the clouds moved up along the coast, bypassing the arid valley completely.

"Rosalie said it will not rain," Francesca muttered in sadness after maneuvering her chair over to where MacLeod stood.

"Did you ask her when the hell it will?"

"Do not be angry with her. It is not her fault she sees these things."

"Well, maybe she can go out and explain this to those poor suffering animals. They're dropping weight with each passing day. We'll still have the hides, but I don't expect them to carry much fat for tallow."

Concannon approached carrying MacLeod's Kentucky rifle, the one his mother had sold a cow in order to purchase after he told her he was going west. She understood it was either that, or he would surely kill his stepfather.

MacLeod reached out for it, unconsciously weighing it in his hands. He threw it to his shoulder and grinned. "Mighty fine work, Sean. I didn't think it could come out as good as this."

"I figured on getting it done soon as I could since you missed that fellow the other day."

"I wasn't meaning to kill him. Although I wasn't aiming to shoot him in the leg either," MacLeod admitted.

Francesca tugged on his sleeve. "Has Jacob talked to you about the water?"

"Why, is he still talking about bringing it out of the mountains?"

Francesca smiled. "He believes it could be done."

"Well, it won't matter much if others have their way. Water for the hacienda will be the least of our worries."

"I believe some of your worries are about to present themselves," Concannon muttered, pointing down toward the river crossing.

Turning his attention in the direction Concannon indicated, MacLeod shielded his eyes and watched as a large group of riders walked their horses up toward the hacienda.

"Is it him again that comes?" Francesca asked.

"Yep, it's him. Looking like a damn peacock. I figure to wipe that grin off his face."

They all waited for Rodriguez and his party to come to a halt. MacLeod nodded to him and waited for what the man had to say.

Rodriguez opened the flap on a leather dispatch case he had slung over his shoulder and pulled out a folded paper. "Our Excellency, the Governor of California, has ordered me here to inform you and Doña MacLeod that she is no longer the owner of this land because she cannot prove it has ever been hers."

"And you came all the way from Monterey to say that. Actually you came twice," MacLeod clarified.

"It is my duty to follow the orders of our governor."

"Well, Rodriguez, I'm afraid you came all this way for nothing. I know you were asked to have me produce our copy of this document. However, it just so happens that someone in Monterey sent the original document you seek to Señor Santiago. I believe that is illegal, is it not?"

Rodriguez looked puzzled. "That is not possible. *Diseño's* must always remain in Monterey. How else would we know who owns the land?"

MacLeod stepped forward and handed the land grant map to the man who still had a confused expression upon his face. Rodriguez quickly unfolded it and read the document. When he was finished he refolded the map and handed it back to MacLeod.

Rodriguez looked over the assembled group in front of him, appearing to come to a decision. "You must come to Monterey and present this to our governor. You will need to explain how you have come to obtain such a document. I am sure our governor will want this information."

"You know," MacLeod paused for a moment. "I was hoping you would do that for me."

Rodriguez shifted in his saddle uncomfortably and stared at MacLeod. "This you trust me to do?" he asked, chuckling.

"I believe these men are hungry and thirsty. Perhaps you can have the women whip up a meal of sorts for them," MacLeod suggested to Francesca, who nodded. He turned back to Rodriguez. "We've had our differences over the years, Captain, but I don't believe you to be a man I could not trust. Why don't you and your men step down and find a spot in the shade to rest a while."

Rodriguez turned in the saddle and looked at the men he had brought with him from Monterey. He could clearly see the weariness upon their faces. He turned back to MacLeod. "I agree that we have not found good in each other. I have had my duty to perform and you have tried to make this impossible for me, but you have my word that I will see this is presented to our governor." Rodriguez reached back into his dispatch case and produced a sealed letter. "Señor Hartnell has asked me to deliver this to you."

MacLeod took the envelope and quickly broke the seal. He turned away to read what was written while Rodriguez and his men dismounted and accepted the gourds of water the two kitchen Indian girls brought them.

"Do you trust him with this?" Francesca whispered as she and her husband watched the soldiers from Monterey wolf down the platters of tortillas and beans cooked with beef.

"Might not like him all that much but I believe he's an honorable man. You can see it in his face right now. His ego is about to burst wide open." The laughter from the group helped to ease the tension everyone had felt during the short confrontation between the two men.

MacLeod read Hartnell's letter once again, a cold chill swept over him.

Will it never end?

Hartnell's letter reported that someone was buying up all of MacLeod's notes held for payment. He knew it had to be Santiago. Clearly, the man wasn't finished yet.

"What is it?" Francesca asked as he folded the letter and walked back to where she sat.

"William Hartnell is confirming a rumor he had told me about. It appears our troubles aren't over just yet."

RANCHO SANTIAGO

Marisol found a bundle, actually two bundles, of letters tied with a narrow black ribbon sitting atop the small desk Santiago used for work. One bundle contained envelopes, the writing unfamiliar to her. The other package, however, looked as if its contents contained various pieces of thin paper. She picked it up and read the top one.

Marisol Montero recognized the name—an American ship captain she had no use for. The man had tried to cheat her on several occasions. Later, she'd heard that he had said he doubted she could understand the business she appeared to be conducting. Marisol knew what he really meant. She was a woman; therefore she was incapable of understanding business. It was fortunate she found others more understanding.

At first, she paid little attention to a signature she found on the top note. Then she studied it further.

Through the open door Marisol watched the young Indian girl race across the field toward the protection of the trees and willows growing along the sandy banks of the stream. She couldn't blame the girl for attempting to escape. At least that is was Marisol assumed the girl was trying to do. Santiago had beaten the girl the night before. Then, early this morning, Santiago ordered Marisol to remain in the hacienda and to be prepared to answer his questions when he returned.

Marisol had no illusions about what his words meant and what his plans for her were.

But now this?

She stared at the signature again in hopes she had read it wrong. Sadly, that was not the case.

Atop the piece of paper was MacLeod's signature. It was on a note for payment on items he had ordered. Quickly she untied the bundle and flipped through each one. They were all guarantees for payment—all items for the ranch, as well as a few books. Glancing at each one, she mentally tallied up the total before retying the package and picking up the second.

There were so many letters it took her most of the morning to go through each of them. Many of them she read twice before picking up the black ribbon and securing them the way she found them.

What she had not discovered was who Santiago was working with in Monterey. Though there was one person she was almost certain she could rule out. The governor.

A moment later Santiago strode through the open door and threw his sombrero across the room. "Where is it?" he shouted in anger.

"Where is what?" she asked, feigning innocence. In reality, she knew exactly what he wanted.

"You are not a stupid woman. Where is the dispatch that was sent by the courier from Monterey?"

Marisol remained silent, a cold chill creeping up her spine. She knew his anger would eventually reach a boiling point and he would react. And the little experience she had with him, she knew it was usually physical.

"I do not have it," Marisol stated confidently.

Santiago walked to the sideboard and poured himself a cup of wine, his hand shaking. "That day you went to see that woman—you gave it to her, or possibly to your lover, didn't you?" he asked, his tone steady.

"Doñ MacLeod is not, nor has he ever been, my lover."

Santiago spun around and threw his cup of wine at her, drenching the front of her dress. "You say these lies to me! I have offered you this hacienda and all of this rancho and still you crawl to this Americano with your dress drawn up to your knees for him."

Marisol held her tongue. No denial would satisfy him. She knew he would react to whatever she said so she opted to say nothing at all.

Santiago yelled for another cup of wine before pointing his finger directly at her. "So you stole this paper that was sent to me? Do you have any idea what you have done?"

At that Marisol could no longer remain silent. "It was not yours to begin with. You are trying to steal the land that belongs to these people."

"Shut up," he bellowed as he stomped across the room and slapped her face.

Marisol stumbled backwards, throwing up her hands to protect her face if he tried to strike her again. She had not been struck since she was selling herself on the streets of Vera Cruz what felt like a lifetime ago.

Santiago lost all control. Wrenching her arm away from her face, Santiago backhanded her once again, sending her sprawling across the floor.

Marisol rose to her knees, a thin trickle of blood sliding down her cheek. She laughed. She knew it would intensify his rage. She also knew she would suffer the consequences. "He is more of a man than you will ever be," she spat. "If you want to live, I would suggest you leave here before he finds out what you have done."

"You whore of a woman. I could kill you and no one would ever know until your bones were found, picked clean by the animals and vultures."

"Then you will be certain to die for it," she spat.

She wiped the blood from her face as she stood. She tried to step away as he reached for her, but he was too quick. Grabbing her by the arm he threw her to the floor. She fought him with everything she had as she felt him tearing away at her clothes. He backhanded her again, causing her head to slam into the hard plank. Her head spun as she crawled backwards and rose to her knees. She touched her lip with her tongue, the familiar metallic taste of the blood now running down her chin. Santiago wrapped his hand in her hair and lifted her onto her feet. Instinctively, Marisol swung an arm out and raked his cheek with her fingernails, only increasing his rage.

The woman Marisol had brought from Monterey tried to pull Santiago away. He turned to her and threw her hard against the adobe wall.

Marisol screamed. "Leave her, she does not deserve to be beaten for what I have done, or do you only attack women?" Marisol taunted.

Santiago's fury raged. With his hand still wrapped in her hair he dragged her across the room toward the bed. Desperate to stop him, she reached out and tried to grasp the leg of a nearby table.

"That will not save your precious honor. This is something you have needed for many years. If he did not have you, I will. Believe me, you will like it." Santiago tore her hand away from the table leg and punched her repeatedly in the side. Not satisfied, he slapped her with such force she neared the point of blacking out. When he picked her up, Marisol tore at his face again as he carried her to the bed and threw her atop it. Rolling her over onto her stomach, he began ripping off her underclothing. Marisol struggled to break away from his grasp but his strength proved to be too much. She felt his hands grasp her nearly naked body and pull it toward him. She screamed.

When Santiago had finally finished she felt his weight lift off her. Her body ached from the abuse she had endured. From that moment on she vowed to never allow him to believe she feared him. Somehow, she knew she needed to escape. Not next week, or next month, but today.

"Remember this," Santiago said through clenched teeth, as if he could read her thoughts. "Tonight, we will do it again. Perhaps more than once, so I suggest you learn to like it." Standing back, he laughed as he watched her try to cover herself with her tattered clothing. There was no humor in his laughter. No, this was the laughter of an evil man.

With his last words ringing in her ears Santiago stomped out of the house calling for Pacheco as Marisol rolled over and pulled the dress up in an effort to cover herself.

What will he do now that he knows about the diseño? Will he ride to Colinas de Oro with all of the men he had gathered around him and demand its return? she wondered.

Marisol knew MacLeod would never back down to him, regardless of how many men Santiago brought. In the end, people would die. She did not want anyone to die for what she had done, but she feared it was inevitable. Marisol knew she must find a way to reach them before Santiago did. She called out to her servant, surprised at how strong her voice sounded.

No, I will never let him touch me again.

Marisol Montero could barely stand, much less walk from the beating Santiago had given her. *Where had he and Pacheco gone?* she wondered. Suddenly, a wave of fear reverberated through her. *Are they still nearby or had they ridden off?* Marisol thought to herself.

Pained, she leaned against the doorway knowing the answers to her questions weren't available. She would have to take a chance. Even if she were able to procure a horse she knew she could not ride fast with her injuries. Her body would not allow it. She walked back to the sideboard and called for one of her servants to bring her some water and a cloth to clean herself. As expected, her face and lip had already begun to swell.

The older woman who looked after the servants for Santiago entered with a dish of water and a clean cloth. Marisol had seldom spoken with the woman so she knew very little about her. In fact, the only thing she did know was that Santiago had brought her down from Monterey with him to supervise the many Mexicans and Indians in his household.

Without a word the woman gently pushed Marisol's hands away from her face and began to wash off the blood and inspect the cuts.

Marisol was slightly taken aback. That was not the treatment she had expected from her.

"My husband has a horse for you," the woman spoke. "It is out by the big tree. But you must leave now and say nothing if you are caught. It would not be good for any of us if you told him."

A horse, ready for me? A chance to escape before he returned? Marisol could not believe her ears.

"What you are doing for me is dangerous," Marisol stressed, taking the woman's hands in her own. "But I thank you. If you ever return to Monterey you must come to me. I will have work for both you and your husband."

The old woman looked at her in disbelief. "You can do this thing for us? How is it possible?"

Marisol shifted a moment in an effort to relieve the pain in her side. "I can do this, believe me," she insisted.

The woman pointed at her and asked, "You?" It was clear to Marisol that the woman was confused.

Marisol nodded. "Yes. Now, please, help me get on that horse. I must leave now while he is away."

Together they made it across the dirt courtyard to where the woman's husband stood holding the reins of the horse. It was obvious to Marisol the man was nervous about what they were doing. She reached out and touched his arm gently to thank him. Working quickly, the woman and her husband helped Marisol up into the saddle. She had little experience riding a horse so she could only hope the man had chosen a fully broken horse for her.

As expected, her body rebelled immediately. She closed her eyes a moment until a wave of nausea passed.

I just need to make it to Colinas de Oro without falling off or being caught by Santiago—or worse yet, Pacheco. God, how I hate them.

She turned the horse's head and urged it forward while saying a silent prayer that she make it to her destination.

As she rode, Marisol's mind continually went over and over the horrors of the morning. After some time the pain began to worsen. Nearly too much to bear, she chastised herself for not paying closer attention to the distance to Francesca and MacLeod's hacienda. Now it seemed so far.

Each step of the way, through low ambling hills of dry grass and scattered oak trees, there was one question that continued to trouble her. *Am I bringing Santiago's wrath down on these people I love so dearly? Should I turn back and suffer the consequences?*

"Oh, Guillermo," she said out loud to no one. "Look what this love of mine for you has done. What will I have done to you if they come for me?"

The trouble was, Marisol knew what MacLeod would do. He would fight. The real question was how many would perish for her troubles?

Under the cruel sun the land baked. The few tufts of grass the grazing cattle had missed lacked the strength to remain upright. Ironically, Marisol felt much the same.

Suddenly, a movement off to her right startled her, sending a cold chill down her spine. She saw a horse standing motionless beneath the shade of an oak tree. In an effort to control the trembling in her body Marisol gripped the front of her saddle.

Are there others nearby? her panicked mind wondered.

She tried to turn and look behind her, but the pain that shot throughout her body was nearly too much to bear. Crying out in pain, she tried to take a breath and calm her quickly fraying nerves. If she had to guess, Santiago had broken her ribs when he punched her. Needing to know if she was alone, Marisol carefully reined the horse to a halt and turned it back to face the way she had come.

Nothing. No riders followed.

Marisol laughed, sending another spasm of pain jolting her body. "Oh, please don't do that again," she muttered to herself.

She turned back in the direction of Colinas de Oro, Marisol could see that the horse still stood beneath the tree. It had not moved. While she watched a tiny figure stepped out of the shadows and grasped the horse's mane. *They are far too small to be Santiago or Pacheco,* Marisol realized. A wave of relief flooded over her as she watched the figure throw itself up onto the horse's back and ride down the slope to where Marisol was positioned.

Marisol wanted to laugh in relief but stopped herself in time. The young Indian girl who had also been beaten by Santiago rode up to her. Her face showed the marks from his fists.

Embarrassed that she didn't even know the young girl's name, Marisol beckoned her to come closer. She smiled at the girl who she guessed to be not much more than a child. It was then she remembered the things Santiago had done to her.

Marisol tried talking to the girl but she didn't seem to understand. Still, Marisol knew she couldn't ride off and leave the child here for them to find. She turned her horse again toward Colinas de Oro and motioned for the girl to follow.

Unable to do anything but walk the horses, due to her injuries, it took most of the afternoon before the adobe buildings of the sprawling enclave came into sight. By the time the two led their horses into the courtyard Marisol could barely hold herself upright.

Sarah saw her first and rushed out to help her dismount, calling for Jacob as she did so.

"Mrs. Montero, what has happened to you?" Sarah asked with concern in her voice.

Before she could answer Marisol collapsed into Sarah's arms and was gently lowered to the ground. Jacob ran forward and picked her up, carrying her to a spot in the shade and held her as Juana ran to them with a cup of water.

Francesca and Rosalie appeared in the doorway. "Who is it?" Francesca asked.

"It is Mrs. Montero," Sarah replied. "She appears to have been beaten and has collapsed."

Francesca gasped in disbelief. "Hurry, bring her in here and place her on the bed," she motioned to them with her hands.

Francesca wheeled her chair away to let Jacob pass, then followed him into the house.

"My God, what has he done to her?" Francesca whispered as she took in the woman's appearance. She instructed Juana to bring water and a clean cloth. Then had her wash the blood from Marisol's face.

Marisol opened her eyes and reached for Francesca's hand. "He learned that it was I who brought the *diseño* to you."

"You can speak more of this when you have rested. He can do nothing to you now. The *diseño* is being returned to Monterey as we speak. We are safe from him," Francesca insisted.

"No, no—you must understand. He has other things he can do," Marisol protested. "I must speak to Guillermo."

Francesca smiled softly. "You must learn to call him William. Why is it so important you speak to him?"

Marisol attempted to turn onto her side while lying in the bed. Suddenly, her body was wracked with excruciating pain. Crying out in agony, she took a moment to try and catch her breath, allowing the pain to subside slightly.

When she had finally composed herself enough to speak, she said, "You both must know of what I have to say. Doñ Santiago will do anything to take your land away from you. Please send for your husband." She collapsed back onto the bad and closed her eyes. *He must be told what is planned for them,* she thought to herself.

Catalina, who had followed them in, stood at Francesca's side. "Go and find your father and tell him to come at once," Francesca instructed the young lady.

Marisol opened her eyes and watched the girl run from the room to do as her mother had asked. Hopefully she would find him soon. Marisol knew she needed rest, but she needed to let MacLeod know what had happened. She also needed him to know that he knew about the *diseño.*

Marisol wasn't naïve enough to think Santiago wouldn't come for her. She knew he would. She felt it. The only question was when.

Lying in bed, awaiting MacLeod's arrival, she tried silently pronouncing Guillermo's name the way Francesca had done. After several minutes of trying and the awkwardness it caused, she decided to continue to call him Guillermo. After all, the name she called him did not matter in this instance. Fact was, he needed to know the information she had gathered in order to be ready.

Is this really what you want to do? Marisol asked herself. *Do you really want him to fight over you?* The answer came to her quickly. *No, that was not what I wish for, but he has to know everything.*

While they waited for MacLeod's arrival, Francesca sat in her wheelchair and held Marisol's hand, pleading with her to tell her what had happened. Through the tears, Marisol recalled the events of the rape. She cried. She told Francesca of her early life, on the streets of Vera Cruz. Even then she had never been forced to have sex. She had done it willingly in order to survive.

Francesca wiped Marisol's forehead with a damp cloth and told her about the Frenchman, Dupré, and how Catalina came to be. She admitted to her that she had never told the girl who her real father was. Her own rape had led to her being banished from her home because her father refused to believe it as truth.

As the two broken woman relived the horrors of their pasts, they sat in companionable silence. Suddenly, Marisol heard the familiar sound of horses outside in the courtyard. Moments later, Catalina rushed in followed by MacLeod. Afraid of what might happen, Marisol buried her face in her hands and wept uncontrollably.

After a few moments Marisol felt Francesca pull her hands away from her face as she carefully wipes her eyes with the cloth. When she looked up, MacLeod gasped.

Marisol held up her hand before he could question her, she whispered, "No, do not ask. It is not necessary."

Sarah interrupted. "Please, the little Indian girl—what would you like me to do with her?"

MacLeod turned to address Catalina. "Go and find Sisquoc. He was with Diego and the horses."

"I forgot about the child. He has beaten her also. I do not understand her language," Marisol admitted, tears filling her eyes once again.

"We'll find out what she has to say soon enough," MacLeod said. "Now, you will stay with us until I can get you to Santa Barbara and onto a ship. We have enough money to get you back to Monterey. Will you be all right there?"

Marisol tried to smile. "Yes, but no more about me. You must listen to what I have to say."

MacLeod and Francesca both nodded for her to begin. The next several minutes were spent telling them about the notes for debts that Santiago had purchased and the sum of the notes, in. case he had not kept track.

"But that is not all I found," she added. "He has received many letters from this place he is from, Argentina. These people are asking questions of him."

"What kinds of questions?" MacLeod asked.

Marisol took a sip of water before continuing. "There is much money involved. The way I understood it, it is their money he has used to buy the cattle and build his hacienda. I know of men in Monterey who he has paid to do things that are not allowed. From what I could discern, these people in his country want their money back."

"Even with our land he may not have the money they ask for, but it could be a convincing argument to hold them off for a spell," MacLeod said in understanding.

Sarah came into the room again. "That big Indian said the girl is like him. A Chumash. At least I think that's what he said. He has found someone here who will take care of her."

MacLeod stood beside Francesca's wheel chair and sighed. "I know I promised, but this has gone too far. He needs to be dealt with."

"No," Francesca said. "You cannot fight him. There must be another way."

"If he takes the fact that we can't pay the notes to the authorities, there's not much we can do. I could try to get a loan." MacLeod shrugged. "At least these people know us."

"And if we cannot find someone to help?" Francesca asked.

"Look, Francesca. I don't know. If he's bought out those notes he did it for a reason. There's nothing we can do about it. Everyone's hurting because of this drought. There are few who will lend money until they know everything is back to normal."

"You mean we could lose our land over this? Do these problems never end?" Francesca cried.

"I'll ride to Monterey and talk to a few people, but I can't do it with the chance Santiago will come looking for Marisol. But even if I did take the chance and rode to Monterey I doubt I could find anyone to loan us enough."

"I will lend you the money," Marisol stated.

RANCHO COLINAS DE ORO

"No," both Francesca and MacLeod voiced together.

A crooked smile worked its way up to Marisol's eyes. "Yes. I will loan you the money. It is all I can do to help destroy this man. Please allow me to do it."

This time it was MacLeod who said. "How can you possibly help? It would take more hides and tallow than we lost to pay off our loans."

"Few know this," Marisol began. "Even he does not know. Guillermo, I am very wealthy."

MacLeod looked at Marisol in disbelief, his gaze bouncing between her and Francesca. Turning to Marisol, he shook his head. "You don't understand—it'll probably take years to pay off this money. That is assuming this drought breaks this year."

"Then it will take years. I do not mind. I have much more money than these notes that he will demand be paid. He does not know this yet, but it will ruin him. It is a better option than killing him," Marisol spat out with a vengeance.

Francesca begged Marisol to get some rest. Marisol reluctantly agreed. After shooing MacLeod out of the room, Francesca followed behind him, leaving Marisol to rest in silence.

MacLeod walked out into the courtyard. He wanted to call for his horse and ride to Rancho Santiago. He would wait for the opportunity to catch Santiago alone and settle the matter one-on-one. Unfortunately, he also knew this would not go unnoticed. Santiago was well known in Monterey and had made many influential friends. Eventually, the authorities would be forced to confront him. He swore out loud and was about to go in search of Concannon when Francesca called him back.

"William, we must think about this before it is too late," she said.

He knew what she was referring to without her even mentioning it. "We can't do this to her, Francesca. I don't know how she could possibly have that amount of money; her husband was not what you might consider wealthy."

"Then why would she make such an offer? Doña Montero would not lie to us," Francesca argued.

MacLeod thought about that statement for a moment. "No reason to lie. Unless she hoped I would do something to Santiago for the beating he gave her? Then again, I don't believe she would do that either."

Francesca rubbed his arm while he stood beside her chair. "If we were to take her money, assuming she does have it, she must understand we cannot promise to return it soon," Francesca whispered softly.

"So you think we should accept her offer?"

Francesca fanned herself with her hat. "Yes, but you must be a part of this decision also."

"What if the rains don't come again this year? I doubt we would have anything left to pay her back."

"Then you must make her understand, William. She must know the truth."

Francesca had Juana push her back into the house so that MacLeod could think about what he wanted to do. It was obvious to him that the events of the day had taken their toll on his wife.

A short while later Marisol came out supported by Catalina, who appeared to be completely taken with her. She led Marisol to the bench in the shade of the olive tree and helped her to sit.

"Guillermo, I must speak with you," Marisol whispered.

MacLeod sent Catalina on an errand and walked over to where Marisol sat, he took a seat beside her.

"She is a beautiful child. She is also completely unaware of it, and very determined." Marisol laughed. "The man she marries will need an open mind."

"She thinks you are the most beautiful woman she has ever seen."

"What a sweet thing to say." MacLeod watched as the smile faded from her face. "But look at me today. I am not what she remembers. Now, before I must rest again, have you and Francesca considered my offer?"

In truth, MacLeod still hadn't made up his mind. "Do you have any idea of the risks you would be taking? If things don't turn around soon we'll never be able to pay you back. What would happen to you then?"

"You need to know something about me, Guillermo. I am not what you remember. The years since Doñ Montero, my husband, died have been about doing business in a country where only men are known to do so."

MacLeod attempted to stop her but she held up her hand.

"Hear me out, please," she pleaded. "I have accumulated much wealth taking chances on people. I have bet on products brought to California by ships. If a ship were lost, I also lost. I am betting on you, Guillermo. And I know you will not fail."

MacLeod stood, walking a few paces away before turning back to face her. "It's a long shot, Marisol. I don't know if I can do it," he admitted.

"Will you accept my offer and at least attempt it?"

Reluctantly, he nodded. "You need to know we're going to get a visit from Santiago and his people. We should probably expect it soon."

Marisol nodded in understanding. "There is something else you need to know. Francesca has told me this in confidence—she did not want you to know about it. But I feel you deserve to know the truth."

MacLeod was puzzled. *What could Francesca have said to her that she would not tell him?*

"It is not Doñ Santiago you must fear. It is this man, Pacheco. He has many men with him."

"I know him," MacLeod said. "He's the one responsible for having the Gomez boy's death."

"But what you aren't aware of, what Francesca has never told you is that he is the one who chased her and caused her horse to bolt. He is the one who fired his pistol at her. Had it not struck the horse she would not have been hurt."

MacLeod was stunned. *Why had she not told me this?*

Marisol, seeming to read his thoughts, continued. "Francesca was afraid of what you would do if you discovered it was he who had caused her accident."

"Then why are you breaking your promise to her?"

"When Doñ Santiago realizes he has been beaten I believe he will send Pacheco after you," she said. "I am more realistic than your dear wife and I realize you must be prepared. For anything."

"But she promised," Francesca cried.

369

"One way or another it was bound to come out eventually," MacLeod said, trying his best to put his wife at ease.

Francesca wiped the tears from her eyes. "Think of what might happen—you cannot fight them all. They will kill you."

MacLeod knew this to be true. He couldn't take them all on alone; he needed a plan. Which was something he had been thinking about since Marisol exposed Francesca's secret. His original anger had finally subsided giving him an opportunity to think more clearly. He needed to separate Pacheco from the other men Santiago had hired. He counted on Pacheco's hatred for him to do just that with little to no effort.

"This fight can't be postponed any longer. Concannon was right—I should have killed him when I had the chance."

MacLeod saw the resignation reflected in Francesca's eyes. "You will do this alone?" she asked, her tone filled with fear for what may happen to her husband.

"Haven't worked that out yet. It'll be up to the others to decide for themselves."

MacLeod reached out and caught Diego as the boy ran past, a handful of tortillas in his hand. Rosalie was right behind him, waving her fist at the boy. With nowhere to run, the boy quickly shoved the tortilla in his mouth while his father waited for him to finish. Shaking his head, MacLeod wondered when the boy would ever begin to take life seriously. Once he had finished his stolen tortilla, MacLeod sent him off to fetch Concannon, Gomez, and Sisquoc. He knew Jacob was nearby, so he decided to go in search of him himself.

They all need to know what I am planning to do.

A short while later the men all gathered beneath the olive tree, questioning the reason for the sudden meeting. Concannon appeared to know immediately that something was about to happen. Gomez, wearing one of the two, often patched but spotlessly cleaned, white shirts, hunkered down on his heels, while Jacob stood by and waited. Sisquoc also opted to stand, still stiff from the lashing he had taken from Santiago's men. MacLeod knew the man was in pain.

With everyone gathered, MacLeod called for his passing son, Diego, to join them. A huge grin spread across the boy's face at being included in the men's meetings.

MacLeod couldn't decide where to begin, so he started from the beginning. He told them of the troubles caused by Santiago, most of which they already knew. He told them about the woman who had arrived the day before, and how, with her help, he hoped to keep Colinas de Oro intact. This brought a combined nods and grins from the group.

Then MacLeod got down to what the meeting was all about. It had not crossed his mind before, but three of the four men in front of him had also suffered at the hands of Pacheco. Only Jacob had not. He informed Sisquoc that those who had whipped him did so under the direction of Pacheco. After taking a deep breath to gather his nerves, MacLeod admitted to Gomez that he had lied about how young Cisco had died and why he did so. He informed the man that his young son had been dragged to death by Pacheco's men. MacLeod expected some kind of outburst, though was shocked when the wiry keeper of the orchards, and all things that grew for consumption on the ranch, took the news with only a lock jawed nod of his head.

Lastly, MacLeod related to Concannon and the rest of the men Francesca's confession. That it had been Pacheco himself who fired the shot that had spooked Bolivar, causing it to throw her from the saddle.

They all waited in silence for him to continue.

"For these reasons," MacLeod said in not much more than a whisper. "I'm going after him. I apologize sincerely to all of you who have suffered at his hand because I didn't do so before."

Concannon was the first to speak. "When will we be doing this?"

"I'm not asking any of you to come," MacLeod stated, trying to make it clear to them that this was their decision. "This fight has been a long time coming. Most of you have families to consider."

"You're not to be doing this thing alone. Someone has to go along to take care of you," Concannon said, his grin showing through his thick red beard.

Sisquoc, a man of few words, simply touched his chest and said, "I go."

"In my heart," Gomez choked, tapping his chest. "In my heart I knew he did not die by himself. I know this."

MacLeod hadn't expected them all to risk their lives, but he was grateful nonetheless. Looking Gomez directly in the eyes, he said, "I surely appreciate your wanting to help, but your wife has already lost a son. I doubt she would like to lose a husband too."

Gomez kicked the dirt with his battered boots. "I must go, Señor. I would not be a man if I did not seek my revenge. For my son. She will understand this."

MacLeod heard Jacob chuckle beside him. "I believe we are going to have a fight. I doubt there is one among you all better with a rifle than I. Given that, you certainly cannot go without me." The men all chuckled.

With their meeting concluded, everyone returned to tell their families or friends of what they had committed to do. Before Diego could run off to do whatever it is he did, MacLeod asked him to remain and moment longer.

Now it is time I do the same, MacLeod thought to himself. MacLeod had put it off long enough and now seemed as good a time as any. The father and son walked out into the orchard and found a spot beneath a young fruit tree giving off a sliver of shade.

"Son," MacLeod began. "I have a story that needs telling. You need to know this in case anything happens to me." MacLeod was surprised that the boy had not immediately started asking questions.

For the next several minutes he told the boy that Francesca was not his real mother. That his real mother was a wonderful woman named Maria Cordero and that she had been killed in an Indian attack near the big river they called the Rio Colorado. He informed Diego how he had been kidnapped as a young child and of the search for him. How it was this search that resulted in MacLeod meeting Francesca. He depicted the fight on the sands of the San Diego harbor with the Frenchman, Dupré.

Overloaded with information, Diego finally interrupted his father to ask a question MacLeod had not anticipated so early in his explanation. "Is Catalina my sister?"

This posed a problem and MacLeod knew it. Francesca had never told her daughter about being raped by Dupré and how MacLeod was not her real father. *It is high time to bring everything out into the open. Secrets can no longer be kept,* MacLeod told himself.

"No, Catalina is not your sister. But you are to say nothing to her about this until Francesca says it is all right."

"What was my mother like? Am I like her?" Diego asked, a sadness in his tone.

"In some ways. You were the most precious thing she ever possessed. In fact, you were responsible for keeping her alive during very hard times."

Diego frowned. MacLeod watched as his young son digested these new facts that had been thrust on his young life.

"I wish I could have seen her," Diego whispered.

MacLeod brushed a tear from his cheek. It took a moment for him to find his voice. "I do to son. I wish you could have known her. But you must always treat Francesca as your mother now. Now more than ever. She needs you to be strong and she loves you very much."

Before they left for the hacienda MacLeod reached into his pocket and withdrew a tiny silver cross and chain. He ran it through his fingers a few times, reliving the dying Maria's final words. He passed it to Diego. "The last words your mother said was that she wanted you to have this when I thought you were old enough. She said, 'Give this to our son. It is all I have of me to give him. And tell him I loved him beyond anything else.'"

MacLeod reached into the same pocket, he retrieved the letter from Doñ Cordero. "There is a man in the village of Taos, across the river in New Mexico. His name is Doñ Cordero. He is your grandfather."

Diego took the letter and stared at the writing on the paper. "Did he love me too?" the young boy asked.

"Very much. The letter will tell you all that you need to know."

The men all gathered again in the late afternoon to go over their weapons and develop a plan to draw Pacheco away from the hacienda. MacLeod figured by doing so it might lessen the number of men available to Pacheco.

Concannon still preferred the muzzle-loading shotgun he had used on a number of occasions, while Jacob chose one of the Baker rifles he was familiar with. Sisquoc sat on his heels apart from the others. In one hand he held a short bow carved from a thick hickory branch. In the other hand half a dozen iron topped cane arrows.

MacLeod hefted his newly stocked Kentucky rifle and, along with Concannon and Jacob, began the task of cleaning and loading their weapons. Always one to carry a backup, just in case, MacLeod also prepared his Bates of London .60 caliber pistol.

Each man double-checked his gear and packed away the wrapped packages of food Rosalie had prepared. She made no attempt to hide her hostility toward MacLeod when she handed him his package. She blamed him for Francesca's accident. MacLeod didn't mind. He blamed himself too.

With everything packed and secured away, they rode out of the courtyard with the blazing sun at their backs. As always MacLeod searched the sky for any sign of a budding thunderhead. And just like every other day, the sky remained cloudless.

Earlier that morning a Rancho Colinas vaquero told of seeing two Rancho Santiago men camped out at the upper end of the valley. MacLeod surmised this pair was there to ensure that RS cattle remained on Colinas de Oro land. Why they would want to return to the pitiful water and grazing on Santiago's land he couldn't understand. But then, he had never really understood cows. Nevertheless, it was those two RS vaqueros MacLeod chose to use to send the message back to Pacheco.

He and Concannon left the others to trail behind. He wanted the Santiago vaqueros to report to Pacheco that they had only seen two men approaching.

As they neared the spot where the two vaqueros had been seen camping Concannon dropped down into a shallow arroyo and followed it toward the camp. MacLeod keeping to the main path casually pulled the Kentucky from its scabbard and double-checked the flint.

"Buenos Dias," he said, catching the men by surprise.

Both RS men jumped up and reached for their weapons. An old musket leaning against a nearby rock belonged to one of the men, while the other man's whip hung on his saddle some distance off. He started for it when Concannon rode out of the arroyo, essentially cutting them both off.

"Oh, keep on reaching, please, so I can send you straight to hell." The man froze at the sight of Concannon's shotgun trained on him.

MacLeod quickly dismounted and walked toward the small campfire set within a circle of rocks. "You have water?" he asked, pointing toward the smoldering coals.

"Si, you do not have any of your own?" the one man asked.

"Douse those coals. All we need now is a damn grass fire, *comprende?"*

"You have more water than we do. You kill the fire yourself," the man spat, causing both men to laugh.

The one standing by the fire turned toward his companion with a grin on his face. He never saw the butt of the rifle that struck his jaw coming. "Get up, *pendejo."* MacLeod ordered.

Taken aback, head pounding, the man pushed himself to his feet and stood on shaky legs while holding his jaw.

This time, MacLeod used his fist, connecting with the other side of his face and sending him sprawling across the hot coals. Panicked, the man screamed as he rolled over into the dirt and whacked at his pants in an effort to brush off the hot coals.

Taking his cue from MacLeod, Concannon drove the butt of his shotgun into the other vaquero's stomach. The man doubled over, his breath knocked out of him. "That's for making me angry." Before the man could catch his breath Concannon kicked him in the side of the head. "And that's for all the other things you people have done." Both vaqueros now lay sprawled in the dirt, each groaning in pain.

"Bring their horses over and let's send Pacheco a message," MacLeod said. He grabbed the one whimpering from the burns he received and walked him to where Concannon held the horses.

They used leather thongs to tie their hands and feet to their saddles. MacLeod picked up the musket and slammed it down on a nearby rock. The old weapon shattered into a number of pieces. Concannon removed the whip from the other vaquero's saddle and sliced it in two.

"Tell Pacheco we'll meet him here tomorrow. Tell him I don't want to have to come looking for him in order to kill him."

One of the vaqueros managed a laugh through his pain. "He will come, Señor. He will come to kill you. Maybe before he does he will come for your wife too."

MacLeod's pistol appeared in a flash.

"No," Concannon yelled stopping him before he could pull the trigger. "With any luck they come back with Pacheco tomorrow. Then we can kill then all."

He knew Concannon was right. Reluctantly uncocking his pistol, MacLeod nodded. Picking up part of the nearby whip,

Concannon cracked it across the hindquarters of both horses, sending them back to Rancho Santiago at a full gallop.

"Now I think we should find us a place close by to wait," Concannon muttered once the men were out of earshot.

A short while later the others joined Concannon and MacLeod and they all sat without speaking, each with his own thoughts and unanswered questions. They lit no fire to ward off the bears that still sought the rancid meat of the slain cattle. Each ate his share of the cold beef and bean enchiladas Rosalie had prepared and drank the cool water from the creek.

MacLeod looked around at the good men surrounding him, his mind plagued with worry for their well-being. *How many will suffer for my cause? Will I be returning to the ranch with bodies tied to the horses? Or will one of them be forced to tell Francesca if he was one of the bodies?*

The cry of a coyote split the silence. Its call was answered and a new hunt would begin. However, unlike MacLeod and his men, the coyote's hunt would be for food, not revenge.

He woke early, and threw aside his thin blanket and pulled on his boots. He walked down to the creek where the cool water slid down over the rocks and formed a shallow pool. He dipped both hands into the water and drank, then threw more water on his face, visions of what the day would bring still foremost in his thoughts.

The muted sounds of the other four men rising from their bedding to do the same greeted him as he began rolling up his bedroll. No words were spoken. No words would quell the tension each man felt. MacLeod's uneasiness rose as he watched the others prepare themselves for what the day might bring.

"Oh, but it's a fine morning for a fight," Concannon said, then he broke into a dry chuckle.

"Let's be hoping it's a one-sided affair," MacLeod replied. "I don't look forward to returning with any of us being losers."

"How many do you believe the man will bring with him?" Jacob questioned.

"Asking myself the same question. Best I can figure, he'll bring as many as he can round up. Could be as many as six, including himself."

"You figure they'll come early or late?" Concannon asked, a serious expression upon his face.

"I'm thinking we might have to cool our heels a spell before they show up. That's if they show up at all."

As it turned out, MacLeod was wrong on both counts.

Sisquoc spotted them first. He grunted and pointed down into the shallow valley MacLeod had chosen.

"Seems he's awful anxious to die this morning," MacLeod shrugged.

Sisquoc, Gomez, and Jacob quickly fell back into the shadows of the oak grove and moved to their pre-arranged places.

MacLeod and Concannon sat on their horses and watched as Pacheco approached.

"I do believe I'm counting nine of them," Concannon muttered. "Sure sign of a man who doubts his own ability."

MacLeod remained silent, eyes trained on the enemy until Pacheco and his men reached the spot MacLeod had picked out the day before. "Let's ride out and see what happens. He'll think it's just the two of us. Then again, never did figure him to be too bright. He'll be happy to think he's got the advantage."

Concannon looked at MacLeod with a puzzled expression upon his face. "I don't know how you figure he doesn't have the advantage. Seems there's a sight more of them than us."

"Only appears that way. They only see two of us. Might be changing their minds when the others show up."

Pacheco and his men stopped and spread out behind an enormous oak that had recently been downed by lightning, just as MacLeod figured they would. The tree was well within hailing distance and gave the men a bit of cover.

"Remember now, they've got to be the ones to fire first," MacLeod said. Although he didn't know Jacob well, he knew he would not fire unless someone took a shot at him first. Which left only Sisquoc and Gomez. MacLeod could clearly see that Gomez had set his sights on revenge...personal revenge. Sisquoc, armed with just his bow, was the least likely to fire first. It would be suicide to be the first to fire with nothing more than a bow.

The thought of Sisquoc had MacLeod's mind racing. *How will the big Chumash manage to pull his bow with his back nothing but a mess of scabs? I suppose we will find out soon enough.*

Concannon spoke up a moment later, apparently thinking along the same lines. "You ever see the Indian use that bow before?"

"A couple of times. The Chumash are considered a peaceful group, but from what I can gather, Sisquoc rebelled against Mission life and wanted to start a war of some kind. Couldn't round up enough followers, I suppose."

Pacheco pointed up at them and shouted, "I see you have come here to let me kill you." A number of his followers laughed. Two of the men shot their muskets into the air and began the slow process of reloading.

"Idiots," MacLeod muttered. "They basically took themselves out of the fight if it were to start now." Shaking his head, MacLeod hollered down to Pacheco, "It's been a long time coming, Pacheco. This fellow here beside me says I should have killed you years ago. Suppose I should have listened; could have saved myself all this trouble. I guess today is your unlucky day."

Pacheco looked on either side of himself to check out his men's position before shifting in the saddle. He laughed.

Concannon pointed down the shallow slope to where they all waited. "The one on the far right there—see him? I believe that's one of the ones we caught whipping Sisquoc."

"I believe you're right. Patched himself up and wants a little revenge," MacLeod said.

Pacheco, feeling secure with his men behind him, moved a step in front of the others and shouted, "When I have finished with you and that little man with you I will go and see your wife again. And that other one—I will do to her what Doñ Santiago did to her. It will be so much fun," he laughed. "But your wife, I'm sure she will be so glad to see me again. After I have finished with her maybe I will kill your little bastard children. Well, not the girl, I think she is ready."

MacLeod's grip on his reins tightened, his knuckles white from the pressure.

"You're doing an awful lot of talking, Pacheco. Is that all you do?" Concannon questioned. "Watch the one on his right. He has the look of someone who has done this before. He will be the one to start it," he whispered to MacLeod.

MacLeod shook in anger from Pacheco's threats. He kneed his horse forward a dozen steps, doubting any of their muskets could reach them. Regardless of Concannon's words he kept his eyes on Pacheco. MacLeod felt Pacheco would be the one to start things.

Once again, MacLeod was wrong.

The man on Pacheco's far left, the one Concannon said looked like one of the RS men who had whipped Sisquoc, circled his nervous horse and exposed himself for a moment. Sisquoc must have recognized him. Before MacLeod could shout a warning a bloodcurdling cry echoed through the valley. Sisquoc screamed a challenge and kicked his horse into a ground-eating gallop down the slope toward Pacheco and his men.

"Looks like the party's about to start," Concannon said, bringing the shotgun to his shoulder.

"Won't do much good with that scatter gun of yours."

"No, but it might get their attention for a bit. Enough to let that damn Indian get away with whatever it is he has in mind." The boom from the shotgun got everyone's immediate attention.

The man Sisquoc appeared to recognize had swung his horse back around at the sound of Sisquoc's horse bearing down on them. He pulled a pistol from his belt and fired at the charging Indian. The ball sent up a cloud of dust in front of Sisquoc's horse. MacLeod watched as the man tried frantically to reload his pistol.

The whole scene took place in less time than it took for Pacheco and the others to react. Sisquoc had his arrow notched and pulled the gut bowstring back as he rode toward the man at a full gallop.

MacLeod watched as the arrow streaked across the distance between the two men. Before the arrow buried itself in the man's chest another was already in flight. To Concannon and MacLeod's shock, both arrows found their mark.

"Jesus, Mary, and Joseph," Concannon muttered. "Remind me to never get on his bad side."

They all watched as the man with the arrows embedded in his chest toppled from the saddle. Caught off-guard, Pacheco and the others quickly turned to fire a volley at the already retreating Indian. Sisquoc had flung himself over the side of his horse, using the animal as a barrier from the balls of the guns. It didn't matter though; all the balls fell short, kicking up dust behind the galloping horse.

"Powder's in mighty short supply hereabouts," MacLeod noticed. "They're using too little to do any damage."

Pacheco's voice rose above the shouts and curses of his men as he directed those who had fired to reload.

"What we be waiting for? Seems they've started this little war."

MacLeod sat silently on his horse, the Kentucky rifle resting across the front of his saddle. Neither Jacob, nor Gomez, had come out of the shadows or fired a shot. However, he figured Pacheco would be rethinking his position once they did. Another ragged volley split the air. But this time the ball from one of the muskets whistled past MacLeod's ear. *That shot demands a response,* he thought to himself. He brought the rifle to his shoulder and chose a man on Pacheco's right. The one Concannon had warned him about.

MacLeod fired and watched his target slump over and slip from the saddle.

At the sound of MacLeod's rifle Jacob and Gomez opened fire. As MacLeod poured powder down his muzzle, a musket ball held in his mouth, he kept a close eye on the enemy at the bottom of the hill. Just as he was ramming the ball down against the powder another man went down. Quickly tapping some powder in the touchhole, he cocked the rifle and prepared to fire again.

"Hate to see men die following a bastard like him," MacLeod muttered before his rifle barked once again. MacLeod watched as Pacheco slapped the side of his chest and attempted to wheel his horse around. "Oh, I'll have none of that," MacLeod said as he quickly reloaded.

Hopping out of the saddle, MacLeod knelt in the dirt beside his horse. Both Jacob and Gomez fired a split second before MacLeod. This time MacLeod's ball struck the man he came to kill. Pacheco fell forward over the pommel of his saddle before slowly falling to the ground.

Four men and Pacheco lay in the dirt behind the low barrier of the fallen tree. Not wasting any time, the four remaining men spun their horses around and drove their spurs into their horse's flanks as they quickly retreated.

MacLeod held his hand up and motioned Jacob and Gomez forward slowly. "Anyone seen Sisquoc?" he questioned, scanning the area around them.

"There," Jacob shouted, pointing to a spot well down the arroyo.

Sisquoc approached at a slow walk, blood running down his side. Obviously the scabs from the whip cuts had been torn away when he charged the man who had tortured him.

MacLeod pulled his pistol and kneed his horse forward until he reached the downed tree. He dismounted. The others follow his lead. Jacob cautiously moved past the tree and proceeded to check on the men who still lay on the ground.

The man Sisquoc had sent his arrows into was dead. Following closely behind Jacob, Sisquoc walked over to the body and pulled his arrows out, leaving the torn flesh exposed for the vultures to feed on.

The first man MacLeod shot was also dead, as was the man Jacob had shot. It wasn't until he went to roll the final man onto his back that the man cried out in pain.

While the other men busied themselves, MacLeod walked to where Pacheco lay on his side, blood dripping from his shoulder where MacLeod's second bullet had found its mark.

MacLeod pushed Pacheco over onto his back with his foot and saw the man's eyes flicker.

"Looks like I missed killing him. He must have moved on me." MacLeod sounded disappointed.

Concannon stood with his shotgun positioned at his side. "I be thinking the man lives a charmed life. You do plan on finishing what you started, don't you?"

Pacheco grunted. The patch covering the hole where his eye had been before Francesca gouged it out lay in the dirt beside him.

"Can never seem to bring myself to shoot a helpless man. May be the death of me one day," MacLeod admitted.

MacLeod stood over Pacheco, his cocked pistol aimed directly at the injured man. Pacheco held up a hand as if to deflect the ball before beginning to plead for his life.

MacLeod watched the fear grow in Pacheco's eyes as if he knew his end was near. MacLeod pointed the octagon shaped barrel at Pacheco's chest, his finger applying pressure to the trigger.

Despite the damage the man had done to most of them MacLeod couldn't bring himself to pull the trigger. Lowering the pistol to his side he watched as Pacheco let out the breath he had been holding.

"Doñ MacLeod," a voice he recognized as belonging to Gomez sounded.

MacLeod turned to face him. This was not the often-smiling man who tended the orchards and gardens. This was the man whose creased and weather-beaten face demanded respect. This was the man whose oldest son was dragged to death by those sent by Pacheco. It was then MacLeod remembered him saying he must come on this mission or lose the respect of his family.

Without a word, Gomez pointed at the pistol in MacLeod's hand. MacLeod locked eyes with the man and nodded his head in understanding.

Pacheco, seeming to understand what was happening, cried out for forgiveness.

"It's only right that you do it, Gomez. It's a debt that needs to be paid." MacLeod flipped the pistol around and handed it butt first to Gomez.

The grieving man bowed his head and whispered, *"Gracias."*

The grim expression on Gomez's face wasn't lost on Pacheco as he began to whimper.

Holding the pistol firmly in both hands, Gomez said, *"Por Cisco,"* and then pulled the trigger.

"I'll be damned if he didn't blow out his good eye," Concannon laughed. "Don't imagine he'll be needing it where he's going."

Gomez handed the pistol back to MacLeod and nodded. *The debt has been paid,* MacLeod thought to himself in satisfaction.

"What you fixing to do with all these bodies?" Concannon asked. "Probably kill the buzzards if we leave them here."

MacLeod walked over to his horse and removed his lariat. "We'll put them on their horses and send them back to where they came from."

"Should we be expecting any trouble from this Santiago fellow?" Jacob asked, speaking for the first time.

"Probably. But I doubt he'll come looking for a fight. He's not the type. Prefers to use others to do his bidding."

Gomez had already rounded up the horses belonging to those on the ground. Working quickly, Jacob helped him load the bodies of Pacheco and the other three dead men onto their horses, tying their hands and feet under the belly of the horses. The remaining man that had been wounded was helped up onto his saddle with the lead rope for the string looped over his saddle horn. As they worked to secure the man to his horse, he profusely thanked MacLeod for letting him live.

"Let Santiago know that Pacheco had it coming for a long time. Tell him that I sincerely hope he was not responsible for killing the boy or for my wife's injury."

The man nodded his thanks again and rode out the same way the nine riders had initially come.

"We best be getting back to the women folk. It's a miracle we all came out of this in one piece. You all know how hard it is for me to say thanks. But you all know that's how I feel. Now let's go home."

When the men returned to the hacienda Juana was singing something she had been taught at the mission before she ran away. MacLeod never understood the meaning, despite her laughingly explaining it to him a number of times.

In fact, everyone seemed to sense the relief felt by the women at the safe return of the men, each giving thanks to whichever God they worshipped that everyone had returned safely.

As soon as everyone dismounted MacLeod immediately summoned Jacob and Rosalie to help tend to Sisquoc's back. "Appears he's not wasting any time," Concannon said.

MacLeod watched as a group of riders approached, a cloud of dust surrounding them. "I believe you're right. Perhaps you should step into the house and let them know we have company coming. And you might bring my pistol out when you're finished telling them."

"You expecting trouble? I do believe he's only bringing two with him, but you can never be too prepared."

MacLeod shrugged. "Santiago's not a fighting man. Too bad though. He's just as guilty as Pacheco was. And you're right, there are only three riders." MacLeod chuckled. "I doubt those he has left are prepared to die for him."

Just then, Diego rode up with Catalina at his side. Both children dismounted and stood to one side to watch. As the riders neared MacLeod turned to see both Jacob and Gomez make their way into the courtyard, both armed.

Santiago slowed his horse to a walk and halted half a dozen paces away. The two vaqueros with him moved to either side, both appearing nervous. Inspecting his visitors, MacLeod saw there were no weapons on any of them except Santiago.

Santiago sat on his golden maned sorrel surveying the courtyard and small adobe MacLeod and Francesca lived in. He shook his head, scoffing, as if in disgust.

"You're not welcome here, Santiago. If you've come to apologize for your behavior then state your peace and be on your way."

Santiago continued to inspect the surroundings, still not acknowledging MacLeod. Then he said. "I have sent word to the authorities in Santa Barbara that you have murdered Señor Pacheco and others. They, I am sure, will forward it on to Monterey. I have asked that you be arrested and brought to Monterey for punishment. I am certain they will believe what I have to say."

Concannon looked at MacLeod as if in shock. "Is he serious?" he asked, pointing to the man with his thumb.

"Appears that way."

"Do you suppose he truly believes that line of blarney?"

MacLeod's eyes remained on Santiago as he watched the man's face for any type of reaction. "You're as responsible as your man Pacheco was," MacLeod stated. "I warned you about him. But then you already knew about the history between us. That's why you hired him." MacLeod turned and pointed at Gomez. "That man lost a fine young boy because of your desire to take our land away from us. My wife—she will never walk again because of you and the man you hired to do the dirty work for you. Consider yourself lucky I don't shoot you where you sit right now."

"You do not think I know what happened? I am told you waited in ambush for my people. They had no chance to defend themselves. That information has been passed along and will go to Monterey." Santiago laughed. "Who do you think the governor will believe? Certainly not you and this gathering of the poor and uneducated.

Why, look at them," Santiago said before pointing at Jacob Morganthau. "You have that man over there, a Jew who does not belong to this country or our religion. And him," he indicated to Concannon. "That one would be hung if his country got their hands on him. And the little one, I believe his name is Gomez, he probably cannot spell his own name. If I'm not mistaken, I believe there was also a member of a primitive group. Do you think they would believe him? You have nothing, Americano."

Jacob stepped forward, his tone serious. "I believe, if this country you are from is civilized, then they would have heard of Cambridge. I spent a number of years there and I resent your implication as a Jew. We are not savages. I believe far more people of my faith have given the world their teachings than that pitiful country you claim as yours."

Santiago bristled. His face reddened as he spoke to MacLeod. "It matters not what you claim. Even if any of it is true, which I doubt, I am sure our governor will believe what I tell him. And just so you are aware—in my complaint I have also accused you of stealing my cattle. This you cannot deny."

MacLeod grinned. "If you are referring to those unbranded heifers grazing on Colinas de Oro land. Who else could they belong to but us? Try proving otherwise."

MacLeod could tell he had hit a sore spot with Santiago. Whoever was in charge of taking care of his cattle had been negligent. Or, perhaps, Santiago himself was responsible.

"You know, those heifers should have been branded a couple of months age, but you were so sure you were going to take our land away from us you didn't bother looking after your own."

"That is of no concern of yours. That woman you are harboring is a thief. I demand you release her to me so I can have her taken to Santa Barbara and turned over to the authorities there. I am sure they will know what to do with her."

MacLeod was about to explode and Concannon seemed to sense it. He put his hand on MacLeod's gun arm and whispered. "There's no need to kill the man. He is finished but is yet to discover it."

Santiago overheard Concannon's remark and sneered. "If you allow this little man to influence you I can understand how you have failed with your place here."

Jacob and Gomez had moved further away from those standing behind MacLeod. Both had their rifles ready. Santiago's vaqueros appeared ready to bolt. MacLeod pointed at Santiago, his tone menacing. "That woman you speak of, Doña Montero, is under my protection. What you claim she stole was not yours. Explain why you paid someone in Monterey to send you the *diseño* for Colinas de Oro? You see, your mistake was not having your paid man destroy it. Not very bright on your part."

Santiago remained silent as MacLeod waited for his denial. Santiago pointed toward the adobe. "That woman is nothing more than a whore. She will answer for her mistakes."

MacLeod felt Concannon's powerful grip on his arm tighten.

Santiago, apparently unaware of his near death, continued. "She has also helped one of my slaves escape. I demand both be turned over to me."

MacLeod couldn't stop himself from laughing. "Or what? What are you prepared to do if they're not returned? You seem to misunderstand something, Santiago. They choose to remain here, under my protection."

"The woman is a thief." This time, his accusation lacked sincerity.

"You had your way with both Doña Montero and that young Indian girl, who is not much more than a child." The more MacLeod spoke the angrier he got. "If it weren't for the trouble it would cause I'd shoot you where you sit and worry about the authorities later. In fact, I believe Doña Montero will be charging you with rape."

This time it was Santiago who laughed. "How can she do this thing you speak of? Did she not come to my hacienda? I did not force her. Who would believe her?"

"I believe her," MacLeod said. "And as far as you're concerned, I'm the only one that counts."

Santiago appeared to regain some of his confidence. "Baa, what you say or think of me is of little importance. If the authorities want to further their investigation of my accusations they will do so, but in this country we will all be old before they come to any conclusion. It amazes me that these people ever get anything done. I want this land and I have been assured by His Excellency, the Governor, that I may consider it mine once you have been removed. You and this assortment of," Santiago looked around at those who stood in the courtyard and watched. "I am at a loss for words in attempting to describe this rabble you have collected."

MacLeod had had enough. "In case you haven't realized it yet you're close to being ruined. Your head man is dead; although I never have figured out why you put him in charge, unless you thought it would frighten me. Your cattle look like skeletons and you've lost half your men."

Santiago did his best to look unconcerned.

MacLeod figured he might as well clue him in about what to expect. "Even if the rains return this year they won't save you, unless your secret backers are expected to contribute more money to support you."

"What is this secret backers you speak of?" Santiago sneered

"The ones in Argentina. The ones who loaned you the money to bribe officials here in Alta California. You know what I'm talking about. And as I understand it, they want answers."

Santiago's stallion pawed at the dirt and fought the cruel bit in its mouth as Santiago pulled hard on the reins forcing the horse to rear back. "Where did you get this information? Has that whore of a woman been reading my private correspondence, as well as stealing from me?"

MacLeod drew his pistol and let it hang at his side. "If you call Doña Montero that name again I'll shoot you. Do you have any idea how long it takes a gut shot man to die? If you want to test me, go ahead."

Santiago pursed his lips and stared at MacLeod.

"Well, I'm waiting. Maybe I'll shoot your sorry ass anyway."

Santiago blanched, but remained silent.

"Well, Santiago? You have a pistol. You can pull it. I'll even give you a chance. But then I believe you're a coward to boot."

"I do not wish to soil my hands with peasants like you. In fact, I am surprised you have the courage to challenge me. You shot Señor Pacheco from an ambush; he would have killed you otherwise."

"If you believe that, you're stupider than I thought. Now, if we're done here, I suggest you ride out of here before I change my mind," MacLeod seethed as he placed the pistol back under his belt. MacLeod couldn't believe he had offered Santiago a way out. He silently chastised himself, knowing that if he didn't, Concannon certainly would.

Santiago turned to one of his men and snapped his fingers as he pointed at him. The man reached into a hide bag that hung from his saddle and pulled out a packet of papers tied together with a ribbon. Santiago took it from him and held it up.

MacLeod had been expecting this. Thanks to the information Doña Montero had given them.

Santiago waved them at MacLeod. "You have brought these debts upon yourself. I have spoken to the governor and he has assured me that he will authorize your arrest if you cannot pay for what you have purchased. This is to be done immediately. Others may be willing to wait, but I am demanding this payment now." A wry grin spread across Santiago's face. "However, I have an offer—I will allow you one week to gather the money, but for this you will turn over the women I requested."

MacLeod shook his head at the audacity of the man. He doubted Santiago had ever missed a meal in his life for lack of money. "I think I covered that request before, and as for the notes of mine, you saw to it we could never pay them by having our hide house put to the torch. I have no doubt that was Pacheco's work also. Under, but under your directions I'm sure."

"Your misfortunes are your problems, not mine. Nothing you have spoken of can be proved. Perhaps there was nothing in this place when it was destroyed. Since you cannot pay I will send someone to Santa Barbara with this letter I have from the governor."

MacLeod laughed, turning to Jacob. "I think the man believes he's been saved." Then to Santiago MacLeod stated, "I expect you've counted your chickens before they were hatched. You're ruined, Santiago, and soon you will realize it."

"I do not know why I am wasting my time. I suppose I wanted the satisfaction of watching your face when I presented these bills for payment. It is you who will not accept this fact that you will no longer own this land. That is the trouble with you Americanos, you cannot accept defeat."

"I suppose you're right there."

Santiago nodded, handing the packet of bills to the man beside him.

MacLeod held up his hand. It had gone far enough and it was time to end this charade. "I wouldn't go putting those away just yet."

Santiago looked around. He shifted his weight in the saddle and spoke to the two RS men. "Do you hear this man? He is telling me what I should do with these debts he has incurred. And, he has no money to pay for them."

"But I have."

MacLeod turned to see Marisol being helped from the house, leaning on the arm of the young Indian girl who had hardly left Marisol's side since they arrived. Santiago, in all of his ranting, had not seen them come out of the house. On hearing her voice he turned to look at her, unable to control the anger that showed in his expression.

"Oh yes, that whore of a woman."

MacLeod's hand was a blur as he pulled the pistol, thumbing back the hammer in one swift motion.

Marisol screamed.

The crack of the pistol echoed across the gathering in the courtyard as the ball passed through the wide brim of Santiago's sombrero. Santiago turned white as MacLeod took Concannon's shotgun and leveled it at Santiago's chest.

"I can guarantee I won't miss the second time should you address Doña Montero with those filthy words."

"Please, Guillermo, do not kill him."

"Why not?"

"Enough people have died because of him. I want to imagine what it will do to him when he returns to Buenos Aires. I am sure they will welcome him home after he has lost all their money."

Santiago had finally regained some of his composure. "You," he laughed without conviction. "And how will you pay this sum of money this lover of yours owes me?"

Marisol moved forward on her own and leaned on MacLeod's arm. "This man has never been my lover, but he is more of a man than you will ever be. As to how I have accumulated the money—I am a businesswoman—one of the few in Alta California who has the respect from the men I do business with."

"Since you stole from me and read my private correspondence I imagine you know how much is owed?"

The bruises on Marisol's face had finally begun to turn yellow. But to MacLeod, she still looked as beautiful as the first time he had laid eyes her. It took every ounce of control he had to not shoot Santiago for what he had done to her.

"I know the sum of these notes you have," she said. "In fact, I have a note right here which authorizes you to receive the amount owed. You may present this to the captain of any American trading ship that is in the harbor on Monterey. Here is also a letter to the governor. He will assist you in receiving payment."

The effort of explaining everything seemed to tire her and the pain in her side made it difficult to stand for any length of time. She handed the notes to MacLeod and allowed the girl to help her back to the house.

MacLeod read the notes and the amounts Marisol had paid for before looking across the courtyard at all the people who depended on him. "I have a better idea, Santiago. Even this money won't pull you out of the hole you've dug for yourself and your cattle are dying without the water and grazing on our land. You have no one left to do your dirty work, or herd your cattle over onto Colinas de Oro land—"

"You are mistaken," Santiago interrupted. "With this money I can hire the help I need. So I lose a few cows," the man shrugged. "So will you if the rain does not come."

"See, that's where you're wrong," MacLeod said. He turned to Jacob who stood off a few paces, his gun still trained on Santiago and his men. "Bring me that quill pen of yours and that little bottle of ink."

Jacob ducked into the house and returned with the pen and ink. "I took a moment and sharpened the quill."

MacLeod took Marisol's letter authorizing the transfer of funds to cover the debts and handed it to Santiago who started to fold it up when MacLeod stopped him. "Wait a minute there…you got something else to do," he said as he handed the pen and ink up to Santiago.

"What is this for? I have no need for it," he explained, trying to hand it back to MacLeod.

"You're going to sign that authorization over to me. Call it payment for my hides and tallow."

Santiago attempted a laugh. "You are the one who is mistaken if you expect me to do as you ask. That would be a foolish thing."

MacLeod handed the shotgun over to Concannon and accepted the charged pistol from Jacob. "What's foolish is risking your life over it. Sign it or be ready to join Pacheco and his friends."

Santiago hesitated a moment until MacLeod leveled the pistol at him and cocked it.

Everyone held their breath in anticipation of what might happen next.

"You will regret this! I can promise you that. You cannot get away with this,." Santiago shouted as he removed the stopper in the ink bottle and dipped the pen in it. After signing the letter and throwing it back at MacLeod he started to rein the big stallion around.

"I don't think so. I've changed my mind," MacLeod began. "These men here are taking you to Santa Barbara. They'll stay with you until a ship stops on its way to Monterey. You can take all your complaints to the governor, although he'll pay much more attention to them when he finds out how you paid someone to send you our *diseño*. Oh, and one last thing before you go," MacLeod walked over to where Santiago sat and reached up, grabbing the man's shirt front and pulling him out of the saddle. Santiago fell heavily to the ground. He pushed himself to his feet, clutching at the pistol beneath his belt.

"I owe you this. You can figure it's better than dying." Before Santiago could even react, MacLeod's fist turned Santiago's eyes skyward. He tried to remain on his feet but the second punch knocked him into momentary unconsciousness.

They men loaded him in his saddle as MacLeod requested Jacob and Concannon to take him to Santa Barbara and load him on a ship. As expected, the two men he brought with him chose to return to Monterey as well.

MacLeod called for Diego. "Get a week's supplies together for yourself and the others and go with them. It's time you started acting like a man."

Diego's eyes lit up in excitement. "Can I take a gun in case I need it? You know, for bears."

MacLeod grinned. "You know how to load and prime it?"

"Yes, sir. Mr. Morgenthau showed me how. He even let me fire his a few times."

"All right," MacLeod nodded. "Grab yourself one of those Baker rifles. And Diego?"

The boy turned, the excitement in his face made MacLeod realize how much his son had grown with all the crises they had gone through in the young boy's life. "Yes, sir?"

"Two things—one, you do what Sean tells you to do. And two, you bring that big stallion back. He's yours now."

Diego rode the big, golden maned sorrel they had confiscated from Santiago, followed by Catalina on her favorite black gelding. After Diego was gifted his stallion, Catalina had elicited a promise from MacLeod that she could have Bolivar when he felt the horse had been broken of its fear of loud noises. In truth, MacLeod hoped that wouldn't be too soon.

MacLeod turned his attention to the west where a gathering of clouds moved closer. Only this morning Rosalie had predicted rain.

A week ago, the two men sent to Santa Barbara with Santiago had returned. A ship, already at anchor in the harbor, had agreed to take Santiago to Monterey.

Marisol Montero, who was still staying with them, was beginning to heal. Satisfied with her progress, she wanted to return to her home in Monterey. She and MacLeod had agreed he would keep the money that she loaned him as the ranch was desperately in need of repairs that had been put off until money was available. With so many people depending upon Francesca and MacLeod, and the fact that their little village was continually growing, they needed to do all they could to keep things running.

Marisol had asked MacLeod to gather the people together after the noon meal so that she could discuss a few things with all of them.

So awhile later they all waited outside in the courtyard for Marisol to join them. While they waited MacLeod turned to watch the darkening clouds moving to the north. They looked as if they would parallel the coast, bringing their life giving water to land far to the north.

Was everything that happened for nothing, he wondered.

Marisol walked to where he stood and placed her hand on his arm. Her touch and closeness excited him more than he cared to admit. Despite the years apart, they had not dulled his feelings toward her in the slightest.

"I have some things I wish to say," she said, moving away from MacLeod to stand alone. "All I ask is that you listen to my offer and allow me to finish." Everyone nodded. "When I return to Monterey I will seek an audience with His Excellency. With Señor Santiago no longer here, Rancho Santiago land will return to Alta California. It is my hope I can convince our governor to grant me this land. I am sure he will agree to this. There are many who will vouch for me."

Why is she so sure of being granted the land, MacLeod wondered, making a mental note to ask her later.

"I will have to ask about the cattle once I have returned to Monterey, but I am sure I can purchase them also." Beckoning Concannon to come closer, she smiled warmly at the man. "Francesca has told me of your plans to build furniture. If you can build this furniture as well as this chair you have made for Francesca I can guarantee that you will do well. That being said, I would like to invest in this new business." Concannon seemed slightly taken aback as a wide grin spread across his face.

She called Diego over and took him by the shoulders turning him around to face everyone. "He is the child I almost had," she explained, her voice filled with emotion. Turning to face MacLeod, she continued. "I have heard you say his grandmother lives in the city of Boston. You have also said you wished he could have an education that he sadly cannot receive here. Is that not true?"

MacLeod wondered where Marisol was going with her inquiry. He nodded. "Yeah, it's true. Why?"

"I have a ship's captain I do much business with—I would like to offer you the opportunity to send him to Boston for a proper education. It would be my gift to him."

Francesca gasped. Neither she nor MacLeod knew what to say to such an incredible gift.

Catalina, who had positioned herself beside Marisol, tugged on her arm and whispered in the woman's ear, "What about me?" MacLeod smiled at the exchange. It was clear to everyone that the young girl adored her.

"Perhaps you can come and stay with me once in a while. If you are as bright as I think you are you can help me make the decisions about what the women of Alta California would like," Marisol suggested. "Would you like that?"

Catalina's smile was all the answer Marisol needed. MacLeod was positive Francesca would approve. After all, it could do her some good to learn the ways of a woman from another woman that was not her mother.

Marisol walked over to where Francesca sat in her wheelchair and placed a gentle hand on her shoulder. "I have also asked Francesca if I might offer Jacob employment. I would like him and Sarah to come to Monterey with me," she explained, turning to look at the shocked expression upon the couple's faces. "My businesses are far too many for me to handle by myself. I hoped Mr. Morgenthau would agree to come and be my business manager. Perhaps Sarah would also accompany me on some of my business trips."

As soon as Marisol indicated that she had finished, everyone broke out into conversation, talking excitedly amongst themselves.

Walking over to where MacLeod stood, she took his arm in hers and began leading him away from the others. "Will you please take me to Santa Barbara so I might catch a ship to Monterey? I have also spoken to Francesca about a few other things I feel you should be aware of. If the governor does me the honor of granting me this land I would like you to move into the hacienda that vile man built. I will call it Rancho Montero, after my husband. If everything is in my favor I would like you to manage it for me." She laughed. "Of course, I would expect to make a profit."

MacLeod didn't know what to say. With the land Santiago once controlled MacLeod would control the entire valley. If the rains came they would have little cattle available next year, but the following year might bring them out of the hole. He only hoped Marisol had taken this into consideration.

And the house—with real windows and the large orchard— *Maybe I can do it. If we did move onto RS land we could give Concannon and Esperanza our current home.*

Marisol took his hand in hers and looked deep into his eyes. "There is also something else. Francesca has given approval for you to visit with me whenever you come to Monterey. Do you understand what she is saying?" Marisol asked, a pleading expression on her face. "I would hope with all of my heart that you will."

A rolling clap of thunder echoed across the valley. Everyone looked up into the sky as the first drops of rain in three years fell onto the thirsty land.

ACKNOWLEDGEMENTS

I thank my close family and friends for their patience while I researched and wrote this tale. The grass doesn't always get cut, the car needs washing, and the to-do list grows longer while the words slowly accumulate on the page.

I need to thank Tiffany Lynne (graypublishingservices.com) for the cover, editing, and interior design of this book.

OTHER BOOKS BY E. PAUL BERGERON

Two Can Play
Available at: Amazon

The blood of ancient warriors courses through his veins.

A woman is dead.

A child is taken.

Only his own death would quell the hatred they feel for him. Can Gray escape his past and quench his bitter memories, or will others die to pay for his mistakes. He must answer the question. Does he flee, or fight? But he has sworn an oath to never kill again.

From the Blackfoot reservation in the north, to the barren lands of the Tonto O'odham in Arizona, this story takes the twists and turns that keep Gray alive. Because the man who deals in powdered death holds the key, and only Gray's death will open the lock.

*****

In the Shadow of Vargas
Book One of A Land in Turmoil Series
Available at: Amazon

When William MacLeod, a member of an American fur trapping party, is forced into Spanish New Mexico to seek help for a wounded companion, he finds love and soon encounters a vengeance that will test his power to fulfill the promises he made.

Maria de Cordero, the beautiful daughter of a wealthy hacienda owner, is promised in marriage to another. That is until she makes the fateful mistake of falling in love with the young American. However, when her secret visit to MacLeod's jail cell is discovered, the man who lustfully awaits their marriage, Miguel Griego, captain of the governor's own militia, seeks his revenge against the insult to his name.

Can MacLeod find a way to escape, and save Maria from what her family believes is a fate worse than death?

*****

THE SEARCH FOR DIEGO
BOOK TWO OF A LAND IN TURMOIL SERIES
Available at: Amazon

In the bowls of a hostile desert, a woman lay dying. As the last vestige of strength seeps from her body she passed the child into his hands. "Save him—for me. He is all I have to give you," were her final words.

Standing in his way is a fanatical priest who would take the child and save its soul instead. But the Frenchman, whose deadly reputation is built on the bodies of the men who challenged him, has other ideas. Filled with hatred for the man whose son it is, he takes the child from the woman paid to keep it, and passes it into the hands of a beautiful woman from the streets and slums of Vera Cruz.

It is 1823, Mexico ahs recently gained its independence, with little conception of how to govern this chaotic land. And in that far away place that is Alta California, leadership is based on the whims of the ignorant. It is here that William MacLeod scours the land in search of his son, while the Church and those in charge struggle to banish this foreign intruder form their land.

Love, hate, treachery, and death stalk his path as he attempts to fulfill her dying request.

A thrilling historical novel in this Land in Turmoil Series.

ABOUT THE AUTHOR

You can contact E Paul Bergeron at: edpbergeron@cs.com

As I remember it, life began on top of a load of furniture in a sleigh drawn by a team of horses on a bitterly cold day. My mother was walking alongside in the snow when the moment arrived. She claims it was Valentine's Day, and of all people, she should know.

I attended a one-room schoolhouse outside of the French Canadian town of Mascouche, Quebec, and later in the metropolis of Montreal. At some point, an overworked schoolteacher wrote a note home to my mother to say that someday I would be a writer. The rest of the family laughed.

I spent long winter afternoons and nights reading, and acquired a love of history. I never realized the depth of this love until, years later, I stood on a street corner in old Montreal and read the inscription etched on a brass plaque attached to the cornerstone of a grey, brick building. It read simply, "Hudson's Bay Company." There stood the company synonymous with intrigue and adventure, and, being of French and Scottish heritage, the people behind those adventures were my ancestors. They were the French voyageurs, or coureur de bois, who traversed the mountains and forests, and paddled the streams and rivers, and the Scots who sent them out in search of the fur pelts, which led to the exploration of the North American continent.

I was sixteen when my father found an old farmhouse, badly in need of repair in West Bolton, Quebec. There I spent a year among people who would become lifelong friends. But my father passed away before he realized his vision for the house.

My mother took us back to Montreal, and I soon left school to find a job to help support the family. Then a Christmas phone call came from California, and the invitation to come west took us to North Hollywood, with palm trees and salt sea air--and word that I was too young to work. I returned to school.

I stood in the quad of North Hollywood High with a recent import from Australia, gazing at the parking lot and wondering how the school could have so many teachers. The Aussie informed me that it was the students' parking lot. Life had certainly changed.

I soon discovered California's lofty Sierra Nevada Mountains and streams filled with wild trout holding below the riffles, as if waiting for the dry fly attached to the end of my line. However, those towering, snow-capped peaks beckoned, and I could not care less if the trout were hungry. Life was wonderful.

With the early beginning of a writing life, and being married to an artist, our two beautiful daughters grew up in a home filled with artistic expression. Later, we moved down the coast to a town in Orange County, until it was time to sell a business and find a place to begin the work put on hold for so many years.

We settled in Hayden Lake, Idaho, with a beautiful home a few miles from the shores of Lake Coeur d'Alene. Now I load my Surly Long Haul Trucker bike on the back of the car and drive to the trail whose path winds its way along the Coeur d'Alene River. I find a spot beside a small lake to watch the ducks and geese feed among the lily pads, or sit in a small clearing beneath a canopy of leafy branches, and there work out the twists and turns of the stories I want to tell.

Visit him online at:

Website: http://www.epaulbergeron.com

Facebook: http://www.facebook.com/EPaulBergeron/

www.ingramcontent.com/pod-product-compliance
Lightning Source LLC
Chambersburg PA
CBHW020505260626
47156CB00006B/1879